THE

BOYS

WHO

BRING

IN

THE

CROP

By: SPIKE NASMYTH

Printed in Victoria, Canada

National Library of Canada Cataloguing in Publication

Nasmyth, Spike
       The boys who bring in the crop / Spike Nasmyth.

ISBN 1-4120-1065-9
       I. Title.

PS3614.A824B69 2003   813'.6   C2003-904394-0

TRAFFORD

This book was published *on-demand* in cooperation with Trafford Publishing.
On-demand publishing is a unique process and service of making a book available for retail sale to the public taking advantage of on-demand manufacturing and Internet marketing. **On-demand publishing** includes promotions, retail sales, manufacturing, order fulfilment, accounting and collecting royalties on behalf of the author.

Suite 6E, 2333 Government St., Victoria, B.C. V8T 4P4, CANADA

Phone	250-383-6864	Toll-free	1-888-232-4444 (Canada & US)
Fax	250-383-6804	E-mail	sales@trafford.com
Web site	www.trafford.com	TRAFFORD PUBLISHING IS A DIVISION OF TRAFFORD HOLDINGS LTD.	
Trafford Catalogue #03-1434		www.trafford.com/robots/03-1434.html	

10   9   8   7   6   5   4   3   2

THE BOYS WHO BRING IN THE CROP

CONTENTS

THE BOYS WHO BRING IN THE CROP

Almost all of what follows really happened. Of course
all of the dialog is as I thought it would have been back
in the seventies.

The names and places have one hundred percent been
changed to protect the identity of those involved.

ABOUT THE AUTHOR

Spike Nasmyth started off life in Billings, Montana on 14 November 1940 as John H. Nasmyth, he legally changed his name to Spike Nasmyth in the seventies. The Nasmyth family moved to southern California in 1945.

Spike attended Rosemead High School from 1954 to 1958, he then went off to college at the University of Idaho. At the U of I he majored in Psychology and was a member of Air Force ROTC. Spike first flew at the controls of an airplane in 1961. He earned his Private Pilot's license in 1962, then went on to US Air Force pilot training. He graduated in 1963 and was assigned to the 555th Tactical Fighter Squadron at MacDill Air Force Base in Tampa, Florida.

On September the 4th, 1966, he was shot down over Hanoi, North Vietnam, he spent the next six and a half years as a Prisoner of War. The book "2355 DAYS" recounts his days as a POW.

After release from North Vietnam, Spike separated from the Air Force and began a life in civil aviation. From 1961 until 2002, he has logged over 20,000 hours in a variety of airplanes including:

McDonnell-Douglas	F-4	Phantom	1000 hours
DeHavilland	DHC-2	Beaver	4000 hours
DeHavilland	DHC-3	Otter	1500 hours
Cessna single engine	180,185, 206, 207		3000 hours
Cessna multi-engine	310, 402, 421		1000 hours
Britten Norman	BN2A	Islander	700 hours
Piper	PA-31	Navajo	900 hours
Grumman	G-21	Goose	1000 hours
Grumman	G-73	Mallard	1500 hours
Grumman	G-111	Albatross	100 hours
Douglas	DC-3	Dakota	600 hours

Spike flew float planes in Canada, Flying boats in Thailand, DC-3s in Asia, Beaver and Islander in Palau, plus he's the survivor of more than 50 ferry flights, most across oceans. "SO YOU WANT TO BE A FERRY PILOT" is a book describing some of the more exciting of those flights.

Presently in the year 2002, Spike is living in The Philippine Islands, he's 61 years old, married to a young Filipina named Lucille, they have a beautiful spoiled 7 year old daughter named Maebelyn, he's still flying airplanes and working on his Nobel Prize winning book.

Chapter I

THE PILOT

Luke Air Force Base, Phoenix, Arizona

It's November, 1973, Slick Adams is half way through his last day as a member of the United States Air Force. Two more stops on his list and the check out process will be complete. All that's left is a stop at finance for his final pay check, then over to the personnel building to pick up his honorable discharge and the final sign out, but that's after lunch.

Slick stops his 55 T-BIRD in front of the Luke Officers Club, steps out and takes a look around, *I'm gonna miss this joint, good food, good booze, some good parties and a lot of good people, but I gotta get out of this place.*

Slick Adams had turned thirty earlier in the month. His birthday had been celebrated right here at the "O" Club stag bar, Slick and his friends had all got a little bit drunk as they toasted his last birthday as one of the Boys In Blue and the start of his new life on the outside.

Contrary to the style of the day, long hair, moustaches and long side burns, Slick's hair is short cropped, his face clean shaven. His entire appearance is that of a young Air Force Officer, trim and fit. You wouldn't describe Slick as handsome, not in the movie star sense anyway, but his image did fit what he is, a highly trained fighter pilot, cool and confident in whatever he set out to do.

As Slick enters the club, he is hailed by some squadron mates, *"Join us for lunch, we'll buy you a farewell burger."*

The lunch conversation is about Slick's impending departure later in the day.

"Why are you getting out? You got it made, you're almost halfway to retirement, shit man, twelve more years of flying around in Uncle Sam's best fighters and you retire with a nice pension for life. You'd be what? Forty two, you could start a new career, fly for one of the airlines."

"I'm tired of people telling me what to do, I want to be my own boss."

Slick's friends persist, *"Telling you what to do? All you got to do is go fly a shiny new Phantom four or five times a week, how hard can that be?"*

Slick is adamant, *"This peace time flying sucks, I'm sick of filling out bullshit forms, filling in stupid squares, being told what to do by burned out majors and colonels who couldn't fly a kite. I guess I just got spoiled over in Nam, no bullshit, just takeoff, find the target, blast it and head for home, get shit faced, get laid and do it all over again the next day. Sorry boys, I'm outta here, I can't handle the peace time military."*

"Listen to me Captain Slick, you've got a good record, more than a hundred combat missions, medals out the ass, you're sure to be promoted to major in two or three years, you could retire as a light colonel after twenty. You'd have a lifetime check over two thousand dollars at the tender age of forty two. Are you out of your mind?"

"You know the peacetime Air Force motto, When the weight of the paperwork equals the weight of the aircraft, you're cleared for takeoff. No thanks, I've had it, unless of course you guys could start up a little war in some exotic place where the weather is good and the girls are beautiful and horny like they were in Vietnam and Thailand."

Looks of reverie appear on all the pilot's faces, *"Yeah, life was good over there."*

"I do miss my little brown skinned dolls."

"Me too, but don't tell my wife."

"You weren't married then."

"Don't tell her anyway, she thinks I was true blue."

"She ain't that dumb."

Slick and his pals have a good bullshit session about the good old days in The Nam. They all agree that nothing can replace the rush of real combat flying.

"Anyway guys, nice try, thanks for lunch, I've got to pick up my check and sign out at personnel, I'll be a civilian in less than an hour, see you all around, I gotta di di mau."

"Adios Señor Slicko, later."

"See ya pals, remember to check ur six."

Slick shakes hands with his buddies and leaves the club, he

has no idea what his next adventure will be except that it will be something of his own choosing.

What's left of 1973 and all of 1974 pass.

Part way through 1975, South Vietnam is collapsing, North Vietnam will soon control the entire country. It is now obvious that Johnson and McNamarra have put together the biggest fiasco in American history, not to mention the billions wasted and the fifty eight thousand American lives squandered.

Chapter II

THE MESSAGE

Slick Adams watches on T V as the last American helicopter lifts off the roof of the US Embassy in Saigon, he salutes the television with his glass of beer, *"Good luck Nughyen, ur gonna need it, ur on ur own now."*

Since separating from the Air Force a year and a half earlier, Slick has gone through most of the few thousand dollars he had saved. Using the G. I. Bill, he has been able to get his civilian FAA commercial pilots license, FAA instructor rating for both single and multi-engine aircraft. He is now in Miami, Florida spending what's left of the G. I. Bill money to add single and multi-engine seaplane ratings to his license.

In another week, after completing the seaplane ratings, Slick is going to have to find a way to earn a buck. Either that or rob a bank, or even worse, sell his beloved Thunder Bird, he will soon be flat broke.

Slick isn't in any panic, all the major airlines are hiring, Western Airlines, Delta, PSAA and Eastern have all sent letters inviting Slick to come for a job interview. They are all eager to hire pilots who have been through the best training in the world, US Air Force pilot training.

But jesus, I'd be right back in a giant organization where people are promoted strictly by longevity, talent be damned. There's got to be some way I can earn a decent dollar without being told what to do by a bunch of people who's only claim to fame is they've been on the payroll longer than me.

Slick took to seaplanes like ducks take to water. After completing the single engine rating in an amphibious Super Cub, he started the multi-engine program in a 1944 Widgeon, his instructor was a crazy Italian named Jerry.

After six hours of instruction, Slick took his multi-engine seaplane check ride, he passed with flying colors. He still had four hours flying time available on the G.I. Bill.

Slick was about to break a lot of laws by using up these

four hours.

First, he and instructor Jerry were going to be defrauding the United States Government. Charging training to the G.I. Bill after completing a check ride is a crime punishable by a big fine and jail time. No big deal, just juggle the paperwork so the check ride is dated after the entire flying allotment has expired.

Second, Slick and Jerry were planning to fly south towards Cuba, find Cuban rock crab traps, land in the water, pull up the traps and steal the crabs from the communist Cuban crab fishermen. This would violate every commercial fishing treaty ever signed between Cuba and the U S.

Third, the flight would take Slick and Jerry out of U S airspace, into Cuban airspace, then back into U S airspace, all without clearance. Of course, no clearance could be obtained, the whole deal was illegal. Who cared, they'd only be stealing crabs from a sworn enemy of the United States of America. Even if they got caught by the U S Coast Guard, no big deal, just plead ignorance. *"So we're a few miles south of U S airspace, how were we supposed to know, there isn't a line painted on the water, is there?"*

Being caught by the Cuban fishermen would be a different story, explaining wouldn't be necessary, Cuban fishermen shoot poachers. But, no big deal, after all, we're in an airplane, we'll just fly a big circle, make sure no boats are in sight, land, steal the crabs and haul ass. Fuck the commies.

Later that evening there was a giant stone crab feast at Jerry's house. Being stolen, the crab claws tasted even better, everybody at the crab orgy had a good laugh as Jerry told his much embellished tale of crab thievery. *"The first trap we landed next to was damn near full, Slick was pulling so hard that water started coming over the bottom of the door. I could just see the headlines, two pilots drown trying to steal crabs."*

"To top off our day of robbery, after we had pulled and emptied the last trap, the right engine wouldn't start, there we were, taxing around in circles, knowing that any minute, armed Cuban fishing boats would appear on the horizon."

"Obviously we got it started or there wouldn't have been a party this afternoon, I just wanted you all to know that Slick and I

risked our butts for your culinary enjoyment."
Everybody applauded, then continued with the feast.

Later when Slick returned to his hotel, there was a message for him at the desk. *"Mister Adams, please call Pete Williams. He will be at this number tonight and tomorrow morning."*
Slick asked the receptionists if she recognized the area code, *"Yes sir, it's the Tampa, St. Petersburg area code."*
"Thank you, I'll call him in the morning."
On the way up to his room, Slick pondered the message, *I wonder if this is the Pete Williams I knew in the Air Force? Must be, wonder how he knew I was here?*
Slick showered and hit the sack, it had been a long day.

Chapter III

THE CREW

With absolutely nothing on his agenda, Slick slept in the next morning. After coffee and a croissant in bed, he asked the front desk to dial the phone number Pete Williams had left the day before, a minute later the operator called back and connected Slick with his party.

"Hello Slick, it's Pete Williams, how's ur ass?"

"Long time no see, how'd you track me down?"

"I talked to your brother out in California, he gave me the hotel number. Hey Slick, how bout you stoppin here in Tampa before you head back to the west coast, I got a business proposition I'd like to make you."

"What about?"

"I'd rather talk to you in person, don't worry about spending any money, me and my partners will cover all your expenses."

"That's good, I'm about tapped, I haven't had a real job since I got out, just the odd charter flight, but shit man, I've got damn near every civilian pilot rating known to man, and you know what a multi-engine seaplane rating and a cup of coffee will get ya."

"Look Slick, I'll get you a ticket organized and call you right back, I'll try to arrange for a mid afternoon takeoff from Miami so you can sleep in."

"Okay Pete, I'll wait for your call, guess I'll see you later today."

The life of Slick Adams was about to make a very large change.

At about five that afternoon, Slick stepped into the Tampa Airport terminal, he was met immediately by Pete Williams, they shook hands, Pete led the way to the parking lot. Slick noticed that no great changes had occurred over the past eight years in Pete's appearance, he was still trim and dapper. There was one thing about

Pete that Slick couldn't help but notice, he was dressed to the nines, alligator skin shoes, tailored slacks and shirt and a beautiful ring with a rather large stone held in place by a lot of gold.

Just outside the terminal in the VIP parking lot, Pete approached his car, a new four door metallic green Mercedes Benz.

"Jesus Christ, what do you do, rob banks?"

"Hell no, robbing banks is dangerous, bank robbers don't make beans, what we do is a lot safer and a hell of a lot more profitable. Fasten your seat belt, I'll fill you in on the way to my house. There's some cold beer in the cooler behind you, grab a pair."

Slick pulled two ice cold cans of Bud out of the cooler, he handed one to Pete, *"Thanks man, looks like life has been treating you pretty good."*

"I got no complaints."

"So what's this business deal you got for me?"

"Before I go into any details, what me and my partners do is illegal. You want me to continue?"

"Sure, lay it on me."

"It goes without saying that whatever I tell you stays between you and me, whether you decide to join us or not."

"You got my word on that."

"First, the reason I picked you, I know from experience that you're a hell of a good pilot, from what I've heard you don't rattle under pressure and you thrive on excitement."

"Somebody's going to pay me a lot of money to fly down to Havana and drop a bomb on Fidel Castro?"

"The flight is a little longer, we're going to Colombia for a load of grass."

"Grass?"

"You know, pot, marijuana, ganja."

"You done this before?"

"Our group has made quite a bit of money bringing in pot by boat, it takes too long and there are too many chances to get caught, we want to switch to airplanes."

"What kind of plane are you planning on?"

"That's where you come in, we want you to investigate light twin engine planes, we want one that can fly one thousand four hundred miles, land on a dirt strip, re-fuel then fly the same

distance back with one thousand two hundred pounds of pot on board. We air drop the pot in the middle of nowhere, come back to the airport and land. Even if the cops are waiting for us, all they have is suspicions."

"What kind of money can we make on a deal like that?"

"There would be four of us involved, one guy who puts up all the money, you know, the cost of the plane, the cost of the pot and the set up money. Another guy on the ground to pick up the dope after we drop it and you and me. We split everything four ways after we take out a little for the guy who paid for everything."

"About how much would I end up with?"

Pete rattled off some numbers, Slick wrote them on a piece of paper. 1200 pounds of dope sold for $340 dollars a pound equals $408,000 dollars. Cost of the pot in Colombia, $60 dollars a pound equals $72,000 dollars. Take out $50,000 each flight for the plane and expenses.

$408,000
-72,000
=336,000
-50,000
=286,000 divided by four equals about $71,000 dollars for each of the four partners per flight.

"Seventy one thousand bucks for one day's work, sounds pretty tempting, when would all this take place if I did decide to get in on the deal?"

"Not until next November after the hurricane season, we'd have seven months to get the plane and set everything up."

"How would I live til then, I'm almost broke?"

"Don't worry about money, our money man has lots of that, you'd be paid a good salary in cash until we made our first run. It's all part of the fifty thou he gets each flight in addition to his quarter."

"You ready for another cool one?"

"Yeah, just thinking about all that money is making my mouth water, where would I live?"

"Stand-by one."

Twenty minutes later, Pete pulls to a stop in front of a modern two story house, the back yard stops at the edge of a small lake. They walk around the side of the house, there's a small dock with a speed boat tied to it. *"I see you're still into water skiing, Pete."*

"Come on inside, I'll show you the pad."

Pete leads the way, *"I live upstairs with my girlfriend Brenda, follow me."*

The upstairs bedroom is sumptuous, the king size bed is the centerpiece. Above and to one side of the bed are giant mirrors. Between huge hi-fi speakers is a large color TV set. An eight foot long window overlooks the lake, there are no curtains.

Inside the bathroom is a sunken tub that's almost big enough to swim in. There is enough closet space to hang all the clothes Slick owns five times over.

"Pretty fancy."

"What money can't buy, it can always rent."

As Slick leaves the bathroom, he bumps into a small movie screen, *"What's this for? You make home movies?"*

"My girlfriend likes to watch porno flicks, I got about a hundred of them."

"I take it she's the babe in all the pictures."

There are more than a dozen photos of the same doll scattered around the room, she's a hot looking chick who isn't afraid to show off her beautiful body.

"She's not shy."

"She's loaded most of the time."

"Loaded on what?"

"Whatever."

"Come on down, I'll show you your room."

"Does my room come with a girl as sexy as yours?"

"No sweat, there are tons of chicks around here."

The down stairs portion of the house appears to have been recently re-modeled. Facing the lake is a large Florida room, it's cluttered with water skies and boat paraphernalia. The kitchen doesn't appear to be used very much, Slick opens the fridge door, no beer shortage here.

"Doesn't look like you eat at home very often."

"*Brenda can't even boil water, grab a couple of beers while you got the door open, here's your room.*"

The downstairs master bedroom is finished in natural wood, there isn't a stick of furniture.

"*If you decide to stay, you can pick ur own stuff.*"

"*This job has a lot of perks.*"

"*What we are planning to do will make us all a lot of money, we want to get and keep the best pilot available, we think you are that pilot, therefore, we're willing to make this as attractive to you as we can. You'll have this house next to the lake, you've got that ski boat at your disposal, tomorrow we can pick up your car. When we buy the plane, you can be sure it will be as mechanically sound as money can make it. Look Slick, we've learned a lot about this business. Why risk four hundred thousand dollars by cutting corners, you know, when we need a part, put in a new one instead of saving a few bucks trying to fix something that's broke.*"

"*We've seen acquaintances lose tons of dope just because they bought cheap radios and couldn't communicate with their people on the beach. I know a sailboat smuggler who lost five thousand pounds of high grade pot, his boat and hundreds of thousands in legal fees just because he refused to give his captain a twenty-five thousand dollar raise. The captain, with several trips under his belt, quit in a huff. The replacement captain got lost and got arrested near Miami, four hundred miles south of where he was supposed to be. The dumb shit couldn't even read a sextant. In fact, the real dumb shit was our cheapskate friend who refused to give the genuine captain a little raise.*"

"*Slick, you join up with us and we'll take care of you, we want this deal to work.*"

"*Pedro my boy, you drive a hard bargain.*"

"*Okay, no more talk about business, we're going out for a few drinks, you'll meet Sam, one of the other partners.*"

"*How bout number four?*"

"*He's layin low for a few months, one of the other deals he financed went sour. He's stayin out of sight, he thinks one of the guys who got busted might sing to save his ass.*"

"*What do you think?*"

"*I don't know anybody involved in that caper, I don't want to know. That's the beauty of our little setup, there's only four of us. Sam would fry before he'd give up a partner, you'll see what I mean when you meet him. The money man has been popped before, he's solid. I'd never squeal, if a man has no loyalty, he has nothing."*

"Let's go, Brenda is waiting for us at our favorite watering hole."

The local watering hole was jammed with yuppies, yuppie wannabees and real people who had made it one way or the other, it was standing room only. Pete led Slick through the crowd to the far side of the bar. Brenda was there with a drink in her hands.

The first thing Slick noticed about Brenda was her eyes, glazed over and droopy. She'd either had a lot of alcohol or she was very high on one drug or another. Well actually the second thing he noticed was her eyes, Brenda was wearing a see through top, her spectacular tits were right there for the world to see, there was no brassier interfering with the glorious view.

"That's Brenda."

"She's got great tits."

"You noticed."

"I'm glad she forgot her bra."

"She doesn't own one."

Pete introduced Slick to Brenda, she gave him a juicy kiss and squished her lovely tits against his arm when she hugged him hello.

Slick couldn't help but wonder why all the guys around Brenda weren't ogling her great boobs like he was. He whispered to Pete, *"I can't figure out why all these guys are pretending not to notice this world class set of tits, are they all fags?"*

"No man, this is the yuppie generation, they're all much too cool to notice."

"Guess I'm not a yuppie, I can't take my eyes off those things."

"Wait until you see what she wears when we go boating."

"I can't wait."

A cute waitress delivered some drinks, Brenda went on about how happy she was to finally meet Pete's old Air Force buddy, Slick tried to pay attention but it was hard.

Sam arrived, it's not that he was some giant muscle man, there wasn't one particular aspect of Sam that you could pinpoint, but his overall appearance simply shouted, *"Don't fuck with me!"*

"Good to meet you, Slick, how you doing? Hi there Miss Brenda Boobs, nice to see you, both of you."

"Oh Sam."

"Slick, you ever seen a set like that?"

Sam wasn't one to beat around the bush, to him, a spade was a spade, Slick liked him instantly.

More drinks arrived, Brenda made several trips to the ladies room, Sam laughed, *"That's powdering your nose in the literal sense."*

Slick looked confused, Pete explained, *"She's snorting cocaine in the head."*

"No shit?"

"No shit, probably half the people in this joint have some coke in their pockets, you want a snort?"

Slick recoiled, *"Fuck no, I don't do drugs."*

"Really?"

"Really."

Brenda introduced Slick to one of her girlfriends. Lola was a hot looking doll, great legs, eight on the breast work, eight and a half face, but who cared, who noticed, this broad was packing a double ten ass. Her skin tight semi mini skirt was tailored to follow every curve of this world class butt.

As they continued talking, Lola snuggled right up against Slick, he didn't resist when she wiggled in even closer, her tits were as firm as a teenager's.

Brenda winked, she and Lola dashed off to the ladies room.

Even though it was three drinks and a couple of beers into the night, Slick was still way too alert to be completely duped, *"I'm either the most irresistible man in this bar or you guys have just offered the perk of perks."*

Sam laughed like hell, *"We just got her here, the rest is up to you, but what about that body?"*

"My boys, between Brenda's tits and Lola's ass, I'm gonna have a tough time paying much attention to anything you two have to say. What's the story with Lola?"

Sam shrugged, *"Just another hard body looking for a little action with somebody who's got cash, she's Brenda's buddy, what's she up to, Pete?"*

"She's been a kept woman for the last couple of years. Some rich heart doctor gave her a new sports car and a condo on the beach in exchange for exclusive rights to her pussy. The doc's wife caught them a couple of months ago, Lola lost her monthly pay check but she kept the car and condo."

The girls returned from the powder room. When Slick's eyes locked on to Lola's posterior, he couldn't help but feel sorry for the heart doctor.

A strange apparition floated across the room, she took Sam's arm and looked angelically up at his face, she literally glowed.

"Slick, meet Sarah."

If Slick could have picked any woman in the world who didn't belong with Sam, it would have been Sarah. Here was this totally natural beauty, not a touch of makeup, dressed in a loose fitting gown that almost touched the ground, obviously mad about her man. Her man, a bad ass looking dude who you'd expect to see with some gun moll, glowed back at his lady. What a match.

Talk about different women, Brenda and Lola exuding sex from every pore, various parts of their bodies exposed to the world, then we have Sarah, the most beautiful girl in the bar, covered from neck to ankle by a simple dress, Slick needed another drink.

"And what do you do, Sarah?"

"I love Sam."

The answer couldn't have been more concise.

Sam snapped Slick back to reality, *"Let's go eat, we've got reservations at Burns Steak House."*

Burns Steak House claims to serve the best steaks east of the Mississippi River, Slick was soon to find that their claim was well founded.

Sam ordered extra dry Beefeater martinis for everybody, the cocktail waitress scurried off.

"You're gonna love the way they serve martinis here."

Minutes later the cocktail waitress rushed back with a pitcher that was so cold it was steaming. The martini glasses on her tray were also ice cold. Without wasting time, she filled each of the six glasses with Beefeaters Gin that was so frigid it had the viscosity of motor oil. Next, she asked, starting with the girls, how dry they wanted their martini. Each response was answered with an eye dropper full of dry vermouth, extra dry got two drops, dry got four, Slick's extra dry martini was the best he'd ever had.

Pete and Sam didn't know it yet, but their recruit had been recruited.

Things just kept getting better, the steaks were perfect, the cheesecake was scrumptious, the fifty year old Napoleon Brandy was almost too smooth.

As they walked outside the restaurant, Slick remembered he had no place to stay, *"Where am I gonna crash, there's no furniture in my room?"*

Sam picked up on Slick's reference to "his room" and smiled.

Lola solved the problem, *"You're welcome to stay at my condo in Clearwater, that is if we can get Pete to drive us home, I'm way too loaded."*

"No sweat, but you gotta promise us one for the road."

Sam and Sarah bid the foursome adieu, *"See you all in a day or two."*

Lola's condominium overlooked a long beach of white sand north of downtown Clearwater, her heart doctor had had a good eye for real estate. Pete and Brenda had stayed just long enough to have one cup of coffee, they then headed for home. Having nowhere to go, Slick had made his coffee the Irish kind. Lola had declined coffee, *"It keeps me awake, excuse me, I have to wee-wee."*

Slick had another Irish coffee, Lola didn't return, her snoring could be heard through the bedroom door.

Slick peeled off his clothes and flopped on the couch, the events of the day passed through his mind, *"These guys really know how to live, guess I'm going to be a criminal."*

The aroma of coffee and bacon awoke Slick from a deep sleep.

Lola noticed that Slick had stirred, *"Sorry about last night, guess I zonked out."*

"Me too, damn that smells good, anything I can do to help?"

"You could massage my neck, I've got a bit of a head-ache."

Slick pulled on his pants and shirt, he then walked around the mini bar separating the kitchen from the front room. Lola was cooking in her shorty pajamas, other than her eyes being a little puffy, she looked great.

"After we have a bite, we can jump in the hot tub, you up to that?"

"Sounds perfect, now let me work on your neck."

Thirty minutes later, Lola and Slick were out on the balcony neck deep in the one hundred and four degree hot tub.

"You want some wine?"

"Sure, why not?"

Lola stepped out of the tub, *"You look better naked than you do with clothes on."*

"Thanks, I guess."

"Few women do."

"Then, thanks."

Slick's eyes followed Lola as she walked inside to get the wine, *"Jesus Christ, look at that fucking body, is this really happening?"*

The wine was real, Lola was real, her unbelievable body was real, when they got out of the hot tub, they had real sex, twice, then the real phone rang bringing Slick back to the real world.

"It's Pete for you."

Slick's new furniture was delivered later in the afternoon. By six, everything was in place, the downstairs master bedroom was ready to live in.

Pete brought two cold beers to celebrate the grand opening of Slick's new home, *"This turned out pretty damn good, only problem is, now you don't have any excuse to go shack up with Lola."*

"I'll miss her ass, but there's nothing ever gonna happen between us except yesterday's roll in the hay. She knows it, I know it."

"No bigee, as you've seen, this town is full of available chicks."

"Look Pete, I guess I've sorta committed to this operation. There's one thing I need to know before I get totally involved."

"What's that?"

"Let's just assume that something goes totally haywire and we get caught red handed with a thousand pounds of pot, how much trouble are we in for?"

Pete went off on a long explanation of the drug laws in Florida, he went into particular detail concerning people who had been caught with large quantities of marijuana. The fate of those apprehended boiled down to one simple fact, those with expensive, big time lawyers almost always got off with fines and or short terms in minimum security lock up facilities.

Pete knew in great detail about a group that had been nabbed with five tons of pot. They had been busted while unloading the dope from their shrimp boat in a little cove along Florida's coast. No case could have been more concrete, the cops had the dope, the boat, the crew, the trucks and drivers who had come to pick up the load, everything, a simple open and shut case.

The big shot lawyers had got most of the gang off with fines, the leaders did a short stay at a famous prison country club in northern Florida. They had played tennis and golf daily with some political big shots who'd been caught with their hands in the cookie jar.

"What the hell kind of defense could they possibly come up with, they caught them with the goods?"

"The lawyers convinced the jury that their clients were just a bunch of young guys having the adventure of a lifetime. They'd seen all these Mafia hoods making millions and never getting caught, they just couldn't resist the temptation."

"And it worked?"

"Slick as a whistle."

"If you're only going to get your hands slapped, you'd think everybody with a boat or plane would give it a go."

"There's more amateur smugglers out there than you'd believe."

"Do we have a lawyer?"

"The same firm that got the boys with five tons off."

"I like it."

"Shit man, you and I are mini war heroes, Sam has never been busted for anything, he has a good reputation with his business, we're lily white. We're only talking about a little over a thousand pounds, we'd barely make the paper if we got popped."

"What about our money man?"

"If we ever get busted, he doesn't exist."

"I still don't know who he is."

"You see, he's non existent."

"So, we're just three clean cut young punks who couldn't resist the urge to try for some easy money."

"Not only that, if they got us, we'd swear it was our first try, then we'd promise never to be naughty again. Look Slick, we're not getting caught, we're gonna do this thing right."

Pete went on with the basic plan that he and Sam had come up with. They would buy whatever aircraft they decided on out west, register it to a fictitious name and use a PO Box in Oregon that had been opened earlier under the fictitious name.

Any modifications that had to be done on the plane would be carried out in the northwest. Florida had so many smugglers working that all airports were on the lookout for aircraft that had extra fuel tanks or had been plumbed for long range tanks. Oregon was way too far from South America for anybody to pay any attention to planes rigged for long flights.

"In the next couple of days, you and I will lay out the flight in detail. After we know exactly how far we've got to fly, we'll be able to find the right plane for the job, then you'll go plane shopping. What twin engine planes have you flown?"

"I got my multi-engine rating in a Cessna 310, it's no good for a deal like this, then I flew a Cessna 421 a little, it's made for comfort, not payload. The charter outfit I was flying for in California just checked me out in a Piper Navajo, it's fast and carries a hell of a load, a Navajo might be perfect."

Outside with two fresh beers, Pete and Slick made plans for

the following days. In the morning they would drive down to Sarasota where there is a pilot's supply shop. There they'd buy all the necessary maps, bring them back to the house and lay out the trip in detail. As soon as they had the mileage, they could begin a serious search for the aircraft best suited for their needs.

Their next task would be to spend a few days visiting airports in central Florida. They would be looking for a busy airport that had a lot of planes and enough light twins so theirs wouldn't bring any unnecessary attention.

Pete pulled a thick wad of cash out of his pocket, *"Here's five thousand, your first month's salary, it's for your personal expenses. Anything you pay for that's for the project, keep track, we'll cover it."*

"So far I like the job."

"You'll earn it next fall."

"How many runs are we going to make?"

"Shit, I don't know, a lot I hope. Let's just see how smooth it goes, wouldn't you like to have a cool million in your Swiss account this time next year?"

"Considering that right now I have zero, it sounds pretty good."

"This board meeting is over, let's hit a couple of bars and check out the action."

"I second the motion."

On the way to where ever they were going, Slick asked Pete some questions, *"Does Brenda know what you're up to?"*

"Hell no! All she knows is that I'm in partnership with Sam."

"Doing what?"

"Sam has a nursery."

Slick can't believe his ears, *"Sam sells flowers?"*

"Yeah, isn't that wild."

"I'd a picked him as a hit man or some kind of Mafia enforcer, but sure as hell not a flower peddler."

"It's a great front."

"How bout Sam and Sarah?"

"Isn't she a beauty, Sarah's a flower child left over from the sixties, she's been watering plants at Sam's place for years."

"What does she know?"

"Between her beloved plants and her meditation and her devotion to Sam, I don't think she ever thinks about anything else."

"They are a weird pair."

"Sam loves her ass, nobody ever fucks with her, not twice anyway."

"Is Sam as bad as I think he is?"

"He's the genuine article."

"Where we headed?"

"A little seafood joint out on the causeway towards Saint Pete."

A few minutes later, they came to a stop in front of a totally unpretentious restaurant, the sign said, "FRESH SEAFOOD."

"This place is always good."

"I remember this place, I came here a million times when I was based at MacDill." (MacDill Air Force Base, located on the south edge of Tampa)

Pete ordered beer, two shrimp cocktails, a dozen oysters on the half shell and some soft shelled crab. He told the waitress to bring a large order of shrimp grilled with garlic and butter when they had finished their hors d'oeuvres.

While eating, they reminisced about the good and not so good old days in the Air Force and some of their mutual acquaintances, some no longer among the living.

"You ever hear for sure what happened to Red Fischer? When I got out in sixty seven, he was listed as missing in action."

"Guess he bought the farm, when the POWs were released in seventy three, he wasn't one of them."

"Too bad, he was a good shit, remember when we all lived in that wild apartment over on Cypress Avenue, what a place, we really had it made."

"What was the name of those two broads who used to hang around the pool with about twenty five pounds of tits between them?"

"Susie and Sally."

"What a pair, how could I forget. I think Red was fucking both of them."

"He wasn't the only one."

"You dirty dog, you didn't? Maybe that's why they call you Slick."

"Wasn't too hard."

"Hey Slick, you remember that cute little broad you were always with, the student nurse?"

"How could I forget darling Rosemary, what a girl. She used to wait til I got home, then she'd sneak over to my apartment and keep me up half the night."

"She lives around here somewhere, I ran into her a couple of months ago."

"No kidding."

"She married some big time lawyer, he died of something weird, left her a bundle."

"How's she looking these days? It's almost been nine years."

"I think she looks better."

"I'd love to see her, you know how to find her?"

The two detectives try to figure out how to track down Slick's old girl friend. Pete can't remember the last name of the dead lawyer husband, but he's sure any Tampa lawyer will know, seems as though he was quite famous in lawyer circles.

Slick fell asleep that night wondering about Rosemary.

The drive from Tampa to Sarasota takes about two hours, it's a scenic trip, first across the twenty mile long Tampa Bay Bridge, then along the shoreline south until reaching Sarasota.

At the pilot supply store, Pete gathered all the necessary maps, Slick picked up a tri-monthly publication called, Trade-A-Plane. Over the years, Trade-a-Plane had become the bible for people interested in buying or selling aircraft, there were thousands upon thousands of planes listed. He was also able to get a pilot's manual for the Piper Navajo and the Cessna-402.

On the way back to the house, they made several stops, first they had brunch at a funky little restaurant called "Toddle House", breakfast, the specialty, is served twenty four hours a day.

Next, Pete parked in front of an impressive looking office building in downtown Tampa, *"Wait a minute."*

Five minutes later he returned with a smile on his face, *"His last name was Street, how could I forget a name like that? Now all we gotta do is find Rosemary Street."*

Their last stop was at Sam's nursery, *"There's your car."*

Pete pointed at a lime green two door Mercedes 450 SL, *"The hard top is removable, it has a rag convertible top if you get caught out in the rain."*

"Who do I thank?"

"Don't worry about it, it's yours to use as long as you want, think of it as another perk that comes with the job."

Slick followed Pete back to the house where they went straight to work on the maps. Pete had bought a variety of maps and charts. One planning map covered the entire area they would be operating in including all of Florida, the Caribbean Sea and the northern coast line of South America. For central and southern Florida he had picked up a stack of sectional charts with a detailed scale of 1 to 500,000. Sectional charts weren't available for northern Colombia, the most detailed he had found were ONC (Operational Navigation Charts) that had adequate detail. The scale of the ONCs was half that of the sectionals, 1 to 1,000,000.

"Don't worry, before we make our first trip south, we'll take a vacation to Colombia, our man down there will take us out to the landing strip we're going to use, I think he even has a plane we can fly around in. Before we go there on business, we'll have seen the place from the air and the ground."

Using the Route Planning Chart, they measured the distances and added up the miles. They assumed the starting point would be one of the many airports located somewhere between Tampa on Florida's west coast and Daytona on the east coast. Mid way between Tampa and Daytona lies Orlando with at least a dozen airports within a thirty mile radius.

The Route

Orlando Area	> Point just south of Ft. Pierce	160 miles
Ft. Pierce	> Point just west of Freeport	80 miles
Freeport	> Great Inagua Island	490 miles
Great Inagua Is.	> Southern Coast of Haiti	210 miles
S.Coast of Haiti	> North Coast of Colombia	460 miles
N.Coast, Colombia	> Landing Strip	50 miles
	Total distance	1450 miles

According to the pilot's manuals, the Navajo and the Cessna-402 would both cruise along at ten thousand feet at about 155 knots true air speed, that means the time in route would be about nine hours and a few minutes. Add an extra hour, make it two extra hours, they'd plan enough fuel for eleven hours at a conservative 30 gallons per hour. They needed a Navajo or Cessna-402 with 330 gallons of gas on board.

Navajo or Cessna-402, no matter, whatever aircraft they selected, they now knew how far it had to go. From the distance, they could calculate the time by the speed and the amount of fuel required by the time it would take to get from central Florida to Colombia.

Slick and Pete, being ex fighter pilots, both knew how to figure down to a gnat's ass, the payload, whatever kind of plane they ended up flying.

"You said we're going to drop the stuff before we land, where?"

Pete pointed to a general area north-east of Tampa, *"Sam knows of a thousand acre ranch around here, he says no one is ever there."*

"We'll have to figure a little extra gas to get from there to our airport."

"We already got two hours, remember, every extra gallon of gas means six pounds less pot at three hundred forty bucks a pound."

"How many passes we gotta make when we drop the shit?"

"I don't know, we'll have to figure that out when we get the plane, I guess we'd better plan on plenty of gas, I don't want to land with a bunch of dope just because we got a little greedy. Like I said, we're going to do this thing right, when we get the plane, we'll have plenty of time to get the exact fuel consumption figured out, then we'll get a long range tank welded up that holds exactly the right amount of extra gas. I know a guy who makes aluminum fuel tanks for boats. He makes all sizes and shapes."

"What if someone looks in the window of our plane and sees a couple hundred gallon gas tank, isn't he going to get a little suspicious?"

"Slicko, you don't think we're going to leave the tank in the plane do you? We'll either take it out after we land or throw it out the fucking door, we can always get another tank."

After finishing with all the charts and manuals, Pete carefully packed everything inside a briefcase with a combination lock, then stowed it in Slick's closet.

"I don't want Brenda seeing too much airplane stuff laying around here, wouldn't want her little pea brain working overtime. She thinks the most daring thing I ever do is prune the roses, let's keep it that way."

Slick laughed, *"You guys must sell a shit load of roses to pay for all these toys, I never saw so many cars and boats and houses, who owns all this junk, anyway?"*

"The same non existent guy who's gonna buy the plane owns all the cars, we got a P.O. Box here in town where the cars are registered. I own the boat, the corporation that owns the nursery owns the house."

Pete went to the kitchen for two cans of Bud, Slick went to the phone to see if information had a listing for Rosemary Street. The information operator said there was no Rosemary Street, but one R. Street. Slick wrote the number down.

"Hey Pete, if I get hold of Rosemary, what's our schedule?"

"We make our own schedule, I'd like to take a look at those airports in the next week, other than that, we're free as a bunch of birds."

Slick dialed the number, after two rings, the unmistakable voice of Rosemary answered, *"Hello."*

"Rosemary, this is Slick Adams."

"Slick Adams, you naughty boy, it's been a long time between calls."

Thus started Slick and Rosemary's re-acquaintance.

"Look Rosemary, you know how I hate to gab on the phone, let's get together and go over the last nine years in person."

They made a date for the following day. There was an art festival being held in Winter Park, a small town close to Orlando, they'd drive over together and get caught up.

"How's she doing?"

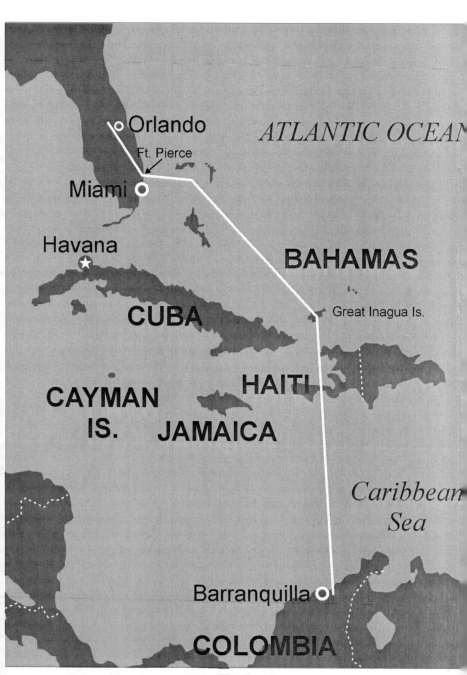

The Route

"She sounds exactly the same, we're going to Winter Park tomorrow."

"That's great, she's a nice broad. We got some time to kill, let's drive over to the Saint Pete Airport and look at planes, I want to see what a Navajo and a Cessna-402 look like, I'll buy you some crab on the way back."

"You got a deal."

The aircraft dealer at the St Petersburg Clearwater Airport had about fifteen planes in front of his office, two of them were Piper Navajos. The dealer had already left for the day but his secretary was happy to unlock one or both of the planes, "You men make yourselves at home, take as much time as you want, I'm here until six."

Slick and Pete made their way up forward to the cockpit and sat in the pilots and co-pilots seats. As soon as the secretary returned to her office, Pete took a tape measure out of his pocket. Slick held one end of the tape, Pete went to the rear of the plane, as they took measurements, Pete was writing them down on a sketch he had made of an airplane cabin.

"We could rip out this potty room and add two feet."

They took careful measurements of the cabin door opening. The long range fuel tank had to be able to fit in through the door.

"You sure this door can be opened in flight? We gotta be able to throw the shit out."

"I'm positive, I think we'd only have to open the bottom half."

Slick demonstrated opening the bottom half of the passenger door from inside the cabin, it fell down with a clunk. They decided that when they did it for real, instead of letting the door bang open, they'd tie a rope to it so the door could be gently lowered before commencing the drop. They also decided to attach a rope or a bungee cord to the top portion of the door to hold it closed, the space provided by the bottom portion was plenty for throwing bundles out.

"You think this will hold a big tank and twelve hundred pounds of stuff?"

"All depends on the size of the packages."

"That's right isn't it, if the bundles are packed loose, we'd be lucky to get five hundred pounds in here, that's something we'll have to be sure about when we take our vacation down south, the size and weight of the average package. Lets get the hell out of here before some DEA sleuth blows our deal before we even get started. I just wanted to see what one of these Navajos looked like, they're cool looking little planes."

On the ride to the crab shack they went over other aspects of the project. The fuel tank was critical, it would need to be engineered to use the least amount of space possible. It would need to be as tall as possible and still pass through the cabin door. Tall and skinny so it would fit snuggly along one side of the cabin and leave as much space as possible for the valuable cargo.

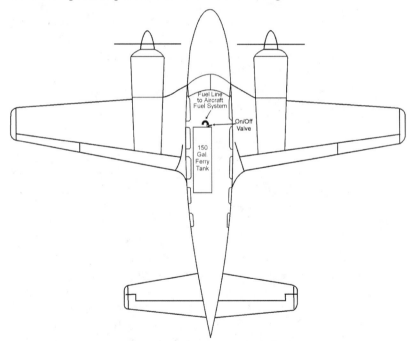

Navajo And Long-range Tank

"Let's have some stone crab, we got plenty of time to figure everything out, but you know, now that I've been in one of those little twins I'm getting excited, this deal is going to work slick as snot, pardon the pun."

Over dinner they discussed what Slick would tell Rosemary. They decided it would be best to say that he was working for a west coast plane broker who had a market for several light twins. That would explain any trips they made to airports and any talk about airplanes.

"Who knows, after tomorrow I may never see her again but I kind of doubt it, we always hit it off pretty good."

The next day at noon, Rosemary Street drove up and parked her car in front of the lake house, Slick watched as she walked up to the front door, no doubt it was Rosemary, but she looked a lot different. Slick opened the door before she knocked.

"Well Mister Adams, what do you think?"

"Like a fine wine, improving with age."

"You lying old bastard."

Slick and Rosemary gave each other a very big hug.

"How old were you nine years ago, nineteen or twenty?"

"Twelve."

"You liar."

"When you went away to war, I had just turned twenty, don't you remember? We celebrated my birthday together."

"Do breasts grow after twenty? These two feel and look considerably larger."

"My husband liked big tits, he bought these for me, now let go of me and quit feeling my body, a girl is allowed to have some secrets."

Still the same old Rosemary, full of piss and vinegar.

They talked and laughed about the times they had spent together all the way to Winter Park.

Rosemary's husband had been a good guy. He'd known he was dying for the last two years of his life. Instead of feeling sorry for himself, he'd tried to do everything, he and Rosemary had traveled all over the world, only the last three months had been bad.

"I'm glad you called, I haven't been out since he died, I wouldn't have any idea how to go about meeting a man, you're sort of like an old pair of shoes."

"Thanks a lot."

"You know what I mean."

The art show was interesting, all the cool people were there. Rosemary bought a little piece that she said reminded her of flying. Instead of driving all the way back to Tampa, they checked into a hotel in Orlando.

A week later they were still together, Rosemary had more or less moved into the lake house. She was just too easy to live with, not always around, but when she was, there were never any problems. Everybody seemed to get along with her, even spaced out Brenda, Sarah adored her, she made Sam laugh. When Slick and Pete would disappear on their mysterious missions, she never asked any questions. Rosemary was just Rosemary.

On one of the mysterious trips, Slick and Pete found what they thought would be the perfect airport. Thirty five miles north of Orlando in the middle of a cluster of lakes and small towns is a peaceful little airport named Leesburg. When Slick looked around he was sure this was their airport. There were airplanes all over the place, more than a hundred. Single engine and multi-engine planes were mixed together on the grass parking area. What really caught Slick's attention was that there were no automobile restrictions. Aircraft owners drove their cars right up to their planes, loaded or unloaded, did mechanical work or washed their planes. If the owner flew off for a few days, he left his car or van or motor home parked in the same spot where his plane had been parked. There were cars and vans and motor homes scattered all over the grass parking area.

There appeared to be dozens of unused parking spaces. Many of the parked aircraft had long grass growing up around the tires and underneath where the mower couldn't reach. A high percentage of the parked planes had reflective foil cloth inside the windows to prevent sun damage to the instruments and upholstery. The foil cloth also blocked any view from the outside to whatever was inside.

"*Pete, look at that Cessna-421. Can you tell me what he's got inside the cabin?*"

"*No way, I can't see a thing through the sun shield, I like it.*"

The longer they hung around Leesburg, the more they liked the place. Nobody seemed to pay any attention to what others were doing.

"Let's go to the office and ask about parking."

A sign over the Airport Office door read, *If I'm not here, call me at home, I live 5 minutes away, Manager.*

The manager was inside playing cards with some of his cronies.

"Hi ya, young fellas, can I hep ya?"

"Yes thanks, we have a friend who's planning on spending next winter here, how much would it cost him to park his plane here?"

"Single or twin?"

"Twin."

"Hundred and fifty a month on the grass, got no hangar space available."

"Do you always have parking space?"

"Always."

"Are the spaces assigned?"

"No, no, nothing that fancy, just grab any empty spot and come on in the office and sign up, if I'm not around, a day or two don't matter much, we're pretty laid back around here."

"Okay, thanks, we'll pass the word along."

"Thanks boys, be seeing ya."

Slick and Pete started walking back towards the car, *"This place is perfect."*

They decided to come back to the airport that night after dark to see if they got the same good vibes about the place.

The good vibes continued. In the cool of the evening there were several groups of people hanging around different airplanes. One group had lounge chairs set up, they were drinking beer and swapping yarns.

"You notice how many vans there are around here?"

"Lots."

"Perfect. If we were going to make a run tonight, we could back our van right up to the door of our plane, take the seats out, slide the tank in, fill the tank from the drums in the van, then drive the van to our hotel. Just before takeoff time, get dropped off here, do our thing. The next night, unload the tank, put the seats back in, then have a couple of cool ones seventy thousand dollars richer."

"All we need now is a van and a plane."
"Soon, very soon, damn, this place is better than I hoped."

During the two hour drive back to Tampa, Slick started making a list of things they would need before the first flight.

1. Van without windows
2. Three, 55 gallon drums
3. Electric gas pump with 20 feet of hose
4. Spare 12 volt battery to drive the pump
5. Reflective screens to cover windshields and windows
6. Selection of bungee cords and rope
7. Selection of tools
8. Duct tape

"Can you think of anything else?"
"I'm sure we'll think of more stuff after we get the plane and do some practice flying."
"How about a couple of thermos jugs for coffee, It's a pretty long haul."
"Good idea, I saw some stainless steel unbreakable ones somewhere the other day. "When you thinking about heading out west?"
"Pretty soon, I might as well go back to my job and get a little more flying time in those Navajos, I could be looking for our plane at the same time."
"Good idea, nothing much left to do here until about September. As soon as you find the right plane, give me a call, I'll be on the way, we'll have some fun."
"Okay buddy, see you tomorrow, it's gonna be a gas."

When Slick told Rosemary he was going back to California, she started pouting like a kid.
"You can come with me if you want."
"I want."
"Then get a packin woman, we're leaving in about a week."
"Where are we going to live? How long are we going to

be? How much stuff should I bring?"
     "Don't worry, we'll find a shack somewhere. Bring what-ever you want but remember the rule of traveling with me."
     "And what pray tell is that sacred rule?"
     "Whatever you bring you have to carry."
     'That's not fair."
     "It's written in stone."

Rosemary was bubbling with excitement, she drove off to her house to decide what to take out west.

     Slick was bubbling with excitement too but he wasn't thinking about what to pack, his thoughts were of the adventures that lie ahead in the not to distant future.

Chapter IV

THE PLANE

Two weeks later Slick and Rosemary moved into an overpriced apartment two hundred yards from the sand at Manhattan Beach about 10 miles south of Los Angeles International Airport.

Slick went right back to flying charters out of Torrance Airport. Every time he took a trip he scouted around for available Navajos and Cessna-402s, there were lots of them. The one he was looking for would have to have zero or almost zero time factory remanufactured engines and newly overhauled propellers. Another required feature was a cockpit door.

Very few Navajos had come from the factory with this feature. For their mission, the cockpit door was imperative.

One day in June, Slick met a guy who told him about a nice looking Navajo that had no engines or props. It was sitting in a hangar at Riverside Airport, the owner was broke, he couldn't afford to put new engines and propellers on the plane, it was for sale as is. The Navajo did have a cockpit door.

The plane sounded perfect. There would be no doubt about the newness or condition of the engines and props, they'd be brand new. Every hour put on the engines would be by Slick, he wouldn't have to take the word of any other pilot as to how he had treated the engines. Slick wanted two motors that were perfect, they would be hauling his ass out of a short dirt runway, in an overloaded airplane carrying taboo cargo in hostile territory over long stretches of unforgiving water.

Two days later, Slick wasn't scheduled for any flights, he and Rosemary drove out to Riverside to have a look see. The owner of the engineless Navajo had taken good care of his plane, too bad he hadn't been as careful with collecting money from his flying clients. For sixty-five thousand dollars he'd throw in the time expired engines and props, they were worth several thousand as trade in cores.

The mechanic who had maintained the Navajo came to the hangar and introduced himself, should a deal be struck, he was available to install and monitor the new engines and props during their break-in and sign the plane off for it's annual inspection.

The propeller overhaul would take about a month, the engines, who knew, it all depended on availability. Sensing a job, the mechanic made some phone calls. Within an hour, he had located two zero time factory re-manufactured Lycoming I-O-540s, whoever had ordered them had not paid the bill. As soon as $36,000.00 dollars was received by the overhaul company, the engines would be shipped to any US address requested.

Slick did some quick calculations:

Navajo	$ 65,000
2 engines	$ 36,000
2 props (approx.)	$ 6,000
installation & annual	$ 3,000
miscellaneous	$ 1,000
	$111,000

"I'll call my client in Oregon, assuming I can reach him, you'll get a definite yes or no before quitting time tomorrow."

"Pete, I think we got it."
"Lay it on me, buddy."
"For a hundred and eleven grand we'll end up with damn near a brand new Navajo with a fresh annual."

Slick explained in detail what he'd found, especially the part about the new engines.

"When could they have it ready to fly?"
"By the middle of July."
"Sounds good to me, what do we need to seal the deal?"
"The engines have to be paid for right now or we might lose them, the props will be C-O-D, the guy who owns the Navajo will sign a deal if we give him five grand now, then pay the rest before the first flight."

Pete said he would transfer fifty thousand to Slick's bank account first thing in the morning. That would be enough to pay for the engines, make a down payment on the Navajo, pay for the installation of the engines, a thousand for miscellaneous and five for Slick's June salary. Pete would bring the balance in cash out west when the propeller overhauls were finished.

Slick's first move the following morning was to his bank. He gave transfer instructions for thirty six thousand dollars to be transferred to the account of the engine overhaul company, got a cashiers check in the amount of five thousand payable to the Navajo owner and picked up two thousand in cash. He then drove out to Riverside and made a down payment on the Navajo in behalf of Mister Allen from Portland, Oregon.

Slick called the engine company and gave them shipping instructions, yes, they had received the money, the engines would be on the way later in the day.

Slick found the mechanic out on the ramp doing something to a plane that wouldn't start, he gave him a thousand in advance, told him the engines would arrive in a day or two.

The mission was on.

Pete called later to make sure that everything had gone as planned, *"Okay buddy, see you in about a month, keep me posted."*

"Talk to you later."

"Rosemary, let's go out for a couple of drinks, it's been a busy day."

"Only if you promise to stop treating me like some kind of airhead. Look Mister Slick, I'm not deaf or blind. I know that what-ever you're up to involves airplanes and drugs, so you can relax and stop trying to talk in some stupid code when I'm around."

"Well I, uh, well shit, I wasn't trying to trick you or out-smart you, we just thought it would be better that nobody not in-volved should know anything."

"Don't worry, I don't care, in fact it's kind of exciting. Be-ing married to a criminal defense lawyer taught me one thing, to keep my mouth shut."

"When did you first suspect?"

"Four or five Mercedes, beautiful lakeside houses, Brenda snorting tons of coke, all supported by one little nursery, it didn't take Inspector Clouseau. Then I took a look at the three of you, Sam, a very scary guy, smooth Pete dressed like a rock star but working in a nursery, then you, the hot shot jet jock shows up, I was sure I knew what you were planning."

"My my, quite the little detective."

"But really, a man from Oregon who you always call in Florida and he sounds exactly like Pete, then you buy him an airplane and Pete gets really excited. You bad boys are planning on flying drugs from somewhere to Florida with your new plane sometime soon."

"Okay kiddo, from now on I'll just be me, no more talking in code or any other bullshit, but remember, mums the word."

"Slick, you dope, I like you, I may even love you, I did nine years ago. I'd never say anything that would get you in trouble."

"Let's get that drink, I might even buy you dinner."

"Now I know I love you."

After their tete-a-tete, Slick and Rosemary's relationship became much closer. Not having to lie, Slick relaxed and became his old easy going self again. Rosemary was relieved that she didn't have to pretend not to see or hear anymore, the proverbial load was removed from both their shoulders.

The new engines arrived and were installed. Slick visited the propeller overhaul shop in Santa Monica. One of the six blades had a bad nick, repairable but bad. He ordered all new blades. The shop foreman promised the props a week ahead of schedule.

Slick continued flying charters, he was beginning to feel quite at home in the Navajo. On one trip he carried nine large fire fighters and their gear from Phoenix to Willows, California. Nine big guys, himself, plus a shit load of stuff, and a full load of gas, the Navajo preformed like a dream. He called Pete that night to report, *"Pete, today I took off from Phoenix way over gross. The temperature was over a hundred, there was zero wind, the plane just roared down the runway and leapt into the air, it felt like it could have handled a lot more weight, these damn Navajos can haul the bacon."*

"The one you were flying is exactly like ours?"

"Shit no, this old piece of junk has high time engines and worn out two bladed props, ours will have tons more power."

"I can't wait to take a ride."

"It won't be long, the motors are all hooked up, the props will be ready in ten days, yesterday I bought two new heavy duty

starters, they were expensive, but like you said, let's not let a two bit item screw this deal up."

"Anything on that plane that you think needs replacing, replace it, you are not on a budget. You want me to send you some more?"

"Better send another ten, I'm about tapped after buying the new prop blades and these starters. Maybe you better make that fifteen, then I can pay for the prop overhauls next week."

"It's done, talk with you later."

There was a big forest fire in northern California, Slick was busy carrying firefighters from all over the Western United States to bases close to the fire. He had been more or less assigned to one of the company Navajos, the more flying time he spent in the Navajo, the more he appreciated the little Piper. Slick was often alone on return trips to pick up more firemen, he got to play with the plane. On one trip he was loaded with equipment that was being returned for repairs. With the Navajo at close to max gross weight, Slick shut down and feathered the right engine, no problem, she flew like a dream with just a little trim adjustments. After restarting the right engine, he went through the shut down and feathering procedure of the left engine. The Navajo definitely flew better on the left, but no big deal, this girl was a very nicely designed airplane.

The prop shop finished the overhauls, Slick got a certified check to pay off the balance, for an extra hundred, they would deliver the propellers to Riverside.

Slick called Pete and told him it was time to pay off the Navajo, Pete said he'd be there in two days.

Later the next afternoon, Slick sat in the pilot's seat of the Navajo, when the mechanic gave the signal, he started the right engine, a minute later, the left, they both purred like kittens. Within an hour and after several minor adjustments, the mechanic was satisfied, *"She's ready for a test flight."*

"We'll have to wait until the new owner pays the balance, should be some time tomorrow."

Slick gave the mechanic another thousand and told him

he'd get the final thousand after ten hours of flying the new engines and everything was to both their satisfaction.

As requested by Pete, Slick approached the Navajo owner and suggested he could get mostly cash for the balance if the sales price could be adjusted on the contract. The guy was ecstatic, he'd put any price they wanted.

Slick picked Pete up at LAX, they drove down to Manhattan Beach. They'd go out to Riverside in the morning to finalize the deal. Pete would be introduced as Jerry Allen, the brother and partner of Carl Allen, the new owner.

"Those guys in Riverside know who you are?"

"No way, they only know me as Roger, I've never mentioned a last name."

"Shit hot, how's your girl?"

"Better than ever. Last week she told me she knew what we're up to but not to worry, she thinks it's exciting."

"I'm not surprised, she's a lot smarter than Brenda, that's pretty stupid, but hey, Sam's dog is smarter than Brenda. You okay with her knowing?"

"She's cool as hell, I'm not worried. Shit, all we can do is forget the deal or kill her or nothing, I'm not into killing her, I like her too much."

"Yeah, you're right, fuck it, she's a good broad, if you're not worried, I'm not. Just remind her how pissed off Sam would be if anything ever happened."

"She thinks Sam is scary."

"He is, I'm glad she sees that in him. They sell alcohol here in California?"

"There's a great joint about two hundred yards from the apartment, we'll throw your stuff in the house and walk, you can't ever find a place to park."

"Any pussy?"

"This place is crawlin with chicks, it's just like Florida, drugs out the ass and happening people. I've never figured out what any of these idiots do for a living, they just hang around acting cool and talking stupid. Guess I'm just out of it."

Rosemary opened the front door, *"Hi there, Mister Smooth, nice to see you again."*

"Give me a big hug you beautiful doll, Slick tells me you're on to us."

"Call me Sherlock."

"Okay Sherlock, let's hit that bar, maybe I can get lucky."

Rosemary laughed like hell, "Mister Smooth, I can almost guarantee that there will be at least three babes after your butt within thirty minutes."

"Didn't realize I was that impressive."

"Sorry, there just isn't much competition, all the guys would rather stay stoned than hustle girls. They're always after Slick."

"That true?"

"Hell yes, can you blame em?"

"Times a wastin, let's hit the road, I'm horny as a two peckered goat."

Pete went home with two hot looking chicks, he drug his emaciated ass back to the apartment a little before ten in the morning.

"I told you so."

"This is a very friendly town."

"Get ur ass ready, we got a plane to pay for and test flight to do. You remember your name?

"I don't even know where I am, but wherever it is, I like it."

"Come along Mister Jerry Allen, you can sleep while I drive."

Pete gave the Navajo owner a bank draft for $20,000 and $40,000 in cash, his eyes gleamed as he counted the stack of one hundred dollar bills. Pete explained that his brother and he were in the retail business and they took in a lot of cash. This deal would save them a lot in taxes.

Carl Allen's name was printed on the FAA Bill Of Sale. The ex-Navajo owner signed where it said SELLER, then he signed the back of the Aircraft Registration. The Navajo was now the property of Carl Allen of Portland, Oregon.

The first flight was for an hour and thirty minutes. Slick followed the engine break-in recommendations of the overhaul shop, he changed power settings and RPMs every few minutes. When they landed, the mechanic pulled the oil screens to check for metal, they were clean as a whistle. The cowlings were both removed, one tiny oil leak was found, the fix was to tighten a fitting half a turn.

They left the Navajo in front of the mechanic's shop, the next day they would fly up to Reno, overnight, check the oil, then return to Riverside to re-check the screens and look for any more leaks. If all was well, they'd pay off the mechanic and hit the road.

"Well, what did you think?"

"Couldn't you tell by the shit eating grin on my face? That thing really hauls ass, I didn't want to say anything in front of those guys."

Pete treated Rosemary and Slick and his twosome to a great dinner. Pete's tag team kept Rosemary in stitches, someone had the term "Dumb Blonde" in mind when these two were made. Before they split up for the night, it was decided that Rosemary would drive Slick out to Riverside in the morning. She'd drive back to meet Pete at the apartment at noon, then they'd drive to Torrance Airport to meet Slick in the Navajo. They'd leave the T-Bird there and fly off to Reno or where ever they felt like going.

Slick and Rosemary grabbed a gourmet breakfast and coffee at a MacDonald's drive thru window, an hour and a half later she dropped him off by the Navajo. No new leaks had developed overnight, there was not a trace of oil anywhere. The gas man topped off the main tanks and checked the oil. Slick paid cash for the gas, he also bought a case of break-in mineral oil.

Both of the beautiful new engines started within seconds of hitting the starter. With two hours to kill, Slick flew southeast, he climbed to eight thousand feet and took a look at Big Bear lake. He followed the mountains on a northerly heading until passing snow covered Mount Baldy. Turning south, Slick had to descend below four thousand feet to stay below the Los Angeles TCA. Passed Long Beach, on out to Catalina Island, turned towards the shore and landed at Torrance Airport. He had added one hour and forty minutes to the new engines.

By the time Pete and Rosemary arrived at Torrance, Slick had filled all four fuel tanks as full as he could get them. The plan was to fly an exact amount of time, then re-fill the tanks so they could get an accurate measurement on fuel consumption. Each engine had used one quart of oil in the first 3 hours and 10 minutes of their new lives. It's quite normal for newly overhauled engines to use some oil until the piston rings set in. This could take anywhere from 5 to 25 flying hours.

Pete and Rosemary arrived, they had stopped at a deli and picked up lunch and drinks.

"Let's get going, we'll see if my lucky streak continues in Reno."

"There's a place in Reno called The Mustang Ranch where it's guaranteed you can get lucky every time."

"That's a whorehouse, I like a challenge."

Rosemary can't believe it, *"They still have houses of ill repute in this day and age?"*

"Hell yes, The Mustang Ranch is one of Nevada's most famous land marks."

"You ever been there?"

"Who, little old me?"

Shortly after takeoff, Pete left the co-pilot seat and went aft. A few minutes later, he returned with two glasses of champagne, *"A toast to the first successful step of a long journey."* They clanked glasses, Rosemary leaned in between them to join the toast.

Three beautiful hours later, they landed at Reno, a short detour had taken them over Yosemite National Park and Lake Tahoe.

The engines now each had 6 hours and 15 minutes since new. A careful examination of the oil dip stick showed that the left engine had used less than half a quart the last three hours, the right about three quarters of a quart.

They had a hell of a night in Reno, Pete had a date with a cocktail girl before they'd even checked in. Rosemary won a hundred bucks on a slot machine while waiting for an elevator, Slick kicked ass on the crap table. Pete went to his room for a quickee, Rosemary hit two numbers in a row on a roulette table, Pete, with a flushed face, returned in time to throw four passes before crapping out. Slick had a pile of chips, Rosemary's bucket was full of dollar coins and Pete's doll looked ready again.

"I hope this is just the beginning of a great year."

"I'll drink to that."

They all staggered off to their rooms.

"How much did you win?"

"Don't know, count it."

Slick had one thousand three hundred and fifty five dollars worth of casino chips, Rosemary had a hundred and thirty seven dollars in one dollar slot machine coins.

"We're rich."

"Guess I better call Pete, see if he's ready to blast off."

Two days later, Slick flew over to Riverside. The mechanic pulled both oil screens, they were still perfectly clean. When the cowlings were removed, they found one tiny drip of oil, they couldn't decide where it came from. The next check would be at 25 hours when the first oil change was scheduled. Slick gave the mechanic his final payment, picked up all the aircraft log books and took off for Torrance.

Pete and Slick started working and flying in earnest. The first project was to remove the potty and potty partition and door. The Navajo was lightened by about sixty pounds.

"Sixty pounds is more than twenty thousand worth of pot. How much do each of these seats weigh?"

Next were the partitions behind the pilot and co-pilots seats, seventeen pounds. They also took out 5 of the 9 passenger seats then arranged the remaining 4 in an executive configuration facing each other. The 4 seats and the heavy carpet would come out just before flying a mission, about a 2 minute job.

They stopped at a marine hardware store and bought a variety of bungee cords, some rope, duct tape and some stainless steel fittings. Within an hour they had rigged a way to tie the top half of the passenger door tightly closed and to lower the bottom part of the door to the fully open position from the inside while flying without it banging open in the wind stream.

Every day they flew out over the desert between Los Angeles and Las Vegas. Pete was soon able to rig the top and bottom halves of the door in minutes. They discovered that the bottom half of the door could be lowered to the open position at almost any airspeed without adversely effecting the aerodynamics of the plane.

One of the mechanics who worked on the planes where Slick flew charters did the 25 hour engine inspection and oil change, he gave everything a clean bill of health.

Slick had continued to fly the odd charter when he had time, but around the first of July he told the charter company that he had a new job.

After the Fourth of July, Pete and Slick and Rosemary packed up for a holiday. They flew up to Hillsbourough, Oregon, a big general aviation airport near Portland. Using Rosemary's Visa card, they rented a car and began their search for an "ask no questions" mechanic. As it turned out, there was nothing to worry about, one of the mechanics at Troutdale Airport advertised at all the local airports that he was qualified to plumb all kinds of planes for overseas ferry flights, his ad also said he welded aluminum long range tanks.

They all drove out to Troutdale to meet the plumbing expert. He explained the job, he had to tap into the crossfeed fuel line. The job was relatively simple, bend and cut to length a couple of pieces of fuel line, tap into the crossfeed line, then come up through the floor so the ferry tank could be connected to the main fuel system. To get the ferry tank to feed, the pilot had to first, turn ON the ferry tank ON/OFF valve, then move the two fuel selector levers to the OFF position. This setting only allowed the long range tanks to feed, when the long range tank or tanks were used up, simply move the fuel levers back to the MAIN or AUX position. The job would take half a day or less. Time and materials would cost $250 dollars.

Oh yeah, the FAA required that he put a notation in the airframe log book about the fuel system alteration, but if the log book wasn't in the plane, he'd just type an entry on a piece of paper that could be stapled into the log book at a later time.

"When do you want me to do the job?"

"It's up to you, when you're ready we'll bring the plane over."

The deal was set, Slick would fly over the next afternoon, the plumbing expert would do his job the following morning.

The plumbing expert was an expert. The only sign that any alteration had been made to the Navajo was an inch and a half hole in the metal floor. Sticking up less than a quarter of an inch was a male plug in the end of the new fuel line that had been added.

When the carpet was rolled back in place, there was absolutely no sign of anything. The plumbing expert showed Slick what he'd done before he re-attached the inspection panel he'd removed to get to the crossfeed line. It was a very tidy job.

The old boy was so infatuated with Rosemary's doctor assisted breasts that he completely forgot about the little note for the logbook.

Pete paid the bill in cash, Rosemary drove off in the rent-a-car, Pete and Slick flew off in the Navajo. It was just too easy, but who the hell was worried about smugglers way out here in the great northwest.

The only official duty left was a bit of paperwork. The FAA Bill of Sale and Application For Change of Registration were both completed, the five dollar fee was enclosed in the form of a post office money order.

Pete and Slick drove out to the post office where their P.O. Box was and mailed the forms. There was a bunch of junk mail and a bill for the next year's rental of the box. Pete paid the rental fee.

"We'll have to get up here once in a while to check Mister Allen's mail, how long will it take for the new registration to get here?"

"Not long, couple of weeks."

"Well hell Slick, looks like we've done everything that needs being done, where do you want to go next?"

"Rosemary wants to see Yellowstone Park and Jackson Hole, Wyoming, let's head over there."

During the following days, they visited Wyoming, Montana, Idaho, Colorado and Utah. The fifty hour mark arrived at Salt Lake City, Utah. Both the left and right engines had stopped using oil, the rings had seated and there were no leaks. Slick hired the Piper dealer at Salt Lake City Airport to do a thorough 50 hour inspection on the engines, they came up with zero problems. Oil was switched from break-in mineral oil to hi-detergent.

When the 50 hour inspection was finished, they flew back to Portland, picked up the new FAA Registration from the post office box, then headed south.

Pete went back to Florida, he and Sam had some hiking to do to be sure about the intended drop zone. He took along 4 hand held marine radios that they would use to communicate with from the plane to the drop zone. They had decided on marine radios because there were so many boats in Florida, nobody would pay any attention to a few more voices coming across the airways. They had tested the marine radios several times, Rosemary could talk to them loud and clear from inside the apartment even if they were 30 to 40 miles away. The only modification they'd had to make was the addition of a small antenna on the outside of the plane. The antenna could be removed in about 30 seconds. Pete left the balance of his cash with Slick, just over 8 thousand bucks, that would buy a lot of av-gas.

Slick wanted to keep the Navajo at Torrance so he wouldn't have far to drive when he took it up for a bit of exercise, it wasn't possible. The airport manager insisted that any plane parked there on a monthly basis had to be insured for public liability and public damage, the Navajo was totally uninsured.

The temporary home of the plane ended up being El Monte Airport, an hour twenty drive from Manhattan Beach. The drive was a pain in the ass, but El Monte was a quite little airport with no insurance requirements and a friendly airport manager who just wanted to be one of the boys.

Chapter V

THE HOTELS

Rosemary called Slick to the phone, *"It's Pete, sounds like he's at a payphone."*

"Hey man, what's happening?"

"Time to take a little trip down south, I've got reservations for next Friday, that give you enough time?"

"Sure, I'll see you in a day or two."

"How's our toy?"

"Perfect, I use it every couple of days."

"We decided not to use the house phone except for normal stuff, if you need to talk to me, call and say something about your car, I'll call you right back from a pay phone."

"Okay."

"Don't forget your passport."

"No sweat, talk to you later."

"Rosemary dahling, I gotta run down to Florida, then take a little trip, you want to stay here or come to Florida with me?"

Two days later Slick and Rosemary flew down to Florida.

Pete had the trip all laid out. Friday morning they'd fly over to Nassau in the Bahamas. It's not necessary to use a passport for travel between the US and the Bahamas. From Nassau, they'd fly to Jamaica, overnight, then catch a flight down to Barranquilla, Colombia.

The Colombian connection would meet them in Barranquilla, two days in Colombia should give them enough time to work out the details of the upcoming flights. Arrangements had been made with Colombian Immigration for the inbound and outbound stamps to be on a separate piece of paper to be removed on departure. No use carrying evidence around saying you had spent time in drug haven.

The return trip would be the flight down in reverse.

Rosemary dropped Slick and Pete off at Tampa's airport. The flight to Miami connected to the Nassau flight with only an hour's delay. After clearing customs and immigration in Nassau, they had a three hour wait before taking off for Jamaica.

Everything went smooth as velvet until Jamaican immigration. There they ran into some real idiots who seemed determined to piss most of the arriving tourists off to the point that the phrase *"Never Again"* was heard many times.

"These are some rude mother fuckers."

"I think they're all stoned."

"Just how I'd want to spend my vacation, surrounded by big black rude assholes who obviously don't want me here on their dog shit island."

"On the way back we don't have to spend the night."

"Let's go find a safe little hotel and have some rum, I wonder if their women are this arrogant?"

The hotel was dirty, the food wasn't fit for dogs, thank the gods that you can't fuck up rum and coke. In the morning, the Jamaican coffee was served cold and stale.

"Nobody in this dump gives a shit."

"Next time I'm here I hope it's on a napalm run."

At least the flight to Barranquilla was on time, of course it wasn't a Jamaican airline.

Señor Luis Leon Lorenzo was waiting outside the Barranquilla Airport, he greeted Pete like a long lost brother.

"Pete my friend, good to see you, how you are mi amigo?"

"Luis, this is my friend Slick, Slick meet my very good friend, Luis Leon Lorenzo."

Luis the Lion Lorenzo looked and acted exactly like what he was, a marijuana exporter, in fact, he referred to himself as "El Marijuanero."

Luis took Slick and Pete to their hotel, a quaint little place way off the beaten track.

"Too bad I didn't bring Rosemary, she would love this place."

The hotel was gorgeous, real flowers in flower boxes adorned the balcony of every room.

"I hope you like the hotel, I bought it for my mother."

The lobby was decorated with beautiful sculptures, behind

the check-in desk were several original paintings by Miro and Degas. It appeared as though the marijuana export business was quite profitable here in Colombia.

The three men agreed to meet in an hour to start going over everything each side needed to know before the first launch.

"Pete, I'm going to take a long shower, hopefully I'll be able to wash off any trace of Jamaica, then a quick power nap. I'll meet you in your room in exactly one hour."

The meeting convened. Luis was there with Carlos, one of his lieutenants. Carlos spoke very good English, he took notes on all the points discussed.

Pete took a bag out of his suitcase. The bag was made of heavy duty tan canvas. Sewn around the top were metal eyelets, through the eyelets was strung nylon parachute riser cord.

"This is one of the bags we'll bring with us on the plane. The bales have to fit in this bag, then we'll close the top with this drawstring. We want each bale to weigh as close to fifty pounds as possible, but they have to fit inside this bag."

"That will be no problem, we will just have to compress the bales a little more. How many pounds can you carry on your aircraft?"

"One thousand two hundred pounds."

Carlos wrote everything down.

"How many gallons of aviation fuel will you need from us?"

"Three hundred and fifty gallons."

"How much oil?"

"We'll bring our own oil."

"That's very easy, when you land we will meet you with one thousand two hundred pounds of our finest marijuana in fifty pound bales that will fit in this canvas sack and three hundred and fifty gallons of aviation gas."

They went on to discuss how to set up the upcoming rendezvous. From a pay phone, Slick or Pete would call a number collect here in Barranquilla, they were to ask for Carlos. If Carlos wasn't there, call back every hour until he was there. Then, tell Carlos they planned to arrive the following morning, what hotel did he suggest? Carlos would tell them which hotel, either the Plaza or the Continental. Whatever hotel he recommended would indicate which of two airstrips they were to use.

"*Tomorrow we will go look at both of the airstrips, we have a Cessna and a pilot standing by.*"

"*Sounds good.*"

"*What time of day should we expect you to arrive?*"

"*It's a nine hour flight, we'll take off between eleven and midnight, we should be here at eight thirty in the morning give or take half an hour.*"

"*Don't worry, we'll be waiting. What time do you want to leave?*"

"*Not until eleven thirty or twelve, we want it to be good and dark before we get back to Florida.*"

"*That will give us plenty of time to load the plane and re-fuel.*"

Only two issues yet to decide, when and money.

Pete told Carlos that the first trip was planned for late September or as soon as the hurricane season was over. Carlos talked with Luis for a minute in Spanish, "*We think that will be too soon, the rainy season will not finish until then and we are afraid the landing strips will still be too soft.*"

They came up with a plan, Carlos would be standing by the phone on the 20th and 30th of September, Pete would call at five in the afternoon, Carlos would tell him the weather conditions and suggest they come on down for a holiday or delay their trip a few weeks due to rainy skies. If he said *come on down,* they would get everything ready, then call Carlos the afternoon before leaving to find out which airstrip was being used.

The issue of money was simple, $72,000 dollars would be deposited in the numbered account of Luis in the Cayman Islands. If they took off with a little more or less weight, the dollar amount would be balanced before each following trip.

Pete had earlier told Slick that the money man had an account at the same Cayman bank, only a phone call was necessary to switch the money from one account to the other.

"*Okay my amigos, we have nothing else to talk of, come along with me and Carlos, we want to show you how beautiful are the ladies of Barranquilla."*

The business meeting was over.

Being rich is almost always better than being poor, but being really rich in the third world is the only way to live. Every where they went, Luis and his companions were treated like royalty. After Luis had shown off his white friends in a few places, they went to a posh bar that had live entertainment and lots of fine looking girls who's job seemed to be making sure the guests were happy, especially the really rich guests. Luis' table was constantly surrounded by a bevy of beauties, any time one of the drinks would get down to the half way point, one of the dolls would dash away for a re-fill. If the girls weren't getting drinks, they massaged necks or just sat there attentively looking beautiful.

"Hey Slick, how do you like this bar? Luis bought it for himself."

"I like it."

"Now, aren't you glad that Rosemary isn't here?"

"Rosemary who? You know how to say, you are beautiful, in Spanish?"

"Sure, Usted quiere dormir con migo? Try that, it seems to have worked for me."

"You lying fucker."

As it turned out, Slick didn't have to dazzle any of the girls with gooey words, they were all employed by Luis and under instructions to hang around and be available if Slick or Pete showed interest.

A little later, Slick went back to his room with a voluptuous nineteen year old named Magda who would have been driving a Ferrari if she'd had the good luck to have been born in the States. Her English was worse than Slick's Spanish but it didn't matter, they had no difficulties communicating.

"Good morning Señor Es-slicko, como esta?'

"Bueno, muy bueno, I think I'm in love."

"I know the feeling."

"I've never seen a girl built like that in my entire life."

"These Latin chicks seem to have gotten more than their fare share, especially that one you were with."

"What do you mean, were? She's staying with me as long as I'm in Colombia, you may have to start looking for another pilot."

"Speaking of pilots, you better grab some coffee and a bite to eat, Carlos will be here any minute."

Slick and Pete rode out with Carlos to a small airport on the outskirts of Barranquilla. There they met Renaldo, their pilot. Renaldo had a detailed map of the Barranquilla area, he laid the map out on a table.

The first landing strip they would fly to was about 10 miles from the coastline, this airfield would be referred to as, the Plaza Hotel. Airstrip Plaza was on the eastern edge of a flat plain. To the east of Plaza, hills began to rise to a height of about 2000 feet. Plaza would be a cinch to find, just fly along the edge of the hills 10 miles inland of the Caribbean Sea until you see the airfield lying perpendicular to the flight path. The magnetic heading of the runways were 080, (zero eight zero) degrees towards the east and 260 (two six zero) degrees to the west. Renaldo advised that the runway sloped from east to west at a downgrade of about 5 degrees, therefore, it was always advisable to land uphill to the east and takeoff downhill to the west unless the effective tailwind was in excess of ten knots.

Runway Plaza was almost 4000 feet long, plenty of room for fully loaded planes of all sizes and description, however, he warned, "There are medium sized trees at both ends of the runway."

Renaldo then drew a circle around another spot on the map. This was the location of airstrip Continental. Continental was located twenty seven miles inland from the shoreline. There were no good land marks close to Continental, Renaldo advised that when they flew out there, they take a good look around and get accurate bearings off the Barranquilla VOR and ADF.

"Even I have problems finding this airfield and I have been there many times."

Slick wanted to know, "Does Barranquilla have DME?" (Distance Measuring Equipment)

"Yes, but our Cessna doesn't."

Carlos told them not to worry too much, they would have to

use Plaza until late November because Continental would be too soft for heavily loaded aircraft until then.

"Continental is flat, water doesn't drain off very fast, so we can't use it until the rainy season is well passed. The slope of Plaza makes it drain fast, you can land there almost anytime of the year. Come amigos, let's go for a ride in the Cessna and look at the airfields."

The Cessna appeared to be nearly new, the engine ran smoothly and Renaldo soon demonstrated that he was a competent pilot.

They flew north from Barranquilla to the coastline, turned right and flew along the beach until they came to a river mouth. The river mouth would be the point where Slick and Pete would penetrate into Colombia in future flights. At the river mouth, they made a sharp right turn and picked up a heading of 170. Ahead, the slopes of the hills could be seen, Slick held the map and followed their course with his index finger. After 6 minutes Renaldo pointed ahead, *"There it is, the dirt of the strip is very red."*

Sure enough, landing field Plaza stood out like a beacon, the bright red clay runway looked like some kid had drawn a red line across the earth with his red crayon. Renaldo flew down the runway to make sure there were no obstacles, *"Sometimes cows are on the runway, keep a close eye."*

Seeing nothing on the runway, Renaldo made a wide left turn until he was on final, flew over the trees and landed a third of the way down the landing strip. They taxied up slope to the far east end of the runway where there was a parking place nicely hidden under the limbs of some huge trees. Renaldo stopped the Cessna under the trees and shut the engine off. *"This is where you will park when you come here to Hotel Plaza. We will be here waiting for you, I will have the Cessna parked over to the side closer to the trees."*

Slick couldn't believe his eyes, *"This place is perfect, even if someone flew right over the top of us, they wouldn't see a damn thing."*

They all piled out of the Cessna, the first thing Slick noticed was that there was enough room under the huge trees to park a DC-3, much less a comparatively small Piper Navajo. The hard packed red clay was really hard, the Cessna had barely left tire tracks.

"Well Señor Slick, what do you think?"

"No problem, Señor Pedro, this runway is better than lots of paved runways I've landed on, let's pace it to be sure of the length, those trees at the west end are pretty tall, but I think we've got tons of room."

Slick walked to the far east end of the landing strip, he then started pacing west in the direction of take-off. At three thousand feet, more than the distance required for a heavily loaded Navajo, there was still enough room to climb over the tops of the trees at the end of the runway.

"No sweat, lots of room, I hope Continental is half as good."

They flew back to the coast before flying down to Hotel Continental. At the same river mouth, Slick centered the VOR needle, the bearing from the Barranquilla VOR read exactly 064 degrees, Slick noted that information on the map. This time, they flew on a heading of 185 degrees, almost parallel to the city of Barranquilla some 10 miles off to the west.

Renaldo was right, Hotel Continental was hard to find. Out in the middle of the flat plain everything looked the same, mile upon square mile of short scrubby trees growing out of drab sandy soil that apparently wasn't very fertile. There were no farms or any signs of grazing animals, just brush and scrub trees.

Finally after flying several circles, Carlos, sitting in the back seat, spotted the runway. Before landing, Slick had Renaldo fly directly over the center of the landing strip so he could get an accurate as possible bearing from the Barranquilla VOR.

When they landed, one thing became very obvious, this airfield had not been used in a long time, the weeds on the runway were so long that the prop sounded like the blade of a mowing machine.

"Don't worry, we will cut the grass before you come to this field, there are also many small holes that need to be filled in. The good thing about this runway is that it's so far out of town, the police never come here. Once or twice each year, the American DEA puts pressure on our police to make some arrests, we know about

this from informants, it's then that we move our operation out here."

"Who do they arrest?"

"Those who don't have informants inside the police."

"Sounds as though Luis is well organized."

"He is, Luis has been in this business a long time and he's good at his job. There are many amateurs in Colombia trying this business, some of them don't make it. You know how it is, if someone has to be sacrificed, it's going to be the one who pays the least for protection. The police and the army generals don't want men like Luis to get in trouble, that's where they get most of their money."

"I told you Slick, we're dealing with the right outfit."

"Sounds like it."

Runway Continental had only two advantages over runway Plaza, it's remoteness and short trees at the end of the runway, everything else was negative. The runway was shorter, the sandy soil was considerably softer, it was rougher, there was a lot more stuff growing on the runway at Continental, it was hotter and more humid than Plaza and there were no trees for shade and hiding under.

"Well, El Señor Piloto, what do you think of this one?"

"At least there aren't any tall trees to get over. We'll know a lot more about how our plane performs after a trip or two over at Plaza. But I'm not worried, I made some really heavy takeoffs in that clapped out Navajo I was flying in California, I never came close to using 3000 feet and it was hotter than hell too, over a hundred and five degrees one day in Phoenix."

Slick and Pete carefully measured the length of Continental. There was almost exactly 3500 feet from where they'd start the takeoff run to where they had to get airborne to make it over the 25 to 30 foot high trees at either end of the runway.

"Should be enough."

"If we ain't airborne by here, we're in the trees."

"Fly or die."

"Speaking of dying, isn't it about time we got back to the hotel, I've got Miss Colombia there waiting for me."

Carlos dropped Slick and Pete off at the hotel, he told them they'd be picked up at seven thirty, Luis was taking everybody to his favorite seafood restaurant.

Magda greeted Slick at the door with a hug and a big kiss, she was wearing only her underwear, but not for long.

He dragged her into the shower under the pretense that she wash his back, in reality he just wanted to ogle her spectacular body, *"Jesus, can you believe this girl, beautiful face, perfect ass, unbelievable tits, and skin as smooth as a new born baby's ass. And to top it all off she can't speak enough English to give me any shit. I must have been very good in my last life."*

"I no understand."

"You perfecto body, bonita face, me like mucho."

"Gracias, you nice."

"Come with me my little angle, just looking at you has changed the location of about a quart of my blood, we got to do something to relieve the pressure before I blow a cork."

"It big again."

"Very observant."

A driver picked Pete and Slick up at seven thirty on the dot, Magda had run home to change clothes, she said she knew where the restaurant was and would be there soon, at least that's what Slick thought she had said.

"How's your girlfriend?"

"Perfecto."

"Hope this place is good, I'm hungry as hell."

"Me too, I'm starving."

"Worked up a little appetite, eh?"

"She is really something, hope she shows up tonight."

Luis and Carlos were waiting at the restaurant, there were several girls from the night before at the table.

Luis was beaming, *"Carlos tells me you had a good day, you like the hotels?"*

"Everything was fine, I especially like the Plaza."

"Yes, the Plaza is our very best."

All the men laughed robustly about their little coded secret.

Before he had finished his first drink, Pete had selected his mate for the night, a sultry dark eyed fox that had passion dripping from every pore. Slick was about to go into depression when

Magda sneaked up behind him and covered his eyes, *"Guess who?"*

Carlos couldn't contain himself, *"I just taught her to say that five minutes ago, she met me by the toilet and asked what to say to surprise you."*

"A very good surprise indeed."

Luis proposed a toast, *"Our good friends from America, hope we see you many more times."*

Pete was next, *"To our most generous host, Señor Luis Leon, the Lion of Colombia."*

"Thank you my friend, but let us not forget a drink to the beautiful ladies of Colombia."

"To the most beautiful ladies in the entire universe."

A sumptuous meal of lobster, crab and grilled dorado was served along with fine French Cabernet Sauvingnon, everything was perfect.

"What do you think Pete, do these rich guys know how to live or what?"

"Slick my man, a year from now we could be sitting on our own tropical island eating caviar and lobster and having it fed to us bite by bite by our own harem of dolls like this."

"If I had a harem of her I wouldn't last a week."

"Could be a lot worse ways to go."

Slick kissed Magda good-by at ten the next morning. As usual, Luis' driver was right on time, he dropped them off at the airport two hours in advance of their one o'clock departure time. They checked in, went through immigration and customs, then went to a cocktail lounge to wait for the flight to be called.

"Well Slick, what do you think?"

"I think I'm in love."

"Yea, that's obvious, what do you think of the set up?"

"I'm a lot more confident about the whole deal now than I was a week ago. These guys seem to have there shit together."

"Good, I don't want you worrying about anything except flying the plane."

In Jamaica, Pete and Slick were directed to the transient

lounge, the wait for the flight to Nassau was only an hour and a half.

They overnighted in Nassau. First thing in the morning, Pete folded the detailed maps of the landing strips into a neat package and wrapped them up for mailing. He then walked to the local post office and sent the package to himself at the lake house in Tampa. No use giving US Customs anything to get excited about, they were now squeaky clean.

The quick flight from Nassau to Miami was barely long enough for the stewardess to serve a drink, Slick and Pete toasted each other with cold cans of Budweiser.

"Blue skies."

"Smooth sailing."

At US Customs and Immigration, Slick was waived through, Pete was asked to step aside, a half hour later he joined Slick in the boarding area for the final leg of their journey up to Tampa.

"What did they want?"

"Mainly they wondered why after a week in Nassau I didn't have a better sun tan."

"Are you shitting me? What did you tell them?"

"Too much sun causes skin cancer."

"Why didn't they stop me? Your face is a hell of a lot browner than mine."

"Never try to out guess the boys of US Customs and Immigration, you have to pass a special series of tests to become one of them, they are a breed apart. Fortunately for us, we won't be checking in or out with them the next time we travel."

They both laughed at Pete's little joke.

Two days later the maps came in the mail.

Pete, Slick and Rosemary drove over to the east coast of Florida to watch a race at Daytona Speedway. On the way back they spent several hours hanging around the Leesburg Airport, everything seemed the same, very low key. They saw the same airport manager driving around in his golf cart, the place still felt good.

They decided to bring the Navajo to Florida the first week of September, that would give them a month to fix anything that needed fixing.

Pete would catch a commercial flight to California in late August. From there they would fly up to Portland, check Mister Allen's P.O. Box, order a long range tank from the plumbing expert, hook up the tank, gas up, then take off for any destination nine or ten hours to the east.

Chapter VI

THE PREPARATIONS

Rosemary and Slick went back to the Manhattan Beach apartment in California, she was happy to have her man back. Little did she know that for a few days her man hadn't been hers. Slick realized he'd probably never see Magda again, but there are no laws against fantasizing.

Their second day back, Slick took Rosemary for a flight out to Catalina Island, they had buffalo burgers for lunch. After a two week rest, the Navajo had flown flawlessly. During the flight back to El Monte, Slick had Rosemary write down a list of tasks he needed to complete before Pete's arrival.

One, take accurate measurements of the passenger door opening.

Two, call the plumbing expert and order a long range tank, be sure to tell him the door measurements.

Three, have someone make some sun reflectors to cover the windshield and cabin windows.

After landing at El Monte, slick measured the door opening, he subtracted an inch from the height to make sure the tank would fit inside.

On the way home, they stopped at a recreational vehicle yard, Slick had noticed that some of the RVs had reflective panels in their windows. Five minutes later they had everything they needed, two large pieces of stiff reflective foil that could be trimmed to fit and several yards of dark blue heat absorbing material that Rosemary had volunteered to make into removable curtains for the cabin windows.

The plumbing expert answered the phone on the second ring, yes, he would be happy to fabricate a ferry tank for them. He repeated the door height measurement, did some quick calculations, told Slick that a tank that tall needed to be 20 inches wide for it to hold 150 gallons. He would use $1/8^{th}$ inch thick aluminum, materials and labor, $400 dollars. The tank would be ready when they arrived in a week or two.

Rosemary took a short walk to help digest her buffalo burger. She came back with a big smile on her face, *"I think I have just solved one of your biggest worries, follow me."*

Four doors closer to the beach, one of their neighbors was assembling his new trail bike. Lying in his tiny front yard was the six foot long, five foot high, cardboard box that the bike had come in.

"I see what you mean, nobody would think twice if they looked in the plane and there was a big box with a picture of a bicycle on the side of it. Just another wealthy northerner bringing his grandson a present from grandpa. Rosemary my dear, you have a devious mind, we'll make a crook out of you yet."

"You forgot who I was married to."

The neighbor said the box was theirs, he was just going to toss it in the trash.

Slick carried the big box back to the apartment and put it in the spare bedroom with all the other airplane stuff they had gathered. There were a lot of square feet of cardboard in the box. It could be cut and glued to the aluminum tank so that it would look exactly like a bike in a box, unless of course, someone crawled in and closely examined the box/tank, they'd never know the difference. If someone was inside their plane snooping around, they were in deep shit anyway.

Pete called a couple of days later to check in. He reported that there was a semi-new windowless van parked at the nursery registered to some non existent person. In the van there was a new 12 volt battery and new 12 volt fuel pump with 20 feet of hose. Stored in one of the nursery sheds were 3 like new 55 gallon fuel drums.

He and Sam had walked and drove all over the thousand acre private ranch/drop zone. The ranch was totally deserted, there were no houses, no roads, no nothing. The only signs of life were the barbed wire fence and the no trespassing signs.

Pete loved the idea of the long range tank camouflaged as a bicycle, *"Why didn't I think of something like that?"*

"Women are naturally devious."

"What's the status of the tank?"

"The man says it will be ready next week."
"Okay, I'll be there the 25th of August."
"Later."

Slick and Rosemary picked Pete up on the 25th, they squeezed into the T-Bird and headed back to Manhattan Beach. During the drive they discussed plans.

The next day they would rent a van, then haul all the airplane parts and other stuff they had accumulated up to El Monte and put everything in the Navajo. While there, they'd fit the reflective foil sunscreens and hang the dark blue cabin window covers.

The following morning, Rosemary would drop them off at the plane and say good-by. From there she'd drive back to the apartment, hang out for a few days, then catch a flight back to Tampa.

Almost everything went off according to schedule, the only delay was caused by Pete, he got waylaid by a blond bimbo and disappeared for one night and half a day. No big deal, they'd left plenty of time for diversions.

"I'll call you tonight from Portland."
"Don't you let that naughty boy Pete lead you astray, see you in a week."

After Slick had both engines started, he blew a kiss to Rosemary and waived good-by, she waived back and left.

"She's a good broad."
"That she is."

At 10,000 feet they had a ground speed of 170 knots, five and a half hours from LA to Portland, the almost empty Navajo hauled ass.

"Let's land at Troutdale, in the morning we'll taxi over, stick the tank in, hook it up, fill it up and get the hell out of here."

"Sounds good, let's buy some tape and glue and a cutter, while we're flying, I'll convert the tank to a bicycle."

"I got all kinds of tape and a cutter in the back, all we need is some contact cement and a brush."

The new fuel tank slid through the door with an inch to

spare. It sat snugly along the left side of the cabin. The 4 left side seats had been removed and stacked in the rear of the cabin where the potty room had been.

A short piece of 2x4 was cut the same length as the width of the tank, it was placed under the rear of the tank so it sloped towards the front insuring it would empty completely. Two more boards were cut, each a little thinner, then stuck under the tank at equal intervals towards the front so the weight would be evenly distributed.

Next, they connected the tank to the fuel system. First, an ON/OFF valve was screwed into the female fitting that had been welded in the fuel tank about half an inch from the bottom. Next, the male plug was removed from the end of the new fuel line, the male end of a flexible fuel line was screwed in it's place. The coupling at the other end of the flexible line was tightened on to the male end of the ON/OFF valve completing the tank hook-up.

The tank installation was polished off with the addition of two, two inch wide straps, one close to the top, holding the tank securely against the side of the aircraft, the second holding the tank firmly to the floor. Both straps were snapped in place with an over center clasp.

"Okay boys, let's fill her up and check for leaks."

The gas man was called, he drove his truck over beside the Navajo. First he filled the new tank, it took 138 gallons.

"Guess my calculations were a little off."

"Never mind, it's close enough."

The plumbing expert turned the ON/OFF valve to ON, he then removed an inspection panel so he could check his plumbing job for leaks, there were none below the floor or in the cabin. The gas man then filled the aircraft fuel tanks to the brim.

Pete paid cash for the gas and for the long range tank.

Earlier in the morning, Slick had checked the weather with Flight Service. The western half of the US was dominated by a high pressure area, clear skies could be expected west of the Mississippi River, after that, the usual afternoon summer time thunderstorm build-ups. East of the Mississippi didn't matter, they'd probably get only as far as Amarillo, Texas, a distance of 1100 nautical miles. If the tail winds were as strong as forecasts maybe Dallas or Houston.

The day's destination wasn't important, what they really wanted was a flight of at least 8 hours so they would have a definitive oil consumption check.

Before departing, Slick carefully added oil to the right engine until the dip stick showed exactly 12 quarts. The right engine required half a quart. To bring the left engine up to the 12 quart mark took less oil, about a quarter of a quart. Slick was thrilled with the tiny amount of oil being used by the new motors.

Pete had borrowed the plumbing expert's car, he returned with nutritious burgers and fries from MacDonalds, he had stopped somewhere and bought a large thermos which was now full of coffee.

"Let's hit the road, we got gas and oil and food and coffee and plenty of empty water bottles to pee in."

After takeoff, Slick turned to a south-easterly heading while climbing to a cruise altitude of 10,000 feet.

They crossed the Cascade Mountains twenty miles south of majestic Mount Hood, then headed out across the vast plain on Oregon's east side. The flight path took them across the south-east corner of Oregon, across the south-west corner of Idaho, across northern Nevada, straight through Utah to the intersection of 4 states, Utah, Colorado, Arizona and New Mexico. They crossed the southern end of the Rocky Mountain Range just north of Albuquerque, New Mexico.

Slick had switched to the long range tank once they had leveled off at 10,000 feet. It took exactly 5 hours and 11 minutes to empty the auxiliary tank, that meant both engines were using a total of 27 gallons per hour at cruise.

Pete had spent a couple of hours in the back messing around with the tank. He had created a beautiful bicycle box. After the long range tank had emptied, he had shut it off and moved it away from the side of the plane so he could completely cover the top, all four sides and the two ends with cardboard from the bike box. When he was satisfied with his masterpiece, he slid the tank back in place and re-attached the security straps.

"Nice piece of work."

"Thanks. Where the hell are we? I'm the navigator, I have a right to know."

"That's Clovis, New Mexico off to the right, we'll be in Texas in five minutes, we got tons of gas, let's keep going to Houston."

"Ur driving."

The Navajo touched down at Houston's Hobby Field after 9 hours and 35 minutes in the air, it was 10:15pm local time.

Hobby ground directed them to transient parking, Slick secured the plane while Pete ran off to get a hotel shuttle van to pick them up.

Twenty minutes later they were checked in at the Ramada Inn, two beers and a snack later, the two tired flyers went off to their rooms.

In the morning, Slick checked the oil while the Navajo's regular fuel tanks were topped off. The engines had used less than a quart of oil each.

Five hours later they landed in Florida's Capital, Tallahassee. Pete called Sam, he would meet them three hours later at the Leesburg Airport.

"How's Sam?"

"He's excited, says he can't wait to see the new toy."

After landing at Leesburg, Slick picked a parking spot that had long grass, he didn't want to take anyone's usual parking place, the whole idea was to fit in as one of the boys and attract zero attention. They signed the plane in under Mister Allen's name paying 3 months parking in advance. While Pete took care of the parking arrangements, Slick disconnected the long range tank. He re-installed the plug in the end of the new fuel line and put a plug in the female fitting of the tank. No use letting any bugs crawl in and clog things up. After de-plumbing the tank, Slick removed the three boards from under the tank, then adjusted the carpet to cover the hole where the tank fuel line connected to the aircraft fuel system.

Sam arrived in the windowless van, since there was no one around, Slick had him back up to the Navajo's door. Five seconds later, the tank disguised as a bicycle was in the back of the van. They then leisurely loaded all the parts that had been removed from the Navajo as well as 5 of the 9 seats. Sam drove off and parked in the regular parking lot, he then walked back to take a look at their airplane.

"Good to see you Slick, when do I get to go for a ride?"

"You name it, you're going to love this plane, she flies like a dream."

"It's a fine looking little aircraft, I was expecting something a lot bigger, this little doll fits right in, who'd look twice?"

"That's the whole idea, step inside, I'll give you the tour."

Slick explained everything to Sam, how they planned to load the dope, how they would throw it out the bottom half of the door, then he picked up a corner of the carpet to show him where the long range tank connected to the aircraft fuel system. Sam helped put the reflective foil covers in place, then they hung the heat absorbing curtains over the cabin windows.

"That's all there is to it, just another family from the north down here enjoying Florida's perfect weather."

"Very tidy, well done."

Slick closed and locked the cabin door, "We're ready, all we need now is the word to go."

They picked up Pete and headed towards Tampa, Sam had been thoughtful enough to bring along a cooler of cold beer.

"How's Sarah?"

"Perfect, I may have her sainted."

"How's my Brenda?"

"Miss Boobs, she's stompin around like a bitch in heat, I almost had to give her one the other day to calm her down, you got ur work cut out tonight."

Slick slid into the driver's seat so Sam and Pete could smoke a joint or two, they talked and laughed and fantasized on ways to spend their upcoming fortunes.

They arrived at the nursery just after dark and unloaded the tank, seats and other aircraft parts. Everything was stored in the shed where Sam had stashed the 55 gallon drums. They covered the van with a tarp, then Sam drove Pete and Slick over to the lake house.

Brenda came flying out the front door, she was almost nude.

"Now that's what I call a welcome home."

"Jesus, look at all them tits and ass."

"Good luck buddy, ur gonna need it."

Sam drove off, Brenda dragged Pete in the house, Slick carried the bags in and went to the phone.

"Rosemary, it's me, we're here, when you coming?"

"I'll be there in the morning, will you pick me up?"

"Bet ur ass."

Slick had to get out of the house, he couldn't stand the sounds coming from upstairs any longer.

The red eye flight was right on time, Slick met Rosemary as she stepped into the terminal, *"How do you manage to look this good after flying all night?"*

"Mister Slick, sometimes you say the nicest things. I think I'm going to ravish your body when I get you to the house."

"Just so you don't do the same thing Brenda did to Pete."

"What was that?"

"I didn't know whether to dial 911 or just get out of the house."

"You exaggerate everything."

"Ask Sam."

Slick told Rosemary how well everything had gone, especially the fuel tank disguised as a bicycle.

"When will you be going?"

"All depends on the end of the rainy season down south, meantime you and I are going to have some fun."

"What do you have in mind?"

"After you have finished ravishing me, how does dinner at Burn's Steak House sound?"

"You're a mind reader."

"Then tomorrow or the next day, we have to go to the Cayman Islands for 4 or 5 days."

Rosemary squealed with delight.

The Cayman trip wasn't all pleasure, Slick would have $300,000 dollars in his suitcase to be deposited to the numbered account of the money man. To avoid as many baggage handlers handling the cash laden suitcase as possible, Slick and Rosemary would drive to Miami, then hand carry the case to the Cayman Airways check in counter.

A certain Mister Smith from the money man's bank would be waiting at Cayman Customs to expedite their arrival. Mister Smith was a white man, he would be dressed in a tropical suit complete with a white hat. He would be looking over the arriving passengers, when their eyes met, Slick was to salute him, Mister Smith would escort Slick and Rosemary through customs, they'd then drive straight to the bank, the money would be counted and deposited. After that, they were at their leisure.

Slick told Rosemary what they were up to as they drove towards Miami.

"Aren't you a little nervous with all that money, what if the cops want to look in your suitcase?"

"Pete and Sam say they do it all the time, nobody ever checks anything leaving the US, it's coming back."

"What if someone in Cayman sees all that cash?"

"Sam says they'll ask why we're in the Caymans, I'm to say, banking. They're used to people bringing big amounts of cash."

"I guess they know what they're doing."

The Cayman flight passes directly over Havana, Cuba on the way to Grand Cayman, total time in route, less than one hour.

As briefed, Mister Smith was waiting. He introduced himself and helped with the baggage. They walked directly to Mister Smith's car, a customs inspector opened the door for them, Mister Smith was the man.

Three hours later they were lying on the beach enjoying a delicious rum punch.

"About three more of these and you'll have to drag me to the room."

"You be good, we're going diving tomorrow."

Five glorious days of scuba diving, snorkeling, sunbathing, drinking, eating and love making passed in a flash, it was time to get back and make the final preparations.

Sam called for a meeting, there were several things that needed going over. He asked Pete to make a list of all the money he'd passed out since Slick had come aboard.

$111,000	Airplane and engines.
$ 8,000	New prop blades, new starters.
$ 25,000	Gas, oil, tank, 25 hour inspection, hotels, food
$ 10,000	The trip from California to Florida via Oregon
$ 40,000	Pete and Slick's salaries for 4 months
$194,000	

Sam looked at the list, *"I guess that's about right, that plus the three hundred grand we put in his account adds up to almost half a million, that's what he gave me, I was just wondering why I was out of cash. I'll hit him up for another hundred so we don't run short before the first go."*

Pete looked in his black bag, *"I still got a little more than seven grand here for gas and anything that comes up."*

"I'll still get the hundred, you never know.'

"What about the van?"

"Shit, I forgot all about it, that set me back six and a half."

Slick was amazed at the way these guys kept track of their money.

The next day, Slick would accompany Sam and Pete to take a look at the drop zone to get a first hand look.

"We'll take a look tomorrow, then the next night you and Pete will make a couple of passes to make sure you can see my signals.

Pete had a road map that he'd drawn several lines on, *"If we cross interstate 4 here, then follow highway 22 to this intersection then follow this road to the right, we should be able to see Sam's lights from here. We turn about thirty degrees to the right, we should be on final approach, the lights will be spread out for about one thousand five hundred feet. If you fly right down the lights as low and slow as you can, I should be able to throw out eight bales a pass, we can unload in three passes, four at the most. There's no buildings or anything on the west side of the ranch, we'll make a left hand pattern. If the moon is out it will be a piece of cake, if it's really dark, it'll be a little harder. If we get a little lost, Sam will have to vector us in with one of the marine radios."*

They continued talking about the drop, they would announce their arrival twenty miles south of the drop zone with the transmission, *"Happy Hooker, radio check"*. Sam would respond, *"I read you Hooker"*, other than that they would keep radio silence unless things went wrong. Sam would use the radio only for three reasons, first, danger, second, if they got lost, third, if they dropped outside the zone.

"Why Happy Hooker?"

"Haven't you noticed, about every third boat around here is named The Happy Hooker."

"You got any questions, Slick?"

"I've been wondering, are you alone down there? What are you gonna do with a thousand two hundred pounds of pot?

Sam and Pete laughed like hell, *"Shit, I thought Pete told you. The guys who buy the stuff will be on the ground with me, they grab the bales, load them in a four wheel drive pickup with a camper, lock the door and head for Boston. They sell all the shit there to college kids, I guess there's a million colleges around Boston. We've been dealing with these guys a long time, they've never burned us yet."*

"When do we get paid?"

"They'll give me two hundred grand that night, and the rest after they get back to Boston and weigh it."

"How much notice do you have to give them?"

"Not much, they got trucks here all the time, they just gotta jump on a plane and fly down."

"Sounds almost too easy."

"It is. Even better, there's no pot around, everybody's screamin for it, these guys will take all we can bring in for awhile, after December boats and containers will flood the market, until then it's only planes."

"So we should make hay while the sun shines."

"Hell yes, as many trips as you two can handle, getting rid of the stuff is no problem."

"You mean like a trip a week?"

"Or more. Even if our buyers aren't around, we can stash

it til they're ready, couple of years back I had three thousand pounds in my garage for two weeks."

Pete brought in three beers, *"Let's really hit this hard right off the bat before anybody starts paying us any attention, about the time they realize we're doing a lot of flights at night, we'll be gone, sell the plane, sit back and count our money."*

"That's right, ten or fifteen quick runs then bail out, this ain't no long term career."

Pete brought out the marine radios and put all four of them in their battery charging units, Sam went for more beers, Slick studied the road map, it was getting down to the wire.

Slick, Pete and Sam met at the nursery the following morning. They left for the ranch in the four wheel drive pickup.

The road along the east side of the ranch was practically deserted, when no cars could be seen in either direction, Pete dashed to the gate, unlocked the padlock and swung the gate open. Sam drove inside, Pete locked the gate and jumped back in the truck, they disappeared behind the row of trees that ran along the road.

Sam followed the trail that snaked through the trees, after about a quarter of a mile they broke out of the trees into a large clearing.

Sam announced, *"This is it."*

He stopped the truck at the southern end of the clearing.

Slick took a compass bearing from where he stood towards the farthest end of the long narrow opening.

Sam showed Slick and Pete where he planned to put the first light, then they all walked in the direction that the line of lights would be laid out in, ten lights in all. Slick noted on the road map that the compass heading down the imaginary line where the lights would be was 18 degrees.

The trees at the northern end of the drop zone were small and scattered for the first fifty yards, then they became taller and quite dense.

"Don't put a light past here." Slick pointed to a spot some one hundred yards short of the trees. *"We'll stop dropping over this light, then none of the bales will go into the trees."*

They walked back to the beginning of the drop zone, Slick

sat on the grass and looked up at an angle in the direction they would fly in from. It was apparent that the first two or three lights would be blocked by trees until they got very close to the drop zone.

"Pete, you'll have to be ready to drop on my signal, when we come in over those trees, the first lights will pop into view pretty fast."

"I'll be spring loaded."

Slick drew a line on the road map where he thought the clearing was in relation to the road.

"I think we'll be able to see the lights off to the right as we fly up this road, at least the last five or six." Slick marked a slight curve in the road. *"By here, you'll be in the back with the bottom half of the door open, I'll have the plane slowed way down with 15 degrees of flaps. About here, I should see the string of lights, I'll turn right and line up on the lights and start descending. The closer we get, the lower I'll be able to go and still see the lights.* Slick pointed up at the trees. *"When we get to those trees, I'll be able to see the first lights, I'll give you the drop signal until we're over the last light, then I'll pull up and make another pattern. How's that sound to you?"*

"Sounds good, you just keep giving me a count down."

Sam asked, *"What's the drop signal?"*

We've decided to signal by yelling, we tried it with the door open and we could hear each other fine, when I turn on final I'll start yelling, Get Ready! Ready! Ready! Go! Go! Go!Go! Until the last light, then I'll scream, Stop! Stop!

Pete broke out three bottles of beer, Sam brought one of the lights from the tool chest on the back of the pickup. The light had an adjustable lamp, Sam placed it on the ground and aimed the lamp in the direction the plane would come from. *"How high up should I tilt the beam?"*

"Just a little higher than the top of the tallest tree, direction is more important than the angle."

"We may have to make more than one pass tomorrow night, I want to get an exact spot on that road to start my turn to final, the curve should be close, a few seconds either side should be right on.

"Make all the passes you want, let's do it right."

They discussed the hand held radios. The plane would start calling Sam at 40 miles, then each 5 miles closer until he could hear them loud and clear. Pete would transmit, *"Five, four, three, two, one."* As soon as Sam heard the transmission, he would reply, *"One, two, three four, five."* That would give them a good idea of the available range of the radios both to and from the aircraft.

"Pete, grab three more beers, I think we've done all the damage we can today, let's go home and take our girls out on a date. Pete, you got that wild animal of yours calmed down enough to go out in public?"

"Maybe I better give her another shot before we meet, she was still foaming at the mouth this morning."

"You better, we don't want her jumpin the waiter."

Sam treated everybody to an orgy of food at his favorite oyster bar. They went through dozens of oysters on the half shell and buckets of steamed shrimp. Brenda ate like a starving dog, Pete must have put her through the paces. Sarah and Rosemary just smiled at each other. Sam was in his glory, bib tucked in, shrimp and oysters all over the place, red wine and beer flowing, people he liked surrounding him, life was good.

They took off at 8:30, Sam was expecting the first radio call at 9 pm.

It was a beautiful summer evening, afternoon thunderstorms had cleansed the air, the sky was crisp and mostly clear, the moon shone at half strength.

Slick flew south to Interstate # 4, turned right and followed the highway at 1000 feet until they reached Lakeland.

Pete made his first radio call, *"Five, four, three, two, one."*

Just past Lakeland, Slick veered to the right following highway # 22.

"Five, four, three, two, one."

"One, two, three, four, five."

"Perfect, that's more than thirty miles."

Slick continued up highway # 22 until he came to a Y in the road, the right hand part of the Y was the road that ran along the west side of the ranch.

By now, Slick had slowed the Navajo down and lowered 15 degrees of flaps.

Ahead in the moonlight, Slick could see the curve in the road, *"Keep your eyes peeled about twenty degrees to the right."*

Five seconds after passing the curve, Pete shouted, *"There they are!"*

Slick had seen them at the same instant, he banked sharply to the right to get lined up, he pulled the power back a little and started descending from 1000 feet.

Slick could count four lights, then five, then six, he pushed the nose even lower.

Ready! Ready! Ready!

Just as the Navajo passed the last of the trees, the first four lights popped into sight.

Ready! Ready! Go! Go! Go! Go! Go! Go! Go! Go! Stop! Stop!

Slick added a little power and pulled the nose up to climb over the tall trees ahead. He then made a climbing left turn until his eyes picked up the road along side the ranch. He continued the left turn until they were flying parallel to the road, when he saw the curve he started another left turn, pulled the power back and started descending.

This time, Pete went to the rear of the plane and opened the bottom half of the door.

Again the lights came into view, *Ready! Ready! Ready! Go! Go! Go! Go! Go! Go! Go! Go! Go! Go! Stop! Stop!* Slick made the second pass as close to the first as possible except he came down a bit lower.

After the second pass Pete came back to the co-pilots seat, he was beaming, *"Jesus Christ, Sam was about twenty feet away from me waving like hell, what a rush, shit man, we'll be able to drop the stuff right in their laps, I had no idea you'd get that low, how close were we?"*

"I don't know, fifty feet."

"Bullshit, try thirty, what a fuckin rush."

"Could you hear me okay?"

"Loud and clear."

"I've seen all I need to see, let's head for the barn."

They met Sam at a pre-planned bar a little after midnight. When he saw them walk in, Sam rushed over and embraced them both, *"Fuck, that was great, I could see Pete's eyeballs, he was laughing his ass off. You crazy fuckers were below the trees."*

"I figured the lower the more accurate the drop."

"It was perfect, I just had no idea you could come in so close."

"If the moon's that bright, no sweat."

"How were my lights?"

"Right on, don't change a thing."

"How bout the radios?"

"I heard you the first time before I answered, but not clear, how far away were you?"

"Over thirty miles."

The three young men looked anything but what they were, perhaps three upcoming businessmen celebrating a successful deal, surely not three smugglers planning to haul drugs into the motherland.

Slick went to the head.

"I told you Sam, that fucker is the best damn pilot I ever saw, he's got some balls, fuck, he can fly that thing."

"You were right, when I saw that fuckin plane come in over the trees I about shit my pants, this is gonna be a piece of cake."

With only a week to go before the first call to Carlos on September the 20th, Pete and Slick made sure that everything was ready. Pete dropped the 12 volt battery off at a gas station to top off the charge. Sam finally got his ride in the Navajo, Slick wanted to fly her at least one more time before launch time. Sam grinned like a kid, *"Wish I was going with you, this is great."*

The 20th of September arrived, Pete and Slick went to a payphone at the Holiday Inn, at 5 they placed a collect call to Carlos in Barranquilla, Colombia.

"Hello, Carlos, it's Pete, how are you?"

"*Pedro, good to hear from you.*"

"*We'd like to come down for a visit, how's the weather?*"

"*The weather is very good, the rainy season is finished.*"

"*Oh, good, I'll call you back in a day or two when our travel plans are complete.*"

"*We can't wait to see you again, I'll be waiting for your call.*"

"*Okay, thank you, we'll see you soon.*"

Pete was smiling.

"*I guess you could figure out what he said, no more rain, it's a go.*"

"*Shit hot, I'm ready. All we need to do is stick the tank in and fill it up.*"

"*Let's go see Sam and get the ball rolling.*"

Chapter VII

THE FIRST GO

Sam was ecstatic, *"Comeon, let's go find a phone, I'll call the buyers and see if they're around."*

Pete and Slick waited in the car while Sam talked on the phone, he was back in five minutes.

"They're hot to trot, they'll be here tomorrow. Let's plan to leave tomorrow night."

"Okay, I'll call Carlos tomorrow and tell them we're coming."

There were a lot of things to get done.

Slick took all the maps out and made sure they were all there, especially the detailed map of the area around Barranquilla and the road map with the drop zone on it.

Pete drove out to the Davis Island Airport and had the three, 55 gallon fuel drums filled up. Had the gas attendant asked any questions, Pete was going to tell him that the aviation gas was for some of his buddies who were going to cheat a little at the next weekend's drag racing event.

That afternoon, Pete and Slick drove to Leesburg, they took the Navajo for a thirty minute flight, after landing, they taxied to the re-fueling area, there they filled the 4 aircraft tanks to the brim. After re-fueling, they taxied to their parking area, locked the plane and headed for home.

Back at the nursery, they put the long range tank in the van. Slick double checked to make sure everything was loaded, tank, fuel pump, battery, plumbing fittings, canvas bags and the three 55 gallon drums. The radios, radio antenna and the maps would be carried in a bag and loaded at the last minute.

Slick took Rosemary out to dinner, she already knew that they were planning to depart the next night. She and Slick had long ago decided that Rosemary would go to her house any time he was off on one of the missions. Perhaps she would be able to provide him with some kind of alibi if things went wrong.

Rosemary seemed to be more excited about the whole deal

than Slick was.

"*I just can't believe what you guys are about to do, it's almost unbelievable that something so illegal and crazy is about to happen right in front of my eyes, yet you act like you're going off to another day at the office.*"

"*It's really not that big a deal.*"

"*Oh you asshole, it's so fucking exciting and you act so blasé.*"

Pete started calling Carlos the next day at noon, he was at the phone on the third try.

"*Carlos, this is Pete, we'll be down to visit you tomorrow morning, is that okay?*"

"*Oh yes Pete, we will be waiting for you, your reservation is arranged at the Hotel Plaza.*"

"*Okay, see you tomorrow morning.*"

"*Tomorrow then, good-by.*"

Pete and Slick drove over to the nursery to tell Sam that they had contacted Carlos and that everything was still "GO". Sam told them that the buyers were in town, they'd all be waiting at the drop zone when they got back, good luck and all that shit.

At 3pm, Pete and Slick left for Leesburg in the van, they had already made reservations for two nights at a close by motel.

"*Well my man, I think we're ready, gas, oil, maps, radios, thermos, food, a shit hot plane and a good weather forecast, what have we missed?*"

"*Nothing I hope.*"

"*What time you want to take the seats out and load the tank?*"

"*About dark, what do you think?*"

"*Yeah, that won't attract any attention.*"

At 6:30. Pete and Slick checked into their motel, at 7, they drove the quarter mile to the Leesburg Airport. Slick unlocked the passenger door, Pete pulled up beside the Navajo. Within a minute, Slick had unfastened the four remaining passenger seats, he handed them out one by one, Pete stacked them in the front of the van in front of the fuel drums. Slick then handed Pete the carpet he had just rolled up. Pete closed the side door of the van and took a look around, there wasn't anyone close by. He opened the rear door of the van and slid the disguised tank out. Slick jumped out of the Navajo to lend a hand, twenty seconds later the tank was inside the plane. Pete closed the rear door of the van, went to the side door, leaned in and pulled out a bag that contained the plumbing fixtures, the three wood blocks, the safety straps and an end wrench that fit the plumbing. Five minutes later the tank was connected to the aircraft fuel system and strapped in place.

"You ready for some gas?"

"Fire away."

Pete climbed in the back of the van, opened the first 55 gallon drum, inserted the fuel pump, hooked the alligator clips to the 12 volt battery, pushed the rear door open far enough so he could get out, then handed Slick the nozzle of the gas hose.

Slick had already unscrewed the fuel cap of the long range tank, he stuck the nozzle in and squeezed the handle, fuel started flowing.

While Slick was filling the tank, Pete threw the 30 new canvas bags in the rear of the plane, he then stood there by the passenger door trying to look as nonchalant as possible while blocking view of the black hose. Nobody came by, nobody paid any attention, just a couple of guys messing around with their airplane.

It was about a fifteen minute process to empty two and a half 55 gallon fuel drums. With the long range tank full, Slick handed Pete the nozzle, tightened the tank cap, locked the door of the Navajo, shut the rear door of the van, got in the passenger seat, took a deep breath and glanced around as Pete drove off the airport parking area onto the highway.

"Slick as snot."

"So far, so good."

Back at the motel, they parked the van in the corner of the parking lot next to the adjoining twenty four hour restaurant, checked that all the doors were locked, then went to their room for a little rest. It was 8:15, they'd walk across to the airport at 10:45 and takeoff just after 11. The only thing left to load was the leather bag with the maps and hand held radios and a sack of sandwiches they'd picked up at a deli.

Slick dozed, Pete watched T.V.

At 10, a restless Pete took the thermos to the restaurant and had it filled with coffee, he had to wait while 2 truckers had their thermos' filled.

The two flyers left their room at 10:40, it took them less than 15 minutes to walk the three hundred yards down the side of the highway and across the airport to the Navajo. The place was absolutely deserted.

Slick unlocked and opened the passenger door, Pete screwed the marine antenna into place, pulled the wheel chocks and threw them aside, he then climbed inside and pulled the door closed behind him. By the time Pete sat down in the co-pilot's seat, Slick had started the right engine. Five seconds later, Pete watched as Slick momentarily turned the left fuel boost pump on, watched as the fuel pressure built up, turned the boost pump off, turned both overhead left magneto switches to on and cranked the left starter. After about 3 turns, the engine fired. As they sat there waiting for the cylinder head temperatures and the oil temperatures to climb up to the green arc, Slick turned on the aircraft radios and switched on the rotating beacon and the navigation lights.

"You ready?"

"Let's do it."

Slick switched on the taxi light, added power and turned left out of the Navajo's parking space. At the end of the parking row, he turned right, a hundred yards later they taxied off the grass onto the paved taxiway.

Leesburg ground and tower are not manned after 9pm so Slick didn't bother to say anything over the radio.

They stopped at the end of the taxiway, did a quick run-up, Pete looked to his right to see if anyone was on final, *"All clear."*

"Okay my man, here we go."

Slick added a little power turned the Navajo 90 degrees left onto the runway, slowly pushed the throttles all the way forward, the Navajo accelerated down the runway. At 85 knots, Slick pulled back on the control column, the Navajo lifted off. Slick raised the landing gear, they flew off into the night. It was 11:12pm.

The route of the first part of the flight was down the east side of Florida, since they weren't breaking any laws yet, Slick left the rotating beacon and the navigation lights on until they needed to be unseen. Slick leveled off at 10,000 feet. The only place that needed to be avoided was the Air Force gunnery range near Sebring, they made sure to stay well east, wouldn't want to violate any restricted airspace, would we.

Slick had switched to the long range tank as soon as they had leveled off at 10,000 feet. The switch required two movements, first, he had Pete lean back and turn the auxiliary tank valve to ON. Next, Slick moved the aircraft fuel control levers, LEFT and RIGHT, to the OFF positions.

"The motors are still running, I guess the tank is feeding."

"How many hours is that supposed to last?"

"Almost exactly five."

They cruised along.

An hour after takeoff they were abeam Vero Beach.

"It's time to start breaking laws."

Slick turned the rotating beacon and the navigation lights OFF.

Just passed Fort Pierce, there is an almost deserted 20 mile stretch of beach, half way down the deserted stretch, Slick made an abrupt turn to the east south east. While planning the flight, Pete and Slick had decided on this route, if anyone was watching them on radar, it would appear that their aircraft was heading straight for Freeport in the Bahamas. Fifteen miles short of Freeport, they'd veer to the right and fly straight down the chain of the Bahamas Islands. There was no radar in the Bahamas looking for intruding aircraft, the farthest thing from the minds of the laid back Bahamanians was an invasion from foreign aircraft.

"Feet wet."

The lights of cars on the coastal highway could be clearly seen as they crossed the coastline. Ahead lay the eerie blackness of the Atlantic Ocean.

"You believe in the Bermuda Triangle?"

"Sure, why not?"

"We're in it."

"Naw, I'm not superstitious, hope I didn't forget my rabbit's foot."

"Looks like we're starting to pick up the ADF at Great Ina-

gua, is that possible? It's almost 500 miles."

"Nothing down there to block the signal, only water and that's flat."

Two hours and thirty minutes after takeoff, 1:35am, the lights of Nassau passed off the left wing of the Navajo. All the instruments were steady in the green, the engines were purring like a pair of happy kittens, Slick was enjoying his second cup of coffee, Pete was telling him some of the crazy antics that Brenda had pulled in the time he had known her.

Fifty or so miles off to the south-east, a huge thunderhead could be seen each time a giant bolt of lightening exploded inside the storm.

"That baby must reach up to 40,000 feet."

"Hope we don't run into anything like that."

"If we do, we'll go around it, way around."

Flying past Nassau, the Morse code identifier from the Great Inagua ADF was coming through loud and clear.

Pete took a short nap, Slick tried to figure out which islands they were passing, with the help of the moonlight, some of the shapes below could be recognized, there weren't too many lights down there.

After passing by George Town on Great Exuma Island, not another light would be seen until Haiti.

Pete woke up, "Where are we?"

'We'll be passing the Great Inagua ADF any minute."

"I slept more than an hour?"

"Brenda must be taking a toll."

The ADF needle swung as they crossed Great Inagua, they'd been airborne four hours and forty minutes, it was 3:52am, their ground speed had averaged 159 knots. The long range tank had been in use for 4 hours and 10 minutes, 40 or 50 minutes to go.

"Pete, would you mind going back there and tapping that tank, there should be about 9 or 10 inches of gas left."

Pete stepped between the seats and knelt on the cabin floor beside the tank, he began tapping the side of the tank, at about 8 inches above the bottom he got a more solid sound, "I'd say seven or eight inches to go."

"Close enough for government work."

Slick carefully folded the map he had been looking at, stuck it back in the map bag, pulled out the next map, opened it, found where they were on the new map and showed the spot to Pete.

"We're right about here." He pointed to a mark on the map just off the southern coast of Great Inagua Island. *"Haiti dead ahead 70 miles, we're half way there."*

Pete broke out sandwiches and some little cans of juice, *"Orange, apple or grape?"*

"Orange."

They crossed over the north coastline of Haiti without seeing a thing, ground fog or an undercast blocked whatever view there might have been. Slick made the first heading change in several hours, from south south-east to almost due south, 174 degrees.

"Keep an eye on the fuel pressure gauges, the aux tank is about empty."

First the left gauge, then within seconds the right fuel pressure gauge started fluctuating wildly, *"There it goes."*

Slick reached smartly down between the pilot's and co-pilot's seats, he moved the fuel selector levers, left and right, from the OFF positions to the AUX positions. Neither engine had a chance to sputter.

It was 4:37, they had been flying 5 hours and 25 minutes, the auxiliary tank had lasted 4 hours and 55 minutes, if their ground speed didn't change, they'd land at Hotel Plaza in about 4 hours.

Slick asked Pete for another cup of coffee.

Whatever had been blocking sight of the ground went away, the lights of Port-au-Prince, Haiti's capital, came into view off to the left side. Beyond the southern coast of Haiti lay 460 miles of the Caribbean Sea, the next landfall would be Colombia, 3 ½ hours to the south.

At 6:05, the fuel gauges read 5 gallons in the aux wing tanks, Slick moved the fuel selector levers from AUX to MAIN. They had a little more than 4 hours of fuel remaining and 2 hours and 32 minutes to go, everything was going according to plan.

Half way across the Caribbean, the Barranquilla ADF started pointing in the right direction, minutes later they could hear the Morse code identifier of Barranquilla.

Slick pulled out the detailed map of Hotel Plaza and their

entry point on the north shoreline of Colombia. As soon as they got close enough to pick up the VOR at Barranquilla, they'd be able to intercept the 064 degree radial that crossed over the river mouth some 10 miles from their destination. From the river mouth it was 170 degrees and about 5 minutes flying time to the red clay runway of Hotel Plaza.

"If our ground speed hasn't changed, we'll be at the river mouth at about 7:30, then 5 or 6 minutes down to Plaza."

"If it stays this clear we're laughing."

At ten minutes to seven, Slick pulled the power back a little, pushed the nose down a hair and started a 250 foot per minute rate of descent that would put them over the river mouth at an altitude of 1,000 feet at 7:30, give or take a few minutes.

The VOR was locked on, Slick dialed in 064, when they hit the shoreline the needle would show which way the river mouth was, left or right. It was so clear that the two flyers felt sure they'd be able to see the river mouth from 10 or so miles off shore.

"Land ho!"

Sure enough, there was a long dark line on the edge of the horizon about 50 miles ahead.

At 30 miles, the hills that sloped up to the east behind Plaza came into view.

"I can see right where the runway ought to be, just stay a little to the right of those hills."

"I'm gonna pretend the weather is shitty and go from the river mouth on a heading of 170 so we can get used to the land marks."

"Good idea."

Ten miles out, the river mouth was in clear sight, Slick altered the heading so as to try to have the VOR centered as they crossed the shoreline like they would have to if it was raining or hazy or smoky.

They crossed the shoreline at 7:32, the river mouth was directly below, it was a great landmark, the river made two sharp bends within half a mile of the coast, there would be no mistaking this obvious landmark should they one day be flogging around in the smoke or rain.

Slick picked up a compass heading of 170 degrees, the river

drifted off to the right. Two minutes from the river mouth, a razor-back ridge jutted out of the hill, it went off at a 90 degree angle to the left of the flight path. Slick penciled it in on the map. Past the razorback was a noticeable rock outcropping, then a little green valley, Slick made some more notations.

"There it is, dead ahead."

The red clay of Hotel Plaza's runway was the best of all possible landmarks, Plaza would be clearly visible in the worst of weather conditions.

Slick slowed the Navajo down, lowered 15 degrees of flaps and flew across the runway at a 90 degree angle, the place looked deserted, the huge trees were hiding whatever and whoever was down there.

"Let's land this thing, my ass is tired."

Slick banked to the left until they were on downwind, at mid field he lowered the landing gear, as he started a left base turn, the flaps came down to HALF and both electric boost pumps were switched ON, mixtures double checked full RICH. Over the trees at the end of the runway, flaps FULL DOWN, power back, point the nose down, flare out, power to IDLE and touchdown.

Now that they were on the ground, the Cessna could be seen under the trees, some men were over by the small plane, their heads turned in the direction of the new arrivals.

Slick taxied under the tree limbs and shut down the engines, Renaldo, the Cessna pilot, was standing in front of the Navajo with a big grin on his face.

Slick flicked the mags to OFF, turned all the radios OFF, then switched the master switch to OFF, he then swung the cockpit door open, they had arrived.

"Como esta Renaldo, how you doing?"

"Good to see you Señor Es Slick, welcome to our country once again."

Pete followed Slick out the cockpit door onto the left wing. One by one they jumped off the trailing edge of the wing to the ground.

"Pedro mi amigo, welcome."

Renaldo took a hand held radio out of his back pocket and said something to someone in Spanish, within seconds, his radio call was answered.

"Luis will be here in 5 minutes, they have been waiting close to here in a hidden place. Come here by the Cessna, we have some Coke in a cooler."

Half way through their drinks, two small trucks came roaring onto the runway. Standing in the back of each truck were several armed men, as they got closer, Luis' face could be recognized as one of the rifle toting banditos.

"Pedro! Es Slick! Como esta? Bienvinedos."

It was obvious that Luis liked the grand entrance, he was reveling in his chosen work of marijuanero.

Luis greeted his guests like long lost brothers, he then ordered his gunmen to disperse to their assigned lookout spots on the airfield.

The second truck backed up close to the front of the Navajo, when it stopped, one of Luis' men removed the tailgate. He started moving fuel drums to the back edge, another man threw an old truck tire on the ground, then one by one they dropped each of the 7 drums off the back of the truck, onto the tire, then rolled them off to make room for the next. After the 7 drums were unloaded, an electric pump was handed down, finally two 12 volt car batteries were passed down. The two workers then started rolling drums up next to the Navajo's wings, they'd obviously done this task before.

Slick and Pete had earlier agreed that Slick would take care of refueling and checking the oil, Pete would be in charge of packing and loading the marijuana. Loading was critical, the bales had to be arranged so as to maximize the available space, he also had to be sure to leave enough room at the top of the load so later, he could wriggle to the rear of the plane to make the drop.

Slick told the guys who were rolling the drums around to put 3 by the passenger door. Once in place, they stood the drums on end, opened the first one, slid the 4 foot long shaft of the pump in until it hit the bottom of the drum, hooked the electrical wires of the pump to one of the batteries, handed Slick the nozzle and finally turned the pump on when Slick gave them the word. Gas started flowing but not very fast, Slick made a mental note to bring Luis a new pump on their next trip.

Even though it was only 9am, Slick was sweating like a

pig. The temperature was about 85 degrees and the humidity was at least 99 percent.

Half way through the second drum the pump quit, changing batteries didn't help, the electric motor had packed it in. Slick stepped out of the stifling Navajo to see what the problem was, by the time he was on the ground, one of his helpers had jumped in the truck, fired up and drove off in a cloud of dust. Slick walked over to where Pete and the Colombians were messing around with the marijuana.

"The pump died, I guess they went to get a new one."

"Don't worry Captain, he'll be back in a few minutes, we always have extras in case of problems."

Slick watched as Pete and Luis directed the marijuana packing operation. First, a bale wrapped in waxy looking paper was handed down from the second truck. The bale was then thrust inside one of the new canvas bags. Next, one of the workers pulled the drawstring tight, wrapped the long end of the drawstring round and round the top of the bag then secured the nylon cord in place with several wraps of duct tape. The sealed bag was then placed on a modern looking scale, Pete read out the weight, Renaldo wrote it down on a pad of paper. The ready to load bag was then placed in a pile on a canvas tarpaulin. Everything seemed to be going smoothly, the bales were weighing in from 40 to 48 pounds.

Now that they'd been on the ground for more than an hour, Slick went to the Navajo to check the oil, he couldn't believe what he saw on the dipsticks.

"Pete, you aren't going to believe this, the left engine hasn't used a drop, I put half a quart in the right."

"I guess the rings have seated."

"Have they ever."

The truck that had left to get another pump returned, the driver had found a rusty old hand pump, someone had borrowed the spare electric pump. Twenty minutes later, they had managed to remove the hose from the defunct electric pump and hook it to the rusty hand pump, they were ready again.

Slick went back inside the cabin, pumping re-commenced.

The rusty old hand pump worked better than it's predecessor, ten minutes later the long range tank was full. Slick handed the nozzle out, then securely closed the filler cap.

By the time Slick was finished filling the two left wing tanks, Pete's group was ready to load the dope.

"We got a total weight of 1218 pounds, 27 bags at an average weight of 45.1 pounds. Luis is generously allowing us 1 pound for paper, canvas bag and tape, so we're paying for 1191 pounds of pot. We got a credit of 9 pounds but I told Luis we'd just call it even."

"How's the quality of the dope?"

"Want to roll a joint and give it a try?"

"Hell no, this shit just makes me sleepy and hungry, I'll take a martini any time,"

"From what I could see it looks good, sure as hell smells good. Don't worry, after a 3 month dry spell, those fucking college kids are gonna go ape shit over our Colombian Gold."

"I wonder how they ever pass anything if they're stoned all the time."

"Don't you remember college, it was just one big party, I spent all my time drinking and chasing pussy."

Slick topped off the 2 wing tanks on the right side then went around to the passenger door to watch the loading.

Pete had very carefully began filling the cabin. Since each bale was a little different in size and shape, it was somewhat like doing a jigsaw puzzle, one bale wouldn't fit, he'd find one that did. With 8 bales to go, Pete had built a neat load with a small crawl space at the top, he then placed 3 bales on the cabin floor beside the opening of the door. When one of the workers handed Pete the next bale, the nose wheel of the Navajo slowly started to lift off the ground, Slick ran under the tail of the plane and pushed it back up until the nose wheel was back on the ground.

"Renaldo, tell one of your men to come here and hold the tail up so this thing doesn't fall on it's ass."

One of the men moved to where he could get his back under the rear of the plane to hold it up, Slick told Pete what was happening.

"We're a little aft of C G, you better tie the top of the door closed then get out, we still got 4 bales to go, that's more than you weigh, I might have to get in the front to hold the nose down."

Pete rigged the top half of the door so it couldn't open, he then hooked a rope to the bottom half so he could lower it open in flight, he got out of the plane.

They decided not to load the last 4 bales until Slick was in the Navajo with the engines running. His weight plus the forward pull of the props would hold the nose on the ground. After Pete loaded the last 4 bales, he would close the cabin door, step up on the left wing and crawl across Slick to his co-pilot's seat.

Before leaving, Pete and Slick wanted to have a little pow-wow with Luis.

"Luis, we want to come back as soon as possible, when can you have another load ready?"

"Call at the same time in 2 days, if Carlos invites you to come, we are ready, if he says wait a few days, you will know I can't get enough marijuana, it's still early in the season."

"Okay, we'll call Carlos day after tomorrow."

"Señor Es Slick, I have a letter for you."

Luis handed Slick a small envelope with flowers along the edges.

"She misses you mucho."

"Believe me, I miss her mucho too."

"Okay Señores, see you soon."

Pete and Slick shook hands with Luis, Slick jumped up on the left wing and stepped into his seat. He looked to see that both propellers were clear and yelled back to Pete, *"Okay, I'm ready to start."*

"Clear to start."

Slick went through the starting procedure, both engines were running in a couple of minutes. He twisted his body and neck so he could see Pete as he stuck the last 4 bales in the cabin door. Pete then closed the door, stepped up on the left wing, carefully crawled across Slick and got into his seat, they were ready to blast off with more than $400,000 dollars worth of high grade marijuana tucked in the Navajo.

Everybody waved as Slick added enough power to start taxiing. He got as close as he could to the trees at the end of the runway before turning the Navajo towards the other end. He carefully went over his mental checklist, flaps down 15 degrees, trim a little forward of neutral to counteract the aft C G load, mixtures and props full forward and boost pumps on.

"Everything's in the green, you ready to give it a go?"

"Let's go drop this shit on Sam's ass and have a couple of cool ones, then we'll do it again, this is more fun than sex."

Slick held the brakes and pushed the throttles forward, at 2500 RPM he released the brakes and went full power. The Navajo accelerated, slowly at first, then she began to pick up speed. Considering the overload, the rate of acceleration was pretty good.

Pete was calling out airspeeds, *"fifty, sixty, seventy, eighty."* At 87 knots the Navajo more or less lifted herself off the ground, the aft C G load negated any need to pull back on the control column. Slick raised the landing gear as they cleared the trees with 15 feet to spare.

"How's it feel?"

"Heavy as hell but no sweat."

Slick raised the flaps, accelerated to 115, pulled the power and RPM back to climb settings, turned the boost pumps off, adjusted the trim, all at the same time he was making a 90 degree right turn towards the mouth of the river 5 minutes to the north on the coastline.

"It's 11:05, we should be calling Sam at about 8:30 or 9:00 tonight."

"With any luck we'll be into our first beer before midnight."

The two smugglers passed over the river mouth and headed out into the vast expanses of the Caribbean Sea for the second time in 10 hours.

Close to the ground where it was really hot, the rate of climb wasn't anything to write home about but after passing 3000 feet, things cooled off and the rate of climb improved significantly.

They leveled off at 10,000 feet, Pete opened the valve of the long range tank, Slick moved the fuel selector lever to OFF and noted the time, it was 11:40, the tank should be empty at about 4:30, by then they'd almost be as far as Great Inagua.

"Pete, you got enough room to move around back there? You gonna be able to throw that shit out okay?"

"No sweat, there's plenty of room, in fact, I think we could

throw two more bales in next trip, you think the plane can handle
another hundred pounds?"

"Off that runway yeah, the other one I don't know."

"Let's ask Carlos for thirteen hundred, that would be an
extra ten grand in each of our pockets each trip."

"Sounds good, you wanna steer this thing for a while, I got
a letter to read."

Pete took the controls, Slick pulled the envelope out of his
pocket and tore it open. Inside was a one page hand written letter
and a photograph of Magda. In the photo, she was dressed in a conservative skirt and blouse, she looked like a bank teller or an office
girl, a very curvaceous and beautiful office girl.

"What's she got to say?"

"She's studying English so she can write me letters and
talk to me better when we're together."

"Isn't that cute, what else?"

"When am I coming back? Do I miss her? Do I really love
her? Here at the end I think she's trying to say that she's waiting
for me."

"Waiting for what?"

"You know, waiting for her lover to return."

"Wow, you really must have knocked her socks off."

"It was a pretty intense three days."

Pete explained his bale tossing plan, he'd crawl to the rear,
lower the bottom half of the door fully open, then put a bale right in
front of the opening. For the first pass he'd arrange the bales in the
rear of the plane so that as soon as Slick started yelling "Go", he'd
shove the one by the door out then start grabbing the ones to his left
and throwing them out as fast as he could. Then as Slick flew
around for the second pass, he'd arrange more bales, this time on
his left and right as well as one in front of the door. Pete figured
he'd get 5 bales out the first pass and 7 or 8 on passes two, three,
four and five if necessary.

They figured there was plenty of gas as long as they didn't
have to make a big detour around nasty weather, when Slick had re-
fueled at Plaza, there were still two and a half hours of gas left in
the plane.

They bull shitted about the good old days in Vietnam where they were getting less than $2500 dollars a month. In The Nam people were shooting bullets and guided missiles at them, trying to kill their asses with real ammo. Here the worst that could happen would be a year or so in some country club jail, at best, they could make 75 or 80 thousand dollars in one day, maybe as much as half a million in one month.

"We must have been nuts. How do they talk guys like us into flying around over some little dog shit country that nobody really gives a damn about, ack ack going off, SAMs whizzing by, every asshole in the world taking pot shots at us and we're trying to hit a twenty foot long bamboo bridge with iron bombs from World War II?"

"Yeah, but it was really a lot of fun, it's the most exciting thing I ever did."

"It was a hell of a rush."

"I remember one time me and another guy were cruising around down by Dong Hoi lookin for anything that moved, we found two trucks trying to hide under some trees. When I lined up on my first pass, they made a run for it, I got off a two second burst on one of the trucks, he just disintegrated in front of my eyes. My wing man missed the second truck but the driver stopped and ran for his life, we blew the shit out of his truck and headed for home, fuck, that was fun."

"One day I shot some two point seven five rockets into a bunch of trees by a bend in the road, don't know what I hit but I never saw such a giant explosion, shit was flying all over the place, must have been a truck full of ammo."

"Too bad so many guys got killed for nothing, what a fucked up war."

"No matter, I'm glad I didn't miss it."

"What the hell's that down there?"

"Haiti."

"Time flies when ur havin fun."

Pete whipped out his E-6B flight calculator so he could do a ground speed check. He hacked the time as they crossed Haiti's southern coastline, rotated the E-6B until the time was under the miles flown, then went to the rate arrow to find the ground speed.

"We're averaging 155 knots including the climb out, not bad."

"You remember what time we switched to the aux tank? I completely forgot."

"Right when we leveled off, whenever that was."

They crossed Great Inagua at 3:23pm, 5 hours until the drop zone.

So far the weather had been perfect, they hadn't had to deviate around anything, ahead as far as the eye could see, nothing but blue skies.

It would start getting dark in a couple of hours, it would be totally dark abeam Nassau. From there they'd make a blacked out low level dash into Florida across the same stretch of deserted beach they'd departed over. After that, just cruise north among all the other private planes that were always flying up and down the length of Florida.

Slick and Pete knew from their Air Force experience that there was no surveillance radar in the world that could pick up a small target 500 feet above the ground at a distance of 50 or 60 miles. If someone happened to pick them up 10 or so miles off shore, no big deal, who would know if it was some local pilot doing night practice or what. All the bragging the Air Force did about how good their radar was, was pretty much a bunch of BS aimed at making Joe Public sleep better at night.

An hour beyond Great Inagua, Slick was engrossed in the second half of a pastrami on rye, Pete was gazing out the window at nothing in particular when both propeller RPMs started fluctuating wildly. The long range tank was empty.

"Oops! Sorry about that."

Slick moved the fuel selector levers from OFF to AUX, within a second or two, both engines were once again purring smoothly.

"Did that get your attention?"

"Scared the shit outta me."

"Would you reach back and turn that valve off?"

Now that the plane was loaded with pot, Pete had to get on his knees facing backwards on his seat, then stretch around the stacked bales to reach the valve.

"Okay, it's off, how we doing on fuel economy?"

"The tank blew at 4:30, we turned it on at about 11:30 when we leveled off almost exactly 5 hours ago, we're right on the money."

"What time does it get dark in south Florida?

"It'll be pitch black by seven thirty."

"That's good, we're gonna cross the coast about eight."

Flying up the chain of the Bahaman Islands in the daylight gave the flyers something to do, picking the islands they planned to buy as soon as they were rich. There were lots of candidates down there, beautiful little Islands with white sandy beaches and not a sign of people.

"Next year you can come visit me right down there, I'll be sitting on my lounge chair with half a dozen chicks bringing me drinks and rubbing sun tan lotion on my body."

Pete had selected a perfect hideaway, it had a beach on one side, a small cove big enough for a boat or two on the leeward side and a deep drop off on the side opposite the beach.

"Just before dinner time I'll strap on a tank, grab my spear gun and go off that drop off about fifty feet and find the catch of the day."

"I'll fly over in my seaplane once in a while to make sure you don't run out of booze."

A few miles beyond Pete's fantasy island, a longer cay with a landing strip came into view.

"Holy shit, look at that, there's a plane in the water off the end of that little strip."

"What is it?"

"Looks like a DC-3 or maybe a Beech-18."

"The guy musta stopped to get some gas then didn't have enough runway to takeoff."

"He was probably loaded to the hilt with pot."

"You'd think they'd know how much runway they needed."

"Maybe they got greedy."

The sun was just above the horizon at 6:40pm. Grand Bahama Island was thirty miles at two o'clock. Slick had been listening to the tower at Grand Bahama waiting for a plane to takeoff or land so he'd hear the tower give the current altimeter setting. When they made the low level dash to the coast it would be totally dark. There would be no way to tell how high above the water they were except the altimeter. It was a matter of life and death that the altimeter was giving the correct reading.

Finally a plane requested takeoff clearance and was given the altimeter setting along with other departure instructions, Slick rotated the altimeter knob to match the new setting, the pressure difference was insignificant, this time anyway. It's conceivable that there could be a pressure differential big enough between Florida and Barranquilla that could result in an erroneous altimeter reading in excess of 500 feet high or low. If the error was the wrong way and the pilot didn't put the new setting in the altimeter, he could think he was 500 feet above the water just as a wave smashed into the windscreen.

'Pete, you wanna drive for a few minutes while I take a leak?"

"I got it."

Pete took the controls, Slick slid his seat aft, undid his seat belt, picked up an empty plastic bottle, unzipped his fly, pulled out his dick, peed in the plastic bottle, screwed the cap back on then placed the bottle in a pouch between the pilots and co-pilots seats. After a good stretch he re-adjusted his seat and seatbelt.

"That's better, guess we'd better start down."

During the descent from 10,000 feet to 500 feet, the flyers made sure that everything was ready for the low level dash across the water, over the beach and into Florida. The auxiliary wing tanks were dry, they were now on the main wing tanks, both altimeters had been adjusted to the altimeter setting at Grand Bahama, all aircraft lights were off, the detailed map of the drop zone was in Slick's lap, everything else, maps, sandwich bags, thermos', pee bottles, etc. had been stowed.

It was show time.

When Grand Bahama Island was off the right wing, Slick turned left, Florida's shoreline lay 80 miles dead ahead somewhere out there in the blackness.

They were now level at 500 feet, Slick was glued to the instruments, there was absolutely no horizon, no nothing, total darkness.

"*Dark enough for you?*"

"*I'm glad you're flying, I've got a wild case of vertigo.*"

"*Trust the dials or die.*"

"*I swear we're in a 60 degree right descending turn.*"

"*Straight and level.*"

"*The way we're bouncing around, we must be in and out of clouds.*"

"*All the better.*"

Lights along the shoreline became visible about thirty miles out, Pete's vertigo was gone the instant he had a visual on the horizon.

"*That better?*"

"*I haven't been that fucked up for a long time, last time I had it that bad was night air re-fueling in the clouds.*"

"*That can do it all right.*"

As the shoreline got closer, Slick aimed at the spot with the fewest lights, the idea was to attract as little attention as possible.

A few minutes later the Navajo zoomed across the beach, if any radar had picked up the small aircraft out over the water, it would now have disappeared in ground clutter, they would stay at low altitude and in ground clutter until several miles inland.

Just passed interstate # 95, Slick banked to the right, climbed up to 3,000 feet and switched the rotating beacon and navigation lights ON.

"*Wouldn't want to violate any air regulations, would we?*"

As far as anyone else knew, the Navajo was just another private aircraft among the thousands of private aircraft that annually flew up and down the length of Florida, some would be on flight plans, most wouldn't. Hell, it was Florida where ninety percent of the time it was VFR, who needed a flight plan, just follow one of the many highways that after dark looked like long snakes with millions of fireflies crawling along their bodies. Nobody could possibly keep track of all the air traffic, planes were zooming all over the place, in fact, nobody tried to keep track, there were no laws against getting in your plane and going somewhere. After all, this is America, the land of the free.

"*About forty minutes to the DZ.*"

"I'm ready to get moving, my ass is paralyzed."

"Won't be long."

Slick listened to the radio as a Delta 727 made it's approach to Orlando, as required by the FAA, the pilot repeated the altimeter setting given by air traffic control. Slick adjusted his altimeter to the new setting, again, the change was insignificant.

At Yeehaw Junction, Slick veered to the left so as to intercept interstate #4 just a little to the east of Lakeland. At Lakeland he'd switch to the more detailed map that they'd used when making practice runs at the drop zone.

Pete was fiddling with one of the hand held marine radios.

"I'll give Sam a try as soon as we see Lakeland."

"Okay, I'm turning the lights off again."

"Happy Hooker, radio check."

"Last time he couldn't understand us til Lakeland."

"Happy Hooker, radio check."

"I read you Hooker."

"Shit hot, there he is."

Since Sam had said nothing other than, *"I read you Hooker"*, there were no problems at the drop zone.

"I'm going to the back and get ready."

Pete unhooked his seatbelt, turned around in his seat, stood as high as he could then started to burrow through the stacked bales of marijuana, after a few seconds, all that Slick could see were his feet, then they too disappeared.

Slick pulled the throttles back and started down towards 1000 feet, a few minutes past Lakeland he made a slight right turn in order to follow highway #22, the Y in the road was less than five minutes ahead.

"About five minutes to go!"

"Okay, I'll be ready!"

A minute or so before the Y in the road, the Navajo was at 1000 feet with 15 degrees of flaps down, Slick had her slowed down to 100 knots.

"How long?"

"About a minute and a half!"

"I'm opening the door!"

As the bottom half of the door came open, Slick could hear the rush of air, it sounded about the same as a car window being opened at 100 miles per hour.

"It's open!"

In the moonlight, Slick could clearly see the Y in the road half a mile ahead.

"Forty five seconds to go!"

"I'm ready!"

Slick banked right to follow the right hand arm of the Y, the slight curve in the road was fifteen seconds ahead.

"Thirty seconds!"

Over the curve, Sam's lights appeared off to the right, Slick banked right, at the same time he pulled the power back and pushed the nose down. With ten seconds to go he was perfectly lined up with the line of lights.

"Get ready! Ready! Ready!"

The Navajo skimmed over the trees at the south end of the clearing, all ten lights suddenly came into view.

"Ready! Ready! Go! Go! Go! Go! Go! Go! Go! Go! Go! Go! Go! Go! Go! Stop! Stop! Stop!"

As Slick started yelling *"Stop"*, he was over the last of the 10 lights, at the same instant he added power and pulled the nose up above the tops of the trees ahead. After climbing and passing the trees, he started a left turn to begin pass number two.

Slick could feel the changes in the center of gravity as Pete began moving bales and getting ready for the next pass.

"I got five bales out!"

"Okay, about thirty seconds to go!"

When Slick saw the curve in the road off to his left, he banked sharply left, the lights came into sight again.

"Fifteen seconds!"

"Okay!"

"Get ready! Ready! Ready! Go! Go! Go! Go! Go! Go! Go! Go! Stop! Stop!

Pete managed to get 7 bales out on the second pass, 8 on pass number 3 and the remaining 7 bales on the 4th and last pass.

"That's all! That's all! We're empty!"

As Slick pulled up after the last pass, Pete closed the bottom part of the door, then came up and started pounding Slick on his shoulders.

"What a rush, what a fuckin rush, every bale right on target."

Pete sat down on the floor beside the tank in the empty Navajo to catch his breath, his eyes were wild.

"What a hell of a rush."

The empty Navajo zoomed up to 3000 feet, Leesburg Airport was dead ahead at 50 miles.

As soon as Pete caught his breath and calmed down, he tidied up the back of the plane. First, he removed the bungee cords that held the top half of the door closed. Second, he untied the rope that had been used to lower the bottom half of the door to the open position. Third, he un-plumbed the long range tank. When his house keeping chores were complete, Pete climbed back in the co-pilots seat.

"Just another day at the office."

"Sit down and relax, we'll be on the ground in about twenty-five minutes."

"I can't believe how smooth the drop went, you didn't seem to have any trouble."

"No sweat with this much moonlight."

Five minutes east of the drop zone, Slick turned the rotating beacon and navigation lights back on.

The flyers went over what they would say in case anyone approached them after landing. If the cops were waiting, they would be semi fucked. All they could do was to deny everything, with no dope on the plane, what could the cops do except make threats? Pete and Slick's best defense would be to stick to their story no matter how lame it sounded, and lame the story would sound because of one serious oversight.

"It's pretty stupid of us to be landing with all these maps showing our route from here to Colombia and back."

"Next time we'll throw them out with the pot, I never thought about it."

"Me neither."

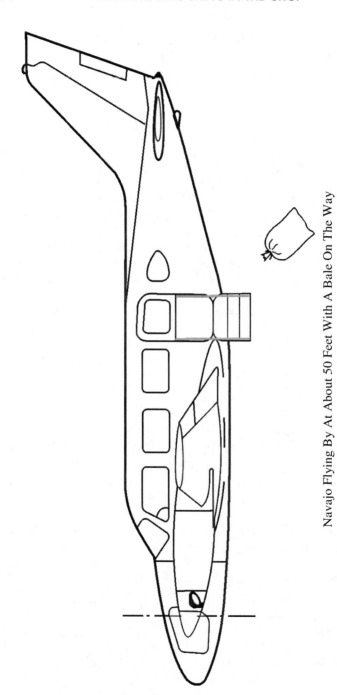

Navajo Flying By At About 50 Feet With A Bale On The Way

"I could get rid of them now."

"We're gonna need them again in two days. What are the odds of anybody being on to us?"

"I'll be ready to ditch all the maps if there's any sign of life at the airport."

The lakes to the west of Leesburg came into view, then the airport. They flew across the runway and parking area, if anyone was down there they were well hidden.

Slick banked into a continuous left down wind, left base turn, half way through the turn he lowered the landing gear and 15 degrees of flaps, on short final, full flaps, landing lights ON and boost pumps ON. Squeak, squeak, they were on the ground, it was 9:52pm.

They turned off the runway and backtracked to the parking area, Leesburg airport was quiet as a mouse.

Three minutes later, the Navajo was sitting in it's usual parking spot with the engines shut down. Pete double checked that the curtains were closed, Slick stuck the sunscreen in the windshield.

Thirty seconds later, the two smugglers stepped out of the Navajo's back door, while Slick secured the lock, Pete put the wheel chocks in place.

"You ready?"

"Let's go."

As nonchalantly as possible, the two tired but exhilarated aviators began walking off the airport, Slick had the bag containing the marine radios, thermos', bungees, rope and plumbing parts slung over his shoulder, Pete had all the incriminating maps in a tight bundle stuck in the front of his pants. As soon as they were off the airport property, they crossed to the other side of the road, the motel was 3 minutes ahead.

"Next time let's find out what's behind us down the road so if a cop stops us we can tell him where we're coming from."

"Good idea."

Two cars passed, nobody stopped.

Pete reached in his pocket, pulled out the room key and opened the door, they had done it. Safe inside the room, Pete gave Slick a giant bear hug, *"We did it, we fuckin did it."*

"No wonder there's so many crooks in this country, that was way too easy."

"Slick my boy, let me buy you a beer."

Pete opened the large cooler at the foot of his bed, only 50 percent of the ice had melted in the last 24 hours.

"You want a Bud or a Bud?"

"Gimmee a Bud."

The intrepid smugglers flopped on their bunks and guzzled ice cold beer, Pete made a list of the changes they needed to make before the next flight south, Slick phoned the restaurant next door and ordered 2 deluxe burgers to go.

"Ready for another beer?"

"Ready."

Slick walked to the 24 hour restaurant to pick up the hamburgers, he stopped at the pay phone to call Rosemary.

"Hello."

"Hi there, I'll see you tomorrow at noon."

"See you then, everything go okay?"

"Perfect, bye, bye."

The burgers were delicious and the beer kept coming, by midnight, not a creature was stirring.

The alarm went off at 8am, there were still several tasks left to perform.

Task number one, wakeup coffee.

Task number two, drive to the airport, look around for any suspicious looking characters, when satisfied that the coast is clear, unload the long range tank and re-install the 4 passenger seats.

Task number three, pick up the flight bag at the motel and head for home.

After coffee, Pete and Slick got in the van and drove the short distance to Leesburg Airport, ten minutes later they were satisfied that nobody was paying any attention to the Navajo.

"What do you think?"

"I think that nobody around here gives a shit about us or our plane, let's grab the tank and hit the road."

Pete backed up close to the Navajo, Slick jumped out and unlocked the door. Within two minutes, the long range tank was in the van and the 4 passenger seats were re-installed in the back of the Navajo.

Before leaving, Pete slid the curtain covering the window next to the door about half way open.

"If anyone's the least bit suspicious about our Navajo, they can take a peak in here, all they're gonna see is four passenger seats."

"Good plan, let's di di mau."

Half way to Tampa they stopped to call Sam.

"He's waiting for us, the dope is on the way to Boston."

When they pulled to a stop in the nursery parking lot, Sam was standing there with a big shit eating grin on his face. The three crooks hugged each other as if they'd just won a gold medal at the Olympics.

"You guys did good."

"You find all twenty seven bags?"

"Hell yes, they were all right on target, all the stuff was on the way to Boston about ten minutes after you made the last pass."

After stashing the long range tank, Sam took his air crew out to lunch, during the drive they congratulated each other and talked about the previous day's events.

"So tell me, how'd it go? You have any problems with the plane or down south?"

"No man, the whole deal went smooth as silk, the plane ran like a clock, how bout ur end?"

"Piece of cake, me an the boys went out to the drop zone at seven, set up the lights, drank some beers, waited a couple of hours, got ur radio call, turned on the lights, hid under the trees, watched you fly by four times about ten feet off the ground, picked up the bags, loaded the truck, picked up the lights and took off. Hell, I was in bed by midnight."

"We're gonna bring an extra hundred pounds next time, the plane has tons of power."

"Shit hot, when is the next time?"

"We'll call tomorrow to see if they can get another load ready, if they've got enough dope we're out of here in two days."

"Now we're talkin."

"Can the buyers be ready that soon?"

"If they ain't, I'll hide the shit til they get here, in those bags there isn't enough smell to give it away. Don't you worry about getting rid of the dope, I'll stash it under my bed until we sell it if I have to."

Over lunch the threesome discussed what had to be done to be ready to go in two days. There were also a few changes that needed to be made. Sam wanted to be told how many bags he was supposed to pick up, they decided to add the number of bags to the radio call, Pete would transmit, "Happy Hooker Two Seven or Two Eight or Two Nine, Radio Check." The number after Happy Hooker would indicate the number of bags to be dropped. There would be one small bag included in the number that would contain the incriminating maps.

The three drums had to be filled, somebody had to call the motel to make reservations, Carlos had to be called to make sure that the mission was on, there were enough bags left for the second go but more would have to be ordered before number three.

"You boys think of anything else?"

"Nope, the lights were perfect, we had plenty of gas, we still got almost a full case of oil, all I need is a piece of ass and some sleep and I'll be ready, how bout you Slick?"

"You get any money from those guys?"

"Oh yeah, I almost forgot, they brought two hundred and fifty grand, they'll bring the balance for the first load when they pick up the second load plus whatever extra they collect by then."

Sam did some figuring on a napkin.

"What say we hold out the fifty for expenses and seventy two for the dope and split the rest four ways, that's thirty two thou each. Then when the next batch of money gets here we'll square off for the first trip."

"Sounds good to me."

After lunch they returned to the nursery, Sam counted out 32 thousand dollars for Slick and Pete, *"I hope this is the first of many pay days, now you guys get home and get some rest, we've got a busy couple of days ahead of us."*

Pete and Slick left for the lake house.

The several small bundles of hundred dollar bills created a new problem that Slick hadn't solved or even thought about.

"What the hell am I gonna do with all this money?"

"You need to open an account in Cayman, in a month or so you'll have quite a pile."

"I never thought I'd be worried about having too much cash lying around."

"We'll make a run to Cayman in a couple of weeks, you open an account, I'll put some more in Luis' account, by then we'll be ready for a little vacation. Meantime, hide your loot somewhere they won't find it if we get busted."

Rosemary rushed out of the house when she saw Pete's car pull into the driveway. She threw a lip lock on Slick that took his breath away.

"Come into my web you crazy idiot, I've got a thousand questions for you, then I'm going to abuse your body."

"A just punishment I'm sure."

Rosemary's plan was carried out but in reverse order, after some torrid love making, she started the questioning.

"Now you tell me every little detail, I can't believe what you just finished doing, it's so exciting, I haven't slept a wink."

As Slick told his tale, Rosemary squealed with delight, the part about dropping the dope was almost more than she could bear.

"No, you flew below the tops of the trees, you are nuts, oh how exciting, I think I just peed my pants a little."

"You aren't wearing any pants."

"You bozo, it's just an expression."

"Now will you let me get some sleep?"

"I just hate you, you get to do all these exciting things while I'm window shopping in the mall like a proper grieving widow, it's not fair."

"There's girl things and there's boy things."

"It's still not fair, I should learn to fly a plane."

"You could start the first all girl smuggling gang, Brenda could be your co-pilot."

"Guess I'll stick to getting my thrills vicariously through you."

Slick dropped his small pile of cash in Rosemary's lap.
"Here, count this, there should be thirty two thousand."
"I double hate you. What's this for?"
"Half a day's work."
"I like your job."
Slick nodded off into a deep sleep, Rosemary didn't notice, she was busy counting.

Chapter VIII

THE SECOND AND THIRD

"Wake up, open your eyes you naughty little boy, it's time to get up."

Rosemary gently shook an almost comatose Slick.

"Wake up, it's seven thirty, time to get up."

"AM or PM?"

"PM, you told me to wake you up before eight."

Slick got out of bed, walked out of his room to the bottom of the stairs and yelled for Pete to get his ass out of bed.

"Pete, get your filthy hands off that woman, let's go out and get some chow, we got a busy day tomorrow."

"What woman? I haven't seen hide nor hair of the bitch."

"The hell with her, let's go have a drink and a bite."

"Where we going?"

"The usual."

Sam and Sarah showed up a little later, Slick had never seen Sam in such a bubbly mood.

"Tonight my friends, everything is on our friends from the north, we got a cool thousand to blow."

The morning's activities started with several cups of coffee. It's hard to spend a thousand dollars on a dinner for five, even at Burns Steak House. There was also the question of Brenda, she hadn't been seen nor had she called. Oh well, no big deal, there were things that needed to be done regardless of how horny Pete might be.

Around nine, Pete and Slick drove to the nursery, got in the van and headed east towards the airport at Plant City to re-fuel the 3 drums. They had decided to try to use a different airport each time the drums needed to be filled to avoid any unnecessary curiosity.

The kid who sold aviation gas at Plant City couldn't have cared less what they planned to do with the fuel, he backed *his* truck up to the van, filled the drums, took the money and drove away. An hour later the van was back in it's place at the nursery.

Sam had been in contact with the buyers, they would be back in Tampa in time to meet the plane, however, because of the fast turn around they wouldn't have any more money until they'd had a chance to sell some of the first load.

The three importers discussed the situation and decided not to worry about the money and go for a third run as soon as possible, that is if all went well on number two.

"They said they'll have sold a lot of stuff in a few days. I guess everybody is begging for the shit, the poor little college brats have been smoking some lousy quality crap all summer. They promised to bring all the cash they can get together before our third dash south."

"Maybe we better plan on a short break after number three, let the money get caught up, me and Slick are gonna have to make a run down to Cayman to stash some loot. Luis' account is gonna need another shot pretty soon too."

Carlos was waiting for the call, he said there would be a 24 hour delay, they were to call the next day at the same time to verify their reservations at the Plaza Hotel.

Sam was notified, Brenda showed up, Pete got laid, Slick and Rosemary got a little drunk and did it in the speed boat in the middle of the lake then had a pizza delivered to the house.

"Hello Carlos, it's Pete."
"Pete mi amigo, we will be expecting you tomorrow morning at the Hotel Plaza, your reservation is confirmed, see you tomorrow."
"Adios Carlos, hasta mañana."
"It's a go, I'll call the motel in Leesburg."

The second flight to Colombia and back was almost a carbon copy of number one, the plane ran flawlessly, the weather was perfect, Luis and his crew were waiting at Plaza, moonlight made the drop a cinch and nobody paid a bit of attention when the Navajo returned to Leesburg.

Sam verified that they had picked up 30 bags, 29 big ones full of dope and one light one that contained the maps.

The load had weighed in at 1325 pounds, 5 passes were required to empty the plane.

Before taking off from Plaza, Luis had assured them that he had enough marijuana ready for the 3rd trip in 2 days, they would call Carlos at the same time to verify.

In 5 days, the crew had earned a total of $848,500 minus $100,000 for expense minus $151,500 for the pot left $597,000 for the partners, that represented $149,000 plus change for each member of the smuggling ring. If flight number 3 was successful, their week's earnings would be about $226,000 each. Not bad. Not bad.

Carlos was called, their reservations were set for the next morning at the Hotel Plaza, number 3 was a go.

The drums were filled, reservations were made at the motel, the buyers were on the way back to Florida with the truck used in the first pick up. By seven thirty in the evening, Pete and Slick had removed the passenger seats, installed the long range tank, filled the tank, parked the van at the motel, had a bite and lied down for a much needed rest. So far, so good.

The flyers were awakened prematurely by a blast of thunder followed by torrential rain that lasted close to an hour, a series of humongous thunderstorms moving from east to west delayed their departure.

The Navajo lifted off at 35 minutes after midnight, the crew was entertained by a spectacular light show off the right side of the plane.

Several detours were required between Orlando and Cape Kennedy to avoid more thunderstorms, it was 4:05 am when they were abeam Nassau, happily, the skies ahead were void of more lightning flashes.

"Well, that was fun."

"Those were some big mothers."

"How much time have we lost?"

"Hour on the ground, hour and half in the air, we'll be there about eleven."

"The gas gonna be okay?"

"We'll have thirty to forty five minutes left if there's no more shit to dodge."

"From now on, we're going to have to sacrifice a little

dope and carry more gas, if we run into another batch of storms we'll be screwed."

"What do you think? A tank that holds another hour's gas."

"At least."

Fortunately, no more storms were encountered, the intrepid flyers pressed on through the night and on into the morning, at 10:55am, the Navajo touched down at Hotel Plaza.

Pete and Slick congratulated each other at having successfully completed the first half of smuggling run number three, little did they know.

"Señor Pedro, Señor Es Slicko, Bienvenido, you have problems? You are very late."

"Como esta, Luis, many big thunderstorms in Florida, you know, tempestos muy grande."

"No problema muchachos, we are glad you made it."

The refueling and loading procedures were once again carried out. Now that everybody was used to the Navajo, things went along quite smoothly. The oil consumption was still zilch, it took less than one quart to top off both engines.

The only problem encountered during refueling was the heat. It was so hot inside the cabin that Slick had to take a short break when the tank was half full to cool off. By the time he had all of the gas tanks full, Pete's crew was almost done putting the bales of marijuana in the canvas bags and weighing the cargo.

"We got a total weight of one thousand two hundred and ninety pounds, thirty bags."

"Sounds good, let's get the shit loaded and get going, we're gonna be late as hell, Sam will think we're floating around somewhere out in the Atlantic Ocean."

They rolled for takeoff at ten minutes before 2, both flyers were sweating profusely, it was really hot. The Navajo didn't care too much for the intense heat and humidity either, her rate of acceleration sucked, by the time she was at flying speed, Pete's eyes were bulging. Slick held her on the runway as long as he dared, rotated and aimed at the tops of the trees ahead.

"Son of a bitch! We damn near hit that tree."

"It wasn't quite as bad as it looked, I held her down as close as I could for speed."

"You did good, I don't see any branches stuck in the wings. Man! It's hot, let's get this fucker up where it's cool."

"Patience my boy, right now we have the aero-dynamics of a bowling ball inside a blast furnace, we'll be okay above three or four thousand feet."

Sure enough, the newly overhauled engines did their job and thrust the overheated and overloaded plane up above the scorching surface of mother earth. At 3500 feet the outside air temperature dropped to a cool 80 degrees Fahrenheit. All of the sudden everything started cooling down, the cylinder head temperatures moved away from the red line, the oil temperatures started a slow descent from the red zone to high in the green and the cabin finally became bearable.

At 8,000 feet Pete broke out a delicious lunch of bagels with Philadelphia Cream Cheese, smoked salmon and slices of raw onion. They had learned on the first trip to keep their food and drinks in a small cooler so it didn't get hot while on the ground in Colombia.

"Damn Pete, this is good, ur a hell of a cook."

"Thank you mon capitane, ur a hell of a pilot."

"Merci beaucoup, got any more coffee?"

"Coming up."

It was dark before they reached Great Inagua at 6:50pm. If all went well from there on, they would make the drop at about 11:30 and land a little after midnight.

The three and a half hour flight up the Bahamas Island chain was uneventful, the first sign of trouble came shortly after they passed abeam Grand Bahama and turned west towards Florida's coast at Fort Pierce.

Ahead in the darkness, bolts of lightning began to brighten the sky every few seconds, the closer they got to the coast, the more frequent the lightning.

Twenty miles off shore, 500 feet above the water, Slick

could see what appeared to be a solid wall of thunderstorms along the east coast of Florida.

"*What's the plan?*"

"*I sure as hell ain't flying into that, we'd come out the bottom in a million pieces. We're gonna have to fly up the coast.*"

"*What about Cape Kennedy?*"

"*If we can't get inland before then, we'll have to go around the restricted zone on the ocean side.*"

In and out of rain and clouds they headed north along the shoreline.

"*What are we going to do if we don't find a way around these storms?*"

"*I dunno.*"

Thirty minutes later, Slick saw the rotating white beacon of a civil airport.

"*You see that light? You know what airport that is?*"

"*We must be up by Palm Bay or Melbourne by now.*"

"*I think ur right, that's got to be Melbourne, looks like there's a gap between storms over there. I'm gonna try to make it over to Interstate Four then backtrack down to Lakeland. What do you think?*"

"*Go for it.*"

Slick peeled off in a steep left diving turn towards the area where there wasn't any lightning. When there were breaks in the clouds or rain, he could see the odd car on the two lane road below that ran east and west. Several times he had to dodge the worst parts of the storms that were lit up by lightning.

Try as he may, he couldn't miss everything, they were getting their asses kicked pretty severely, the Navajo was leaping around like an enraged bucking bronco.

Then it was over, as fast as they'd got in the shit, they were out of it.

"*Hallelujah! I see stars.*"

"*Good thing, we're getting pretty low on gas.*"

As the ruffled flyers worked on the fuel problem, they intercepted Interstate #4 a little south of Kissimmee.

"*We have two choices, go straight to Leesburg and land with the dope or go drop it and land at Tampa. You got any better ideas?"*

"Fuck it Pete, we need a bigger tank anyway, let's drop the shit, throw the tank out and land at Tampa, get some gas and go back to Leesburg. I don't want to risk landing with all this pot."

"I agree, there ain't shit they can prove if we don't have anything in the plane."

"You gotta try and get all the bags out in four passes, we're gonna be running on fumes."

"I'll be throwing my ass off."

"Happy Hooker Three One, radio check."

"Happy Hooker Three One, radio check."
"You think they gave up and went home?"
"Not Sam, try em again."
"Happy Hooker Three One, radio check."
"I read you Hooker."
"Shit hot, there he is."

Pete crawled to the rear of the plane to get ready for the drop, Slick couldn't keep his eyes off the fuel gauges.
"Five minutes!"
"I'm almost ready!"

"Two minutes!"
"I'm ready!"

Slick heard the rush of air as Pete lowered the bottom half of the door open.

Sam's lights came into view exactly when Slick anticipated them.

"Get ready! Ready! Ready! Go! Go! Go! Go! Go! Go! Go! Go! Go! Go! Go! Go! Go! Stop! Stop! Stop!"

Slick pulled up to start the second pass, he was keeping the pattern as small as possible to save time and gas, he'd also lengthened the drop pass about one second in the hope Pete could get all 31 bags out in 4 passes.

"You okay?"
"I got eight out!"
"Three more passes!"

Slick almost fucked up the second pass by cutting the last corner too close to the drop zone, Pete lost his balance as Slick maneuvered to get back on track but he still got 7 bags out the door.
"Sorry, I won't do that again!"
"No sweat!"

Pete threw 9 bags on the third pass, his adrenaline had really kicked in.
"I got seven more!"

Slick pulled up after the 4th and final pass, he made a climbing left turn directly towards Tampa International Airport.
Pete gasped, *"Hand me the tools."*
Slick passed the small bag that contained the tools, within two minutes, Pete had disconnected the long range tank.
"I gotta open the top half of the door to get this out."
"Tell me when ur ready, I'll slow way down."
"I'm ready."
Slick pulled the power back and turned slightly towards a totally dark area on the ground, he could hear Pete moving things around in the rear of the plane.
"You ready?"
"Go ahead!"
"Shit, I can't get this fucking tank out, the wind is twisting it in the door!"
"Hold on, I'll pull the nose up and slow this fucker way down!"
Slick pulled the nose up about 30 degrees above the horizon, he could hear Pete grunting in the back. As the Navajo ran out of airspeed and started stalling, Slick gently lowered the nose back towards the horizon.
"I got it, it's gone! Let's get the hell out of here!"
As Slick turned towards Tampa, he could hear and feel the rear doors close, a minute later Pete slipped into the co-pilots seat.

"How we doing?"

"Tampa is twenty two miles dead ahead, if they don't let us land immediately, we'll just have to land on Davis Island and figure it out from there."

"I hope those gauges leave a little room for error."

"Tampa tower, Navajo Two One Two Two Bravo, twenty miles north east for landing."

"Two One Two Two Bravo, no reported traffic, report right base runway three six right, winds three four zero at eight knots."

"Two One Two Two Bravo, roger."

"So far so good."

As soon as Slick picked up the rotating beacon at Tampa International, he headed straight for it. The fuel needles kept on their relentless march towards the big E.

"Two One Two Two Bravo, report the runway in sight."

"Two One Two Two Bravo."

"Pete, I'm gonna stay as high as I can as long as I can in case this thing flames out."

"I dig."

"Two One Two Two Bravo, runway in sight."

"Two One Two Two Bravo, clear to land runway three six right."

"Clear to land three six right, Two One Two Two Bravo."

"Come-on baby, two more minutes."

Abeam the end of runway 36 right, Slick dropped the landing gear, pulled the throttles to idle and started a steep diving right turn to final, when he was sure of landing, he lowered the flaps to half, then full down over the end of the runway. They touched down about 1,500 feet down the runway, it was 2:40am.

"Hail Mary."

"Fuck me, that's calling it a bit too close."

"Two One Two Two Bravo, stay on this frequency, where are you going?"

"We need directions to any FBO where we can get fuel."

"Okay, exit the runway at Delta, follow taxi way Delta to the Shell sign, they're the only FBO open at this time."

"Two One Two Two Bravo, thanks."

"Two One Two Two Bravo, be advised, we've had several reports of severe weather on the east side of the state in case you are headed that way."

"Thanks for the info, we're only going as far as the Orlando area."

"Two One Two Two Bravo roger, talk to you later."

"Shit, I thought he was going to say they had reports of falling fuel tanks."

"I don't think anything's up, his voice sounds totally normal."

The all night gas man directed them to park with lighted batons.

"I can't believe this thing is still running, look at those gauges."

"My eyes have been glued to them since I sat down, what would we have told them if it had quit on the runway or taxiway.?"

"I would have blamed it on you. I wish I had a camera, you look like a wild man."

"You have to admit, that was pretty intense."

Slick pulled the mixtures to Idle Cutoff and turned all the switches off, *"Let's get some gas and haul ass."*

"Hi ya guys, what you boys doing out this time of night?"

"Same as you, trying to make a living."

"You need fuel?"

"Yeah, fifty gallons each main then we're outta here."

"Just a minute, I'll bring my truck over."

Twenty minutes later Slick called Tampa Tower on the radio. They were given taxi instructions to runway 36 right and cleared for takeoff. Ten miles to the east of Tampa Airport, Slick informed the tower that he was clear of their zone, tower cleared Two One Two Two Bravo to change radio frequencies.

"Can you believe that, we just broke about a million laws then landed at an international airport, gassed up and went on our merry way."

"I guess most people never suspect that anybody would

ever do anything this bold, not right under their noses anyway."

"That first beer is gonna be sweet."

"And the second."

"You think we'll get any attention landing this late?"

"I'm gonna come in quite as possible, I'll come in over the lake at idle, I won't switch the landing lights on til the last second, doubt if anybody will even notice, they should all be asleep."

"It's a good thing we're taking a break after this one, I need a rest."

"I think putting two hundred and fifty thou in my Cayman account followed by a week of sun and fun sounds pretty relaxing."

The exhausted duo jabbered on about their plans for the next ten days, Slick made his silent approach and landing then taxied to the Navajo's parking spot, indeed, everybody in Leesburg was fast asleep.

Pete stuck the key in the motel room door, *"What time you got?"*

"It's four forty four."

"Allow me to buy you a beer."

"Thank you very much."

"I'll grab the beer, you call and order a couple of greasy burgers, I'm starving."

"Oh man, that may be the best beer I've ever had."

"You got that right."

After two fast Buds, Slick walked over to pick up the burgers, as always, he stopped at the payphone to call Rosemary.

"Hello."

"Hi, it's me, see you around noon."

"Thanks for calling, you okay?"

"Fine, lousy weather, bye-bye."

Chapter IX

THE BUYERS

Sam met them at 2pm, he was grinning like the Cheshire Cat.

"We had a hell of a time finding bag number thirty one, it was way off in the trees."

"You're lucky it was only one, we damn near ran out of gas."

"Let's go get a drink, I want to hear all about it."

For the next hour, Pete and Slick regaled Sam with the wild tale of their flight, Sam just kept shaking his head and saying, *"Holly shit."* The bartender must have thought he had three escapees from an insane asylum the way they were laughing and pounding on the table top.

Sam had a bit of good news, the buyers had brought 425 thousand with them and a promise of another 400 thousand in a few days. Their dope selling network was once again in full swing.

Sam did the arithmetic on a napkin as usual.

"What say each of the four of us takes eighty, that's three hundred twenty, we set aside one hundred for expenses and hold the five that's left over to the next payment."

It was agreed.

The three smugglers discussed the problems that had arisen. First, they needed a new bigger gas tank. Pete would take care of the new tank with his buddy who made odd shaped fuel tanks for racing boats. Second, the weight of the extra gas would cause them to go back to the original 1,200 pounds of pot. Nothing they could do about that. Third, would Slick fly up to Boston to pick up the next pile of money? Slick accepted the assignment. Fourth, Sam wanted Slick and Pete to figure out where all the monies had gone, he admitted he was losing track of who got what for what and why, how long they had to keep holding out 50 thousand per trip for expenses and how much had been set aside for the dope.

The meeting was adjourned, half an hour later, Slick and Pete drove to the lake house with 80 thousand each.

"If we get that four hundred grand in the next few days, each of us will have about two hundred thousand free and clear."

"Six months ago when you called me, I was flat broke, now I got a garbage bag full of hundred dollar bills, there is a Santa Claus."

Rosemary was waiting, *"You both look like you could use a shower and a good night's sleep, I've never seen such bags under anyone's eyes."*

"I just hope I can stay awake through the shower."

Pete staggered upstairs alone, Brenda was missing again.

Rosemary led Slick to their room. *"Let me help you get undressed you poor baby, you must be exhausted."*

"It just hit me, guess I'm out of gas."

Three minutes after Slick stepped out of the shower he was sound asleep. Rosemary couldn't believe her eyes when she peeked in the black plastic garbage bag, *"Oh my, that's a lot of money."*

Thirteen hours later, Slick's body came back to life, at first he couldn't remember where he was, a glance at Rosemary's ample breast snapped him back to reality. It was 6am, he was hungry as a bear.

"Rosemary, how do you want your eggs?"

"Poached."

"I meant, how do you want them fried?"

"Over medium. My my, aren't we domestic today."

"Run up there and tell Pete his breakfast will be ready in five minutes."

"On the way daddy."

After breakfast, Pete left for Clearwater, he had a fuel tank to order, a tank that held at least 170 gallons of gas. That would be 32 gallons more than the one they had kicked out over some unsuspecting orange grove. The extra 32 gallons would weigh 224 pounds and would give them about another hour and 5 minutes flying time, time that would have made their last flight a hell of a lot less frantic.

When Rosemary was done having her way with him, Slick

worked on the crew's financial statement. What he came up with probably wouldn't pass a CPA's audit but he felt sure it was close enough for a guy like Sam who had forgotten about the 7 grand of his own money he'd spent on the windowless van and who knows what else.

Sam called, he said he'd be by in thirty minutes.

Sam rambled as he drove to the local coffee shop.

"I talked with the boys in Boston, a guy we call Nevada will meet you in your room at the Boston Yale Hotel three days from now. They still don't know how much loot will be ready, but we'll get all they can collect by then. Nevada will also have the weights from each load so you can come up with the exact amount they owe us and how much more we have to transfer Luis to square up his account."

"When I get to Boston, am I supposed to act like I'm someone else or what?"

"It's up to you, you can tell them anything you want, those guys don't give a shit who you are, they're just some guys like us trying to make a buck. You'll probably hit it off pretty good with Nevada, his partner is a little out of control."

"What about the weights, what if what they give me is way off our weights?"

"I don't think they will be, those guys have always been straight with us, if they're off a little, negotiate to something close, we don't want to get too excited over a couple of pounds."

Sam gave Slick a few traveling tips that would come in handy on future commercial airline flights, especially if he was carrying lots of cash in his luggage. First, never attract any attention to himself, always dress like ninety percent of other travelers. Second, never pay cash at the airline counter for tickets, plan ahead, buy the tickets a few days ahead from a travel agent. Young men who throw lots of cash around attract unwanted attention. Maybe most important, always go non-stop even if you have to wait around for the right flight. The more plane changes, the greater the chances of lost luggage.

Over coffee, Slick showed Sam the financial breakdown he'd put together with Pete's help. Sam liked it, especially the

5,000 dollar a month salary that he'd forgotten to pay himself for 6 months. (Now that everyone was flush, no more salaries.)

1st Load   1218 lbs   27 bags   each bag 1 lb equals 1191 lbs of stuff
2nd Load   1325 lbs   29 bags   each bag 1 lb equals 1296 lbs of stuff
3rd Load   1290 lbs   30 bags   each bag 1 lb equals <u>1260 </u>lbs of stuff
                                                    3747 lbs

 3747 pounds X $340 = $1,273,980 rounded off to $1,274,000
Expenses:
1. $ 90,000 Six months salaries Sam, Pete, Slick
2. $111,000 Plane
3. $ 8,000 New prop blades and starters
4. $ 25,000 Break-in trip, plumbing job, gas, hotels, food, etc.
5. $ 10,000 Calif to Florida (Pete still has a little over $4,000 cash.
6. <u>$ 7,000</u> Van
   $251,000 Of the $251,000 in expenses, $150,000 paid off,
                                              $101,000 left.

Cash in: $250,000   Cash out: $ 50,000 expenses deduction
         <u>$425,000</u> $ 72,000 stuff
         $675,000 $128,000 $32,000 X 4
                                    $100,000 expenses deduction
                                    $320,000 $80,000 X 4
                                    <u>$ 5,000 cash</u>
                                    $675,000

$1,274,000 Total amount owed for 3747 pounds at $340 per pound
<u>- 675,000</u>   Amount received so far
 =599,000 Amount still due
<u>- 150,000</u> $72,000 + $72,000 + a little,_Amount due to the man
$ 449,000   Amount to be split 4 ways minus some expenses

   "This is perfect, details have never been my forte, I better have you take care of the numbers from here on out. I forgot about most of this stuff, our man woulda thought I was rippin his ass off, not that he'd miss a couple grand here and there. Remind me when we get back to my office, I'll give you that five grand left over for ur trip to Boston, whatever's left you guys can use for the trip to Cayman. I also got a metal suitcase with good locks for you to take to Boston, it's good for haulin money."

The waitress brought another round of coffee and bagels, they talked some more about the first three flights, Sam swore he was going to take Pete's place on one of the future runs down south.

"You guys don't get to have all the fun, I'd kick myself in the ass if when we quit doing this all I ever did was pick up the dope and load it in a truck, couple of more trips and I'm going."

"You'll love it, it's a real kick in the ass."

During the drive back to the nursery, Slick reminded Sam that they were down to about 10 canvas bags, Sam said he'd order another 100 as soon as he got to his phone.

The metal suitcase was perfect, it was covered with scuba diving stickers, the 3 number combination lock was solid. There was a 4 inch wide strap that circled the case, the strap would keep the case closed even if the lock or hinges failed. It looked exactly like the sort of suitcase you'd want to carry your expensive under-water camera and other dive gear in.

Slick stuck the $5,000 in his pocket and left, Rosemary was going to barbecue mahi-mahi, it was his job to make the salad and boil corn on the cob.

"Can I go? I've never been to Boston."

"I don't see why not but let me check with Sam. Where's Pete?"

"He told Brenda to either come home at night or get out so she's upstairs fucking him so he won't be so mad."

"She is some space cadet. I'm gonna call Sam, I have to make sure he ordered some stuff, see you in ten."

Slick drove to the corner 7-11 and called Sam. Yes, he had remembered to order the bags and yes, it sounded fine for Rosemary to go along, *"Nothing more innocent looking than a nice young couple visiting some of America's historic sights, take her to Cayman too, she can help pack some of the diving stuff."*

"Sam likes the idea, he's even planning to put you to work."

"Doing what?"

"I think the word is mule."

"Another word for mule is ass."

"Well, that fits."

"Be serious."

"We're going to need an extra bag or two to haul money to Cayman."

"I can see the headlines, Grieving widow jailed for helping crooks smuggle money."

"It's up to you, I'm sure there'd be a buck or two in it. Speaking of money, where the hell can I hide all this loot until we stash it in the Caymans?"

"My dear departed shady lawyer husband left me a giant safe, there's plenty of room in it."

"Ur house safe?"

"Safer than yours. There aren't any stoned zombies wandering around my place, does she know anything?"

"Pete swears she doesn't have a clue."

"She must be denser than I thought."

Brenda went out to dinner with one of her girlfriends, she said she'd puke if forced to eat fish. Pete said he'd meet her later.

"God, she's a pain in the ass, but god, she's a good lay."

"Slick, am I a good lay?"

"The best."

"You think I'm as good as Brenda?"

"One sure way to find out, Pete, you wanna swap tonight?"

"Sure, why not?"

"You dogs."

"Strictly in the interest of science my dear. Come-on, let's eat, she's not my type but I must admit I like looking at her tits."

"So do I, they're unreal."

"Do girls get turned on by other girl's tits?"

"I've seen whole bars get turned on by her's, boys and girls."

"Pete, now that we've dissected your woman, you ready for a beer?"

Pete had been busy, he had spent the morning with the fuel tank fabricator, they had drawn about a zillion tanks before they came up with the right one. It would hold 175 gallons and fit in the door with two inches to spare. The new tank would be almost 18 inches longer than the one Pete had kicked out the door, but because it was narrower, it would still make it inside the Navajo. The new tank would be ready the next day after lunch. After he had arranged the tank, Pete had hid his pile of money in the house of his ex wife where he kept a bunch of personal things.

"Hope she ain't the nosy type."

"She thinks I'm a loser who's only interested in smoking pot and chasing broads."

"Sounds like she's got you pegged."

"Hey, I resemble that remark."

Pete volunteered to go to his travel agent in the morning to arrange airline tickets for both upcoming trips. They decided that it was imperative to make sure the new tank fit inside the Navajo's door. Pete would pick the tank up after lunch, they would then drive to Leesburg for the acid test. It would be beyond stupid to discover that the new tank wouldn't fit through the door just before departure.

The mahi-mahi was delicious.

The house was alive at 8am, Rosemary cooked breakfast while Slick and Pete bullshitted. Brenda was still in bed, no one could remember ever having seen her downstairs before noon, except maybe coming home.

At nine, Pete left for the travel agents office, Slick and Rosemary locked themselves in their bedroom and played with money.

The black garbage bag had 16 little bundles of 50 one hundred dollar bills, each bundle was $5,000 dollars, the total, $80,000 dollars. The first payment of $32,000 was in a brown paper sack, Slick had removed $2,000 for pocket money. Since the trips to Boston and Cayman were paid for, Slick decided to put the entire stash in Rosemary's safe, $110,000 dollars or 22 little packs of hundred dollar bills neatly secured by colored rubber bands. Rosemary stacked the bundles of money in an empty shoebox, there was room for plenty more.

"Let's go bury the treasure."

Rosemary was right about one thing, her safe was big. If

anyone tried to steal it, they'd have to bring a truck and crane inside the house. Slick wondered out loud how it ever got where it was.

"They had to take out the front door and the door frame, then a bunch of men scooted it in on little rollers, it cost more than a thousand dollars to repair the scratches on the floor."

It took several tries before Rosemary could get the safe open, she couldn't remember if the first turn of the combination was right or left or how many revolutions of the wheel were required before going the opposite direction. Finally, they figured everything out and the heavy door swung open revealing two things, a jewelry box and a pristine nickel plated Colt 45 semi automatic pistol.

"That thing loaded?"

"Of course."

"You know how to use it?"

"Indeed I do, I used to practice all the time."

After the shoebox full of money was locked up, Rosemary gave Slick the cook's tour of her house which was more of a museum in honor of her dead husband than a house. Momentos and photographs of past trips were everywhere, Rosemary and hubby with Zulu warriors, Hottentot lion hunters, spear toting Masi, head hunters from Borneo, Eskimos, Mongolian horsemen, Tibetan Sherpas and Amazonian natives to mention a few. In the place of honor on the mantel over the gas burning fireplace was a large picture of President Nixon with his right arm around Rosemary and his left arm around her husband, all three with big smiles on their faces.

"Wow, you guys got around."

"I told you, when he found out he was dying he quit working and we took off. It wasn't until the last few months that he was too weak."

"At least he didn't have time to worry about whatever he had."

"He very seldom mentioned it, he was a tough cookie."

"I think I would have liked him."

"You would have, he would have wanted to fly to Colombia with you just for the experience, he did lots of crazy stuff. You should have seen some of the wild things he ate, bugs, monkey brains out of the head of a live monkey, it made me sick."

"Along with being tough, he might have been a little nuts."

"In Borneo he handed me a piece of meat that he said was monkey, after I took a bite he and all the half naked tribes people started laughing and giggling. I had just taken a bite of human flesh. They had killed an enemy warrior and were eating certain parts of him to get his strength."

"How was he?"

"If they hadn't all laughed I would have eaten the whole piece, it wasn't bad at all."

"What you're saying is that I live with a cannibal."

"I only did it once."

"Let's get going, we gotta meet Pete and go check out our new tank."

On the way to Leesburg, Slick told Pete some of the stories about Rosemary's husband.

"I heard about that monkey brain thing but I never believed it, you actually saw it?"

"Right in front of my eyes."

"You didn't barf?"

"I didn't eat any."

"No, not sweet Rosemary, she just nibbled on some poor guy's liver."

"One way or the other, these chicks are all cannibals."

The tank slid right in the door at an angle.

"That's a relief, I was afraid it was too long and would get jammed against the other side."

"Now that we're here, let's go for a little ride then fill her up."

After putting the new tank back in the van, they checked the Navajo, fired her up and taxied off towards the runway. After takeoff, Slick gave the controls over to Rosemary, Pete was regally sitting in one of the passenger seats sipping on a cold can of Budweiser.

"We got her doing everything else, why not teach her to fly this thing and Ill stay home and guard all the money."

"If you don't mind, I'll stick with you."

"Why Pete, don't you trust me?"

"Of course I trust you, I just trust him more."

"Come-on Pete, all you do is rave about what a great pilot he is, nobody's that good."

"He's that good, I bet my life on him every time we launch. You think I'd crawl to the back of a plane overloaded with pot, open the door, throw bundles of shit out the door while making multiple passes at a tiny drop zone below the tree tops while it's pitch dark with just any pilot. No thanks my dear, I'll stick with the best."

"Slicko, I'm getting jealous, I think Pete likes you."

"I like him too, he's a marijuana throwin mother fucker. Pete, pass one of those beers up here."

"What about eight hours bottle to throttle?"

"This is probably the smallest infraction of Federal Aviation Regulations we've made this month."

"Naughty boys."

"Pete, you think you could keep this thing in the air long enough for me to initiate Rosemary into the Mile High Club?"

"Sure."

"You dope, we joined the Mile High Club over Catalina Island several months ago."

"How bout re-validating your certificate?"

"How bout we go home and do it in our bed, last time I cut my knee on one of those switches."

After landing, they had all 4 of the fuel tanks topped off, the Navajo was ready for her next mission.

Pete treated to a fantastic feed of ribs at a far-out little joint in Lakeland. Two huge black ladies sang religious songs as they cooked, they were really good. From the looks on the faces of some of the patrons, you could tell that they came here as much for the music as for the food.

"Where'd you hear about this place? I love it, those two dolls can really sing."

"I never heard nothin, just saw a sign that said ribs."

Rosemary woke Slick, *"Get up you bum, it's nine thirty, we're having scrambled eggs and toasted bagels."*

After the late breakfast, Pete called his travel agent to see if the tickets were ready, they were. Slick rode along to pick them up.

"You know something, we need another twenty gallons of gas in the van to fill the new tank, you think we should get another drum or a bunch of five gallon jerry cans?"

"Another drum, it'll be easier to pump from. After we get the tickets we'll grab the van and go get another drum. Good thing you thought of it, hell of a lot of good the hundred and seventy gallon tank would have done us if we only had a hundred and fifty gallons to put in it."

Pete's travel agent had everything arranged, Slick and Rosemary would leave Tampa the next day at 1:20pm non-stop for Boston, their return non-stop flight was the next morning at 11:30am. They all left from Miami the next afternoon at 2:20pm for the Cayman Islands. The very attractive agent had three nights reserved for them at the Cayman Holiday Resort on Seven Mile Beach, everything was set.

"That broad has her shit together."

"Not bad legs either."

"I liked her mouth."

"When I dump Brenda I'm gonna make a move on her."

"Don't blame you."

Sam met them at the nursery, the new canvas bags had been delivered that morning, they agreed to meet on the causeway in two hours for a seafood lunch.

"You and your girl all set for tomorrow?"

"She's hot to trot, never been to Boston."

"I doubt if you'll have much time for sightseeing, those guys will probably drag ur asses out to Worchester for a big party, don't stick too much coke up ur nose, you won't be able to get it up."

"Sam, you ever seen me snort any coke?"

"That's right, the pure pilot."

"I drank six cans of Bud last night."

"WOOOEEE!"

"The hell with Sam, Slick, you be a good boy, you got some very important luggage to get home and twenty-five percent of it's

mine."

"If I really feel wild I'll have a dry martini."

"I'll see you and Straight Arrow in two hours."

"You think it bugs Sam cuz I don't do drugs?"

"Are you kidding, as long as you keep bringing in the loads he don't give a shit what you do, he's just pulling ur chain. Why do you think we're sending you anyway?"

"Why?"

"Because you won't get fucked up and do anything dumb."

"Would you?"

"Picture this, a scrumptious doll, naked as a jay bird, kneeling on the floor beside a table with a glass top, she's making little lines from the biggest pile of coke you ever saw, a scene like that can make me act a little dumb, make that a lot dumb."

"Sounds like it could be fun."

"Those guys are mad as hell, last time I went up there it took me three days to pry myself away."

Pete paid $20 dollars for the empty 55 gallon drum, now they had a 200 gallon capacity in the back of the van. They beat Sam to the restaurant by one beer.

Sam was in a festive mood, lunch dragged on until 5pm, they decided to continue the going away party at the lake house. Pete ordered 5 dozen shrimp and a quart of cocktail sauce to go, Sam said he'd pick up Sarah and meet them around 7. After dropping off the van, Pete and Slick picked up some beautiful aged New York steaks at the meat market, it was going to be a feast.

Rosemary put together a mouth watering green salad, Brenda came downstairs in all her glory, she looked as though she'd painted her clothes on, she hadn't used much paint either.

"You know Pete, a guy could get used to this line of work. I never ate and drank so much good shit in my life, plus, the hours are good."

"I know what you mean, wonder what the poor folks are doing tonight?"

Sam and Sarah arrived. As always, Sarah looked angelic. Pete lit the charcoal, Slick served drinks. Brenda greeted Sam from the lounge chair where she was sitting cross legged.

"Hi Sam, how you doing?"

"Hi there Brenda, nice to see you, I didn't know you shaved your pussy."

"How did you know?"

"Well, half of it's hanging out the bottom of those shorts and it's bare as a baby's ass. Could me and Sarah borrow ur bedroom, I'm getting horny watching that thing twitch."

"Well sure, I guess."

"Just kiddin."

Slick and Rosemary watched as Sam put Brenda on, they were both giggling out of control. Brenda was either a great actress or one of the more dimwitted broads on earth with those knowing her leaning towards the dimwit category.

"Can you believe that bimbo?"

"Every party needs a Brenda, now that she knows everyone is paying attention look at the show."

Very ladylike, Brenda squirmed to cover her exposed labia, all she succeeded in doing was to almost totally expose her pussy and one and a half of her lovely breasts.

"Pete, tame that beast, if that god damn alligator sees her like that he'll rip her ass apart and eat our steaks."

"She'd throw the poor beast on the ground and fuck him to death."

"Guess you're right, he wouldn't stand a chance."

The dinner party was a great success, they wined and dined like kings and queens.

Pete dropped Slick and Rosemary off at Tampa International at noon. The big metal suitcase on loan from Sam was half full of Slick's smaller bag and some of Rosemary's things. Rosemary had her expensive Nikon slung around her neck, a nice young couple off to the land of America's birth.

The taxi ride from Boston's airport to the Yale Hotel took 25 minutes, they checked in at 5pm. There was a message waiting for Slick, the receptionist handed him a small envelope. The note read, "I'll pick you up between 6:30 and 7, don't eat, dinner is on me. Nevada"

A few minutes before 7, Nevada called from the lobby.

When they met downstairs, Slick was surprised, Nevada looked like a potato farmer from Idaho or a cowboy from Wyoming but certainly not a wholesale marijuana buyer. Faded blue jeans, a plaid shirt and well worn cowboy boots. The only things missing were the Stetson hat and a straw between his teeth.

"How you doing Nevada, this is Rosemary."

"Hi yaall, hope you like Greek food."

"Love it, ur name fits."

"Yeah, I'm a good ole boy from outside Elko, just tryin to get by."

During the 45 minute drive to the Greek restaurant in Worchester, Nevada went over all the numbers, he had written everything on the inside of a matchbook cover which he referred to with the aid of the overhead light.

"We rounded off the total weight to 3750 pounds times $340 equals $1,275,000 minus the $675,000 already paid leaves a balance due of $600,000. How does that sound to you boys from Florida?

"Sounds good to us, your weight is within three pounds of ours."

'That's good, nothin makes me happier than a happy Sam."

"You obviously know him."

"We're old friends. We can give you all six hundred thousand if you don't mind carrying about two hundred thousand in twenties, we just haven't had enough time to gather up enough hundred dollar bills."

"I'll have to see how big a pile and how much it weighs, we'll take as much as we can, twenties spend as good as anything else."

"Enough business talk, let's eat, one of my partners is waiting for us with his wife, she's cool."

"How did you know I was cool, Nevada?"

"Sam said so and Sam don't bullshit."

"Why thank you, I take that as a very nice compliment."

Rosemary was beaming.

Nevada's partner was introduced as Ronnie, his wife's name was Linda. The first thing Slick noticed about both of them, especially Linda, is that they were both stoned on something. Linda had the same droopy eyes that Brenda usually had so she'd probably just dropped a quaalude, Ronnie's pupils were the size of a pin head, the same as Pete's when he was snorting cocaine.

The restaurant was jammed, it had become an in place for the throngs of Boston. Because of the crowd, service was slow, the longer they waited for food, the edgier Ronnie got, finally he left the table in disgust muttering something about fucking Greek idiots.

When Ronnie returned he had a smile on his face, whatever he had done outside had certainly calmed him down.

Nevada winked at Slick and Rosemary, *"Nothing like a little hit of opium to calm the old nerves."*

"I thought you could only get opium in some smoky little den in China."

"You've seen too many old movies, the best opium comes from Pakistan, I buy it by the pound."

"You're kidding."

"Remind me to give you some sticks when we get back to the house, it's by far the best drug around."

"How so?"

"It doesn't make ur heart pound like coke, it doesn't make you hungry or paranoid like pot, it just makes you feel good all over, mind and body. But best of all, if you run out it's no big deal. No matter what anybody tells you, opium is totally un-addictive."

"No shit, maybe I'll try a little, I'm sure as hell never gonna smoke any more pot and I don't like the effect coke has on people."

"We'll fix you up later."

Dinner came, it was different but good. The owner of the restaurant had an ace in the hole, his floor show. No matter how slow the service or even if the food wasn't too hot, you'd leave his establishment remembering one thing, the unbelievable gyrations of the incredibly beautiful and sexy belly dancer.

"You ever seen anything like that?"

"She's something else, it's like certain parts of her body aren't connected to other parts."

"She's beautiful too."

"Imagine what she could do to you in the sack."

"I have been."

"Slicko, you trying to make me jealous?"

"Just imagining."

Linda hadn't paid much attention, in fact she hadn't done much of anything, eat or observe, she was in a semi-trance. Nobody except Rosemary seemed to care, she whispered to Slick, *"What's with her?"*

"Maybe she's related to Brenda."

"I hope she doesn't die at the table."

Nevada paid the bill, Ronnie led his zombie out, Slick and Rosemary marveled at how much liquor the already stoned Ronnie had consumed.

Slick sat in the front with Nevada, *"She always like that?"*

"No, she's pissed off at Ronnie, she caught him fucking some other chick so she's showing him by staying stoned. It's not the first time."

"Couple of times I thought her heart had stopped."

"Downers are bad shit."

Nevada briefed Slick on what to expect, *"We live on a small farm, there's usually a lot of people around, they all work for or with us so don't worry. Nobody but me and Ronnie know anything about you and nobody's gonna ask you anything. First we'll count up the money then maybe you want to try a little O, I'll get you back to the hotel before it's too late."*

"Sounds good."

The farmhouse was hidden from the country road by trees, a perfect place to operate an illegal business. Even though it was dark, Slick could see the barn and several other buildings besides the main house.

"Man, this place is perfect."

"Yeah, as long as we're cool and don't attract any attention, we can do pretty much what we want out here."

Nevada led Slick and Rosemary to the 2nd floor of the farmhouse. He unlocked the door to one of the rooms, it turned out to be the master bedroom. Nevada locked the door after they were all inside.

"Let's see how many hundreds we got."

Nevada opened the closet door and pulled out a large Samsonite suitcase, he carried it to the queen size bed and dumped the contents on the bedspread.

"I'll give you stacks of five bundles, you keep count."

Nevada carefully piled 5 little bundles of one hundred dollar bills on top of each other, each stack was $25,000 dollars. When they were done making piles, there were 18 stacks of 5 bundles, $450,000 dollars in one hundred dollar bills.

"Here, use this hat box for the hundreds."

Rosemary packed the piles of money neatly in the hatbox, there was still room for half a hat.

Nevada pulled out another suitcase, this one contained bundles of 20 dollar bills. Each bundle held 100 twenties or $2,000 dollars. The bundles were exactly twice as big as the bundles of hundred dollar bills that were worth $5,000 dollars. Forty bundles filled the hatbox, they still needed 35 more bundles to bring the total to $600,000 dollars.

"You got any more hat boxes?"

"How about a canvas bag that once upon a time held about fifty pounds of pot?"

"Why not, as long as it doesn't smell."

"It's been washed."

They threw 35 more bundles of twenties into the canvas bag.

"No sweat, that's not as big a pile as I thought."

"I've carried more than a million lots of times, you won't even close to the max weight for one suitcase, let's have a couple of drinks and a taste of O."

Slick and Rosemary followed Nevada downstairs and into the kitchen.

"What you want to drink?"

"Beer's okay for me, how bout you, Rosemary?"

"Vodka tonic."

Nevada pulled a beer from the fridge, he pointed to a bunch of bottles on the kitchen counter. *"Whatever you want is there little lady, help yourself."*

Slick watched in amazement as Nevada prepared the opium. First he turned the electric stove up to max hot, as soon as the element was red-hot, he put a kitchen knife on the red portion of the burner. As the knife blade heated up, Nevada took something out of his pocket that looked like a tootsie roll, from the end of the long dark roll he pinched off a small piece and put it on a plate. Next he opened a cabinet door and removed a white tube, closer examination revealed that the tube was the two pieces of a Tampax applicator taped together with scotch tape. By now, the knife blade was red hot, Nevada picked up the knife, put the Tampax tube in his mouth, put the red hot end of the knife on the small piece of opium, pressed down hard. The hot knife caused the opium to start smoking, Nevada sucked in the smoke through the Tampax tube.

"You want to try some?"

"What's it like?"

"You won't feel nothin until you take several hits, then you'll just feel a little mellow, I think you'll like it."

"Why not."

In the next five minutes, Slick and Rosemary both took four or five hits of opium, at first there was nothing to report, then the drug started taking effect.

"Wow, I see why you like this shit."

"I told you."

"Well doll, what you think?"

"This stuff is smooth, how long will it last?"

"When you feel like another hit, just turn on the stove, you feel like going to bed, just hit the sack, you feel like making love, just do it, there ain't no bad side to this stuff, you'll feel good as new in the morning."

Slick had another beer, Rosemary had a couple more hits from the Tampax tube.

"I hope we get to bed while I'm feeling like this, I'm really horny.'

"We could go up and do it on that pile of money."

"I'm serious."

Nevada drove them back to the hotel, they were in bed by 2am, Rosemary was serious, she had her way with Slick, he didn't object. The hatbox and canvas bag were safely under the bed.

The eight o'clock wakeup call came way too soon, the two

opium fiends drug their tired butts out of bed. Slick ordered a pot of coffee and sweet rolls, they then got to work packing.

The hat box was too tall to fit in Sam's metal suitcase, Slick neatly piled the stacks of money in the middle of the case, then he packed clothes around the money to keep things from rattling around.

"How heavy you think this is?"

Rosemary hoisted the big suitcase, *"Not much more than forty pounds, I'm sure it's okay, diving gear is heavy."*

Slick double checked that the locks were locked and that the strap was tight. He then applied a ten inch long strip of white tape from a roll he'd carried along for just that purpose. Tape in place, Slick opened a black waterproof marker he'd also brought and carefully wrote his name and TAMPA FLA. in bold letters. Now, if the destination tag somehow got ripped off, the baggage handlers would know where the suitcase was supposed to end up. Most people who checked valuable cameras and things dear to them, like a favorite diving outfit, took extra precautions with their bags.

"Let's go, all we can do now is hope."

"What was in that little box Nevada gave you?"

"I dunno, it was taped shut, I'm sure it was a couple of those sticks of opium. I stuck it in with the money."

"I sure hope so, I don't remember ever being that turned on."

The phone rang, it was Pete calling from a payphone, he wanted to make sure that everything was kosher.

"We're leaving for the airport in half an hour, we got everything we came for."

"Excellent, I'll see you at the airport."

The check-in agent was a little on the swishy side, *"Oh, I see you've been to the Caymans, I just adore it there."*

Rosemary chatted with the flaky agent as she arranged the baggage and seat numbers. *"We're going on to the Caymans tomorrow afternoon with our friends from Tampa."*

"Do you dive?"

"Yes, my gear and underwater camera are in this big suitcase so please don't lose it."

"Don't you worry sweetie, it's in good hands. Where are you staying?"

"Slick, darling, which hotel are we booked in?"

"I don't remember, somewhere along Seven Mile Beach."

"I'm so jealous, you're going to have a divine time, you be careful of those nasty barracudas, they have terribly long teeth."

"We'll be careful, thanks for your help."

"Ta ta my dear, your man is very handsome."

"You devil, don't you steal him."

The agent gushed, then placed the heavy bag on the moving baggage belt, Slick and Rosemary watched it disappear then walked towards their departure gate.

"What were you doing, comparing bra sizes?"

"He wanted to know if I was willing to share you."

"As soon as we get home and smoke a little opium, you'll want me all to your self."

"Ooo, I can't wait, you sexy man, tell them to fly fast."

Rosemary slept all the way to Tampa, Slick couldn't fall asleep, he had about six hundred thousand things on his mind.

After deplaning they walked straight to the baggage pickup area, Pete was standing by one of the exits, finally the baggage carousel started turning. One of the first bags to appear was Rosemary's containing zero dollars.

"I guess it's a test of our nerves."

"I don't think they mix soft bags with big heavy ones."

Slick snatched Rosemary's small suitcase off the carousel and waited. When he finally saw Sam's big metal suitcase appear, the hairs on the back of his neck stood on end. Rosemary almost couldn't contain herself, *"There it is."*

"I see it, relax."

Slick kept his eyes glued on the big bag until it was safely in his hands, *"Let's go my dear, the driver is waiting."*

Rosemary had to show the baggage stubs as they left, Pete motioned for them to follow him outside. They walked without talking until reaching Pete's Mercedes.

"Let's get the hell away from here, I had the feeling that

everybody in the whole terminal was watching my ass."

"Well, how was your trip?"

"Mission accomplished, we got it all."

"Shit hot, Sam will be over about five."

"Good, that'll give us enough time to figure everything out."

"What did you think of that crowd?"

"Nevada's a good guy, Ronnie is a certified nut, his old lady is a real worry, she's so loaded all the time, I don't think she has a clue what's going on. I guess she found out he's banging some other broad and she's mad as hell. If I was those guys, I wouldn't want some pissed off broad hanging around who knew where they kept all the loot, what if she wanted to get even?"

"I know what you mean, we shouldn't let them get too far behind again."

"I can just see that stoned out broad getting busted and an hour later about a hundred cops crawling all over the farm, fuck, they'd find all kinds of dope and money all over the place, I wouldn't want too much of it to be ours."

"If we keep the flights a little farther apart, they should be able to bring almost all the cash the day of pickup."

"We'll see what Sam thinks."

"Speaking of Sam, he asked me to have you bring your dollar chart up to date so he knows how much loot to send south tomorrow."

"Okay, as soon as we get home we'll fix it up."

"Rosemary, what did you think of that bunch?"

"When we were at dinner with Ronnie and Linda both of us thought she'd died a couple of times, you know, we never did see her again that night, maybe she did die. I liked Nevada, we smoked some of his opium."

"Slick too?"

"I have to admit, I tried a little."

"You old druggie."

They laughed about the Boston crowd during the rest of the drive to the lake house, how the hell did that bunch of space cadets manage to operate such a high risk operation while under the influence and stay out of jail.

The conclusion was simple, who cared what they did or how they did it as long as the cash kept flowing and no unwanted attention came south.

As soon as they got home, Slick and Pete went over the numbers:

1st three loads 3750 lbs.

3750 pounds X $340 = $1,275,000

Expenses:

1. $ 90,000 Six months salaries Sam, Pete Slick
2. $ 111,000 Plane
3. $ 8,000 New prop blades and starters
4. $ 25,000 Break-in trip, plumbing job, gas, hotels, food, etc
5. $ 10,000 Calif to Florida (Pete's cash now spent for Boston &
6. $ 7,000 Van   Cayman tickets)
   $ 251,000 Of the $251,000 in expenses, $150,000 paid off,
                           $101,000 left to go.

Cash in: $1,275,000 Cash out: $150,000 expenses, $50,000 per trip
                                      $225,000 total weight X $60 per lb.
                                      $128,000 $32,000 X 4
                                      $320,000 $80,000 X 4
                                      $ 5,000 cash
                                      $400,000 $100,000 X 4
                                      $ 47,000 cash held for next flight
                                      $1,275,000

We have a little over $4,000 cash from the Boston trip and $47,000 cash from last payment for the next trip. Slick will take $7,000 of that for Cayman expenses.

What we need to take to Caymans for the Man
$150,000 $50,000 X 3 expenses
$ 32,000   ¼
$ 80,000   ¼
$225,000   paid by man for stuff
$100,000   ¼
$587,000

Plus we need to transfer from the man's acct $9,000 to Luis for 150lbs extra:

That should leave Sam with $32,000 + $80,000 + $100,000 = $212,000, the same as Slick and Pete.

"How much you gonna take to the Caymans?"

"I'll take two hundred grand, that'll leave me about ten. Man, that sounds good."

"I can't take quite that much, ex wife and kids still take a bite."

Sam arrived, Slick and Pete went over the "financial statement". Sam agreed with all the numbers, he volunteered to take the majority of the twenty dollar bills so they wouldn't have such a big pile of money to carry south the next day.

Slick opened the big metal suitcase and began separating the money into 6 piles. In the 1st pile he placed 23 bundles of twenties, he then removed the rubber bands from another bundle of twenties, counted out one thousand, put one rubber band around each small pack of one thousand, put one of the small stacks with the 23 bundles of twenties. The 1st pile now totaled $47,000 dollars.

"That's the forty seven thousand we'll keep around for expenses."

In the 2nd, 3rd, 4th and 5th piles he started tossing bundles of hundred dollar bills. When he had 20 bundles of hundreds in each pile he had Pete double check his tally. After Pete had counted each pile, the loot was separated. Slick put his hundred thousand in a paper bag, Pete dropped his in a pillowcase, Sam put the hundred thousand that belonged to the Man on the corner of the bed. Sam put his hundred grand together with the Man's, it was just a hundred thousand less he'd have to bring back for tomorrows run to the bank.

Rosemary couldn't keep her eyes off the small taped up cigar box that Slick had removed from the suitcase. What had Nevada given them? She hoped she knew.

Slick did a little math on the back of his "financial statement".

$$\$100,000 \times 4 = \$400,000$$
$$\underline{\$\ \ 47,000}$$
$$\$447,000$$

$$\$600,000$$
$$\underline{-\$447,000}$$
$$\$153,000$$

$153,000 left in metal suitcase
+$200,000 Man's ¼ plus Sam's ¼
=$353,000 $587,000 Man's deposit
+$234,000   - $353,000 in pile
=$587,000 $234,000 needed from Sam's stash

Slick exchanged ten thousand in hundreds for ten thousand in twenties. Pete traded forty thousand of his hundreds for twenties, that left Sam with a hundred grand in twenties. Now Sam needed to bring back $334,000 in hundreds to make the Man's deposit of $587,000.

"I'll go to my stash right now so you guys can get started early tomorrow, I'll be back in about an hour."

Sam left with a black garbage bag bulging with twenties, he put the other half of the split pack of twenties in his pocket, he'd return with $335,000 in hundreds.

The books were balancing.

Slick and Rosemary drove to her house and opened the big steel safe, removed the $110,000 in hundred dollar bills, stuck in the $10,000 in twenties and returned to the lake house. Slick's neat pile of $200,000 fit in a medium size paper bag from the grocery store.

Slick and Pete had just begun their second beer when Sam returned with yet another bulging black garbage bag.

"Gimme one of those fuckin beers, I'm exhausted from all this counting."

"It's the kind of work I don't mind as long as some of it belongs to me."

"I couldn't believe it when I counted up my stash, you guys were right on, it's the first time I've ever felt like I knew what the score was."

They took their beers into Slick's room and got back to work. Sam dumped the contents of the garbage bag on the bed, there were 67 little bundles of 50 one hundred dollar bills, or

$335,000 dollars. That plus the $252,000 in the Man's pile equaled $587,000. Everything was square.

Rosemary started packing the money in grocery bags, Pete went for beer, Slick put Sam's big metal suitcase on the bed and put his brown paper bag full of money in the middle surrounded with the two bags full of the Man's money. Rosemary helped Slick finish filling the case with cameras, dive gear and beach clothes. After locking and strapping the case, there was nothing left to do but hope Cayman Airways was careful with this $787,000 dollar suitcase.

The gang retreated outside where it was now cool.

"Pete, where's that goofy broad of yours?"

"I don't have a clue, I think she's found somebody who's willing to let her do as much dope as she wants. I think it's time to unload."

"Too bad she's such a slut, I'll miss those tits. When you boys due back?"

"We're staying three nights so we look like tourists and not bankers, we'll be back in Miami Friday, four days from now. We can call Carlos the next afternoon, if they're ready, leave that night. That'll give us a chance to run over to Leesburg, fly the plane and make sure everything's okay."

"Sounds good, I'll get hold of Nevada and tell him to be ready in about five days."

They all had a long chat about the zany bunch from Boston, Sam laughed like hell when Rosemary told him that she thought Linda had died during dinner.

"She is dead, brain dead."

Sam didn't seem a bit worried about the antics of their buyers, *"I've known Ronnie and Nevada for a long time, they haven't changed a bit, besides, who else do we know?"*

Sam did agree to space out the trips a little or if they did two back to back to hide the dope until the buyers could get back with money, that way they'd never have more than a couple hundred thousand owed to them.

Rosemary went for another round, Sam motioned Pete and Slick closer, *"What do you think, she's been a lot of help, why don't we drop seven grand on her, that leaves forty for expenses. It really is a lot safer traveling as a couple, nobody thinks of broads being* criminals".

"Sure, why not, what do you think, Slick?"

"She'd love it, she loves being part of this."

"Okay, it's done, where's that forty seven?"

"It's in your garbage bag, I thought it would be safer with you than in this empty house, I'll go get seven."

"Get twelve, you guys take five for spending money."

Rosemary brought the round of beers, Slick went to the bedroom and reached in the garbage bag, he brought out six stacks of $2,000, split one stack in half, stuck $5,000 in his pocket and walked back outside.

"Rosemary dear, we wanted you to have this little token for all your help."

Slick dropped the seven grand on her lap, Rosemary literally glowed, "Why thank you gentlemen, I'll mule for you boys anytime."

After a couple more beers, Sam left with the thirty-five grand in the garbage bag. Pete went to get takeout Chinese food, Rosemary looked for a place to hide her money, she couldn't remember feeling so good. Slick reproduced the last financial statement on a small piece of paper, then stuck the paper in a bottle to be buried later. He tore up the two original balance sheets and burned the scraps, they had all agreed not to leave anything incriminating lying around. The paper in the bottle was only in case the Man ever had any questions.

As they were eating chicken fried rice and sweet and sour pork, Slick told Pete where he'd buried the bottle.

"As soon as we're done, let's see what he gave us, I'm so excited I'm about to pee my pants."

"Bring it out here, Pete's over twenty-one."

Rosemary returned with the cigar box, she used a sharp knife to cut the tape that sealed it.

"What's that?"

"Nevada gave us a going away present."

Rosemary opened the lid of the little box, "Oh jesus, look at all this!"

There were at least 20 sticks of opium lying there.

"Wow, Nevada is a generous guy."

"Is he ever, you have any idea how much that stuff costs?"

"Not a clue."

"I'd say there's several thousand worth."

"He told me he buys it by the pound."

"Still a nice gift, it's all yours, I'd rather snort a line any-time which I believe I'm about to do, want to join me?"

"No thanks, think I'll go to the den for a little touch of opium."

Rosemary dashed inside to turn on the stove, she was ready. After a few puffs Slick was ready, life was glorious.

Chapter X

THE BANK

They left the house a little earlier than necessary, Pete wanted to stop at his favorite place for brunch. The truck stop at Yeehaw Junction had been a trucker's favorite for years, it had recently caught on as a tourist attraction. The breakfasts were legendary.

Rosemary ordered biscuits and gravy with a side order of grits, Pete asked for corned beef hash, the specialty of the house, Slick ordered a cheese omelet with grits on the side. It was going to be a feast.

"What did you do with all that opium?"

"I put it in a mayonnaise jar and buried it next to the other bottle."

"Good, I was a little worried about you know who getting into withdrawal and snooping around looking for dope."

"As soon as we get back, we have a good place to hide it."

"What say we check in separately, I'll drop you two off with the money, then I'll go park and check in by myself. Sam's right about a nice young couple looking more touristy than a single man."

"You want us to check ur suitcase too?"

"If you don't mind."

"What difference is an extra couple hundred thousand gonna make, I'll take ur bag and you take mine."

The waitress interrupted with the food, it was indeed a feast. The early departure was well worth the effort.

It was 12:45pm when Pete stopped in front of the terminal, Slick took the big metal suitcase and Pete's leather case out of the trunk. As he walked inside the terminal he figured he had about a million dollars between his left and right hands. Rosemary, the ultimate tourist had her overnight bag in one hand and her trusty Nikon slung around her neck. Slick looked at her and smiled, *"She's one cool broad."*

When their turn came it was 1:15pm, an hour and 5 minutes until departure.

"Is our flight on time?"

"Yes sir, they landed a few minutes early, we plan to depart on schedule."

Slick took one of the stick-on labels from the counter and wrote his name, the date, flight number and Cayman Islands, then stuck the label on Pete's bag. He had earlier put the white strip of tape on the metal suitcase. Rosemary got the boarding passes and baggage stubs, they were all set. Pete winked as they walked to the departure area, Slick wanted to sit close to the window so he could watch as the baggage was loaded, Rosemary went looking for coffee.

The big metal suitcase with the strip of white tape was very obvious as it went up the conveyor belt and disappeared inside the Cayman Airways 727, Pete's leather bag wasn't far behind. Slick strolled over to join Rosemary, *"Both bags are inside the plane, I'm going to the bar for a Bloody Mary, maybe a double."*

"I'll join you."

Pete was already there, he had a tall drink decorated with a piece of pineapple and a cherry in front of him, probably a rum punch. When their eyes met, Slick gave him a secretive thumbs up, Pete smiled.

The first announcement for their flight came halfway through the Bloody Mary, five minutes later Slick and Rosemary boarded the aircraft. Pete was still working on his second rum punch.

"I'll be a lot happier when we're on the way."

"Here comes Pete."

Pete's seat was 5 or 6 rows aft, he couldn't help but smile as he walked past.

"Just another happy young guy heading off for a few days in paradise, what could be more normal, we look like all the rest of the passengers."

"I'd hate to have to try explaining to Sam what happened to all that dough."

"Sam trusts you one hundred percent, if anything went wrong he'd back you all the way."

The cabin door closed, a stewardess started the departure briefing as the plane was pushed back. The captain started the 3 engines and they taxied away towards the runway while the stewardess continued with the safety briefing.

"Ladies and gentlemen, this is the captain, we're number one for take-off, please be sure your seatbelts are fastened. I'll be back after we're in the air to tell more about our short flight down to the beautiful Cayman Islands."

Twenty-five minutes later they were over Cuba.

"Half way there, if Fidel doesn't shoot us down I think we got it made."

"In the shade."

The 727 touched down at Cayman right on time, 5 minutes later the plane stopped outside the small terminal, 2 minutes later a set of stairs was rolled up to the front passenger door, finally a stewardess opened the door. Everybody stood up, gathered their belongings and started filing out the front door and down the stairs. At the same time, baggage handlers had opened the cargo door and were unloading the aircraft by hand. As each suitcase was handed out by one baggage handler, it was placed on a small 4 wheeled cart by a second baggage handler until the cart was full. The full cart was pulled by hand to the baggage area where the bags were unloaded from the cart and placed on the cement floor.

Pete joined Slick and Rosemary as they waited for their suitcases.

"Mister Smith is waiting for us over there, these baggage guys don't seem to be in too big a hurry."

"Easy there Pedro, this is the tropics, tranquillo."

Rosemary elbowed Slick, *"Here comes the big one."*

· As soon as they had claimed the 3 checked bags, Pete led the way to customs and immigration. They were intercepted by a uniformed officer who asked that they follow him. He led the trio to the head of one of the three lines, collected their passports and handed them to another officer.

"Welcome to our islands, we hope you enjoy your stay."

The officer had a very nice British accent.

The first officer then led them to the departure door, he insisted on carrying the big suitcase. Outside the terminal he walked directly to a light colored sedan, the trunk was open, Mr. Smith was at the wheel.

"Throw your bags in the boot and hop in, it's hot."

The uniformed officer refused the offered tip, he saluted and returned to his post.

Pete and Slick shook hands with Mr. Smith, *"Good of you to meet us."*

"Just another service of our bank."

"Is having our own private customs officer another of your services?"

"Yes of course, banking is the Cayman's largest industry, it's government policy to extend every courtesy possible to foreigners who use our facilities."

Georgetown, the capital, is a very small town, Mr. Smith had pulled to a stop in front of his bank before he'd finished extolling it's virtues.

"I'll have the guard bring in your luggage, join me in my office where it's cool, we'll get right to work."

Once in the office, Mr. Smith motioned for everyone to take a seat, he then offered drinks, all opted for iced tea.

"How can I be of service?"

Pete and Slick had worked up a list of their banking needs, item by item Pete read the list.

"One, I will deposit one hundred and fifty thousand to my account."

"Two, my associate wishes to open a new account, he'll make a deposit of two hundred thousand."

"Three, we'll make a deposit of five hundred eighty seven thousand to my friend's numbered account."

"Four, we'll transfer nine thousand from his account to Luis' numbered account."

"Five, we'll transfer another seventy two thousand from his account to Luis' account. That's it. Sorry about the two transfers, but we want him to know we've made two separate transactions."

"No problem at all, I'll bring in my staff and we'll get to

work. One question, what about any counterfeit we find?"

"Just give it to my associate, he'll replace it with real money."

Mr. Smith excused himself and left his office, seconds later he returned followed by three bank employees, two men and a woman, all three natives of the Cayman's.

Pete opened his leather suitcase and removed his pillow-case full of $5,000 dollar bundles. He dumped the money on top of Mr. Smith's desk.

They watched as the deposit procedure began. First, one of the Cayman men piled the bundles in stacks of fives, there were six stacks of $25,000 dollars. If each bundle had exactly $5,000 dollars in genuine money, the total would be $150,000 dollars.

Second, the other Cayman man took a bundle of hundreds, removed the rubber bands, then expertly fanned the bills under a lamp with an ultraviolet light bulb. Any fake bill would glow bright white. In less than thirty seconds he was satisfied that there were no counterfeit bills in the first bundle, he then handed the stack of bills to the Cayman lady. She began counting the bills, meanwhile, the first man was checking the second bundle under the ultraviolet light, the second bundle was handed to the other Cayman man when it had passed the counterfeit test, he began counting.

When the lady had finished counting the first stack, she wrapped the bundle in a paper band that had the number 5000 printed on it. The accepted bundle of $5,000 dollars was tossed to the other end of Mr. Smith's desk.

The dexterity of the hands and fingers of the three banking employees was amazing, they had obviously had a lot of practice.

Mr. Smith kept an eagle eye on his staff, as each accepted bundle was tossed in his direction, he added it to the rapidly grow-ing pile of money.

In less than half an hour, Pete's deposit was checked, counted and accepted. No fake bills had been found.

The bankers took a short break while Slick opened the big metal suitcase, his deposit was next. Mr. Smith asked him if he wanted his name on the account or did he prefer a numbered ac-count?

"What do you suggest?"

"If you use your name, then only you can authorize a transfer or withdrawal, if you choose a numbered account, anyone you give the number to can make a transfer or withdrawal."

"How safe is it to have your name on an account, the IRS is pretty snoopy."

"It's against Cayman law for any bank to divulge any information on our account holders, not one name on any account has ever found it's way to your tax people."

"I think I'll go with my name, I probably won't forget that."

Mr. Smith passed the necessary forms across to Slick, *"Just sign here and here and your new account will be opened in the amount of two hundred thousand US dollars, as soon as we finish counting that is."*

Slick signed where indicated, the deposit procedure began.

"Oops, here's a bad one."

"Let me see what it looks like." Slick went around to where the man was checking the bills with the ultraviolet light. Sure enough, in the middle of the fanned out bills, one glowed brightly, it appeared as though it had been painted with luminous paint around the edges. *"I'll be damned, sticks out like a sore thumb."*

The bill checker handed the fake hundred dollar bill to Slick, he exchanged it with one from his pocket, the bill checker checked the new bill, it passed. He then passed the stack of bills on to one of the counters.

Before long Mr. Smith handed Slick a deposit slip, he was now the proud owner of a $200,000 dollar account in one of the safest banking systems in the world.

It took two more hours to check and count the big deposit for the Man's account. When they left for their hotel it was 7:30. Mr. Smith's last banking duty of the day was to drop them off, *"Happy diving, call when I can be of assistance."*

"Thanks again for everything, we appreciate you and your staff working so late, we'll be in touch."

With that, the crooks became tourists, nothing to do but enjoy their next three days on the white beaches and blue waters in and around the Cayman Islands.

Pete had called the hotel from the bank so there was no problem with the late check-in.

"I'll meet you two at the bar in fifteen minutes, it's been a long dry afternoon, think there's any pussy around this place?"

"Wow! What a view."

"Nothing too good for my wealthy young pilot."

"Speaking of wealthy, how much are you worth?"

"Remember what Queen Victoria said, a girl can never be too thin or too wealthy."

"How much?"

"You'll have to fly several more trips to catch me."

"Glad to hear that, If I get caught you can bail me out."

"You don't think I learned anything all those years with my shady lawyer."

"Guess I won't pursue that, Let's drink rum, maybe if we get a little drunk I'll tear your clothes off and we can do it on the beach."

"In that case I'm not wearing any expensive underwear, or for that matter, not any underwear."

"My kind of girl."

"Would you look at that, he's already got one."

"Us pilots is pretty cool."

Sitting with Pete was an obvious newcomer, her skin looked like she'd spent the summer somewhere where the sun never shines.

"Rosemary, Slick, meet Claudia, she was on the same plane with us."

Claudia explained that she had arrived quite depressed, she had been informed a month earlier that her 10 year marriage was over and that her husband, who she had put through medical school, would be living with his new young sexy receptionists.

"Pete has already made me feel better, he has a very positive attitude."

Rosemary whispered to Slick, *"Wait until later when he gets her in bed, then she'll really feel better."*

Drinks came, a steel band started playing the local noise,

more drinks came, they dined at the seafood buffet put on by the hotel. Slick and Rosemary strolled on the beach but decided against any shenanigans because of the hordes of sand fleas.

"You think she'll have sex with Pete the first night?"

"Hell yes, she's gonna show that fucking doctor a thing or two. They're probably already in the sack."

"Sounds good to me, I'm exhausted, wish we had some of that opium."

"Now now, you know the rule, no sex the night before diving."

"Rules are made to be broken."

The dive shop sent a van to pick them up at 9am, surprise, surprise, Claudia was with Pete, she looked extremely happy.

At the dive shop Pete arranged the day's activities, a boat and driver for just the 4 of them, enough dive tanks for 2 dives for the 3 divers and plenty of cold drinks. It was imperative that the boat have a top, otherwise Claudia would be overcooked by noon.

The only boat available with a canvas sunroof was big enough for a group of 8 and double the price of the smaller ones. Pete told the dive shop operator not to worry, they were on expenses and the boss could afford a few extra bucks. In fact, he reserved the boat for the following day to make sure some group that got sunburned today didn't grab it.

"Boat, driver, hats, tanks, dive gear, food, cooler, ice, drinks, a beautiful sunny day, couple of nice looking babes, life ain't too shabby."

"Wait til you see Claudia in her Bikini, she ain't too shabby either."

"Let me guess, hubby dumps her, she goes on a big diet and exercise program so she can snare a new man."

"Slick, you are amazing."

"Rosemary is the prophet."

"She'd know."

"I bet that's a new hair-do too."

"Yep, right again."

"She's a damn nice looking broad, guess the doc just

needed some new pussy."
"Don't we all."

They were in the water by 10:30am, because of the tide, they had decided to do Cayman's famous canyon dive first. This dive is through a natural canyon which is really just a big crack in the sea floor. When the tide is ebbing, you simply get in the water at the end of the canyon closest to shore and let mother nature propel you from one end to the other. Because of the semi-strong current, there is an abundance of sea life hanging around waiting for the current to bring them something to eat. The Canyon is most famous for a large school of barracuda that are almost always there.

The boat driver had probably dropped divers off and followed them through the canyon a thousand times, anyway, when Slick and Rosemary popped to the surface, he wasn't 20 feet away. Pete was just a few seconds behind.

"What a great dive, must be two million fish swimming around down there, you got to learn how to dive Claudia, it's like being in another world."

"There isn't much warm water in Puget Sound."

Pete broke out two bottles of beer, popped the tops and passed one over to Slick.

"How bout you girls?"

"Beer is definitely not on my diet."

"Too early for me, besides, don't I remember my diving instructor saying something about absolutely no drinking while diving."

"He must have been a real rookie."

The driver dropped the foursome off on a short stretch of beach with their lunch basket and cooler. He said he'd be back in about an hour and if he had any luck fishing, he'd fix them all a plate of very fresh sashimi or even better, a bowl of the island delicacy, seviche.

Behind the beach was a sheer cliff of sandstone, thousands of years of erosion had created an overhang where they retreated for shade. The lunch basket contained many goodies left over from last night's buffet plus cold cuts, cheese and half a loaf of French bread. The girls laid lunch out on a big boulder that served as a table, Slick and Pete sat in the shade and drank ice cold beer.

"After the hunt the women prepare the food."

"I like the costumes those native girls are wearing."

The boat driver returned, he had caught a beautiful wahoo, while the divers did their second dive he cut it up in thin bite size pieces for sashimi and seviche.

Wahoo sashimi is tasty, but wahoo seviche is out of this world, especially when it's so fresh it's still quivering.

"Hell of a day."

"Ain't over yet."

"Want another beer?"

"Why don't we bust open that bottle of Chianti?"

"Good idea."

The combination of too much sun and several glasses of Chianti had Claudia in an extremely amorous mood, by the time they got back to the hotel she was almost out of control.

"You two have time for a cocktail before we run up for a nap?"

"Claudia, you want a drink?"

"Later, right now I have plans for you."

When Slick got to the room he called room-service and had a bottle of Champagne sent to Pete's room.

"You guys, two days ago she was a poor distraught woman who's life had just fallen apart, you two have turned her into an alcoholic sex fiend."

"I prefer the tipsy horny sexy Claudia to some down in the dumps broad moping around making everybody else depressed. Don't you?"

"Of course. I just hope she can find some fun guy like Pete when she gets back to Seattle."

"At least now she knows she isn't doomed to a life of being pissed off at the doctor. Shit, she's a hot chick, she'll do alright."

Slick answered the phone.

"Who was that?"

"Pete, they're starving."

Somebody at the dive shop had recommended a casual little out of the way restaurant called the Blue Marlin. There was no menu, dinner was whatever the owner caught that day and whatever he caught was cooked by his wife. You could buy beer at the Blue Marlin, if you wanted wine, you brought your own.

All the rumors were true, the blackboard said, "Grilled Skipjack" and nothing else.

"Sounds good to me."

"Me too, whatever skipjack is."

"You'll like it, skipjack has white meat a lot like wahoo except it's a little firmer."

"If it's half as good as the wahoo we had today, I'll love it."

The meal was served family style, a big platter of fish accompanied with another platter of baked potatoes and carrots. When they were finished, both platters were clean as a whistle, there were also two empty wine bottles littering the table. Diving and screwing do wonders for one's appetite.

Claudia had provided most of the evening's entertainment, the more she drank, the looser her lips became. Half way through the second bottle of wine, she laid into a tirade about how glad she was to be unburdened from that no good doctor who also happened to be the worst lay in the world and she couldn't wait to tell him just that. She planned to bring her camera along the next day, she wanted Rosemary to take lots of sexy photos of her and of her and Pete so she could show the idiot how much fun she was having now that she was finally free from him and his boring life style. Slick volunteered to snap some nude shots to really piss the doc off, he even promised not to look.

"Why not, Rosemary, will you pose with me?"

"Sure, I've got no secrets from these two bozos."

Pete had a great idea, they'd get a shot of Claudia with her super white skin standing topless next to their boat driver who's skin was as black as coal, let the ex make any inference from the photo he wanted to. Rosemary had an even better idea, a photo of Claudia surrounded by the entire staff at the dive shop, they were all big strong young black guys, they'd probably be thrilled to have their pictures taken with a topless Claudia, naked would be even better. Make sure the doc sees the group photo and let his imagination run wild, pretty soon they'd have the poor bastard in the nut house.

Back at the hotel the party continued, before the two couples went up to their rooms, Claudia was ready to ride a white horse naked up and down the streets of the Cayman Islands. She probably wouldn't be so brave in the morning when she was sober.

When the dive shop van arrived at the 9am pickup time, everybody was bright eyed and bushy tailed with one exception, Claudia. She complained of a severe headache behind her eyes, she even tried to beg off the day's boat ride, but Pete would hear nothing of it.

Finally after an Alka Seltzer, 3 aspirin and 2 cups of coffee, Claudia felt well enough to join the others with the condition that no-one force her to drink any wine.

"A little of the hair of the dog that bit you might be your best bet."

"If I see even one drop of wine I'll throw-up all over the place."

"Again?"

"Don't tell them."

"At least you made it to the bathroom, too bad you missed the toilet."

"It's all your fault, you're the one who got me so drunk."

They all had a good laugh at Claudia's expense and amazingly enough, by the time they got under way she was looking like she might make it through the day.

Pete had instructed the guys at the dive shop to load only 3 dive tanks, they had decided to do the canyon dive again then hang out at the same beach for a relaxing couple of hours.

After the canyon dive, Pete and Slick had a little powwow with Felix the boat driver, the big smile on his face indicated beyond a doubt that he liked whatever they had told him.

"What are you guys up to?"

"Here's the plan, you sit in Felix' lap, he'll get the boat going full speed ahead and we'll click a bunch of pictures with your hair flying in the breeze, it'll look great."

"*I don't know.*"

"*It was ur idea.*"

Anyway, a few minutes later, Claudia was sitting in Felix' lap, her hair was flying back, she was smiling, her bare white breasts were a total contrast next to Felix' ebony skin, Felix was grinning like the Cheshire Cat, it was quite a scene.

Rosemary was the cameraman, "*I took about ten shots, one of them ought to be great.*"

"*I wonder if Felix will give her back?*"

"*The sixty four dollar question is does she want to come back?*"

Felix dropped the foursome off at their beach, he promised to be back at 3, that gave them 4 hours to eat, drink and play around.

After a bite to eat, Claudia felt so good that she helped polish off a bottle of red wine.

"*I've never done so many naughty things in my life, sex with a man I've known less than half a day, running around half naked in a boat sitting on a black man's lap, drinking wine with my bare boobs hanging out, what's happened to me?*"

"*Not only that, you're about to have sex in broad daylight right here in the sand.*"

"*Where?*"

"*Right over there behind that rock.*"

"*That little rock?*"

"*It's the only one.*"

"*Okay, if I must.*"

"*Rosemary, if they have sex on that side of the rock, how about us on this side?*"

"*Okay, if I must.*"

Felix was right on time, "*Did you have a nice picnic?*"

"*We had a wonderful time, this has been a perfect day.*" Claudia was beaming.

They met for dinner at 7, everybody's faces were glowing.

"*My boobs are sunburned.*"

"*Mine too.*"

"Big deal, I have a sunburned dick, I may not be able to touch it for a week."

"You liar, it worked fine thirty minutes ago."

"It hurt."

Sometime during the day, Pete had invited Claudia to stop by Tampa on her way back to Seattle, she'd have to juggle her tickets but she said she'd be there in 2 days. Pete would take the 2 rolls of film they'd shot earlier and have them developed, the photos would be waiting when Claudia arrived. While the girls were in the powder room he told Slick of the new development.

"Pedro, you're gonna be a busy boy, you forgotten about you know who?"

"She's out, this is just the push I needed."

"Don't forget, we've got work to do."

"She's only staying two days, she has to go back to work."

"Ur the man."

Pete ordered 2 extra dry Martinis, 5 minutes later the girls returned.

"Where you been? Looking for Felix?"

"We've been rubbing lotion on our tits if you must know."

"I could use a little myself."

"Me too."

Rosemary tossed the bottle of lotion on the table, the Martinis arrived, lotion was applied, dinner was ordered, more drinks were ordered, life was indeed hard.

The next morning was a flurry of activity, 9am wake-up call, toss the few items of clothes in the now almost empty metal suitcase, dash down for coffee and a quick breakfast, check out, call a taxi, kiss Claudia good-bye and head for the airport.

The tired trio pulled up in front of the lake house just as it was getting dark, there was no sign of Brenda.

Pete turned on the central air conditioning, Slick dumped the metal suitcase in his room and headed for the fridge, Rosemary winked at Slick and pointed outside in the general vicinity of where the opium was buried. Pete came down stairs with a smile on his face, *"She's gone, all her stuff is gone, this is too easy, she even left her keys."*

"We should still change the locks, you never know."

"Guess ur right, we do have a lot of shit laying around here from time to time, I'll get a locksmith over tomorrow."

Sam came over to get a first hand report on the banking trip, he had several messages to pass on. The boys in Boston were hot to trot, they'd almost sold their complete stock, this early in the season, their's was the only game in town, their buyers were bugging the hell out of them for more pot. They would be able to pay for the next shipment C.O.D. Brenda had stopped by to tell Sam she was leaving, she had met mister perfect and by now was somewhere in The Big Apple snorting her brains out.

"When can we be ready to go again?"

They went over what had to be done prior to the next launch. First, the next morning, Slick and Pete would drive to Leesburg and take the Navajo for a short flight to make sure it was okay. Next, assuming the plane was ready, they'd call Carlos, tell him about the 2 bank transfers and ask him if his people could be ready for them 4 mornings later. That would leave plenty of time to get the buyers in place and to show Claudia around. They decided to go for another quick turn around. Sam would hide the marijuana from the turn around until the buyers could get back to Florida, he didn't think it would be very long the way they were clamoring for the stuff. After trip number 5, they'd have to plan a short break in the action. The Navajo would have over a hundred hours since it's last inspection, they'd have to remove the illegal fuel lines, then have a mechanic give the plane a good going over before the next mission could be scheduled.

"Don't forget we've got to cover the new tank with card-board."

Finding another big cardboard box with a bike on the side was added to the list.

Pete passed Mr. Smith's regards on to Sam, then gave him the counterfeit count.

"Out of all that money, they only found eight fake hundreds."

"That's not bad. You keep em?"

Slick laid the 8 counterfeit bills on the table, 3 were pretty obvious, 4 were damn good and 1 was unbelievably good.

"I'd never have picked this one, looks real to me."

"It glowed white under the blue light."

"The light don't lie."

They decided to burn the bad fakes and pass the good ones some time later on, Sam suggested out of town grocery stores with a purchase of close to or over a hundred dollars.

"Looks like another job for our happy young couple, what could be more natural than stocking up on meat for the freezer, buying case lots to save a little, keeping an eye on the pennies so the kids have enough for college."

"Grieving widow jailed for passing counterfeit notes."

"Just make sure you never have more than one on you at a time, it ain't ur fault if some bastard gave you a fake hundred dollar bill, the FBI should be doing a better job of catching crooks."

Sam laughed when he heard the story of Claudia's conversion from distraught jilted wife to oversexed beach bimbo. He got an especially big kick out of the photos with the black boat driver episode.

"When do I get to see the pictures?"

"Tomorrow, she was really nervous about getting arrested for having naked pictures of her developed."

"Speaking of naked pictures, you better sanitize your room, I doubt that Claudia will be too turned on by a room full of Brenda's tits."

"Already taken care of."

"Sam, you want to smoke a little opium?"

"No thanks, I never mix my drugs, you want some coke?"

Rosemary turned on one of the burners of the stove and stuck a knife between two of the elements, Sam passed his vial of cocaine over to Pete, Slick went outside to retrieve the stash of opium.

"Pete, you gonna turn ur new girl on to coke?"

"That might be a little too much for her to handle."

"Why not slip her a lude?"

"Jesus Sam, a month ago this chick was married to a doctor in Seattle."

"Time she caught up."

The gang did a bunch of illegal drugs and laughed about

ways to further be of bad influence on unsuspecting Claudia.

"You wanna know something, I like having a lot of money."

"Beats the shit out of the alternative."

Chapter XI

The Fourth And Fifth

In the morning, Rosemary headed over to her house to stash most of the opium and her $7,000 dollars in the big steel safe. Pete and Slick drove to Leesburg to fly the Navajo. During the drive they went over the cash situation.

Pete still had a little over $2,000 that belonged to the project, Slick counted his project money and came up with $1,800. Sam had $35,000 in twenties from the night they'd divided up the six hundred thousand Slick had brought back from Boston.

"You know Pete, we only owe the Man a hundred and one thousand, two more trips and we don't have to deduct anything but the price of the dope. That's gonna be an extra twelve grand for each of us each trip."

"Sounds good, I can start snorting a better grade."

"Where do you think Sam will hide twelve hundred pounds of pot?"

"He'll drive right in his garage with it, when the buyers show up he'll have them back up to his garage door and load the shit out of his four by four right into their truck. He don't sweat nothin."

"He ever been busted?"

"Not for dope. They arrested him once for slapping around some dipshit lawyer."

"What did the lawyer do, lose a case?"

"No, nothing to do with a case, he just pissed Sam off."

"What happened?"

"Nothing, the lawyer dropped the charges, I think Sam scarred the shit out of him."

"Fuck, that's funny. What about passing those counterfeit hundreds?"

"It's no big deal. When I did it before, I bought a bunch of stuff, at least two hundred dollars worth, I paid with one good hundred and a bad one. I always made sure the store was busy so the checker didn't have time to look too hard at my money. Let's get

rid of one on the way home today, you got those phonies with you?"

"The five we kept."

"We'll stop in Lakeland later in the afternoon. It doesn't take many good cuts of steak and bottles of wine to add up to a couple hundred, before we're done with you, you'll be a genuine all round crook."

"It'll look good on my resume."

"I'll do the first buy, you wait outside with the other fakes. Sam's right, it would be pretty hard to bullshit the cops if we got popped with more than one phony hundred."

"Ur the head crook."

The Navajo ran like a clock, they flew around for fifty minutes then landed and topped off the four aircraft wing tanks. Pete couldn't believe that an airplane could fly that many hours without mechanical problems.

"You got to remember, most of our flights are ten hours long, the thing that's hard on planes is a lot of stopping and starting, in the hundred hours we've flown the landing gear has only gone up and down about twenty times."

"That makes sense, let's get a bite to eat."

The fearless aviators had a late lunch in nearby Leesburg. Slick told Pete he was seriously thinking about taking a two week holiday after the next two missions.

"I've been thinking about meeting Magda in Costa Rica for a couple of weeks R and R. You think Luis could get her a passport and set it up?"

"Probably take him about two phone calls."

At 4:45pm, the counterfeit bill passers pulled into a busy parking lot in front of a Publix grocery store. Slick gave Pete one of the counterfeit hundred dollar bills, *"I'll meet you over there by that drug store."*

"Okay, I'll load the groceries and drive out of the parking lot, stop over there at the Foster's Freeze, get a vanilla cone then come back to pick you up. By then you'll know if anybody is paying any attention to me, If I'm being followed, just ignore me."

Half an hour later, Pete came out of the market pushing his shopping cart, he loaded his groceries in the Mercedes truck, re-

turned the cart to the front of the store, got in his car and drove
away. No one paid the slightest bit of attention. Out of curiosity,
Slick went inside Publix and bought a 12 pack of Budweiser, the 4
grocery checkers all seemed as normal as can be expected for people with such maddening jobs.

When Slick left the store, Pete's Mercedes was just pulling
out of the Foster's Freeze across the street. Five minutes later they
were on the way home with a trunk full of Publix's best cuts.

*"The guy never even looked, he just stuck the two bills in
his drawer and give me my change, I could have given him all
five."*

"What you get?"

*"They had some great looking New Yorks, I got about
twenty steaks and four bottles of French wine, the bill was a hundred thirty."*

That night they had a barbecue.

Everybody was wild about the Cayman pictures, one of the
ones with Claudia sitting in Felix's lap was sensational. The camera
had caught Felix slyly peeking out the corner of his eyes at Claudia's snow white tits.

Sarah thought the doctor would be most upset with one shot
of Claudia on top of Pete, they were both stark naked, *"It looks like
you two are doing it."*

Sam laughed, *"What do you mean, looks like."*

*"Pete, you devil, oh here's one of you boys with your cute
little dicks hanging out for the world to see."*

"Which one you like best, Sarah."

"Sam's."

"Good answer."

*"Rosemary, what happened to the ones I took of you and
Slick?"*

"I hid them."

"Common, we want to see."

"No! You can see everything."

"What's the difference, I took the pictures."

"Sam and Sarah weren't there."

After a little prodding Rosemary brought out the other pictures, all but one.

"*My my, quite the little perverts.*"

"*I told you.*"

"*Shit, they're great, I'm not criticizing, I'm appreciating, you look good naked.*"

"*Thanks, big fella.*"

"*I was talking to Rosemary.*"

"*Oh shucks, in that case I think I'll smoke some opium.*"

Slick and Rosemary got the paraphernalia ready, Sam and Pete had already snorted a couple of hits from Pete's solid gold coke spoon. Sarah made her way to the kitchen, "*Could I try some of your opium? It's been a long time.*"

When they parted company, Sam knew he was in trouble, Sarah had that look in her eyes.

"*It's going to be a long night, last time she looked like that she almost killed me.*"

"*Don't forget to call Carlos tomorrow.*"

Claudia would arrive at Tampa the next afternoon, Pete would get to the airport early enough to put a couple of calls through to Carlos. Slick and Rosemary would look around for another bicycle box and maybe pass another fake hundred dollar bill, there was plenty of room in the freezer for more meat and wine doesn't spoil.

"*See you in the morning.*"

"*Goodnight. Rosemary, what happened to that close-up? I put a lot of effort into sneaking up on you two, I'd like to see it.*"

"*Never, I burned it.*"

"*Liar.*"

"*What's he talking about?*"

"*You'll see, it's a real porno shot.*"

"*Can't wait.*"

"*Jesus, that bastard got close, guess we weren't thinking about spies at the time. What did they say when you picked up the film?*"

"*Nothing, but they were all starring at me.*"

"*No shit, wow! That's a hell of a photo, let's get it blown up and framed.*"

"*No way, now stop admiring your penis, I need it for a*

while."

"I'm admiring what it's in."

The salesman at the first bicycle store they tried sent them to Sears where he had worked a year earlier, he was positive they could get any number of empty boxes there.

Half an hour later they had the folded bicycle box jammed in the back seat of Rosemary's car. Two hours later the new long-range tank was converted to look like a bike in a box.

Pete left the house at 4pm, Slick and Rosemary weren't far behind, they had some shopping to do. The grocery store in North Tampa was a beehive of activity. The redneck checkout girl totaled up their cart full of groceries at a hundred and fifty five dollars and a few cents. Slick handed her the bad hundred and 3 twenties, she never batted an eye, handed him 4 ones and some change and went on to the next person in line like she had a million times before.

"That was too easy, maybe we should start printing money."

"If they catch you making fake money you are in real trouble, if they catch us with a little marijuana, we get our hands slapped, pay a fine and at worst we do a few months, I'll stick to the import business."

Back at the house Rosemary laid the Cayman pictures out on the dining room table so they would be the first things Claudia would see when she stepped in the door.

"We have a full freezer and plenty of wine, wow, that's quite a montage, you left out some of the juicy ones."

"I'll show her in private."

Claudia and Pete didn't get to the lake house until a little after 7, her connection in Miami had been delayed, late or not, she looked happy.

"Wow! Look at you, you're brown as a berry."

"Hi Rosemary. Oh my, what's this?"

"Our pictures, aren't they great."

"I'd forgotten how bad I'd been. This is the best one by a

mile, that boat driver looks really savage, doctor asshole will flip his lid. I hope he has a massive coronary."

Rosemary took Claudia upstairs to get settled, Slick and Pete went to the kitchen for a beer.

"Did you talk to Carlos?"

"It's all set, they'll be waiting at Plaza three days from now. I'll call Carlos again Friday afternoon before we leave for Leesburg to make sure nothing has changed."

"Shit hot! I'm ready to rock and roll."

The girls came back downstairs.

"Claudia wants a steak, you want to fire up the barbecue?"

"Up to you girls, we can stay here or go out, no bigee."

Claudia's decision was to stay at the house and eat steak, then go for a romantic boat ride in the moonlight. After dinner, while Claudia and Pete were out on the lake being naughty, Rosemary heated up the stove. She and Slick smoked a healthy pinch of opium, then they went to bed and were naughty themselves.

The next morning was devoted to teaching Claudia to water-ski, after a million or so falls, she finally got the hang of it. After lunch she really got in the groove, by mid afternoon she was an exhausted but competent water-skier.

Sam and Sarah were coming over for cocktails around 5, then they were all being treated to dinner anywhere Claudia wanted to go. Since she knew nothing about where to go in Tampa, it was easy to sway her vote towards Burns Steak house.

"Nice to finally meet you Claudia, I feel like I already know you."

"You saw the pictures?"

"All of them."

"What did you think?"

"You're hot."

While Rosemary, Sarah and Claudia tinkered with their martinis, the boys surreptitiously brought themselves up to date on preparations.

Sam was first, *"I talked to the boys from Boston, they'll be here with a bundle of cash."*

"Me and Rosemary decorated the tank, the bike is ready to be loaded."

Pete added, *"All we got to do is call Carlos tomorrow afternoon, he says the word and we're out of here."*

"Don't forget, we gotta fill the drums."

"I drop Claudia off at ten in the morning, I'll meet you at the nursery at eleven thirty, that will give us plenty of time to load everything and gas up."

As always, the dinner at Burns was superb, their claim of being the best steakhouse east of the Mississippi might well be true.

Claudia bid her new friends a tearful farewell, *"I hope I'll get to see all of you again, why don't you guys come visit me in Seattle, we could go skiing or salmon fishing or hiking in the mountains. You could even go scuba diving if you had wet suits. We have the best crabs and prawns in the world, Washington is a pretty cool place."*

"It's a date."

By the time Pete dropped Claudia off and got to the nursery, Slick and Sam had loaded the drums in the van, all he had to do was park his car and jump in and they were off for the airport at Plant City.

"I guess we should check in with Carlos before gassing up, no use carrying a bunch of gas around if we're not going anywhere."

"I'll pull into that Texaco and put some gas in the van while you call Carlos."

After Slick had gassed up the van, he drove over by the pay phones and waited for Pete who was apparently having trouble with his connection. Finally, he walked towards the van with a smile and thumbs up.

"We're all set, they'll be waiting for us at the same place, the weather has been good."

"Let's get some gas and haul ass."

The same young gas kid parked his fuel truck next to the van and passed the hose in to Pete, he then dashed off to answer the phone. By the time he got back, the 4 drums were full, *"Sorry about that, my girlfriend talks a lot."*

"No sweat, man."

Back at the nursery, Slick and Pete slid the new long range tank in the rear door of the van, then loaded the pump, the 12 volt battery and the tool kit.

"All we need now is the map bag and something to eat, we'll fill up on coffee just before take-off."

"I'm starving, let's hit the causeway for shrimp and crab."

They checked in to the motel next to the Leesburg Airport at 6:30pm, left the map bag in the room and drove the short distance to the waiting Navajo. There were two guys unloading a plane two rows away so there was a short delay. After the coast was clear, they went through the same routine. Remove the 4 passenger seats, slide the long range tank in place, plumb the tank, elevate the rear of the tank with boards, secure the tank with straps and finally, fill the tank with gas from the 4 fifty five gallon drums in the back of the van. When the long range tank was full, Slick handed the nozzle out to Pete, he stuck it in the slightly ajar back door of the van then closed the door. Pete jumped in the van's side door, unhooked the pump from the 12 volt battery, removed the pump stem from the fourth drum, and screwed the cap back on the drum. By the time Pete had tidied up inside the van, Slick had capped the long range tank in the Navajo's cabin, stepped out of the plane and locked the door.

"Okay my man, let's get a quick bite, we're ready to split."

"You check the oil?"

"Three times."

"Let's di di."

Three and a half hours passed, the smugglers walked down the street from the motel, crossed the street and approached the Navajo. It was 10:50pm, there was one other airplane taxing either in to park or out to takeoff.

Slick unlocked the cabin door and lowered the bottom half, put the map bag and cooler inside on the floor, stepped on the first step and raised the top half. He entered the Navajo, went forward to his seat, opened the pilot's door and started his mental pre-takeoff checklist. Pete removed the chocks, screwed the small marine radio antenna in place, then hopped in the plane closing the two door halves behind him. By the time Pete was in his seat, both engines were running, a few seconds later Slick added power and they were away.

"What happened to that other plane?"

"I don't have a clue, his lights were blocked by the trees."

"You worried about him?"

"Fuck no, just another northerner with a plane getting away from the cold."

Forty seconds later they were at the end of the runway, there were no signs of any other airplanes.

"Okay my man, everything looks good, you ready to blast off?"

"Let's get the fuck out of here, I'm getting a little paranoid."

Slick smoothly advanced the throttles, the Navajo accelerated down the runway and within a few seconds flew off into the night.

"Okay my man, we're on the way, gear's up, climb fuel flow is set, how bout a hot cup of coffee?"

"Coming up mon capitaine, weren't you a little nervous back there?"

"I think you been sticking too much of that coke up ur nose, it's fucking up ur head."

"Yeah, fuck it, why would anybody give a shit what we're up to. Shit, when that other plane taxied in I didn't suspect he was bringing in a load of dope, why would they think we were up to anything illegal."

"Relax, we got a long night ahead, there ain't nobody following us. Where's that coffee?"

Nobody followed them, nobody even noticed as the small plane flew south down the east side of Florida, then changed course to east south east a little past Fort Pierce.

Nobody in Florida had the slightest clue that the Navajo had departed, nobody in the Bahamas knew it had arrived, hell, nobody in the Bahamas even cared.

At 10,000 feet the noise made by the Navajo's engines could barely be discerned on the ground, since no one was listening, what little noise there was didn't matter anyway.

The same slight noise that reached sea level in the Bahamas reached sea level in Haiti. Nobody in Haiti noticed, the Haitians had more urgent things to worry about than airplanes high overhead such as where their next meal was coming from or who was sticking pins in voodoo dolls that looked like them.

The approach control radar at Barranquilla was so primitive that if an incoming or departing aircraft wasn't squawking an assigned code on it's transponder, it could not be seen on the radar screen. Therefore, the Navajo approached the northern coast of Colombia totally un-noticed, it's whereabouts known only to the two pilots.

"Land ho."

"Yeah, I see it, this flight has been a piece of piss, we're gonna land before eight thirty."

The pot was bagged, weighed and loaded by 10:30, Slick had finished refueling by 10:00, they had a little more than an hour to kill before take-off.

While they were all waiting under the trees, Slick had a chance to chat with Luis.

"Luis, we're going to take a couple of weeks off after the next flight for aircraft maintenance, I'd like to meet Magda somewhere, maybe Costa Rica, you think it could be arranged?"

"Sure, why not. I think you can fly from here to San Jose two or three times a week, she only needs a passport, Carlos can arrange that."

"I appreciate your help."

"We help each other, it's how we live."

"Thanks Luis, you are a good friend."

"Gracias mi amigo. Magda will be very excited."

Five hours later they were approaching Great Inagua Island, the first half of the return trip had been uneventful, just the way the pilots liked it. Slick had even allowed himself the luxury of a nap.

"Whew, I was out like a light, where the hell are we?"

"Great Inagua dead ahead about fifteen minutes."

"What did Luis say about a quick turn-around?"

"The crop is starting to be harvested all over Colombia, he says there won't be any shortage for the next several months. The only problem we might have is scheduling us to fit in with other planes."

"It's a good thing we got those first three trips in early, pretty soon everybody and his dog will be flying around down here looking for dope."

"If this strip gets too busy, I'm sure he'll switch us to Hotel Continental."

"Suits me, I don't like crowds."

"You want a bite to eat?"

Just as Pete was about to break out the food, both engines started sputtering, the long range tank was empty. Quickly, Slick moved the fuel selector levers from OFF to AUX.

"Damn, no matter how hard I think about that tank, it always catches me by surprise and scares the shit out of me."

The little Navajo droned northward along the long chain of the Bahaman Islands, it was dark before they were abeam Freeport on Grand Bahama Island, the days were getting shorter as winter approached.

Before descending to dash in altitude, the smugglers made sure everything was set. They had used all the fuel in the auxiliary tanks and had switched to the mains, so there were no more changes necessary with the fuel selector levers. All the maps were stowed except for the sectional covering south Florida and the roadmap with the drop zone details on it. The only wrench necessary to disconnect the long range tank was in the pouch on the back of Slick's seat about a foot from where it would be needed. Pete had one of the marine radios out, turned on and plugged into it's antenna, as long as the weather didn't go to hell or a wing didn't fall off they were laughing.

"You ready to rock and roll?"

"Let's do it."

Slick pulled the power back and started down, it was dark but not pitch black as they turned inbound towards the beach.

"I wish we had some clouds to hide in, I feel naked."

"This suits me fine, last time when it was so black and we were in the clouds I would have bailed out if I had a parachute, that's the worst case of vertigo I ever had."

"Jesus, I can already see the glow of lights on the shoreline."

The Navajo roared across the beach at 500 feet, if anybody heard her they didn't pay any attention, airplanes were always buzzing the beach around Fort Pierce, no big deal.

"Happy Hooker 28, radio check."
"I read you Hooker."

The remainder of the flight went silky smooth, the intrepid smugglers were guzzling beer in their motel room long before midnight. While Slick and Pete were drinking beer, Sam and the buyers traded the 27 bags of marijuana for one duffel bag full of money, and bid each other bon voyage. By one a.m., Sam was home in bed with Sarah while the pick-up truck load of dope was headed north.

"Well my man, that was a piece of cake."

"You got that right, four or five more just like this one and I'm outta here as a retired gentleman."

"Another Bud?"

"Let me run over and get those burgers, I gotta call Rosemary too."

In the morning Pete was suffering from a severe case of paranoia. He wanted to walk across to the airport and hang around for half an hour to make sure no one was paying too much attention to the Navajo. Slick shrugged and went to the restaurant while Pete checked things out.

Forty minutes later, Pete entered the restaurant shaking his head, *"Quite as a mouse, but I still think we should start taking more precautions."*

"Like what?"

"I don't think we should leave the van sitting around here when we're gone, the same van parked at the same motel this many

times could start somebody's brain to work overtime."
    "Let's go get the tank and put the seats back, we'll talk on the way home."

Nothing happened at the airport, the only unusual thing Slick noticed was Pete constantly looking over his shoulders.
    "Relax man, you look like your doing something illegal."
    "Sorry, I'm trying to look normal."
    "Ur not, take it easy."

Pete finally relaxed about half way back to Tampa, *"This is really stupid, if they were on to us they'd just arrest our asses."*
    "Fuck em, what can they do to us, we never land with any dope in the plane, the most they can do is tell us they know what we're up to and then we just quit."
    "Guess ur right."

Sam was waiting at the nursery, the big smile on his face told the whole story.
    "Howdy boys, let's unload this shit then lunch is on me."

As always, Sam demanded a blow by blow description of the entire flight, Slick even threw in a little of Pete's paranoia, then it was Sam's turn.
    "We found all but one bag right away. The one we couldn't find had bounced way off to one side and was hidden in the bushes. After we loaded up and left the DZ, I took Nevada to his car where he left it over by Bush Gardens. He gave me a duffel bag full of money and said his mob would be ready for more dope in about a week. I asked him what the fuck that was about, he said they had bought a ton from some other outfit and they needed the time to get the money together."
    "Those assholes, for a month we've been their lifeline, now they're gonna treat us like the rest of the fair-weather smugglers."
    "I told him something like that, they'll be ready for our next load."
    "What you tell him?"
    "I didn't tell him nothin, I asked him a question."

"What?"

"I asked him how much dope he thought he could buy with two broken arms and a shoe up his ass."

"How'd he take that?"

"Nevada's a good guy, I'm sure it was Ronnie who got a little greedy and decided to buy more than they could afford, you know what an idiot he is. Nevada guaranteed they'd be ready with fifty percent down on the next load."

"How much he give you last night?"

"The whole schimoli, four hundred K, anyway, that's what he said, I haven't counted it yet. I'll bring it over to the house after dark and we can divi it up."

Sam waived for the bartender to bring another round, "When you boys gonna be ready to go again?"

"What you think, Pete, couple of days?"

"Yeah, fuck it, why not, maybe if I lay off the coke I'll stop hearing little voices."

They decided to meet later, barbecue some of their illegally gotten steaks, figure out what to do with the money they'd just earned by breaking all kinds of laws, then do some illegal drugs. But first they'd have one for the road so they could illegally drive back to the nursery while under the influence. Life was a gas.

Back at the nursery, the pilots jumped in Pete's car and drove across town to the lake house, on the way they talked and laughed about their partner.

"You think that's what he said?"

"I bet he just stared at Nevada until he got the picture. Fuck man, he scares me and I'm his partner and friend."

"He is intense. Now poor Nevada has to deal with Ronnie the drug freak."

"Don't worry about Ronnie, he's known Sam a long time, they'll just have to deal with the lesser of two evils and stall the other outfit until they get the money collected."

Rosemary was dutifully waiting when her quasi-faithful man returned from the smuggling wars. She greeted Pete and Slick with a pair of ice cold Buds, "Hard day at the office gentlemen?"

"Actually not, this was the easiest one yet, a little power nap and I'll be ready to kick ass."

Rosemary took 5 New York steaks out of the freezer then drove off to the store for salad ingredients and baking potatoes, Slick and Pete were sound asleep before she left the house, hauling the crop to market is hard work.

Rested, Pete and Slick put their heads together and came up with a new dollar chart.

Slick had given all his project cash to Pete to pay for gas, food and the motel, Pete still had thirteen hundred project money in his black bag.

$ 1,300 cash black bag	1220 lbs total
$35,000 cash twenties	27 wt of sacks
$36,300 from before	1193 wt of stuff = 405,620
	-$400,000
	$5,620 due

$400,000 received	new	$ 1,300	for man $ 50,000 exp.
-$ 50,000 expenses	cash	$35,000	$ 72,000 stuff
$350,000	total	$18,000	$ 65,000 1/4
-$ 72,000 stuff		$54,300	$187,000
$278,000			
-$ 18,000 cash			
$260,000 divided by 4 = $65,000			*only $51,000 exp. to go

Sam and Sarah arrived, the boys went into Slick's room to take care of business.

There were 80 bundles of hundreds, each bundle was supposed to be exactly $5,000 dollars. Sam approved the new distribution chart, 13 bundles were put in 4 stacks, 1 bundle was divided into smaller bundles of $2,000 and $3,000. Sam put the Man's $187,000 in a black plastic garbage bag, he put his $65,000 in a brown paper grocery bag, Pete dropped his $65,000 in his trusty pillow case while Slick stuck his cut in a shoe box.

Pete suggested they buy a new ultraviolet light to check their cash, no use getting busted in Florida for passing counterfeit money from Massachusetts. Sam said he thought the original light was somewhere in his house, he'd check. They decided to pay the up-coming mechanical bills with a mixture of hundreds and twenties after everything had been carefully gone over with the light.

Slick guessed that the hundred hour inspection would cost from 2 to 4 thousand even if nothing was found wrong with the Navajo. He'd insist on new spark plugs no matter how good the old ones looked. Slick had done a little scouting around and had found a Piper dealer in Lakeland, the dealer had a good reputation. No doubt the inspection would cost more there than if they used a private mechanic, but also no doubt, the dealer's mechanics would be more thorough, after all, their specialty was Piper aircraft. The Piper company in Lakeland was decided on, they didn't want to jeopardize hundreds of thousands because of a few pennies. Slick would meet Sam in the morning to pick up the twenties and the light if he could find it, if not, they'd just get another one, the meeting was adjourned.

The girls had laid out a dish of hors-d'oeuvres and mixed a pitcher of martinis, moonlight was reflecting off the lake, thick steaks were ready to be barbecued over hickory charcoal, Rosemary was glowing just thinking about her after dinner treat, Sarah looked her usual angelic self, how much more could these three crooks handle?

There is no saturation point when things are going your way, during the evening Sam thought about a bigger plane, Pete thought about pussy and Slick's brain had wandered a thousand four hundred miles south.

Slick picked up the twenties, Sam hadn't been able to find the ultraviolet light so Pete went off to get another one. They went over all the twenty dollar bills, there were a lot that glowed, out of $35,000 dollars or 1750 bills, they found 35 fakes. People who make counterfeit money obviously think it's safer to pass small denomination bills, nobody pays much attention to a twenty dollar bill. Some of the bad ones were so bad one had to wonder how they had gone unnoticed, Pete figured Ronnie had just passed them along so he didn't have to eat the loss. Of the $700 dollars in fakes, $220 was too bad to pass, Pete burned them in the barbecue.

The $18,000 of new hundreds only produced one phony, it was added to the small stack of money to be passed later on.

Because of the relatively high percentage of fake twenties,

Pete and Slick decided to check the twenties they'd stashed earlier, Pete went to his ex wife's house to get his and Slick met Rosemary at her house to get his stash.

"From now on I'm going to check every dollar before I spend it, I wonder how many bad twenties we paid bar bills with at our watering hole."

"Let's go tell Sam, I wouldn't want him to pay his bill at Burns and get his ass hauled off, he'd be pretty pissed off."

Sam met them at his house, they went over his entire stash and got rid of the bad bills.

"Next year when I pay my taxes for the nursery I ought to send all this phony shit to the feds, fuck em, they let these fucking counterfeiters get away with this shit, they ought to eat it."

"Good idea, Sam, I'm sure the FBI will be very sympathetic."

"Okay, I won't but it's a good idea, you boys ready for tomorrow?"

"We're on the way to Leesburg to give our girl a quick run and fill her up, we'll take care of everything else tomorrow."

"I'll see if Nevada's still around, if he's not I gotta find a helper."

Slick took his money to Rosemary's house and put it in the steel safe, then he went back to the lake house to wait for Pete. They were on the way to Leesburg by 3pm.

"You got any money?"

"I still got the thirteen hundred."

"Remind me to grab five K before we leave tomorrow, if we get stuck in Colombia we'll need a little cash."

"The right oil is down a quart, the left only a cunt hair, there's some oil on the bottom of the right cowling, we got a little leak."

"You think it's enough to worry about?"

"Naw, after ten and a half hours flying, most pilots dream of oil consumption like that. When they do the hundred hour we'll remind them to tighten everything up."

After a quick spin around the patch, they filled the Navajo to the brim and put her to bed, so far she'd been an incredible machine.

Launch day's routine of filling the 4 drums, loading the empty tank in the van, loading the battery and gas pump went off without a hitch. There were no delays at Leesburg, the Navajo lifted off and headed south at 11:05pm.

The mid October weather was as it should be that time of year, perfect. Everybody knows about Florida's beautiful weather from October until April, that's why there are so many people down there.

The clear skies combined with the flawless operation of the newly overhauled engines provided for a flight free of problems, they flew across Hotel Plaza at 8:25am, 9 hours and 20 minutes after take-off. There were no signs of life below, Luis and his men were probably relaxing under the trees. In reality, it didn't matter, there was no where else to go, the Navajo was down to about 2 hours fuel.

Slick flew his usual left hand pattern and lined up on final heading towards the east. Just over the trees at the end of the runway, he pulled the power back and pushed the nose down towards the red clay runway. The Navajo touched down and rolled to a stop. Plaza was deserted.

"Where the hell is everybody?"

"I don't know, you think they forgot?"

"No way, maybe they had a flat or a wreck, doesn't matter, there's nothing we can do but wait and hope the right guys show up."

After parking in the usual place under the trees, Slick shut the engines down, he and Pete got out to stretch their legs and see what the hell was going on.

"What do we say if a bunch of Colombian cops drive up? Oh, hi, we're a little lost, is this Venezuela? Sorry to be a bother, could you get us a little gas and show us on the map where we are?"

"I'm sure that will work, I might as well see how much oil we used instead of standing here with my finger up my ass worrying about something I can't do anything about."

Slick grabbed some paper towels from the back of the plane

so he could hold the hot dipsticks and checked the oil levels.

Not bad, a quart and a half.

Slick opened the nose baggage compartment and removed a funnel and 2 quarts from the case of oil carried there. He took the dipstick out, put the funnel in the filler hole and poured the first quart in. Since it was hot, the oil poured almost as fast as hydraulic fluid. He added half of the second quart, removed the funnel and replaced the dipstick, making sure it clicked into place. The left engine was down less than the half quart remaining, Slick poured it all in and replaced the dipstick.

Nothing to do now but sit down in the shade and wait.

Suddenly the eerie silence was broken.

"Somebody's coming and they're haulin ass, that engine is screaming."

Not knowing what else to do, the two pilots just stood there and stared in the direction the noise was coming from. Seconds later a truck roared onto the runway from the opposite end normally used, there were several men in the back of the truck waiving frantically. In a few seconds the truck was close enough that Luis could be recognized, he jumped down as the truck skidded to a stop.

"Pedro, Es Slick, sorry, there are soldiers close, we have sent them on a goose chase but they will find this place soon, we must be very fast."

The team went into action without any other greetings, first, the tarp was laid out, then bales of marijuana were thrown off the truck on the tarp. Pete had run to the plane for the canvas bags, Slick was about to ask about gas when he saw Luis's other truck come through the trees at the far end of the runway. He removed all the fuel caps, everyone was obviously in one hell of a hurry.

By the time Slick had filled the tank inside the cabin, Pete's gang had all the bales stacked by the door ready to load, the truck that had carried the dope left in a cloud of red dust. When Slick jumped out of the cabin and started filling the wing tanks, Pete jumped inside and yelled for bags to be passed in to him.

Slick could tell from the worried look on Luis' face that this was no joking matter, he wished the pump would pump faster but it didn't.

About half way through the left wing tanks, Pete came running, *"It's all loaded, let me finish gassing up, jump in and get ready to go, Luis is shitting his pants."*

"Okay, make damn sure those caps are on right."

Slick climbed up on the left wing and slid into his seat, he was sweating like a pig and puffing like a marathon runner.

Pete yelled, *"About twenty gallon to go, start the right engine!"*

Slick cranked the right engine, for the first time in it's life since overhaul, it didn't fire right away. Slick re-primed the engine and started cranking again, nothing.

What's with this fucking thing?

"What's the matter?"

"I'll try a hot start."

Slick gave the right engine a large dose of prime, then pulled the right mixture to idle cut-off and began cranking the starter, after about twenty rotations the engine barked, sputtered then roared to life as Slick slowly advanced the mixture to full rich. Slick gave Pete a thumb's up and took a deep breath. Pete closed the last fuel cap, ran around behind the left wing and jumped on, he then crawled across Slick and took his seat, his face was beet red.

"Let's get the fuck out of here!"

Slick used the hot start procedure on the left engine and it started on the first try, Luis was in the back of his truck waving for them to get the hell out of there. Slick goosed the throttles and sped down to the end of the runway, he closed the pilot's door as he turned in the direction of takeoff. As the Navajo neared the takeoff heading, Slick pushed the throttles ahead, slowly at first, then rapidly to full power. Ahead, the marijuana truck disappeared in the trees. Slick reached up to turn on both boost pumps, then lowered the flaps 15 degrees, so far no one was shooting at them.

The little plane accelerated down the runway and lifted off with room to spare, Slick raised the gear and flaps, then reduced the power, he lowered the nose to stay just above the tree tops so that nobody on the ground could get a good look or good aim at them.

"Holly shit, was that a rush or what."

"How come this thing wouldn't start?"

"The engines were still too hot, I had to use the hot start technique."

"My fucking heart is pounding, I wonder how close the bad guys were."

"Luis sure hauled ass, they must have been pretty damn close."

"You know we got some more problems, it's only ten, we're gonna hit Florida at six, it'll still be broad daylight. We'll be at the DZ at seven, Sam won't even be set up."

"I'll take a Florida jail to a Colombian jail anytime."

The two smugglers drank several bottles of water and juice as they climbed out over the Caribbean Sea, their heart rates were almost back to normal about the time the Navajo leveled off at 10,000 feet, by then they had decided how to handle their early arrival. They would make a daylight penetration into Florida at wave height. They knew from their Air Force experience that there was no radar outside the military that could see a target as small as the Navajo if it was hidden in ground clutter or in this case, wave clutter. After crossing the shore line, they'd stay low until it got dark, after dark, climb up to 5 or 6 thousand feet, power back and cruise up close to the drop zone. If there was no weather to dodge, there'd be 2 hours gas remaining at Lakeland, then it was a simple matter of flying around in circles at a low power setting until Sam came up on the radio. Better to be close to the DZ with a lot of gas then to waste time over the Bahamas, then run into some thick shit and have to eat the root.

"Pedro, how bout a steaming cup of coffee?""

"Coming up Señor Es Slicko."

The morning turned to afternoon, for the first time since he could remember, Slick caught the fuel pressure fluctuation and switched fuel tanks before the engines started sputtering.

The Navajo was starting to smell like marijuana, there hadn't been time to seal the tops of the bags with duct tape.

"How many bags we end up with?"

"I don't have a clue, we were in such a panic stuffin bags and throwin shit in the plane, I got no idea about the weight either."

"When you call Sam on the radio don't give him a number, he'll figure it out."

"The load is pretty fucked up back there, the first pass will

be a real goat fuck, there's bags stuck all over the place."

"No sweat my man, we'll get her done."

Hours droned by as the Navajo cruised along high over the beautiful chain of the Bahaman Islands. Grand Bahama Island appeared on the horizon 5 minutes after 5pm, descent to wave height in thirty minutes, it was almost show time.

"Well, at least we got to see this end of the Bahamas in daylight."

"As long as nobody sees us it's cool."

"Seeing us and figuring out what we're up to are two different things, whoever sees us will just think we're some more asshole pilots showing off in front of our girl friends."

Slick pulled back a little on the throttles, the Navajo began her gentle descent towards the sea below.

At 5:45, Slick banked left to the run-in heading and continued down to sea level plus a few feet.

"If a fish jumps, we're gonna nail it."

"Yell if you see any boats and I'll divert, wouldn't want to run into some Coast Guard cutter out here guarding America."

Skimming across the ocean a few feet above the waves at over a hundred miles per hour takes total concentration on the pilot's part, one hiccup could be game over and sudden death. Slick had both hands firmly attached to the control wheel, his eyes were fixed on the near horizon ahead. All Pete could do was to keep an eye open for boats, periodically glance at the engine instruments and hope that his complete faith in Slick's flying skill was justified.

"Twenty minutes to the beach."

"Roger, how's the heading?"

"Right on."

Pretty soon the coastline came into view, when Slick could make out the shoreline, he picked what looked like the most unpopulated stretch of beach and headed there. A quarter mile or so off the beach, Slick climbed up high enough to miss the power lines that ran up and down the coastal highway. Within seconds Highway 1 then Interstate 95 passed below the Navajo. Slick altered his heading a little to the right and dropped down again to tree top altitude. On this heading there was nothing ahead for 50 miles but the vast Okeechobee Swamps. The sun was on the horizon, it would be dark in 20 minutes.

When Yeehaw Junction was about 5 miles off the right wing, Slick added power and began a climb up to 4,000 feet.

"If anybody's following us now, they know something we don't."

"No way, even gun control radar can't stay on a target going between trees, those two deer we passed could jump higher than we were. Good job El Slicko."

"Thank you El Thrower of Pot, would you fly this thing for a minute so I can take a pee?"

"Sure, you go ahead and take a break, you been workin ur ass off."

Slick took the cap off one of the empty water bottles, unzipped his pants, pulled out his dick and pissed in the bottle.

"That feels better."

At 4,000 feet, Slick slowed down to the lowest power setting and fuel flow possible that would keep the Navajo in the air. The objective now was to burn as little fuel as possible while killing time, hopefully, Sam would be ready for them at the drop zone within an hour. Slick picked an area to loiter just north of Interstate 4 and Lakeland. The land below was sparsely populated and it was well within reach of the DZ by marine radio.

At 7:15, Pete made the first radio call, *"Happy hooker, radio check."*

A few seconds passed, *"I read you Hooker, can you call back in fifteen minutes?"*

"Happy Hooker, Roger."

"He sounded surprised."

Slick continued in a lazy orbit, if Sam cleared them to drop within 45 minutes there would be no problems with fuel, the Navajo was only using 22 total gallons per hour at this reduced power setting.

"I'm going to crawl back there and try to straighten out the mess."

Pete began burrowing through the bags of pot, within a minute his feet disappeared aft.

Slick could feel the center of gravity shift aft as Pete stacked bags in their pre-throw positions. As soon as the top layer of pot was dragged to the rear, the two flyers could communicate with each other by shouting.

"How's it look back there?"

"It's okay now, I'll be able to get it out in four or five passes, I'm coming back up front."

Five minutes after Pete got back in his seat it was time to give Sam another call.

"Happy Hooker, radio check."

Nothing.

"Happy Hooker, radio check."

"I read you Hooker."

Since Sam said nothing other than "I read you Hooker", the coast was clear.

"Shit hot, we're in business."

Slick banked sharply off in the direction of the drop zone, it was time to rock and roll. Pete crawled back to the rear as Lakeland passed the left wing, "Let's kick some ass, I'm ready for a beer or six."

"Five minutes!"

"Two minutes!"

"Door's coming open!"

"Get ready! Ready! Ready! Go! Go! Go! Go! Go! Go! Go! Stop! Stop! Stop!

Slick pulled up and began his second pattern, Pete could be felt rearranging bags for the next pass.

"I got six out!"

"Get ready! Ready!' Ready! Go1 Go!--------------------------
--------------------Stop!

The Navajo was empty after 4 passes, as Pete tidied up in the back, Slick flew off towards Leesburg, there was an hour fuel remaining according to the gauges.

"There are seeds and shit all over the place back here, this thing needs a good vacuuming and a scrub."

"Nothing we can do about it tonight. Let's get the tank out first thing, then come back later for a cleaning party."

The plan was laid, get the long range tank and all the paraphernalia safely hid in Tampa then come back to Leesburg in one of the Mercedes, have a couple of beers while giving her a good cleaning. Hardly a day went by that at least one plane wasn't surrounded by it's owner along with relatives and friends washing or polishing or just admiring. The ritual gatherings around the expensive aircraft seemed to be another status symbol of the wealthy visitors from the north. The smuggling gang would fit right in, just another celebration of having made it in a dog eat dog world.

When Slick switched the radio to Leesburg Tower, another pilot was talking, he was about to land and was asking for instructions.

"This is the first time we got back before the tower shut down, it's only eight forty."

Like a good little aviator, Slick called Leesburg tower when they were 10 miles away, gave his position and asked for landing instructions, after landing he called clear of the runway before switching to Leesburg ground. Ground control asked if they were familiar with the field, then cleared them to their usual parking spot. Slick shut the engines down just as Leesburg Tower announced that it was going off the air until the next morning at 8am.

There was one other car parked on the grass, somebody else was out there flying around, everything looked 100% normal. As soon as the plane was secured, the happy flyers walked rapidly across the street and headed towards the motel.

"May I offer you a beer mon capitaine?"
"Merci beaucoup mon ami."

Halfway through his beer Slick had an inspiration, *"Why don't we grab the tank and hit the road, it's still early enough for people to be coming and going over there."*

"Yeah, fuck it, I'd rather sleep in my own bed anyway, I'll go pay the bill and tell her we're leaving early in the morning. We always leave the key in the room anyway."

Thirty minutes later the van was racing along towards Tampa with two smiling smugglers sitting there bullshitting and drinking beer. Slick had called Rosemary, she would be waiting at the lake house, what could be easier?

"As long as nobody breaks in and sees all those seeds we're laughing."

"After we sweep the seeds up, we'll wash everything with some really smelly soap, nobody will ever know the difference. Jesus Pete, What are we gonna do with this fucking van?"

"Let's park it in the garage, I'll leave my car at the nursery. You park in the driveway right up next to the garage door."

And that's what they did. It took a little shuffling, Rosemary backed out of the driveway and parked her car in the street, Slick opened the garage, backed out in to the street, Pete drove the van inside the garage and closed the door. Slick carefully nudged his Mercedes up next to the door to keep any intruders out, work finished, Rosemary drug Slick inside where the stove element was glowing red.

"Why are you so early? Is everything okay?"

"It's a long story which will come out a lot better after a few hits of opium and another beer. You agree, Pedro?"

"Absolutely."

The flyers were still wired from the day's excitement so Rosemary got a long blow by blow description of the mission, she squealed with delight as Pete and Slick took turns re-living the entire episode, she may have even got a little embellishment here and there.

"Do you think they were shooting at you?"

"We could hear the bullets whizzing by the window."

"Really?"

"No, not really, we never saw anybody coming after us, but Luis and his men sure hauled ass out of there."

"It's still pretty exciting."

Pete and Slick met Sam in the morning, he shook his head in disbelief as he listened to the tale, *"I thought Luis owned the military down there, must be some new general trying to make points with the D.E.A."*

"Something was fucked up."

"No shit, the first time you called, me and Nevada were

still driving out to the drop zone. We couldn't believe our ears."

"How come you had the radio on?"

"Nevada was just fucking around with it, then boom, "Happy Hooker, you read me?" I about shit my pants. We hauled ass out there to the DZ and set everything up, we were almost ready when you called back."

"Slick and I were damn happy to hear your voice, the day had been bad enough without having to land somewhere with a plane load of dope."

"I guess you can't expect every flight to go totally perfect. Anyway, you guys did good, the pot is safe and sound in my garage, Nevada will be back in a couple of days with half the money, let's go clean that plane and get it ready for the big inspection. We got lots of work to do in the next month or so."

Pete chuckled and looked at Slick, *"I told you."*

"You told me what?"

"Where he'd hide the pot."

It was decided to take Sam's big 4 door Mercedes to Leesburg, seems it was registered to the same fictitious Mr. Allen as was the Navajo and the van. If somebody was watching, might as well have them looking for someone who doesn't exist.

"Gee Sam, I didn't know ur car belonged to Mister Allen."

"He owns a lot of shit."

On the way to Leesburg, Sam pulled in to the parking lot of a shopping center, Pete and Slick ran in to get cleaning supplies and enough beer for the cleaning party. Slick peeled off a bunch of twenties including one fake to pay the bill, not even Pete noticed.

At the airport, they lurked around for half an hour to decide if the Navajo was under surveillance, it didn't seem to be. Sam parked at the 24 hour restaurant next to their motel, everyone but Slick went in to get a sandwich. He walked down the road then across to the airport parking lot. There were several groups of people around various parked airplanes, a couple of guys waived and said hello. Slick took a close look at the plane, if anyone had tampered with her, they had left no signs, he unlocked the door and swung the 2 halves open. It was exactly as he and Pete had left it.

Ten minutes later, Sam pulled up and parked his Mercedes beside the Navajo. Slick ate his pastrami on rye while the others got to work. It only took a minute or two to sweep up the seeds and stems that littered the floor. With the carpet removed, the floor of the plane was smooth aluminum. Sam carefully put the tale tale seeds in a sack and carried them away. Pete went off with 2 new plastic buckets in search of water. An hour later, the Navajo smelled like a hospital room. Next, the carpet was re-installed, the cleaners took a break to enjoy a beer.

"What you do with those seeds?"

"I threw them under that expensive looking plane at the end of the next row, the owner is probably a fucking lawyer from New York, he'll have some questions to answer in a few months when those seeds sprout to life."

"Sam, you are a beauty."

"I don't much like lawyers."

The next operation was to take out the illegal fuel line that connected the long range tank to the aircraft fuel system. Slick had bought a special tool to speed up the removal of the several dozen screws that held in place the inspection panels that had to be removed in order to get at the fuel line.

Slick crawled under the plane, laid on his back under the panels and started unscrewing with the drill like tool, he dropped the screws in a plastic container as he removed them. As soon as the 2 inspection plates were off, it was a simple matter of removing a "T" fitting, replacing it with the original "U" fitting, then pulling the illegal fuel line out and finally replacing the inspection panels. Now, the only hint that an illegal fuel line had ever existed was the small hole in the floor of the cabin, who would know the reason for such a hole, it could have been put there for any number of reasons.

While Slick had been working under the plane, Pete had removed the few fittings in the cabin that had been installed for attaching ropes and bungee cords and straps. All the parts were put in one of the plastic containers and carefully stashed in Sam's trunk, they would all be needed again, soon, very soon. The Navajo was now ready to be flown over to the Piper dealer in Lakeland, she was once again squeaky clean.

"I'll drive over there tomorrow and make an appointment

for the hundred hour, hopefully we'll be able to bring her right over."

"Even if there're not ready to do the work, tell em you want to park the plane there while you're off somewhere on business, then we don't have to fuck around with the plane."

"Good idea, maybe I'll just fly it over there tomorrow after I talk to them, it'll be good to have it away from Leesburg for a couple of weeks. Pete, what you up to tomorrow?"

"Fuck-all, I'm ur man. Sam, can we use ur car?"

"Sure."

"That settles it, how bout another beer."

"Speaking of plans, you still planning on meeting your Colombian sweetie next week?"

"Everything was such a turmoil, I didn't get a chance to talk to Luis about her, maybe I'll just take a trip to Barranquilla and surprise her."

"Somebody needs to go down there and find out what we do next anyway. After the fiasco yesterday, we need more than a phone call to get everything straightened out."

"That makes it easy, I volunteer."

Pete drove Slick to the Piper dealer in Lakeland, the manager said they were quite busy but could promise to complete the 100 hour inspection in 2 weeks unless of course a serious problem was uncovered that required parts not on hand in Lakeland. That scenario would be rare since the dealership had a very complete parts department on the premises.

There would be no parking fee starting today until the inspection was complete, after that, $20 dollars per day. The manager went over the inspection procedure followed by his company. The inspection sheet gave an estimated number of hours required for the job, that multiplied by the shop rate of $35 dollars per hour equaled an inspection labor cost of $3,200 dollars plus all parts that needed replacing including oil and spark plugs.

Slick told the manager that he or Pete would check in with him twice a week by phone to see how things were coming along.

"The old guy who owns this plane really hates flying. We only fly him in good weather during daylight hours. What I'm say-

ing is, he doesn't like the thought of anything going wrong, so don't worry about cutting corners. If you think something needs replacing, replace it. The old fart is happy to spend a few bucks to keep his ass safe and sound."

The deal was made, the Navajo along with all the logbooks would be in front of the shop later in the afternoon. Payment was simple, all bills would be paid in full before the aircraft left the ramp.

"Okay thanks, see you in a couple of hours."

On the way to Leesburg, Pete asked about the logbooks, *"I've never even seen the logbooks. What's in them, a bunch of flights back and forth to Colombia?"*

Slick laughed, *"The aircraft log doesn't need to say where you went, it just shows the number of hours flown, I've put in a bunch of entries that add up to a hundred and five hours since our last inspection. The prop and engine logs all have a single entry showing a hundred five hours, don't worry, we're legal as shit."*

Pete stayed with his partner as the gas attendant put a hundred gallons of fuel in the Navajo's almost empty tanks. While Pete paid for the gas, Slick climbed in the plane and started the engines. When Slick started taxing towards the runway, Pete jumped in his car and drove off towards Lakeland.

Twenty minutes later as Pete was cruising along a deserted stretch of State Road #33, he was startled when the Navajo cut right across the road in front of his car no more than 20 feet above the ground. Pete watched as the Navajo pulled up sharply and into a tight barrel roll.

"That is one crazy bastard."

Chapter XII

The Man

Rosemary had two messages, Sam would be by at 6pm and Claudia had called. She was waiting at her house in Seattle for Pete to call back.

"What's she want?"

"Call her, she want's to talk to you."

Pete dialed the number that was written beside the phone, Rosemary led Slick outside, she was wearing a big smile.

"You'll never guess."

"She's pregnant."

"No you jerk, she's back with the doctor."

"No shit. The pictures did the trick?"

"He never saw them, he met her at the airport and begged her to forgive him, she's happy as hell. She just wanted to tell Pete herself."

Pete came outside, he was laughing and shaking his head, *"Guess what."*

"Rosemary told me."

"Now they're gonna try to have a baby."

"She's a lot better off with the doc whether he's a lousy fuck or not, she never came across as a party doll."

Rosemary couldn't resist, *"Pete, after being with you, maybe she can teach the doc a trick or two."*

"I'm sure he's not all that bad, Claudia was just pissed off, I wish her well, she's a nice broad."

"I hope she got rid of the pictures, the ole doc might not be that understanding."

"Don't worry, she burned them."

Sam had some interesting news, *"The Man is in town, he wants to meet with us later."*

Apparently most of the heat was off from whatever else he was involved in, not completely though, they would meet in a hotel room and not go out in public.

"He wants whatever cash that's his, you remember how much we got?"

"Yeah, the hundred eighty seven you took in the garbage bag."

"Bring ur dollar charts along so we can show him where everything's gone. How bout you two meet me at the causeway seafood joint at eight, I'll go get his loot."

After feasting on shrimp and soft shelled crab, Sam led the way to where the Man was holed up. Three quarters of an hour later, he parked in front of a little beach front hotel in Clearwater, Pete parked at the other end of the parking lot, he and Slick followed Sam up to the second floor, he knocked on the last door at the end of the balcony.

Slick couldn't have been more surprised, he was expecting a bad looking dude with at least one scar on his face from a knife fight, instead they were ushered in by a young slender man who greeted them with a rather high squeaky voice.

The Man embraced Sam and Pete, he then extended his hand to Slick, *"Good to finally meet you, they tell me you're a mighty fine pilot. I'm Ramon, everybody calls me Ray."*

"How's it going, Ray?"

"You don't want to know."

Ray opened the door to the adjoining room, *"Tina, bring some beer over here."*

Seconds later Slick discovered what you can buy with a lot of money. Tina was unbelievable, she looked around 17 years old, was about 5' 7" tall, had a perfect model's figure and the face of an angel. After she had served beer to the smugglers, Tina dutifully went back to her room, she hadn't said a word.

"She's still looking scrumptious."

"She ought to, she lives in spas and beauty parlors, spoiled little bitch."

"Slick, what you think of that?"

Slick could only mutter, *"Amazing."*

"If she's so much trouble, maybe you should unload her."

"I'll handle her Pete."

Slick could tell Ray didn't like Pete's suggestion.

Sam told everybody to sit down and relax, there was work to do.

Slick broke out his dollar charts to show Ray what they'd done with the money he'd advanced and where his ¼ share of the profits had gone.

Ray used the numbers from Slick's charts to tally up how much he'd sent out, this he put in one column. In the next column he jotted down the amounts that had been either deposited in his Cayman account or was in the black garbage bag at Sam's feet. After adding his share of the approximately $50,000 in stand-by cash, he was satisfied that the books balanced. Sam dumped the contents of the garbage bag on the coffee table. Sure enough, the pile of money totaled up to $187,000 dollars.

Sam told Ray that there would be a $200,000 dollar half payment for the 5th trip in a couple more days. From that, he'd get his final $51,000 for the expenses plus $72,000 for the cost of the pot plus his ¼ of whatever was left. From then on he'd get repaid the amount transferred to Luis for the dope plus his ¼ share. When they had made as many runs as they thought they could get away with, he'd get ¼ of whatever cash was left over plus ¼ of whatever they were able to sell the Navajo and van for.

Ray had one request, could the others front him the $51,000 expense money, *"I got some legal bills I got to settle tomorrow."*

Sam said he'd bring fifty over in the morning from his stash, everybody settled back to enjoy the spectacle of Tina serving more drinks. Besides being beautiful, Tina demonstrated skill, she rolled the most perfect joints Slick had ever seen. Ray lit one of the joints and passed it around, everybody partook except Slick.

"You fly this shit but don't smoke it?"

"I don't like what it does to me."

"He only smokes opium."

"Classy guy."

The party continued, somebody broke out a vial of cocaine, the room was full of marijuana smoke, Ray and Sam started talking about some way out things. Slick sat back and with his beer and listened to some amazing discussions.

"Whatever happened to Big John?"

"Yeah, Big John, the stud, the tough guy who always said

he'd take all secrets to his grave. When the narcs threw his ass in the slammer he didn't last long. Within six months he was a born again snitch. That mother fucker gave up more than thirty names including mine, if they ever mix him with the rest of the prisoners he won't last ten minutes."

"You worried?"

"Not too much, our lawyers have proven he's a liar who'll say anything to save his ass but I ain't taking any chances. You won't see me walking down main street while he's still shooting his mouth off."

Slick assumed that Big John, whoever he is, was the reason Ramon was hiding out here in Clearwater, one of Florida's many tourist traps.

From what Slick could glean from what he heard, it sounded as though Ray and Big John had been bringing in large quantities of marijuana for a long time, he heard them mention one shrimp boat load that weighed more than 5 tons. Slick did some fast math in his head, 10,000 pounds times $300 dollars a pound equals three million dollars. They then talked about some problems Ray's mob had had with a barge that had carried 12 tons. Jesus, that's seven and a half million.

Ray was reminiscing about the good old days when they brought in 3 tons twice a month in an old C-46 cargo plane, then drove away with the dope in U-Haul trucks. He and Sam agreed that those were the days, nobody paid any attention, nobody gave a shit, the D E A's only job was trying to bust heroin rings who brought in the really bad shit from Turkey or wherever heroine comes from.

Ramon switched the topic, he was now talking about buried money. Slick tried to listen more closely without being obvious, what he heard was beyond belief.

If he understood correctly, one afternoon at Big John's place somewhere in central Florida, Ray and Big John had got loaded, real loaded. They had decided to hide some of their cash because of a rumor that the narcs were getting ready to make a raid. They had buried more than half a million in various places around Big John's property. The money had been buried in about 10 different locations, each bag of money contained about $50,000 dollars.

Ray and Big John had gone to a lot of trouble preparing each bag for burial. First, they had jammed the money in a pillowcase or wrapped it in part of a sheet. Next, the package of money was put inside a black garbage bag, the garbage bag was then wrapped in a ball with duct tape. Next, the ball of money was put in several more black plastic garbage bags. Finally, the whole black ball was again tightly wrapped with duct tape. Of course, all the time Ray and Big John were preparing the money to be hidden, they were snorting cocaine, smoking pot and drinking large quantities of beer.

Ray yelled for Tina to bring some more beer, all the cocaine he had snorted had made him extremely thirsty.

Tina brought the beer, after she placed it on the table, she helped herself to a large snort of coke from the vial. While she was bent over to get at the vial of coke, Slick received a delicious view of the crack of her ass and pussy, the tiny panties she was wearing nicely disappeared in the lovely cleavage. Tina returned to her room, she still hadn't uttered a single word.

Ray guzzled half a beer and got back to the saga of the buried treasure.

Now that Big John was in jail and had turned on him, Ray decided he needed the money more than the chickenshit turncoat, so the day before he'd snuk over to Big John's now deserted house to retrieve the half million.

"It didn't dawn on me until I was standing there in the over grown yard that things looked a lot different than I remembered. The first two bags were easy to find, we'd buried them at the base of the two cypress trees that held up Big John's hammock. One of the cypress trees still had a rusty chain around it where the hammock had been tied."

Ray had dug up the 3rd bag next to the barbecue pit, then things got tough.

"I went into the workshop where we'd put the money in the bags and tried to visualize where we buried each bag, I tried to retrace my steps out of the shop to the spot where we buried each bag. All I could remember was that each bag was buried next to something obvious, you know, a tree, a barbecue, something permanent. I dug about a hundred holes and only found one more bag. By then I had a dozen blisters, look at my hands. Ray showed his

sore looking hands to Sam. *"I was so tired I could hardly move my arms, so I came back here."*

"At least you got a couple hundred grand, that's better than nothing."

But that wasn't the end of Ramon's tale of woe, two of the four bags he'd dug up had leaked, leaked bad. Over the months the soaked bills had more or less adhered to each other.

"What I got now are two balls of money that feels like it's all glued together in a solid lump, when I tried to peel off some of the bills, they just tore in my fingers. I don't know what to do, it's almost a hundred grand, I hate to just trash it."

"What you think Slick, you got any ideas?"

"Maybe if you ran warm water on the top bill, you could slowly peel them off one by one, then dry them. When the bills were dry, you could take small amounts to the bank and tell them you'd washed ur pants with the bills in ur pocket, it happens all the time."

Ray liked Slick's idea and made him an offer, *"You take the money and work on it, I'll split whatever you can salvage fifty fifty."*

"It's a deal."

Ray went into Tina's room, he returned with 2 big lumps in garbage bags, *"It's all yours."*

Sam brought the meeting to an end, *"Let's hit the road, I think Ray has better things to do than sit around bullshitting with us."*

"Okay you guys, keep up the good work, I may be needing the money to pay off all these fucking lawyers. I wish I'd been more careful with all the cash that's gone through my hands the last ten years, then I wouldn't have to worry about a lousy fifty grand to pay off the leaches."

Driving back to Tampa, Pete and Slick marveled at the several fortunes apparently squandered by the Man.

"How many millions you think he's blown?"

"Lots, he used to charter Lear Jets all the time, he's blown zillions on that fucking broad, they've gone to Europe about a dozen times."

"She is something."

Pete answered with a vile tone in his voice, *"She's a no good little coke whore, when Ramon first met her she'd fuck anybody for a line, now she thinks she's hot shit hanging around with the big guys, but trust me, she's still a no good bitch."*

"Ray sure seems to like her."

"Ah bullshit, he don't give a flyin fuck about her, those macho Cubans always got to have some good lookin pussy hangin on their arm so everybody knows they're cool. It's all a macho deal."

"No shit?"

"Yeah, no shit. Who's got the best lookin slut, who can blow the most money on bullshit, all macho crap. One night we were all at dinner at some fancy joint, I forget where. That little prick got loaded as usual and really made an ass of himself. He ordered a case of the wine we'd had with the meal at three hundred a bottle. You can get the same shit in any liquor store for eighty. He lit his Cuban cigar with a hundred dollar bill then threw Tina on the table and drank some brandy from her belly button. The place was jammed, if there were any cops sitting there, they would have known in a second what was going on, I tried to hide under the table. The macho crap has got him in a lot of trouble, if we hadn't needed his money to get started I wouldn't have anything to do with him."

"What about Sam?"

"Sam thinks it's funny but don't worry, Ramon won't set foot anywhere near our operation, Sam would rip his fucking balls off. I'm really surprised he let you meet Ramon."

"Guess I really miss-read the whole deal, him being Cuban never crossed my mind and I thought Tina was a classy little society girl."

"I saw her give you the full pussy shot, you think that was by accident?"

"I see what you mean."

"Just look at that hundred grand he gave you, the lazy fucker could have done just what you're going to do and saved himself fifty grand, but he had to be the big shot and pass it off to one of the underlings, what a macho prick."

"How much trouble is he in?"

"According to Sam, a lot. He could do some heavy time if

they can pin the barge deal on him, Louisiana laws are a lot stiffer than Florida."

"Does Big John know enough to hurt him?"

"Fuck yes, they were partners, it was their deal, he knows everything."

"You don't like him do you?"

"Not a bit and he knows it."

"Now that I think about it, you sure were quiet over there tonight."

"Him and the slut are so phony, she tried to fuck me more than once, I loved telling her to fuck off."

Pete and Slick came to at least one conclusion, if they heard anything about Ramon getting busted, they would instantly stop operating, sell the toys and get the hell out of Dodge. This conclusion was based on Pete's strong feeling that Ramon would start singing like a canary as soon as it looked like he might be facing hard time.

"That little macho prick knows damn good and well that his cute little ass would become a punching board for a bunch of big black cocks if he ever landed in a real prison, he'd sell out his mother and the Virgin Mary to stay out of jail."

"Why doesn't he just haul ass?"

"He still thinks his crooked lawyers can keep him out of jail."

"You think they can?"

"They'll keep fighting as long as he keeps paying."

"I see."

"Now you know why we're as small as we are, if you don't know nothin, you can't tell nothin."

"You know Pete, a couple of months ago you told me that the mysterious money man would never rat."

"I admit I lied, I wanted you to join us. That's the only lie, I promise."

"Shit man, I'm glad, this whole deal has been a real gas, plus I've earned more money in the last month than the rest of my life put together."

"Cool Hand Slick."

"Why don't we go dig up all that cash, there must be some kind of money detector we could buy."

"I don't have any idea where Big John's house is, I think

Sam knows."

"For that kind of money we could take a backhoe to the whole fucking yard."

"Let's wait til they've all been in jail for a year or two, then we'll buy the house and start digging."

When Slick told Rosemary about the wet money, she got so excited she had to take a look. Within a minute she had covered the bed with newspaper and dumped the contents of the 2 bags between Slick's legs.

"That's not as bad as I thought, I was expecting mush."

"No kidding, let's take it over to your house tomorrow so we can spread it out and figure out what to do, this could be the easiest fifty grand in history."

Slick and Pete met downstairs around 11am, they had some decisions to make about who was going to do what between now and the resumption of flying. Their first decision was to do nothing until one of them spoke with Carlos, Pete would try to get through later that afternoon.

Rosemary and Slick headed for her house with the soggy money. Step one was to try to separate the little bundles. Some bundles on the outside of the ball that were dryer came away from the mass with just a little steady pressure. Since the dryer ones came apart, Rosemary decided to take one of the balls of money out on her balcony where they would get the full effect of the afternoon sun. Slick tried the complete opposite technique, he held his ball of money under the kitchen sink tap and adjusted the water temperature until it was lukewarm. He discovered that if he kept a steady gentle pressure on one bundle while aiming the stream of water between the two bills that formed the bond, slowly but surely they came apart. He assumed that this same procedure would work on individual bills but the first job was to separate the bundles of $5,000 dollars. It was going to take some time but what the hell, damn few people he could think of earned a hundred dollars a minute.

Rosemary came in to observe, she started working on the first one hundred dollar bill that was on the outside of the first bundle Slick had separated from the mass. She found that by holding the bundle under water, she could slowly but surely peel it away from the bundle. As soon as she had a free bill, she took it outside to dry on a towel.

"When it's almost dry, I'll iron it, it's going to be as good as new."

"Good work."

As Slick got closer to the middle of the glob, the condition of the money got a lot worse, the center of the ball was just that, a ball. Slick decided to just let the ball soak to see if the bills would begin to separate.

Rosemary continued peeling off one bill after another, by the time she'd got the 10th hundred dollar bill separated, the 1st one was almost dry. She then brought out her ironing board and steam ironed bill number one. Like she had said, after ironing, the bill was almost as good as new, a little stiffer than your average bill, but one hundred percent useable.

The sun had had an interesting effect on the 2nd ball of money. Some of the outside bills had dried and curled up like potato chips, the curling had popped some of the bills away from each other. The driest bill felt so brittle that it might break if it was straightened out. Rosemary sprayed it with a mist of water, flattened it out and finally steam ironed the note.

The money separating team soon discovered that the sun dried the bills too quickly and too dry, with their new knowledge, they began hanging the separated wet money on a string Slick had strung the length of the kitchen. Before long, there were several strings of drying hundred dollar bills strung along one side of Rosemary's kitchen.

There was no doubt that Slick's warm water method was far superior in separating bundles and single bills, so Rosemary brought the money that was outside in out of the sun, they would use the warm water technique later when ball of money # 1 had been dealt with.

By 5pm, Rosemary had ironed 162 one hundred dollar bills, there were another 59 wet bills drying on strings in the kitchen. That meant that in the last 4 hours, Slick and Rosemary had salvaged $22,100 dollars from the 1st wet mass of recovered buried treasure. If half of it was theirs, they had earned $11,050 dollars or $2,762 dollars and fifty cents an hour, not a bad wage.

Slick figured they could get about the same amount from the 2nd wet blob of money in the same amount of time the next day, after that, the process was going to slow way down. The money on the inside was going to be a lot harder if not impossible to get apart.

"Let's go see if we can spend one of these, I think I could eat just about a hundred dollars worth of shrimp right now, I'll call Pete and see if he'll meet us."

Pete met them on the causeway at the usual seafood place, he had not been able to talk with Carlos but was pretty sure he'd got the message across that he would call in the morning and would continue to call every hour until Carlos was at the phone.

Slick told the restaurant owner that he had put his pants in the washing machine with some money in the pocket, that was the reason the hundred dollar bill looked like it had been washed and ironed, indeed, it had been washed and ironed. The restaurateur said he didn't care, money is money.

Pete laughed, *"This is going to taste great knowing it's on you know who, how'd that work out?"*

"We got a little over a third of the first bag separated, it's gonna be slow going from now on. I think about half the money is fucked."

"Too bad, but can you imagine those two stoned out idiots losing half then burying the other half under the level of the water table. If I was you, I'd give him back twenty-five percent of what you recover, fuck him."

"I don't want him having any reason to ever look me up, like you said, he's bad news."

"It's up to you but he'd never know."

"A deal's a deal."

Rosemary was surprised at the tone of their voices, *"I thought he was the Man."*

"More like a fucking mouse."

"Pete doesn't much like him."

"That's obvious."

"Speaking of money, Sam says Nevada will be here tomor-

row to pick up the shit, he'll have half the money with him."

"How's he gonna make the switch?"

"He wants you and me to help him unload his four by four, seal up the bags and weigh the dope, then Nevada will back in to Sam's garage and we'll throw it in his truck and he's out of here."

"Sounds okay to me, what do you think?"

"I don't like being in the same place with that much pot any longer than I have to but I guess we gotta get it outta there, we can't expect Sam to do it all alone."

The deal was set, the next day Pete and Slick would meet Sam at his house just before dark, unload and weigh the dope and get it ready for Nevada. When Nevada backed his pick-up inside Sam's garage, it would take the 3 of them less than a minute to throw the 27 or 28 bags in the back of the truck, Nevada would head north and the coast would be clear. As soon as Nevada left, they'd clean up the garage, then drive over to the lake house to split up the cash.

"I'll be at Rosemary's most of the day messing with soggy money, give me a call if anything changes, now let's go home and smoke some opium."

"What a good idea, you're a mind reader."

Rosemary got started on the second batch of money while Slick went back to work on number one. There was no more simply peeling off one wet bill after another. Now, after peeling back the corner of the top bill, Slick use the sharp edge of a fillet knife to gently cut, then peel, cut a little more, peel then cut, all the time running warm water at the point of the operation. Slowly but surely, he was able to separate more bills, not all of them were perfect, some had holes where Slick had been a little too aggressive and sliced through the bill. Others had little patches of the bill missing, the missing patches simply refusing to be detached from one of the bills on either side. Regardless, Slick was positive that he would be able to exchange the damaged money a little at a time at any bank. Banks always set aside worn out or damaged notes to be swapped for brand-new bills from the US Treasury, everybody knew that.

A little after 2pm, Slick figured he'd separated every bill

from the ball of money that was separable, the remaining glob was just too solid, in fact, the last 4 or 5 bills he'd been able to remove were in pretty rough shape. His take for the day was 44 one hundred dollar bills in varying stages of condition. That brought the total amount rescued from the 1st ball of wet money to $26,500 dollars. By counting the ends of the remaining bills in the remaining bundles that were bonded together, Slick estimated that there was approximately $20,000 dollars remaining in the 1st mass of money, $20,000 that he knew of no way to change into spendable cash.

Oh well, every hundred dollar bill they were able to save was fifty dollars free ass money, not a bad deal.

While Slick had slaved away for 5 hours over the almost solid core of his ball of money for a miserly $4,400 dollars, Rosemary had kicked ass. It turned out that the 2nd wet bag of money wasn't in nearly as bad condition as the first. Rosemary had separated and hung to dry 205 bills and she was still peeling at a steady rate.

Having done all he could, Slick wrapped what was left of his money ball in a towel and began assisting Rosemary.

"Compared with what I had, this is a piece of cake."

"I think we'll be able to get most of this one, it doesn't seem to be getting any harder towards the middle."

"I'm tired of this shit, a few more bills and it's time for a couple of beers, then I gotta go meet Pete and Sam, we got work to do."

While Slick peeled off hundred dollar bills, Rosemary steam ironed the dry and almost dry bills, before leaving, she was able to lock another twenty grand in her big steel safe, the remainder they left hanging to dry in the kitchen.

"Who's buying tonight?"

"Who do you think?"

"The Mouse."

"You got it."

Slick and Rosemary were back at the lake house before 5, Pete was there. *"Let's hit the road my man, Sam is waiting."*

During the drive over to Sam's house, Pete filled Slick in on his day's events. He had been able to have a long talk with Carlos. According to Carlos, everything was okay in Colombia, the little episode with the military had been handled with a rather large payoff to a new regional general. The new general was now on the payroll and had promised full co-operation in the future. Carlos had insisted that a trip was totally unnecessary, but if any of them wanted to visit, they were more than welcome.

"He say anything about Magda?"

"You say the word, she's on the way, he even had the schedule for flights to Costa Rica."

"I'll be damned. Fuck it, I'm going down there as soon as we get rid of this pot and I get this wet money straightened out."

"Not sure I blame you."

Sam was ready, he had been to the hardware store where he'd bought a large blue plastic tarp, several rolls of duct tape and 4 cans of deodorizing spray.

Slick helped Sam partially spread the tarp out behind his 4X4 truck, there wasn't enough room between the rear end of the 4X4 and the back wall of the garage to spread out the tarp so Sam opened the garage door and drove the pick-up half way out. As soon as there was enough room, Pete and Slick spread the tarp out and began unloading the canvas bags of marijuana. When the pick-up was empty, Pete swept up whatever seeds and stems had fallen out of the bags into the back of the truck. Sam then drove completely out of the garage, he came back inside closing the door behind him.

It only took a minute or so for the threesome to prepare each bag. First, Sam stood the bag on end, next he made sure the drawstring was tight, then he twisted the top of the bag as tight as he could. Pete then made continuous wraps around the neck of the bag with duck tape until it was sealed. The sealed bag was then set on a scale where Slick was waiting to accomplish several steps. First, he sprayed the bag with deodorizer, second he slid the weights of the scale until they balanced, third, he wrote the weight of the bag on a piece of paper. Slick's final step was to carry the sealed bag to the far end of the tarp where he started a neat stack.

Twenty five minutes later there were 26 sealed and sweet smelling bags of dope stacked against the rear wall of the garage, Slick totaled up the weight, 1170 pounds. Pete rolled up the end of the tarp where they'd sealed the bags to trap any debris, Slick moved the scale to the far side of the garage and Sam opened the garage door.

"You guys follow me over to the nursery, he should be there by now."

Sam drove off in his 4X4, Slick followed in Sam's Mercedes and Pete tagged along in his Mercedes. Sam purposely left the tailgate and camper shell doors open so any seeds or stems they'd missed would blow out.

Nevada's red Ford pick-up with it's distinctive red camper shell was parked in front of the nursery, Nevada and one of his drivers were standing by the rear of the truck. Sam parked his pick-up and went over to talk with Nevada, Pete parked his car and hopped in with Slick. A few minutes later Sam walked over with the plan.

"You guys go first, park my car in front of the house and be ready to open the garage door as soon as we back in the driveway, we'll throw the shit in and the driver will haul ass. We'll drop Nevada off at his hotel, he's got a plane to catch a little later on."

"What about the money?"

"It's in the back of his truck, only one ninety."

"Okay, see you at ur place in ten minutes."

When Nevada's truck backed into the driveway, Slick opened the garage door, Nevada continued half way inside the garage. The driver went to the rear and unlocked the camper shell door, he then pulled out a large white sheet of canvas exposing a cardboard box. The driver slid the box to the rear, Sam grabbed it and put it on top of his washing machine. Everybody started passing bags of dope in to the driver, he made as neat a load as could under the circumstances. When the 26 bags were loaded, Pete handed the driver the piece of white canvas, he tucked the canvas around the edges of the bags, made sure that the little curtains on the side windows of the camper shell were drawn, jumped out and locked the back door.

"I'm outta here."

"Don't get no speeding tickets, ur not in any hurry."

"No sweat, later."

The driver left, Sam took the blue plastic tarp out on the lawn and shook it, they were once again clean as a whistle.

"*Last time the fucking idiot got stopped for speeding, I'll kill him if it happens again.*"

"*Was he carrying a load?*"

"*Yeah, ur stuff.*"

"*I'd a shit my pants.*"

"*He's pretty ballsy.*"

"*Let's get going.*"

Slick tossed the cardboard box in the trunk of Sam's Mercedes, Pete ran in the house for a six-pack, Sam sprayed two cans of deodorizer in his garage, the end of another hard day's work.

They had a little powwow in the cocktail lounge of Nevada's hotel, Slick gave him the weight.

"*Bags and all it's eleven seventy, so there should be about one thousand one hundred forty pounds of stuff. So, you owe us three hundred eighty seven thousand six hundred plus five thousand six hundred from the last load for a total of three hundred ninety three thousand two hundred. Three ninety three is close enough, minus the one ninety in the box equals what?*" Slick grabbed a napkin to do the math problem on:

$$1140 \times 340 = \$387{,}600$$

387,600		393,000	
+5,600	from last load	-190,000	in the box
393,200	total	203,000	bal. Due

"*Another two hundred three thousand and we're square.*"

"*Looks good to me, when's the next go?*"

"*About two weeks, we're down for maintenance.*"

"*Good. That will give us a chance to catch up, that fucking Ronnie bought a ton of real crap, we can't even give some of it away.'*

"*Can't you just give it back?*"

"*It's a totally fucked up deal, I hope he's learned his lesson, I buy, he sells, but don't worry, you'll get paid off. I won't let him pay for that other shit with the money we get from ur stuff.*"

"Okay Nevada, good luck with the brain surgeon, we'll be in touch when we're ready to go."

Sam dropped Pete off at the nursery to pick up his car, they all met at the lake house to figure out who got what part of the money and to barbecue some steaks.

Slick still had the chart he'd shown the Man or Mouse 2 days earlier.

Everything was almost still the same, the only change was a reduction in the amount of available cash.

The $54,300 cash reserve was now $48,000. Pete had taken $1,300 to buy gas for the fuel drums, he still has $700 plus a little change. Slick had taken $5,000 in hundreds to carry on the last flight in case of problems. He still had the entire $5,000 and threw it back in the reserve cash bag. The cash reserve was back up to $53,000.

Sam dumped the contents of the cardboard box on Slick's bed, there were 38 bundles of hundreds, 38 X $5,000 should equal $190,000, it all depended on how much fake money Ronnie had unloaded on them.

$ 190,000 received
-$ 51,000 last expenses
$ 139,000 bal.
-$ 72,000 stuff
$ 67,000 balance to be divided by 4

Sam suggested they make the last balance an even $80,000 by taking a little out of the cash reserve, he liked even numbers.

Slick took thirteen thousand in twenties out of the reserve bag, each partner got $20,000 or ¼ of eighty thousand. The rest went to the Man who they all now referred to as the Mouse. The $190,000 was now completely accounted for, from now on, the Mouse was due no more expense money, everything was paid off. Future deductions would only be to compensate the Mouse for money transferred from his Cayman account to Luis for the cost of the marijuana. The cash reserve was now an even $40,000.

Sam borrowed 2 paper bags to carry his and the Mouse's

cash, he didn't forget to take $50,000 of Mouse's $51,000 for the loan he'd made to the Mouse earlier in the day.

"I hope I got this straight, he gets seventy two thou for the pot, twenty for his one quarter and the one left over from the fifty one for the last expenses. That seem right?"

"It's right on, you should have ninety three in his sack and seventy in yours."

"I'll get it to him tonight, he's up to his ass in legal bills, those crooked fucking lawyers are really screwing his ass."

Slick broke out the ultraviolet light. *"We better check this shit before one of us tries to pay a parking ticket with a fake hundred."*

It didn't take long, the twenties had already been gone over. There were three bad bills, two of them were right next to each other in Sam's grocery bag, all three were excellent specimens of forged money. Slick added them to his little pile of fake money to be passed around later on.

While the boys had been sorting out the money situation, sweet Rosemary had been busy getting diner ready. She had tossed a green salad, cleaned half a dozen ears of corn and marinated four thick New York steaks. When the money shuffling was complete, she turned on the burner under the corn and lit the barbecue.

"This place sure is dull without Brenda, I miss seeing those fine hooters she was so proud of showing off."

"I have to admit there are certain parts of her I miss too."

"What are you doing for pussy these days, Pete?"

"Rosemary sneaks upstairs when you're asleep.'

"I do not!"

"Don't worry about me, I got a lawyer's wife who's always on standby, I saw her again this morning."

Rosemary was incredulous, *"Is that true?"*

Sam, the lawyer hater loved it, *"It's true, he's been fucking that asshole's old lady for years."*

Rosemary was hard to convince, *"How do you know?"*

"A year or two ago I caught them red handed coming out of a hotel room, ain't that right, Pete?"

"You sure as hell did, I thought she was going to piss her pants."

"You know her?"

"She's my next door neighbor, I see her all the time, nowadays Pete usually fucks her in my house, she just jumps over the fence."

"You guys are terrible. Sam, I have to ask, what were you doing at that hotel?"

"Shit, I don't even remember, probably dropping off or picking up some money, Pete's the pussy hound, not me. Since I've had Sarah I don't even think about other broads."

"Where is darling Sarah?"

"She's home, sometimes she likes to be alone, you know her, she's different."

As soon as Sam finished eating he left, it was a long drive to Clearwater and back. Pete took off in search of female companionship, Slick and Rosemary smoked opium and had a not so quiet night at home, the American dream was no dream, they were living proof.

By two o'clock the following afternoon, Slick and Rosemary had unstuck every bill they thought could be unstuck without totally destroying the paper notes. From the 1st ball of money, which was in worse condition by a mile, 265 one hundred dollar bills had been salvaged.

Wet ball of money #2 had been in remarkably better condition, every bundle had been separated and only part of one bundle was in such bad shape that all the individual bills refused to come apart. Slick came up with a total of 393 bills, $39,300 dollars with about $3,000 still left in a mushy glob.

Not counting the $200 they'd spent, fuck it, make that $500, their three days work had produced $65,800 dollars, half of that was $32,900.

"How many hours do you think we spent on this?"

"Four the first day, five yesterday and seven so far today, sixteen all together."

"Let's make it fifteen, what say I give you a thousand an hour."

"A thousand dollars?"

"What do you think, peanuts."

"Gosh, thanks, that's more than big time call girls get."
"Don't worry, you're going to earn it."
"When can I start?"

Slick opened the big steel safe, he needed to count up his cash and try to remember where it all came from and stash the recovered money he and Rosemary had been working on.

$ 10,000 in twenties left over from the first deposit.
$ 65,000 in hundreds from Nevada's payment of $400,000
$ 20,000 hundreds from the $190,000 plus some twenties
$ 95,000 total   from cash reserve
$ 17,900 Slick's share of the damaged money.
$112,900 total

Slick felt certain that if he offered the Mouse $25,000 of undamaged money, he'd accept, he couldn't see Mister Macho Man going in and out of banks turning in damaged money. That would earn him another $7,900 easy bucks. The last load owed him about $50,000 plus his ¼ share of the plane plus $200,000 in his Cayman account. Shit! He was worth four hundred thousand mother fucking dollars and they were just getting this smuggling shit down pat.

"What are you going to do with what's left of the wet money?"

"I don't know, I think I'll dry it and save it, some bank might give me a few bucks for it one of these days. I don't have any idea what they do with money this fucked up."

Slick put the remains of the wet money on a small towel in a cardboard box and put the box out on the enclosed balcony, he figured a week in Florida's sun would make it as dry as a bone, he'd deal with it later.

"You need any cash before I lock this up?"

"Guess not, I just stole another three hundred from the Mouse, I got about a thousand in good forgeries, we got a ton of steaks and wine, everywhere I go is on the tab, I got a rich old lady, whenever we go out Sam always pays the bill, somebody gave me a Mercedes and a plane, I got no rent, my only financial problem is a girlfriend who charges a thousand bucks an hour."

"I'm worth every cent, aren't I?"

"*Sure, doll, let's hit the road, me and the boys got business to discuss.*"

"*Don't forget your apartment rent in Manhattan Beach.*"

"*Fucking Pete paid six month's in advance before we left plus I got two or three thousand in my pocket, shit, I don't even know where it came from, we hardly ever work, this is the best damn job anybody ever had.*"

CHAPTER XIII

THE BROWN EYED GIRL

"What's the plan?"

Slick pulled a small calendar out of his pocket that he'd made notes on. *"I'll call Carlos tomorrow, see if he can put the girl on Friday's flight to San Jose, if it's okay, I fly down Wednesday or Thursday, there's two or three direct flights every day from Miami. Friday's the twenty eighth, she and I can hang around in Costa Rica til the fourth of November or if you guys think it's necessary, I could fly down to Colombia on the second, talk with Luis and Carlos, fly back here on the fourth. We grab the plane and we're ready to go again by the sixth or seventh."*

"I think you ought to go see them, you get a better idea of what's going on in person. You could show Luis on paper where every cent has gone, you know, compare the weights with deposits, we want those guys to trust the hell out of us. What do you think, Pete?"

"Yeah, you're right."

"Okay with you, Slick?"

"Sure, maybe I could get them to fly me out to the other landing strip again, I'd like to get another look at it before the real thing."

"Good, that settles it. We'll pay for your tickets and throw in a couple of grand for expenses, that sound okay?"

"Hell yes, more than fair."

The meeting continued, Pete would be in charge of keeping tabs on the Navajo, he would call Slick in Costa Rica from a pay phone to keep him posted on the plane's progress, they set a day and time for the call.

Slick would buy his tickets to Costa Rica from Pete's ticket agent friend, he'd buy the tickets to Colombia in San Jose, no use advertising that you're going to the marijuana and cocaine capital of the world. Sam would hold the next payment if he got it before Slick got back from down south.

The cocktail waitress brought another round of drinks, the

three smugglers toasted the hectic and profitable past 30 days.

"Speaking of money, you still in touch with Ramon?"

"Yeah, he's still over there."

"Could you tell him I got everything I can out of his wet money, about sixty two thousand. Some of it's pretty fucked up, tell him I'll give him twenty five thousand good money so he doesn't have to fuck around with trading the damaged shit. If that doesn't fly, I'll bring the whole pile over and we'll split it up, it's up to him."

"He'll take the twenty five, he ain't taking no chances of some cop asking where he got a bunch of fucked up hundred dollar bills, I'm so sure I'll take twenty five of my own along when I give him the message."

"You think he'll want to see what's left?"

"Fuck no, you say it's trash, it's trash."

"In that case, this round's on me."

"It's still on me, I'm only gonna give the little fucker twenty, I pick up a fast five for driving to Clearwater and back."

Pete was obviously pleased to see the Mouse getting fucked over. *"That little prick is just gonna give it to those fucking lawyers, they must really have him by the balls. I wonder how much he's got left."*

"I don't think it's all that much, he's always been a big spender and there's a whole law firm living off his ass. Bet he doesn't have a million bucks to his name."

Pete added, *"We'll know when he's getting low on dough, that little whore will be out on her ass."*

When Slick got back to the house he told Rosemary he was going down to Colombia to make sure both sides were clear on what had happened and what they would do in the future. He'd be gone about a week.

"That's okay, I'll drive up to Atlanta and visit my mom and sister, I should be able to trade off some of my new found wealth, there are hundreds of banks up there."

"Slowly, slowly, there's no hurry, don't draw any attention to yourself, you'll be able to spend it just as well ten years from now."

"Don't worry, I had good training from my ex."

"Let's not forget to run it all through the ultra-violet light before handing a counterfeit hundred over to some stuffy banker."

They settled on a nutritious dinner of Kentucky Fried Chicken with mashed potatoes and gravy, 2 bottles of red wine and several hits of opium.

"I think I've become a hedonist."

"You've become a what?"

"A hedonist. Hedonists follow the doctrine that the pursuit of pleasure is the highest good."

"Where in the world did you ever learn a word like that?"

"Philosophy course in college."

"That's all they do is pursue pleasure? I could get hooked on that."

"That's it, that's all they do, the constant search for things that taste better, look better and feel better. That's the whole idea behind trying to make all this money."

"I think what you are doing is part of it."

"What do you mean?"

"I mean, you guys love this whole deal, I've never seen three grown men turned on so much, you know, the adventure, the danger, breaking all those laws right in everybody's face and getting away with it."

"I never thought about it like that, maybe you're right."

"I know I'm right, you should see the looks on your faces when you get back, like kids at Christmas."

"It is a rush."

Slick went with Pete to a Holiday Inn to make some phone calls. Pete called his travel agent friend to see if she could book a round trip flight to San Jose, Costa Rica in the next two days. Slick phoned the Piper dealership to check on the progress of the Navajo. Pete found out that either day had plenty of seats available on either Eastern or LACSA, Costa Rica's national airline. The manager of the dealership told Slick that they'd finished the airframe and were about to start on the engines, so far they hadn't found any major problems, Slick said he or Pete would call back the following Tuesday. Pete put the collect call through to Colombia, someone on the other end accepted the charges, a few seconds later Carlos was on the line, he promised he'd personally put Magda on the flight to San Jose Friday the 28th. He asked that Slick call him at the same number to confirm he would be arriving in Barranquilla, November the 2nd so he could make the necessary arrangements at Immigration.

"Everything's set, when do you want to leave?"

"Think I'll go tomorrow, I've never been to Costa Rica, this'll give me a couple of days to check the place out before she gets there."

Pete called the travel agent back, he told her his friend wanted to travel the next day, she said she'd have the tickets ready in about an hour, Pete told her he was on the way.

After picking up the tickets, there were a few more tasks to be taken care of. Back at the house Slick took five grand from the cash bag, then gave the bag to Pete for safe keeping while he was away.

"You think of anything else?"

"I have to make a quick run over to Rosemary's, after that all I got to do is pack. I think we'll hang around here tonight and burn a steak, you want to join us?"

"You two have a romantic night, I think I got a date."

"You dog, you didn't."

"I'll know a little later."

Slick called to make sure Rosemary was at her house, when she answered, he told her to hang tight, he'd be right over. He wrapped the ultra-violet light in a towel and left.

Being soaking wet for months had had an interesting effect on the money, it all had a dull glow when under the light. They were only able to find one obvious fake in the bunch, there were several that seemed to glow a little more than the others but they looked perfect after a close examination by eye. Slick burned the counterfeit outside on the balcony. It was a good fake, but it's stiff and ultra clean appearance would make even the most novice handler of money suspicious.

The remainder of the money that was drying was now as hard as a rock on the outside, but still made squishing sounds when

Slick pushed on it, he decided to leave it in the sun. Nothing but fire could make it any worse off.

They went through all of the money that had been salvaged, several of the bills needed repairs with scotch tape, others had wounds that couldn't be repaired.

Slick tried to pick the best of the lot to make up Rosemary's $15,000, he didn't want her to have any trouble when trading in the damaged money, trouble for her would probably mean trouble for him.

Slick sorted his pile of recovered money into small stacks of $2,000 dollars. He put each little pile into an individual envelope, his thinking was that the envelopes would protect the bills from any further damage until someday later on when he would begin the slow process of trading the damaged money for virgin bills. He ended up with 25 envelopes for a total of $50,000 plus the best 7 one hundred dollar bills he'd been able to find after giving Rosemary her share. He figured he'd be able to trade these 7 in at his leisure after returning from Costa Rica. Rosemary helped with the final step in protecting the fragile $50,000. She carefully folded the ends of the envelopes so they would fit crossways in an empty shoebox. After all 25 envelopes were snugly stacked side by side in the shoebox, Rosemary filled the empty spaces with toilet paper, the paper would prevent the envelopes from bouncing around and would also absorb any moisture. Finally, she held the shoebox while Slick wrapped it with masking tape, she then stuck the neat little package in the big steel safe, a job well done.

"I gotta go see Sam. I'll meet you at the house around six, let's have another of those steaks paid for with counterfeit money, they seem to taste better than legal ones."

"See, I told you, you think being a crook is cool."

"We're not crooks, we're just the boys who bring in the crop."

The three partners met at the nursery to go over anything Slick needed to pass on to Luis and his crew. Sam wanted to make sure Slick let Luis know how happy they were with the way things had been handled and what a professional outfit Luis had assembled. Also, so far, the quality of the marijuana had been outstanding, just make sure it stayed the same. The most important item was how much weight they had paid for. A careful check of Slick's miniature charts showed that Luis had received payment for 60 pounds that he hadn't shipped, they decided to call it close enough, after all, Luis had taken damn good care of them on various trips south.

Slick made up a little chart showing on one side the weights they had brought in on the first 5 flights. They were the exact amounts recorded in Colombia before loading the plane with the exception of the last flight where there hadn't been time to do anything but load up and haul ass. On the other side of the chart were the dates and the amounts of money transfers to Luis's account.

#1	1191 pounds	Sept. 20	$72,000 phone transfer
#2	1296 pounds	Sept. 23	$72,000 phone transfer
#3	1260 pounds	Sept. 27	$72,000 phone transfer
	3750 pounds	Oct. 4	$ 9,000 from Cayman
	3750 X 60 = $225,000< ⋯⋯⋯ >		$225,000
#4	1193 or 1200	Oct. 4	$72,000 from Cayman
#5	1140 or 1200	Oct. 15	$72,000 phone transfer
	60 X 2400 = $144,000< ⋯⋯⋯ >		$144,000
	total $369,000< ⋯⋯⋯ >		$369,000

"How's that look, simple enough?"

"Clear as a bell, if I can figure it out, those Colombians can too, let's have a couple of drinks."

Everybody took their own car, later on they would all be going off in different directions.

Sam got there first and had three cold Buds on the table when Slick and Pete walked in the bar, "I forgot to tell you, Mister Mouse took the twenty and said thanks."

"You want me to run and get your money?"

"Naw, I'll just take it when Nevada brings the rest for that last load, relax, have a beer."

"Pete, you got a date tonight with that set of legs?"

"She's going to meet me, she's bringing her own car, guess she doesn't trust me."

"Smart girl."

"Who you talkin about?"

"Pete's got a hot new chick he's hustling, she's got great legs, she even has a brain."

"I miss Brenda's tits, what you gonna do with a brain?"

"I think she might end up with a pretty hot body, you know, one of those slender babes with curvaceous legs and ass and ski jump tits."

"How bout your Colombian doll, Slick?" She must be *something special for you to go running off all the way to South America."*

"Sam, if I described her body, you'd think I was lying."

"It's that good?"

"Better."

"I gotta see this, take some pictures."

"Your heart in good shape?"

"She that hot, Pete?"

"I never saw her naked, but what I saw was fucking mind bending, not only that, she's beautiful."

"You fucking bastards! God damn, you gotta bring her up here, I wanna meet this broad." Sam yelled for another round.

"I might just do that."

"Okay you horny fuckers, screw ur brains out for the next week or so, then we got some work to do. I think we might pull off another five to ten runs before we start attracting any heat, let's kick some ass. We'll never get a chance like this again."

The meeting was over, the three happy smugglers took off in their separate directions.

Slick got back to the lake house at 7pm, Rosemary had everything ready including a red hot burner on the stove.

"You already into the opium?"

"I didn't turn it on until I saw you drive up, besides, you're going to be gone all next week and you know what this stuff does to me. You too."

Opium, beer, salad, opium, beer and a quick blow-job, opium, barbecued steak, beer, opium topped off with opium, what could be better? The two hedonists feasted then made opium induced love then had some more opium and did it again. The fucking Greeks had nothing on Slick Adams and Rosemary Street.

Luckily, Rosemary had set the alarm or Slick would have missed his flight. As it was, she dropped his hung over ass off at Tampa International with forty-five minutes to spare. As soon as he had checked in, Slick made a beeline straight to the bar for a double Bloody Mary. It was going to be a hell of a trip, but even though he was fucked flat and felt like shit, Slick was already feeling aroused just thinking about his Colombian beauty.

He changed planes in Miami, then sat back and relaxed for the two hour flight down to San Jose. Pete's travel agent had been to Costa Rica several times, she had recommended a small hotel right in the middle of San Jose called the "El Presidente." According to her, it was clean, reasonable and within walking distance of everything. Slick decided he'd check it out, big American style hotels gave him a big pain in the ass.

The taxi driver wanted 900 Colones for the ride to town, that turned out to be ten dollars at an exchange rate of ninety to one. During the thirty minute drive, Slick discovered that his driver was also a part time pimp, he rattled on endlessly about all the beautiful young ladies he could provide for Slick's enjoyment, of course, he would need a small fee for his services. He finally shut up when Slick stepped out of the cab, taxi drivers the world over are pains in the butt.

For 2,000 Colones a night, Slick could have a room on the second floor with a small balcony overlooking the street. After being shown the room, Slick reserved it for the next three, maybe four nights, the place was perfect, quaint, quiet, big soft bed and a great view.

By 7pm Slick was ready to rock and roll. He felt almost human after a long hot shower, now he needed something to eat and a couple of drinks. From the balcony, he'd noticed a little bar just opposite his hotel, that's where he headed.

"Lucky's Piano Blanco" was almost full. The eight bar stools were all occupied, there was one small glass table next to the floor to ceiling window, it had the only empty chair in the house. When Slick took his seat, the two pretty girls at the next table smiled broadly, Costa Rica seemed like a friendly place.

A stunning girl approached Slick's table to take his order, *"Como esta señor, que quieres?*

"Una cerveza."

"Que clase?"

Slick had no idea what the local beer was, *"Cerveza de Costa Rica."*

"Imperial?"

She returned in a few seconds with a bottle of Imperial Beer, he'd obviously gotten the message across, Costa Rica was going to be a good place to polish up his Spanish, damn, that bartender was hot.

Slick finished his beer then boldly asked one of the ladies at the next table if she spoke English.

"A leetle."

"Where can I find a good restaurant?"

The girls giggled and talked to each other in Spanish, they talked so fast that Slick didn't understand two words. He figured that when the thinner of the two said, *"A Leetle"*, she should have said, *"Very very leetle."*

One of the foreigners sitting near-by offered assistance, *"Maybe I can give you a hand."*

"Thanks, I just got here, where's a decent place to grab a bite?"

"Depends what you want, this town's got a little of everything."

"Nothing fancy, something local."

The stranger suggested a little joint around the corner that specialized in roast chicken with side orders of rice or black-eyed peas or a combination of rice and black-eyed peas which Slick would soon learn was one of the local favorites called gallo pinto. The same stranger introduced himself and told Slick where he could find the action after he'd eaten.

"You gotta take a look at Key Largo while you're here, there's usually fifty or sixty babes hanging around up there, the place has been around since the days of Hemmingway."

"What's Key Largo, a whore house?"

"No, no way. It's a big old bar where available ladies hang out. You catch the eye of one you like, buy her a drink and if you

can strike up a mutually acceptable deal, ur all set."

"How bout these girls?"

"They're available."

"How bout that doll serving drinks?"

"Roxanna, if she likes you she'll go with you, if she doesn't, she won't."

"What's the going rate?"

"The really hot ones think they're worth a hundred bucks, you drop in here after eleven and you'd be able to get a date for a thousand Colones, that's only ten bucks."

Slick thanked the stranger for the info and left, he was starving. As he walked away, the thin girl gave him a big wink, she looked a lot like a skinny Sophia Loren.

Slick had a great evening, he pigged out on delicious chicken and gallo pinto, bought several girls drinks at Key Largo, discovered another bar called Nashville South where he tried to pick up one of the waitresses but failed and ended up back at Lucky's Piano Blanco. He was about to call it a night when the Sophia Loren look-a-like came back in the bar. Slick offered her a drink, she accepted.

Eva was thirty one years old, had two little girls who were home with her mother. Her father had died in a car accident six years earlier, her husband had taken off around the same time. She had been supporting her mom and kids ever since using the only skill she possessed, her ability to please men. For more than a year she'd had a steady American boyfriend but he'd gone back to the States and died.

Anyway, that's what Slick thought he'd understood, Eva spoke zip English but she was smart enough to use basic Spanish words and speak slowly and only in the present tense. When she displayed photographs of her girls, Slick knew he'd misunderstood at least part of the conversation, one of her girls was less than two years old. After several minutes of rough Spanish and lots of arm waiving he understood that the dead American had fathered the baby, he wondered what else he'd missed.

Just after midnight, Eva's Sophia Loren lips took over Slick's alcohol sodden brain, she accompanied him to his room at the El Presidente where she demonstrated her skills as a "mujer de la noche". She was still there when he woke up at 10:30am, Slick couldn't remember her name but he remembered what she'd done to him well enough to want to do it again.

Room service brought coffee and sweet rolls to the room, Slick was wild about the thick dark black coffee that Costa Rica was famous for. He thanked Eva for a "noche fantastica" and handed her a hundred dollar bill, the ensuing lip lock was an obvious genuine thank you. Slick promised he'd see her later that night at Lucky's, she kissed him again and left with a smile on her lovely face. These Latin chicks were fine.

The girl at reception told Slick where to find a good travel agent so he could set up his tickets to Colombia and back. She also gave him directions to a book store where he could find all kinds of books that would help communicate in Spanish, Slick took off to run his errands and to take in a little of Costa Rica.

At the book store he picked up a pocket dictionary and a booklet of useful Spanish phrases, there were some important messages he had to get across that night to keep his young ass out of a sling. The travel agent said he'd know by late in the afternoon if he could confirm seats to Barranquilla on the 2nd and return the 4th of November. He would leave a message at the El Presidente, if there was room on the plane, Slick would come back in the morning to pay for the tickets.

The plaza down the street was perfect for people watching, Slick sipped coffee, studied his Spanish and checked out the locals. Costa Ricans are a friendly lot, several people approached offering assistance, apparently they thought he was having problems communicating, the book on Spanish phrases being the clue. Slick did ask help from one attractive girl who was in her final year of college. She spoke almost perfect English and of course Spanish was her native tongue. He wrote out several sentences in English for her to translate into Spanish.

1. My girlfriend from Colombia arrives tomorrow.
2. Please don't tell her that we had sex.
3. I want you to be our friend.
4. We want to go to a beautiful beach.
5. Where should we go?
6. What hotel should we stay in?

The girl laughed out loud as she read what Slick had written.

"You are a bad one."

"I couldn't control myself, you Costa Rican women are too beautiful."

"You are very bad, you see, you are flirting with me and I haven't even told you my name."

"What is your name?"

"I am Julia de la Cruz."

"Nice to know you, Julia, I am Slick Adams."

"Let me write the sentences, my mother will be here soon and she will be angry if she sees me talking to you."

"Am I that bad?"

"You are a foreigner."

Julia de la Cruz wrote the 6 sentences out in a beautiful script like hand writing, she bid Slick adieu and departed. When she glanced over her shoulder in Slick's direction he winked, she dashed off.

"Damn, I like this place."

There was a note from the travel agent waiting at the hotel, there were plenty of seats available on the flight to Barranquilla the 2nd of November. The agent would be waiting in his office the following morning.

Slick went for a long stroll around San Jose, he took his books and notes along. By 4pm he'd memorized the sentences Julia de la Cruz had written for him plus a lot of other phrases that might come in handy, he'd also developed quite a thirst. A fat guy wearing a T-shirt with a big CANADA blazoned across the front gave him directions back to the El Presidente.

Lucky's Piano Blanco was empty with the exception of Roxanna, the sultry bartender, her first question was, *"Donde esta Eva?"*

"I don't know."

"I don't believe you."

Roxanna was a wicked one.

"I came to see you."

"I don't believe you."

"It's true."

"I don't believe you."

Slick finally talked her into bringing him a beer but flirt as he may, she wouldn't buy any of his program. No matter, it was a pleasure just being in the same room with this fiery Latin beauty.

He tried some of his new Spanish on Roxanna, most she answered with a laugh and a haughty toss of her head or, *"You have Eva."* She acted like Slick had jilted her for the evil Eva, maybe she thought that every man who came in the bar was hers, hell, she didn't even know his name. Whatever, he liked playing the game.

Lucky's started to fill up so Slick went across the street to his room for a shower and a power nap, having fun is hard work.

Eva didn't show up until a little after 10pm, when she walked in to Lucky's, Roxanna caught Slick's eye and pointed towards the door, *"Su novia."*

Eva seemed to understand everything Slick told her, she promised not to cause any problems when the girlfriend arrived. What she couldn't understand was why Slick had gone to all this trouble, after all, she was only a "mujer de la noche, una prostituta." Slick did his best to explain that prostitute or not, he liked her and hoped she and Magda could be friends.

Eva told Slick about a place she'd been with other men, she described it as one of the most beautiful places on earth, Manuel Antonio Beach and Nature Reserve on the Pacific side of Costa Rica. There was a divine little resort close by called the Tucan that he could call for reservations. What the hell, Eva was so helpful, Slick kept her for the night.

The front desk put a call through to the Tucan, Slick reserved the only available room for the last 3 days of October and the first day of November. The travel agent called, Slick said he'd be right there.

The travel agent was able to give a small discount if the tickets were paid for with U.S. dollars, *"no problema"*, that could be arranged. The agent made a call to check on the arrival time of the flight from Barranquilla, as far as anyone at the airport knew, it would arrive on time that afternoon at 3:30. The handy agent was also able to set up a rent-a-car for the following day with another sizeable discount if paid in U.S. dollars, again, *"no problema."* The car would be delivered to the El Presidente at noon the next day, was there anything else he could assist with? Slick thanked him and shook hands good-by, the agent said, *"Muchos gracias, para sevirle."* Slick had never heard the expression before but he liked it, *"Thank you, in order to serve you."* The so-called Third World was starting to grow on El Señor Es Slick.

At 3pm, Slick grabbed a cab to go pick-up Magda, he wondered if she would be as stunning as he remembered, he wondered what she'd been doing the past month. After all, she'd been one of the covey of dolls employed by Luis to entertain his guests. What the hell should he expect, a poor girl who just happened to be lucky enough to turn out beautiful with a sexy body. Regardless, girls like her who'd grown up with absolutely nothing certainly seemed to appreciate it a lot lot more when someone was nice to them. Maybe he had a bit of "The Knight In Shinning Armor" complex, he sure seemed to derive a lot more pleasure from being with girls like Magda and Eva, probably because they tried so much harder to please. What was the word, hedonism, that's it, hedonism, he'd become a hedonist and was liking it.

The flight from Barranquilla was forty minutes late, the passengers started coming out of the customs and immigration area in another thirty minutes but no Magda. Maybe the customs idiots had noticed her tits and decided to do a body search, who could blame them.

Finally she came through the door, she was wearing the same outfit as in the photo that was in the letter Luis had handed him a few weeks earlier. She looked great.

"Magda, over here!"

She rushed into his arms and gave him a bear hug that took his breath away.

"I miss you too much, they ask me many questions."

Slick snatched Magda's suitcase from the hands of one of the self appointed porters and led her off to the waiting taxi. One negative thing about third world countries that is a continuous pain in the butt is the ever present horde of people hanging around public places looking to pick up a few cents doing nothing. However, the positives of the third world far outweigh the negatives.

Safe inside the taxi they finally got a chance to talk, *"How are you?"*

"I'm fine, my first time in a airplane, I am very afraid."

"You speak English very good now, you have been practicing."

"Yes, I go to school to learn. Señor Luis give me a new job in the hotel of his mother, I am reception."

Slick was amazed at Magda's new level of English, a month earlier they could barely communicate, in words anyway, now she was jabbering away like a bored housewife. Between her new English skills and Slick's improved Spanish, they were yakking back and forth like a couple of parakeets long before the taxi dropped them off at the hotel.

"Enough English practice, follow me upstairs, I have plans for you."

"Si Señor, you are my boss."

After a quick shower, Magda made her entrance wrapped in a bath towel which Slick unwrapped, he then stood back to admire mother nature's work, what he saw was better than anything ever created by man.

"I look okay? I lose two kilo."

"You are perfecto, fantastico."

Standing in front of Slick was the world's most potent aphrodisiac and it was working, man was it working. It worked the first time then a second, twenty minutes later it worked the third time, had starvation not been just around the corner it might have worked a forth time.

After dinner Slick took Magda to the Piano Blanco for a couple of drinks and to show her off in front of Roxanna. It was about time that Her Highness discovered that she wasn't the hottest item in town. They spent an hour discussing plans for the next several days, their talk had become a mixture of English and Spanish, rarely was a sentence completed in one language only, the blend was quite effective. Slick was even able to get the idea across that if possible, he would like to hire a boat for half a day's sports fishing, Magda was excited, she'd never tried to catch a fish in her entire life.

They arrived at Tucan resort the next afternoon just before cocktail hour, Eva was right, the place was divine. Their room was on a steep hillside, through gaps in the branches of fruit trees one could see the ocean and the long strip of white sand that was called Manuel Antonio Beach. They were far enough back from the road that the only sounds heard came from the thousands of birds flying around and roosting in the trees. The resort was arranged so that each room had it's own patio, trees and shrubs separated and kept each room and patio private.

Ten minutes later, Magda and Slick were swinging in a hammock enjoying the surroundings when a large bird with a huge beak landed on the back of a bench not 10 feet away, it was a Tucan, the national bird of Costa Rica. They now knew where the resort got it's name.

Thus started four of the happiest days in the life of Slick Adams, a perfect place and the perfect woman to share it with. The only problems encountered while at Manuel Antonio were the near riots among the macho Costa Rican men each time Magda showed up on the beach in one of her bathing suits. The third morning they did manage to hire a rickety old boat along with it's owner and chug out a few miles in search of Dorado and Wahoo. The old man knew his stuff, when they returned to the shore at 2pm, the cooler was full, Slick took 4 of the fish back to the resort, the cook was thrilled, the day's special was changed to ultra fresh Dorado.

Magda actually shed a tear when on the morning of November the 1st they left their little heaven and started driving back to San Jose, she snuggled up next to her man and didn't make a sound for the next hour. During the 5 hour drive her melancholy mood slowly changed to one of excitement as they talked about the upcoming trip back to Colombia. There probably weren't two other people in the world who could understand the private English/ Spanish mix with which they communicated, no matter, Slick and Magda had become quite fluent.

Once checked back in at the El Presidente, Slick's first task was to call the nursery and leave a message for Pete to call him at 6pm, task number two was to submit to a sensual massage by his adept and naked masseuse. The massage didn't last long, the sight of Magda's curvaceous body made his mind wander from one head to the other.

Pete's call came through right on time, the Navajo would be ready before he got back, there were no major problems with the plane to report, Nevada had delivered and everything else was cool. Pete was at a noisy pay phone so they cut the conversation off short.

"Come mi amour, we have nothing to do now but pack, eat a biftec grande and drink several cervezas."

"Okay love, you numero uno."

After dinner they hit most of the joints Slick had discovered earlier, Eva was sitting in Nashville South looking available, she gave Magda a good looking over then a nod of approval. Slick sent Eva a drink and invited her over to chat. He explained that she was the girl who had suggested Manuel Antonio and the Tucan Resort. Eva gave Magda a soft kiss on the cheek and welcomed her to Costa Rica, the two girls then raced off in rapid fire Spanish of which Slick understood maybe half, he was surprised at how fast his Spanish was coming up to speed.

Later, Magda asked a few questions about Eva that Slick answered as best he could without incriminating himself. He said he'd met her at Lucky's and she had told him about the resort and the beach, yes, he knew she was a "mujer de la noche" but he'd only talked to her. The look on her face said that she was a little skeptical but she didn't press the matter. It seemed to Slick that it's harder to bullshit these third world girls, they must have extra keen senses.

Carlos was waiting when they landed at Barranquilla, as before he had arranged with immigration for the entry and exit stamps to be placed on a separate piece of paper so there would be no permanent record of Slick's visit in his passport. Luis would be at the hotel at 7pm, the three of them would talk, then Slick could get Magda and they'd all go out for the evening.

It never dawned on Slick that he was in the same room where he and Magda had first made love, she scolded him for missing this very important and romantic part of their love affair. Slick figured the more he knew about women, the less he understood them.

Luis greeted Slick like a long lost brother, he hoped that the semi-screw up at their last meeting hadn't messed up the relationship.

Slick went into great detail to make sure Luis understood exactly how happy he was with the entire operation. He brought greetings from Sam and Pete and relayed Sam's thoughts on the first 5 missions, especially thanking Luis for the high quality marijuana and the expectation that nothing would change in that regard. He handed Luis the chart he had drawn up with the weights of the dope and the dates and methods of payment.

Luis and Carlos studied the chart for a moment, Carlos asked how they would like to balance the account, take sixty more pounds or pay a little less for the next load.

"No, no, we want to call it even, you have been more than generous with us, we will both start at zero balance on the next flight."

"You tell Pedro and Señor Sam how much we appreciate doing business with caballeros like you three, of all the groups we deal with, yours is the one we talk about as amigos as well as business partners."

"Thank you, we are honored and believe me, the feeling is mutual."

When Slick mentioned the probability of a flight out to landing strip Continental, Luis's answer was immediate, *"Of course, what time?"*

Luis was in a festive mood, calling the two accounts even had apparently been a pretty big deal to him. They'd obviously made the right move, Sam did have good gut instincts. Like he had said, *"It's important that these guys like and trust the hell out of us."*

What really pleased Slick was the way Luis and Carlos and everybody else they ran into treated Magda. It was like she had made a magical transformation from one of Luis' hired hands to the lady of the friend from the north. Slick was pleased, Magda was floating on a cushion of perfumed air.

The next morning, Carlos picked Slick up at 9am, thirty

minutes later they were at the small airport on the outskirts of Barranquilla, Renaldo was waiting, the Cessna was ready.

Slick flew the Cessna from the left seat so he'd have the same view as during the upcoming real thing. He flew north to the coastline, then east to the river mouth, from there he followed the course that he and Pete had plotted earlier to Hotel Continental. On the first attempt they missed the landing strip by about half a mile. On the second run they came right across the runway by altering the heading 2 degrees. The third attempt was also right on the money. Slick was now certain that he could fly directly from the river mouth to Continental even if the weather conditions were marginal.

"Okay, I've seen enough, I'm sure I can get here now, you want to land and check out the runway?"

"Yes, for sure, we sent a truck load of men out here to cut the weeds and fill holes, let's see how good a job they did."

The runway was dry and in pretty good shape. After the work gang had chopped weeds and filled holes, they had drug a big log up and down the runway behind their truck. The heavy log had smoothed things out considerably. Slick gave Continental his vote of approval.

That night Luis invited Slick to be his guest any time for as long as he wanted at a small resort hotel he owned at Santa Marta.

"You and the lady stay there to relax, it's beautiful, twenty meters from the sea, the seafood is very fresh. Bring Pedro and Sam, I will join you, it will make me very happy to be with all of you."

"I accept the generous invitation for all of us. I also thank you mucho for giving Magda the job at the hotel, she is very proud."

"Anything for your lady."

Later a tearful Magda confessed that she knew what Slick's job was, she begged him to be careful and come back to her soon. They made plans to meet again as soon as possible. She promised to send him a letter via Carlos each time he flew to Colombia, Slick promised to be careful and to send copies of some of the photos of their stay in Costa Rica. He gave her a thousand U S dollars so she could continue studying English and a couple of business courses. Luis had promised her a promotion to the hotel office when she completed the courses. Slick also explained that Carlos and one of Luis's lawyers would be helping her create a lot of phony documents so that she could qualify for a tourist visa to the States sometime on down the line.

"You want me to come to America?"

"Sure, why not."

"I can do that? It is okay?"

"Yes of course, but after I stop flying."

"When is that?"

"One or two months more."

"I hope it is one."

"I will tell you in my letters."

"Te amo."

"I love you too, but first I have to make some money, you know, mucho dinero."

The flight from Barranquilla to San Jose was delayed three hours for reasons unknown, whatever the reason, Slick had no chance of making his connection to Miami. Oh well, there are a lot worse places to be stranded.

Slick missed Magda so much that he tracked down Eva to keep from thinking about his Colombian love. Eva did her best to keep him detracted, damn, these Latin women are understanding.

He arrived at Tampa the next evening a little after 7pm, Pete was waiting at the airport.

"I take it you got my message?"

"Yeah, no problem, how's the doll?"

"Absolutomente fantastico, I'm going to be spending a lot of time in the third world, those Latin dolls are where it's at."

"Let's go, Sam's waiting."

CHAPTER XIV

THE START OF THE 2nd HALF

"What's the word on the Navajo?"

"Ready to go, we can pick it up tomorrow, the bill is six thousand four hundred, parts and labor."

"How's Sam?"

"He's hot to trot."

"How's Miss Legs?"

"She's hot to trot. How's Miss Colombia?"

"She's hot, Luis is going to help get her a visa so she can come up here for a visit."

"Your bed is gonna be crowded."

They met Sam at the usual place.

"Slick, good to see you, where's my fucking pictures?"

"Four rolls, I'll get them developed tomorrow, there should be some hot ones."

"How was it? How's our pal, Luis?"

"He invited all of us to his resort on the beach at Santa Marta."

"Hell, let's go, when we've finished up we'll need a little holiday, it would be a gas."

Slick gave Sam and Pete a rundown of his meetings with the Colombians and the flight in the Cessna. Sam was extremely pleased to hear how Luis had reacted to their plan of calling the account even. The only change, really an addition, to the way the flights were to be handled was that from now on, Renaldo would be in the Cessna either flying or on the ground with his radio on so they could be pre-warned of any problems.

"That's about it, they're happy, the alternate airfield is ready, all we got to do is get the plane and give em a call."

Sam ordered another round, *"I'm glad you went, you made a lot of points, being amigos is a big deal with those Latinos."*

"It's good you flew out to that other strip, I was a little worried about finding it if we couldn't land at Plaza."

"It's no sweat now, I've been there four times."

"Hey! You want some money, those fuckers finally paid us off."

"You got it all?"

"Nevada brought two ten, seven thou towards the next load."

"No shit, I was a little worried that Ronnie had fucked things up beyond repair."

"They're okay now, I'll meet you two at the lake house in about an hour."

On the way to the house, Pete clued Slick in on his new romance with Miss Legs.

"She's very independent, she only stayed overnight once, last Saturday. I'm not allowed to sleep at her pad, she doesn't want the neighbors thinking she's some kind of slut."

"She a good lay?"

"She's a moaner."

"A fucking moaner, oh shit, I like that, I haven't had a good moaner since Thailand. A soft moaner or a loud one?"

"Don't worry, you'll hear her."

"I can't wait, I'm getting turned on just thinking about it. When's she coming over?"

"I think tomorrow."

Sam walked through the door with a taped up cardboard box under his arm.

"I brought it all so we could give it the light treatment."

Slick set the ultraviolet light up on the kitchen counter. Sam spread the 42 bundles of hundreds out on the counter, Pete brought 3 beers, they got down to work.

Half an hour later the money had all been double checked, only one fake hundred had been discovered and it was a beauty.

"That's better, I told Nevada we were tired of so many bad fakes, guess he took me seriously."

"Next time he's here, give him one of these lights."

"Don't worry, they got one, that fucking Ronnie is just trying to unload some of the fakes so they don't have to eat them. He sends us any more and I'll take em up there and shove em up his

ass."

"I think he got the message."

"How you want to split this up?"

Slick wrote down some numbers. *"We still got thirty five thousand cash, I got two thousand left from my trip, we owe six thousand four hundred on the plane, that leaves a little over thirty thousand cash, that ought to*

be plenty. Why don't we just split the two ten	$35,000
four ways, we don't owe Mouse anything else."	+$ 2,000
"Sounds good to me, okay with you, Pete?"	= $37,000
"Yeah, sure."	- $ 6,400
"Gimme that phony hundred, I'll keep it	= $30,600

with the rest of the fakes."

"How much counterfeit you got left?"

"About a thousand, I only kept the good ones."

"That ain't bad."

Sam made 4 stacks of 10 bundles, he then tossed Pete one of the two remaining, *"Split it with Slick."*

Sam scooped up two of the stacks and tossed them back in the cardboard box, Slick took five of his bundles and handed them to Sam. *"Here's the twenty-five I owe you, thanks for the loan."*

"My pleasure, that's the easiest five I ever made."

Pete ran upstairs and returned with the cash bag, he dumped the contents on the counter. There was a mixture of hundreds and twenties.

Slick counted 11 packs of twenties and 2 packs of hundreds, $32,000. There were also 24 hundred dollar bills, $2,400 and 28 twenties, $560.

"Close enough, that's thirty four thousand nine hundred sixty."

"Here's the two grand I owe the bag."

Slick counted out twenty hundreds and dropped them in the cash bag.

"You guys take what you need to pay off the plane and get ready for the next go." *"Ten grand ought to cover everything, wha-da-ya think, Pete?"*

"Plenty."

Slick took out one pack of hundreds and five thousand in

mixed hundreds and twenties, he then dropped two twenties back in the bag.

"That should leave an even twenty seven grand in the bag."

Sam announced the end of the meeting by inviting his two partners out for drinks and a late dinner. They agreed to meet at one of the joints they frequented in an hour.

Pete dumped his money in his trusty pillowcase and went upstairs. Slick put his remaining $25,500 in the metal suitcase along side the cash bag, then stuck the suitcase back in the closet and locked the closet door. He then went out to the kitchen, got a paper bag from beside the fridge, stuffed in the $9,960 cash and put it in a dresser drawer. After a quick shower, he locked the door to his bedroom, Pete was waiting, they drove off to meet Sam.

In the morning, Pete called the Piper dealer and told them they would be there to pay the bill and pick up the plane before noon. Slick called Rosemary's house but no one answered. He had Pete stop so he could drop off the 4 rolls of film.

"I can't wait to see the pictures, if they're as good as I think, Sam will shit his pants."

"You took some of her naked?"

"About fifty, on the beach, in our room, in a hammock, in the jungle, everywhere."

"You can hide the pictures in my room so Rosemary doesn't find them. I'll check em every day to make sure nobody has been snooping."

"You're a real pal, but seriously, I might take you up on that, no use stirring up a hornet's nest."

The manager at the Piper dealership spent almost an hour going over his bill and showing Pete and Slick exactly what his men had done. Basically, they had followed the Piper Maintenance Manual Annual Inspection procedure to the "T". Every part that had been removed, including the 24 spark plugs were in the back of the plane in a cardboard box. The only surprise was the electric flap motor. The old one was weak so it had been replaced as per instructions with a new one. The minor oil leaks had been fixed by simply tightening everything up.

"*Everything we do is under warranty, if you have any prob-lems, give us a call, we stand-by our work.*"

"*Thanks, we appreciate your professionalism, who gets the money?*"

They followed the manager inside, Slick counted out $6,400 and handed it to the cashier, she stamped the bill PAID and thanked the 2 gentlemen. Slick asked her to call for a fuel truck and bid her good-day.

Pete waited until Slick had re-fueled and had taken off be-fore he left for Leesburg, Slick planned to fly around for at least an hour and a half to make sure everything was tight so they'd both get there at about the same time. If the plane was okay, they planned to re-install the plumbing for the long range tank, take a quick hop then fill her up before parking. All they would have to do before the next mission would be the same as usual, remove the seats and the carpet, toss them in the van and stick in the tank and gas up."

When Pete drove on to the airport, Slick was underneath the Navajo, he had almost completed the re-plumbing job. All he needed was for Pete to lower the fuel line down from inside the cabin so he could attach it to the T fitting he'd installed.

"*How'd she run?*"

"*Like a clock, I couldn't find a drop of oil, looks like we're ready to go.*"

"*What-da-ya think, we call Carlos tomorrow?*"

"*Fuckin A, let's get the ball rolling, I'd like to be a million-aire by January the first, this fucking year.*"

"*Wouldn't that be a hoot, drop a load on New Year's Eve, everybody would be drunk, we could drop the shit in Sam's back yard and nobody would notice.*"

"*Let's go fly this fucker and check my plumbing job, then I gotta find Rosemary, I'm getting horny as a two peckered goat.*"

As soon as they were in the air, Pete checked the new con-nections with his flashlight, there were no leaks, they landed, topped off all 4 of the Navajo's tanks and parked the plane.

Just for good measure they stopped on the way home and bought a hundred and fifty dollars worth of wine and steaks with one phony and one real hundred dollar bill. Slick called Rosemary from one of the pay phones in front of the supermarket, she was home and would wait there until Slick called her from the lake house.

"I've got some very interesting things to tell you."

"Good or bad?"

"All good."

"That's my girl, we should be back about six."

Slick put another call through to the nursery and left a message for Sam to meet them at 7pm. Pete called Legs at her office, she accepted his invitation to join him and some friends for a barbecue at the house, she said 7:30 was fine.

"Is she okay with drugs?"

"She snorts a little coke."

"I think everybody in Florida snorts coke, the shit's everywhere."

"Yeah, the fuckin cops bust some sap, then they snort the shit themselves."

"An what they don't snort, the sell to the same people as the guy they busted was going to."

"It's fine with me, the more cocaine there is floating around, the less the fuzz is worried about a little pot."

Back at the lake house, Slick set aside 6 steaks, then loaded the rest in the freezer, after that he called Rosemary, she said she was on the way. He grabbed a cold beer, took a couple of gulps and jumped in the shower. Ten minutes later while he was drying off, Rosemary burst through the bedroom door.

"Perfect, you're naked."

"You're not."

"Give me about ten seconds."

"Counting."

"I'm going to come as soon as you touch my pussy, it's throbbing."

Rosemary wasn't lying, after about two and a half strokes of his tongue she had a massive orgasm.

"Oh god, that felt good, thank you, I was getting desperate."

"Twas my pleasure, now excuse me, I'm going to slip my dick in there while that thing's still quivering."

"Oh man, it's happening again."

"Wow, that didn't take long."

"I couldn't wait."

"What's the good news?"

"Let me catch my breath."

A few minutes later Rosemary went on to explain all she had found out about the US Treasury and damaged money. Anybody could take money that had been damaged in any way to banks that were federally insured. The bank would forward the damaged bills to a department of the US Treasury that specialized in determining the amount. Later, the bank would be given a credit in the same amount, then the customer would be reimbursed. If the amount was less than $10,000 dollars, the only paperwork required was just a note saying what had happened to the money.

"I bet you get at least ninety percent of what's left in those two globs, now aren't you glad you kept all that mush which is now two balls as hard as rocks."

"That's good news, I told you I thought I'd get something out of it but I never figured on anything close to ninety percent. How about the stuff we separated, you try to exchange any of it?"

"I took a little over eight thousand to my sister's bank, we told them that our house had flooded and the money had been under mud and silt for a long time. The bank manager traded all of it for us, all he said was for us to be careful with our money and keep it in a bank."

"We'll have to have a toast in honor of our little Cuban friend, he's made us a bundle."

Sam and Sarah arrived a little after 7pm, the boys went outside for a short powwow. They decided to fill the drums in the morning then give Carlos a call in the afternoon. If he gave them the go-ahead, they'd launch that night. Sam would take care of contacting the buyers, if they couldn't make it with such short notice, he had a trusted employee who would help out at the drop zone.

Legs arrived, turned out she was a nice smart broad named Gayle. As soon as she was on the scene, everybody switched their demeanor from crooks or accomplices to crooks to social beings. It was amazing how the arrival of one outsider could completely change the topics of conversation.

"Nice to finally meet you, Gayle, thanks for arranging my trip to Costa Rica, the Hotel Presidente was perfect."

Rosemary led Gayle inside for a glass of wine.

"Jesus Pete, I almost asked her to moan a little for me, she looks hot."

"You should talk, I heard some moaning and little yelps coming from downstairs a little earlier, what the hell was going on down there?"

"She missed me."

Sam and Sarah left early, as soon as the mess was cleaned up, Pete and Gayle slithered upstairs. Rosemary and Slick smoked some opium in the kitchen and listened for moans, they weren't disappointed.

"You hear that?"

"About two more of those sounds and one more hit of opium and you're in for it, this time I'm the one with the throbbing problem."

"Me too."

In the morning, Slick sent Rosemary off to her house with $25,000 of his money to be put in her safe. Pete pulled over at the film developing shop on the way to the nursery, Slick ran inside.

"You gotta see these fucking pictures, I bet that little prick who gave them to me has jacked off ten times since he developed some of these. Oh fuck, this one is great, Sam is in for a real shock."

Of the hundred or so pictures Slick had taken, there were five or six outstanding shots, Magda nude, twisted in a hammock was Pete's favorite. Slick liked one where she was leaning against a tilted Palm tree, her amazing body made it a tough selection between the top five.

"No wonder you want to get back with her, she is fine, I've never see tits that perfect not to mention a world class ass and legs, plus she's got the face of an angel."

"Yeah, she is something else, here's the topper, she's the most passionate chick I've ever been with."

"Does she moan?"

"No, she has her own little sounds, but man, that broad you had last night was wild, after five minutes of moans and groans, Rosemary was out of control."

By noon they had the drums filled with aviation gas and everything else loaded in the van. Sam had finally tracked down Nevada, he would be arriving in two days, they decided to delay the mission one day.

"I'm going to give Carlos a call anyway and tell him we're planning on leaving tomorrow night, that way we'll know for sure everything's set."

"Good idea, where's my fuckin pictures?"

"In the car."

"Go get em, I've been waiting two weeks for this."

"Holy shit! Look at this broad, Slick, you dirty bastard, you don't really fuck that beautiful little doll do you?"

"As often as I can."

"You rotten prick, son-of-a-bitch, I can't believe that set of jugs, makes Sarah look flat chested. She's a cute chick too, if the little broad was up here, she'd have it made."

"I take it you approve."

"You got that right."

"Okay Sam, you relax for a couple of hours, we'll meet you at the bar at six, you wanna hang on to one of these pictures?"

" No way, Sarah would cut my cock off, just let me take a peek once in a while."

Pete was able to get through to Carlos on the 3rd try, everything was set for the next mission. Right now it looked like Hotel Plaza but they would speak the following afternoon for confirmation, plus, Renaldo would be standing by in the Cessna with the final word.

After the short meeting at 6, Slick drove over to Rosemary's house to check out the 2 dried balls of money, and that's exactly what they turned out to be, two dried balls.

"How much you think in each wad?"

"I'd say the small one is around three thousand, the big

one eleven or twelve."

"I can't wait to see what they give me but it'll have to wait until I'm in California and totally retired from this."

Slick did an inventory of his cash, including the $50,000 in recovered wet money, his total was a little over $170,000 dollars. He removed the nine hundred plus counterfeit and the 7 hundred dollar bills he'd set aside from the recovered money. Rosemary produced another shoebox from her closet, five minutes later they had neatly packed the mixture of twenties and hundreds in the box. After taping it closed, Slick wrote the number 120,000 on top of the box.

"I'm going to take this seven hundred to a bank tomorrow and test your theory."

"Just tell them you were fishing at the beach and you got wet, it's no problem. What are you going to do with all that counterfeit?"

"We'll spend it a little at a time, I just don't want it laying around here, come on, let's go get some soft shelled crab."

Slick walked into a busy bank in downtown Tampa, at the New Accounts desk he explained his problem. The new accounts clerk led him to a woman sitting at a desk that had a sign announcing her as the ASST. MGR.

"Yes, how can I help you?"

"I was on a five day diving trip in Belize, a pair of my pants with all my cash spent four days under water in the bilge, the money is not in very good shape. I was----"

"Let me see it."

Slick handed the assistant manager an envelope, she pulled the 7 hundred dollar bills out and examined them. After a cursory check, she picked up her phone, in a few seconds a young lady approached.

"Please check these bills, if they are okay, exchange them for this gentleman."

"Yes ma'am."

That was it. The teller led Slick to a chair and asked him to have a seat, five minutes later she returned with 7 fresh hundred dollar bills. She handed Slick the money and wished him a nice vacation.

Shit, that was easy.

Pete called Carlos at the appointed time, the mission was on with one precaution, there was another plane that would be taking off at about their arrival time, so keep a sharp lookout and listen on the agreed radio frequency.

The three smugglers met at their watering hole to make sure they were set. Nobody could think of anything they'd forgotten so they drank beer and bullshitted. Sam was still threatening to go along on a flight but they all knew it would be stupid to disrupt the smooth operation.

"Okay you guys, good luck tomorrow, I'll be waiting for you."

They left for Leesburg earlier than usual, both Pete and Slick wanted to spend a little time scoping out the airport to make sure no one was scoping them out.

After parking the van at the 24 hour restaurant next to their motel, they casually strolled down the highway towards the airport. They walked across the highway and cut across the corner of the parking lot, then down the roadway towards the airport office. Just past the office were some chairs from which they could watch planes taking off and landing, the Navajo was also visible from the vantage point, they sat and observed.

When an hour had passed and boredom had set in, Pete suggested something to eat.

"I haven't seen anyone who looks even a little copish, let's get a bite and pick up some sandwiches for the flight."

"Yeah, fuck em, even if they were watching us, we never have anything in the plane that can land our asses in the slammer, suspicion of smuggling don't mean jack."

The tank was slid in the plane and filled by 7:30, they were back in their motel room watching TV by 8.

"It just doesn't feel quite right this time, I guess I'm a little edgy."

"Relax, Pete, we haven't seen one sign of trouble."

The Navajo lifted off at 11:20, no suspicious characters were encountered at the airport, everything had gone as smooth as silk. Pete was still a little on edge but happy to be in the air and away from Leesburg. By the time they'd passed abeam Nassau, Pete had relaxed completely, in fact he was sound asleep, the Navajo droned on.

"Pete, wake up you no good fucker, I need some coffee."
"What time is it?"
"It'll be daylight in about an hour, you slept damn near all night, what's that fucking broad been doing to you?"
Not long after Slick had finished his coffee it was time to start descending, the north coast of Colombia was dead ahead at a little over a hundred miles. Slick switched the radio to the frequency that Renaldo was supposed to be standing by on.
"You ready to rock and roll?"
"Fucking A, let's load up and head for home."
Twenty miles out the shore line was clearly in sight, the winds were calm, the sky was clear, it was a pilot's dream, CAVU, Clear And Visibility Unlimited. Slick adjusted the rate of descent so that they crossed the river mouth at a thousand feet above sea level, seven minutes later the Navajo approached Plaza. As Slick banked left to start the traffic pattern, the aircraft radio came to life, it was Renaldo's voice.
"Can you circle for five minutes, there is a plane about to take-off?"
Slick looked at Pete.
"I guess he's talking to us."
"Who else?"
"Roger, we'll orbit over the field."
"Thank you."
Slick started a slow orbit over the landing strip, due to the giant trees beside the runway, there was no sign of what could be causing the delay. Within two minutes the mystery was solved.
"You see that?"
"Looks like a DC-3, those fuckers are probably carrying

about five thousand pounds, how much is that worth?"

"That's what Sam wants to get, something big."

"Big things attract a lot of attention."

The large aircraft below reached the end of the runway enclosed in a cloud of dust, it turned towards the take-off heading. As the aircraft started it's take-off run, the red dust billowed behind it's tail, slowly the plane emerged from the red cloud, within seconds it accelerated to lift off speed and climbed over the trees at the end of the runway.

"I guess it's our turn, let's get down there and fill this thing up."

Just as Slick started to line up on final, a very American voice came over the radio.

"Eh, hello to the other plane, how do you read?"

Slick looked at Pete and shrugged, *"He talking to us?"*

"I guess."

"Go ahead."

"We got a little problem, I forgot to take the landing gear pins out, we got to land again, you got enough gas to give me fifteen minutes?"

"Yeah sure, go ahead, we'll orbit."

"Thanks a million, I owe you big time."

"No sweat."

Pete and Slick laughed at each other, *"He sounded a little embarrassed."*

"No shit, I wonder how that old tub likes to land with a full load?"

"Don't have a clue, never flew one of those things."

The DC-3 came back to the field and landed, when it had stopped at the east end of the runway, the cabin door opened, somebody could be seen running under the front of the plane, in a few seconds, the person dashed back inside the aircraft and the door closed. Ten seconds later, there was another cloud of red dust as the old plane thundered down the runway for it's second take-off in five minutes.

"Thanks guys, we're out of here for real this time, it's all yours."

"No sweat, have a good one."

Slick banked to the left, lowered the gear and flaps, turned onto final and landed at the busy Plaza International Airport. Luis and his crew were all waiting under the trees with smiles on their faces.

"Amigos! Como esta?"

"Luis! Good to see you, Carlos, como esta?"

It was 9:25 in the morning.

By 10:45, the Navajo was refueled, the dope had been bagged, weighed and loaded, the total weight of the cargo was 1210 pounds in 28 canvas bags.

"What time you want to blast off?"

"Any time's okay now, daylight savings time is over, the days are getting shorter, it'll be dark by six thirty, if we take-off at eleven, we won't cross the shore line til seven, let's haul ass."

The Navajo lifted off at 11:10, all things being equal they'd fly into Florida a few minutes after 7, make the drop a little after 8, then land back at Leesburg around 9. Hell, at this rate they would be drinking beer by 10, not to mention the fact each of them would be almost a hundred thousand dollars richer. This smuggling shit is way too easy.

The return flight went according to plan, mother nature co-operated completely, the law co-operated by being invisible, the Navajo co-operated by not missing a beat, Sam co-operated by having everything ready at the drop zone including a big smile and a wave as they made the last pass.

Pete popped the tops off a pair of ice cold Bud's at 11:20, *"Well, shit, that went off okay, here, you earned this."*

"Thanks, I'm dry as a bone."

"What did ur girl friend have to say?"

"She loves me, when am I going to see her again, you know the drill."

Things continued without a hitch the next morning. The flying duo slid the long range tank out of the Navajo and into the van, locked up the plane and were on the road by 9:30am, nobody had looked twice.

Sam met them at the nursery, after stashing the tank and parking the van, the trio went out to the causeway for lunch.

"Nevada gave me two hundred, he'll have the rest plus another two hundred when he picks up the next load. He says they need it fast, Boston is low on dope, they're selling the shit like wildfire."

"We can go again in two or three days, okay with you, Pete?"

"Might as well, can't dance."

"Luis says they got lots of pot."

"Fuck it, let's make hay while we can."

"I got the two hundred in the car, after we give it the light treatment, I'm gonna take Mighty Mouse what's his, the fucking lawyers are on his ass for more. What do we owe him?"

Slick jotted some numbers on a napkin.

```
200,000                          72
- 72,000                        +32
=128,000 ÷4 =32,000             =104
```

"He gets a hundred and four thousand, the three of us get thirty two thousand, that sound right?"

```
                                 32
Pete did a quick problem on another napkin,      + 32
"That's right."                                  + 32
"We're still okay with cash, there's twenty seven   + 32
thousand left in the bag and I still got a little more than   + 72
two grand in my pocket."                         = 200
```

"Okay, we're all set, let's check the money right now so I can get his to him today.

There were 3 counterfeit bills among the $200,000. All 3 were very good fakes, they were all exactly the same, obviously from the same counterfeiter. Nevada needed to be warned that one of his buyers was paying them with bad money. Sam figured a broken kneecap or two would probably solve the problem.

CHAPTER XV

THE PROBLEM (S)

Two days and eight hours later the Navajo lifted off Leesburg Airport on it's seventh mission south. The pre-flight tasks had all gone off as planned, it was beginning to look like they could make smuggling flights out of laid back Leesburg indefinitely. Even Pete who usually had a case of jitters prior to launch was cool as a cucumber.

"No bad feelings today?"

"Not a one, I been so damn busy running around getting ready and hiding money plus trying to keep Gayle satisfied that I haven't had time to worry about anything."

"Two days between flights isn't enough, from now on let's take a week, this is supposed to be fun."

Five hours later they were approaching Great Inagua Island, it was almost time for the long range tank to run dry. Pete was at the controls, Slick was sipping coffee and thinking about his Colombian doll when one of the engines lost power causing the plane to yaw noticeably.

Assuming that the long range tank had run out of gas, Slick reached down and moved the fuel selector levers from OFF to AUX. The powerless engine remained powerless.

"What's wrong with this fucking thing?"

"I don't know, I got it."

Slick took the controls, the left engine was running but producing zero power. Slick turned the left boost pump on, advanced the mixture a little and switched the fuel selector lever to the main tank, no change.

"I don't know what's wrong but we better head for home, the left motor is kaput."

Slick made a 180 degree turn, he had to add some power and increase the RPM on the right engine to keep the Navajo from losing any more altitude, they were now level at 8,500 feet above the ocean.

"I'm going to feather the left prop, it's not doing anything out there but causing drag."

"Okay, you're the expert."

Slick reduced the prop control lever to the FEATHER position, the left propeller turned until the blade edges were knifing through the air, the prop stopped turning. Slick secured the engine by pulling the mixture lever back to IDLE CUTOFF, mags to OFF and throttle to IDLE.

"What do you think went wrong?"

"I don't have a clue, it just sort of ran out of power like the gas got cut off ninety nine percent. Maybe one of the fuel filters got clogged."

"I haven't seen any shit in the gas when we checked, have you?"

"Nothing unusual."

"You think we can make it all the way back on one engine?"

"I don't see why not, these fucking Navajo's are great on one engine."

The two flyers put their heads together, flying on one engine, the airspeed dropped back to 120 knots, they were well over 6 hours from home. By the time they were abeam Nassau, they'd know for sure if there was enough gas to make it all the way to Leesburg, if they had to land somewhere short, they'd kick the fuel tank out, throw out all the incriminating maps and pick an airport.

Definitely they wanted to go to Leesburg if at all possible, everybody there was used to them and the Navajo, it would be mid morning when they arrived which should cause little or no notice.

"What if there is something in the gas and the right one stops too?"

"If it happened right now, we'd be fucked, there ain't no such thing as a successful night ditching. If it happened after sunrise, we'd splash down next to a sandy beach and hail the next boat."

"It is pretty damn black out there."

"Only one more hour, hand me the pilot's manual, I got to figure out how the cross-feed works, were going to need all the gas we got."

The hour passed, the sun finally started creeping over the horizon, the right engine droned on, the two flyers breathed private little sighs of relief as the islands below became visible.

Over the airport on the island of Great Exuma, they switched back to the long range tank to finish off what fuel remained. The right engine ran 45 minutes before the fuel pressure started fluctuating, Slick's eyes had been glued on the fuel pressure gauge so he was able to switch tanks before the engine began sputtering.

Pete went aft to de-plumb the tank in case it had to be dumped. While he was back there, he got everything ready in case they had to land at some airport where things were a little hostile. Within a few minutes he had the plumbing to the long range tank disconnected, as well as all the fittings, ropes, boards, straps and bungee cords removed and stashed in the tool bag.

Next began a series of using gas from one side until the other wing felt heavy, then switching via cross-feed to the other side to balance the fuel load. Since it was daylight and there were plenty of islands below, they ran both auxiliary wing tanks completely dry, as slow as the Navajo was going, gas was going to be a premium.

By the time the auxiliary tanks were empty, they had passed Nassau, as long as the weather stayed clear, there was no doubt that there was enough fuel to make it to Leesburg. The next obstacle was penetrating the coast of the United States without being intercepted by the US Air Force, dropping down to 500 feet was out of the question on one engine.

"Well my man, here we go, let's hope that the Three Stooges are manning the radar screens this morning, we're going to be a pretty fat duck sitting up here."

"I remember one time when I was based in Okinawa, the navy launched a practice attack against us at Naha. The first thing we knew about it was when a bunch of Navy F-4s and F-8s roared overhead, most of that shit you hear about radar is pure bullshit designed to make Joe American sleep better at night. What are they going to do even if they do see us, launch a bunch of fighters against a single target moving along at a hundred and twenty knots,

I doubt it."

"Yeah, I guess ur right, but I'll be feeling a lot better when we're all alone over central Florida."

An hour and forty five minutes later they were all alone over central Florida, apparently nobody was too worried about an invasion from the Bahaman Islands. With a little more than an hour to go it looked almost certain that they'd flown in unobserved.

There were a couple more problems to be addressed. A twin engine plane won't taxi on one engine unless it has nose wheel steering, Navajos don't.

"After we land, I'll taxi off the runway a little faster than usual, we should be able to coast almost to the beginning of the grass, then you're going to have to get out the back door, open the nose compartment on the left side, take out the steering bar, hook it to the front wheel and steer me to the parking spot. If we're lucky, nobody will notice, just be sure to close the door so nobody can see inside.".

"Then what, we get the tank and haul ass?

"I guess, then in a couple of days we'll get the Piper guys over here to find out what went wrong."

"Don't forget, we gotta call Sam and let him know we had to turn back, I wonder what the hell happened to that motor."

"Damned if I know."

Things on the ground started out according to plan, Pete had steered the Navajo to it's parking spot, Slick had shut down the engine, they were about to walk across the parking area to the highway when Pete whispered to Slick, *"There's a cop watching us from his car."*

"Where?"

"Behind you in the trees."

"Are you sure he's watching us?"

"He's looking right at us and he's talking on his radio."

"Fuck! Let's grab our shit and walk away as normal as we can. We'll have to come back for the tank later. I don't think they'll stop us unless they think we got some dope."

The police car didn't follow them to the motel. From the window of their room they watched the entrance to the airport parking area. Five minutes after they'd entered the room, the police car pulled on to the highway and left in the direction of Leesburg. The nervous flyers drank a beer while deciding what to do. The plan was simple, get in the van and get the hell out of Dodge. They'd pull off the road somewhere along the way to see if anyone was following them, if not, give Sam a call and set up a meeting to discuss this recent dog shit turn of events.

"We gotta give Carlos a call too, what are we gonna tell him?"

"Tell him we had an engine problem and we had to turn back, we'll call when it's fixed."

Pete dug out his Florida road map, they decided to head south on a minor two lane road so it would be easier to determine if anyone was following them. State road 19 joined state road 33 then passed through the town of Eva and on to Polk City before intercepting Interstate #4. One of these little towns would surely have a gas station with a pay phone where they could make their calls and check the traffic behind them.

An hour later, Pete pulled in beside a Texaco Station on the north edge of Polk City. The van was hidden from the road, there was a pay phone sign on the front of the station. From inside the gas station they could keep an eye on the road, not one car passed in the next five minutes. Sure that no one was behind them, Pete called the nursery, Sam was on the line within a minute, he agreed to meet them at the little seafood place on the causeway. Next, Pete put a collect call through to Carlos in Colombia, five minutes later he hung up, Carlos had the message, he would be expecting another call in about a week to set up the next flight.

Sam couldn't wait to hear what had happened, *"You two look like shit, you been on a week long coke binge?"*

"I wish, sit down, you ain't gonna believe what we're about to lay on your ass."

In the next forty-five minutes they filled Sam in on the previous 12 hours happenings, he congratulated them on their flying prowess and coolness under fire.

"There's only one way to be sure if the heat is on, we got to

get the plane fixed and do another flight exactly like all the rest. If the cops think we're hauling in dope, they got to catch us with the goods or they got nothing, if they're on to us they'll set a trap. If the cop at the airport was just a coincidence, we continue like nothing happened."

"You mean we go back there and land just to see if they bust us?"

"No, Pete, we have someone there on the ground with a radio, if they see anything, you guys fly off, shit can the tank, land somewhere for gas, load up and head west. These fucking cops aren't smart enough to figure out we're dropping the shit before landing, they think they're gonna make a big bust when the plane lands. No dope, no bust."

"What-da-ya think, Slick?"

"Yeah, I guess it's the only sure way to know. We'd have to make some other changes, somebody would have to take off in the van, we couldn't leave it sitting around."

"Fuck it, leave it at the same motel, if the cops are waiting, just leave it, we'd never be able to use it again anyway."

"Yeah, that makes sense, if everything's cool, we just land and walk over to the motel like normal, if the airport is hot, we're not going back there anyway."

"That's right, if the place is hot, we're out of business."

"At least until we get a new plane and a new airport."

After lunch Sam ordered another round of beers.

"That ain't all the bad news, are you ready for this?"

"What else?"

"They lost our last load, the stupid fucking driver got pulled over for running a red light, he made a run for it and got away but of course the cops wondered why he took off, so they looked in the back of the truck and found the pot."

"Jesus fucking christ! I thought after they had it, it was their problem."

"They want to make a deal and split the loss."

"Meaning?"

"Meaning we're even, the two hundred we got is all we get for that load, what do you two think?"

"What choice do we have, it's gone."

"How bout you, Pete?"

"It's okay with me as long as Mighty Mouse only gets half for the dope."

"Okay, it's done, after the next load I'll only give him half of seventy two thousand, we'll split the rest."

The only other problem was what to do with the van. If the cops were on to them, the van was hot. Sam said he'd hide it in the back of the nursery until it was needed. The meeting was over, Pete followed Sam and Slick to the nursery, they covered the van with a big tarp and said adios, everybody was exhausted.

Back at the house, Slick called Rosemary, she said she was on the way, Slick took a shower and hit the sack. When Rosemary arrived, all she heard were snores, her man was out for the count.

Two days later, Slick and Pete went to Leesburg to retrieve the tank, there was no sign that anybody had been messing around with the plane. No cops or suspicious people were seen around the airport, Pete backed up to the Navajo, they slid the tank in the back of the van and were long gone in a matter of seconds. On the way back to Tampa, a careful check behind them came up empty.

Slick called the Piper dealer in Lakeland and explained what had happened with the left engine, the manager felt sure that the problem was with the servo. He said the symptoms that Slick had explained are exactly what happens when a servo fails, he also said servos are generally extremely reliable. Slick arranged to be at Leesburg Airport the next morning at 10 where he'd meet one of the mechanics from the dealership.

Pete would drop Slick off near the airport at about 9, then he'd cruise around the area looking for anyone who might be looking at Slick and the Navajo. Assuming that the new servo solved their engine problems, Slick planned to hitch a ride with the mechanic to a restaurant about 5 miles down the road where he and Pete planned to meet.

Rosemary couldn't get enough of the story of the last flight, she was absolutely convinced that Slick and Pete were the two bravest and coolest men in the entire universe.

"You flew seven hours in that plane on one engine?"

"It wasn't that big a deal."

"Now you two are going to march up to the plane, load it up with gas and take-off for Colombia knowing that the cops are probably watching you, are you nuts?"

"We don't think the cops will do anything until we come back, they'll think we're landing with a load of dope. The plan is that we have a spy in Leesburg with a radio, if the spy sees anything that looks like a trap, he gives us a call and we go somewhere else."

"How about me, I'm a pretty good spy, I used to find out all kinds of good stuff for my husband, nobody ever suspects a broad with big tits."

"You might be right."

"I could go over there in the afternoon and ask about flying lessons, I could probably get some young instructor to tell me all about his flying experiences, I might even take an introductory lesson. What could be more natural, I wouldn't attract the slightest bit of attention. Meantime, I'd be listening and watching what was going on. Besides that, you know guys can't resist telling some girl everything they know if it'll make them look like a big shot."

"Pete, you like the idea?"

"Why not? She already knows how to use the radios and we wouldn't have to bring an outsider in."

"Let's run it by Sam."

The servo is a part of the fuel injection unit, it only took the mechanic half an hour to remove the old one and install the new unit. After checking that everything was properly hooked up, he told Slick to fire it up. The engine started normally, after the temperatures came up into the green, Slick ran the power up, everything checked out, the problem was solved.

Thirty minutes later Slick was having a cup of coffee at the restaurant where he was to meet Pete, when he saw the familiar Mercedes pull up outside, he paid his tab and left.

"Simplest little part you ever saw, took the guy fifteen minutes to change it, he said the odds of another servo failure in the same plane are zero. The fucking thing cost us six hundred dollars."

"Let's go see Sam and figure this next mission out."

Sam liked the idea of using Rosemary as their spy, they came up with a rather elaborate plan to warn the flyers if there was danger waiting for them at Leesburg.

The afternoon of the night the Navajo was due back, Rosemary would hang around the airport as long as she could without being conspicuous. If she heard or saw anything that convinced her that things had gone to hell, she would get to a phone and call Sam at the Nursery. If Sam had already left for the drop zone, Sarah would be standing by the phone. If Sarah got the call, she would drive out by the drop zone and warn Sam with one of the hand held marine radios. If Sam was warned by a phone call from Rosemary or by radio from Sarah, he would tell the flight crew to "look for a new fishing hole" after they had checked in. Even if Rosemary saw nothing out of the ordinary during the afternoon or evening, she would drive by the airport every fifteen minutes or so until she had been contacted by the returning Navajo, hopefully no later then midnight. Pete would give her a call when they were within ten miles of Leesburg, if she saw any police activity she would just tell them to go away.

If the flyers had to go somewhere else, their destination would depend on the amount of remaining fuel. If they were very low on gas, it would have to be Tampa International or Orlando Executive, if they had a medium amount, Daytona would be their refueling stop. If the flight went off without any diversions and Sam warned them at the drop zone, they would be able to easily make it to Gainsville in northern Florida. Slick had checked, Daytona, Orlando and Gainsville, all had 24 hour fuel service, they knew from experience that gas was always available at Tampa. Other than that, they planned to do everything else just like they had in the past, if they were being watched, they didn't want the watchers to know that they knew.

"Well, when do you guys want to give it a go?"

"Two or three days, that okay with you, Pete?"

"Yeah, let's get it over with, the suspense is keeping me awake at night."

"Okay, let's get going, Slick, you get Rosemary ready, I'll take care or Sarah, make sure all ur money is hidden in case we get

busted. We better split up that bag of cash in case we have to get out of town, how much is left?"

"Twenty seven thousand, plus I still got two in my pocket."

"I'll take ten, you guys take the rest in case you need cash, we'll square it away later."

"Come on over tonight, we'll charge up all four of the hand held radios and give the girls a little practice, I'll burn a couple of steaks."

"Sounds good, we'll be there around seven."

On the way back to the lake house Pete and Slick swung by the nursery to pick up the marine radios and the battery chargers.

"Well El Señor Piloto, what are your thoughts on all this shit?"

"I don't know about you, but if the cops are on to us, I'm going to head west and lay very low for a long while. If we're hot, I'd probably get out of the country for a few months, Costa Rica comes to mind. Even if they can't charge us with anything, they gotta know who we are and where we live, they're going to be watching our asses and my ass ain't gonna be around to be watched."

"Hopefully we're taking all these precautions for nothing, maybe that cop was just taking a break under the trees."

"We're gonna find out in a couple of days."

Back at the house, Slick took the metal suitcase out of his closet and removed all the cash, he handed Pete $10,000, put another $10,000 in a sack to give Sam later that night and put the remaining $7,000 in a drawer. He called Rosemary and told her he was on the way over to her house.

"Well my dear, if you want, you're our spy."

Rosemary squealed with delight, *"I can't wait, this is going to be exciting."*

Slick went over the plan, she would use one of Sam's vehicles which was registered to Mister Allen so nobody could find out who she was via the license plate. She was under no circumstance to do anything that could get her in trouble. If she determined that the place was hot, she was to get out of there and phone Sam or

Sarah, if she had to warn the plane at the last minute, she could do it while 10 miles away as well as if she was right on the airport.

"I don't want you getting arrested, you have all my money in your house."

"Thanks, I'm thrilled to know how worried you are about me."

"Just teasing, but don't take any chances."

"Don't worry, I'm just going to find out about flying lessons and have some handsome young flight instructor tell me all about the manly art of flying, I bet if I show him a little cleavage he'll give me a free demonstration ride."

"If you girls didn't have pussys there'd be a bounty on you."

"But we do and don't you forget it."

"Open that safe, after I stash the rest of my money I'm going to demonstrate why we keep you around."

"You sexy devil, you really know how to turn me on, you are so smooth."

Rosemary and Sarah drove off with 2 of the marine radios, in a few minutes they took turns calling back to the house, Sam answered on one of the other 2 radios, Pete manned the 4th one. Within five minutes, Sarah had mastered the use of the hand held radios, Rosemary had been using them for a long time.

The quintet sat around and went over the plan in detail. If there was a problem, they figured that Rosemary would see signs early enough in the day so that the plane could be diverted by Sam at the drop zone. He wouldn't leave the nursery until 6pm. Surely the cops would be buzzing around the airport long before then if they were planning to capture the returning plane.

"You know what fuck-ups these country cops are, Bubba and his brother will be roaring around all over the place, they'll probably have snipers in the trees, cops will be hiding in other planes, it'll be a real Chinese fire drill. If they're on to us I'm positive our little spy will see plenty of signs. She calls me, I give you guys the word, you land somewhere for gas and ur over Mississippi headin west while those dumb fucking cops are still waiting for you to land."

"What do you think the odds are that we're hot?"

"Less than fifty fifty."

"That cop was looking right at us."

"Well, no matter what, we're ready, let's eat, I'm starving."

Slick and Rosemary had a few more chores to complete, they had to hide the opium and all the counterfeit money. If the law ended up raiding the house it would be pretty stupid to go to jail as counterfeiters or opium dealers when they were only small time marijuana smugglers. They decided to bury the opium in the mayonnaise jar in Rosemary's flower garden, the counterfeit money would fit in the same jar. A wealthy young widow could explain away $200,000 dollars in cash but there would be no excuses for more than $2,000 dollars in fake money and even less chance of talking one's way out of possession of that much opium.

"Slick honey, Let's smoke some before we hide it, I'm feeling a little horny."

"After what I did to you this afternoon?"

"That was just a quickie."

"It satisfied me."

"A fast fuck in the back seat of a car satisfies you men, sometimes I just want that thing inside me for a long time."

"God, a fast fuck in the back seat of a car sounds pretty exciting."

"Turn on the stove, I need that big penis of yours, I won't take no for an answer."

"Well shit, if you put it that way, okay."

Slick buried the opium and counterfeit money between two rose bushes, he kissed Rosemary goodbye and went off to help Pete, they were going to fill the four 55 gallon fuel drums and give Carlos a call. If the Colombians were ready, they'd launch the following night.

It was D Day minus one.

The same young kid at Plant City Airport filled the drums, as usual, all he did was talk about his girl friend, he couldn't have cared less what they were going to do with the gas. An hour later the van was re-hidden in the back of the nursery. Next task, put a call through to Colombia.

Carlos was home, he was very happy to hear that the mechanical problem had been solved, yes, as far as he knew they would be ready, but please call the next day at exactly noon, he'd be waiting by the phone.

Pete and Slick went to meet Sam so he could alert Nevada about the upcoming mission.

D Day morning arrived, the smuggling gang and their ladies were briefed and ready. The only thing left to do was to place the call through to Carlos at noon. Rosemary cooked brunch for Slick and Pete, they were both a little on edge but glad the time had finally arrived, not knowing is the shits.

"You ready for this?"

"I guess, we hid the opium and fake money, all my cash is stashed I think the house is sterile, my car is registered to some unreal person, I've got ten grand in my pocket in case we have to make a run for it. I dug out all my maps between here and California, I don't know what else we could do, do you?"

"Nope, either they're on to us or they're not, it's that simple."

Carlos answered the phone on the second ring, he said they were expected the next morning, their reservations were confirmed at the Hotel Plaza and be sure to listen on the same radio frequency in case Renaldo had any changes or other information.

They shook hands with Sam in front of the nursery at 2:30pm, *"I'll see you guys when you get back, if things go to shit, get as far away from here as you can, that plane's worth more than a hundred grand."*

"Don't worry, if we have to make a run for it, our next call will be from way out west."

"Tell those idiots from Boston to be careful with our dope."

"I will be very clear with them, two strikes and they're

out."

During the 2 hour drive from Tampa to Leesburg, the nervous flyers had plenty of time to consider what might be facing them at the airport.

"You know, we've almost concluded that we're hot and all we know for sure is that one cop was parked in the trees looking at us."

"Maybe putting that big fuel tank in and out of the plane more than fifteen times finally caught someone's eye."

"I still don't think they'll fuck with us til we come back."

"I'm counting on that."

> *"Theirs was not to reason why,"*
> *" Theirs was but to do and die"*
> *"Into the Valley of Death"*
> *"Rode the six hundred"*

"Jesus, Slick where did you learn all that crap?"

"I've got a head full of totally useless shit, I used to memorize quotes from the bible just so I could bug my so-called religious friends."

"Like what?"

"As a dog returneth to his vomit, so a fool returneth to his folly."

"That fits this deal."

They had decided earlier to go straight to the Navajo, remove the seats, slide in the tank and fill it with gas, then they'd go to the motel, wait until take-off time and haul ass. The plan was to leave to room looking like they were coming back, some clothes lying around and the ice chest complete with ice and half a dozen cans of beer.

The van rolled onto the grass parking area at 5:40, there was no one else visible, nobody was working on a plane, no cars were moving around, nothing.

"Let's get this done as fast as we can, this place is fucking spooky."

"Try not to look around too much, it's got to look like we think we're cool."

Slick stepped out of the van, walked over to thc Navajo and unlocked the door. Pete backed the van up close, by the time Pete was at the door, Slick had the 4 seats un- fastened, he handed them out one at a time. Pete then opened the back door to the van and slid the long range tank part way out. Slick jumped out of the plane to help slide the tank in to the plane. As soon as the tank was inside the door, Slick crawled back inside, Pete threw in the boards and the bag that contained the plumbing attachment, tools and retaining straps.   While Slick connected the tank to the fuel line, Pete climbed in the back of the van, opened the drums and hooked up the pump to the 12 volt battery, he then handed the gas nozzle in to Slick, in a few second the fuel was flowing. Pete stood straddling the gas hose in an attempt to block it from view should anybody be watching, he tried his best not to look around but the effort was futile.

"Pete, the first drum is empty, I'm pumping air."

Fifteen seconds later, gas was flowing once again.

"Anybody snooping around out there?"

"Not a soul, the place is deserted."

The first 3 drums required about 6 minutes each to empty, when Pete switched to the last drum, Slick started paying attention to the level of gas in the big tank. As he heard the fuel nearing the top, he stuck a finger about an inch inside the filler hole of the tank, when the finger started getting wet, the tank was full.

"Okay, it's full, shut her off, let's get the hell out of here."

By the time Slick had put the cap back on the tank and locked the plane's door, Pete had thrown the gas hose in the back, closed the back door, climbed in the side door, shut off and disconnected the 12 volt pump. After he replaced the cap of the 4th drum, he slid in the driver's seat and started the van. The second Slick took his seat, they were on the way.

"That was probably the fastest we ever did that, but it seemed to take an eternity."

"Like we discussed, if the cops are out to get us, they just need to know when we leave, then they set up the trap. They would know about how long our trips take so they got about twenty hours

to get their act together. In fact, they'd be better off not having any-
one on the airport until they're ready to spring the trap."

"Ur probably right."
"I didn't sleep worth a shit last night, I need a nap."
"No way, Jose."

Slick slept, Pete fidgeted, sure enough, 10 o'clock rolled around. Pete woke Slick, then walked over to the 24 hour restaurant to fill the thermos with coffee. At 10:30 on the dot, the flying duo left their room and started the walk down the highway towards the airport."

"Slick my man, this is nuts."
"Comeon! Do you want to live forever?"
"Haven't heard that since The Nam."
"This ain't near as dangerous, plus we're getting paid a hell of a lot more."

The airport was eerily quiet, there wasn't a breath of wind, no other planes could be seen or heard and there were no signs of cars on the ramp or taxi ways. Slick and Pete marched right up to the Navajo, opened the door, attached the antenna for the marine radio, threw the chalks aside and stepped inside closing the door behind them. Thirty seconds later, both engines were running, in another thirty seconds they were taxing. Two minutes later the Navajo pulled out onto the runway, *"You ready?"*
"Let's get the fuck outta here."

The Navajo rolled down the runway, lifted off and disappeared in the darkness. It was 10:58pm.

When Rosemary woke up, the clock on her bedside table read 9:11am, she knew that if the plane had left at 11:00 the night before as planned and hadn't run into bad weather along the way, they would have either just landed or be about to land in Colombia. She hopped out of bed and ran to the bathroom, she had a busy day ahead.

A thousand five hundred miles to the south, the Navajo was about to cross the shoreline of north Colombia, the flight had gone almost one hundred percent according to plan, they'd had to divert around one big thunder storm over Haiti, the diversion had cost them thirty minutes. As they crossed over the mouth of the river, Renaldo's voice came over the aircraft radio.

"Calling to the Navajo, do you hear me? Calling to the Navajo."

"Navajo answering, go ahead."

"Oh, glad you are here, there is a change of plans, the hotel has been changed to the Continental, do you understand?"

"Yes, I understand, the hotel is changed to the Continental."

Slick turned to the heading that he'd perfected during his trip with Magda.

"I wonder what's up this time."

Nineteen minutes and twenty seconds later they flew directly over landing strip Continental, the Cessna could be seen parked at the east end of the runway. Slick lowered the landing gear and flaps, then landed, Luis and his men were waiting.

"Bienvenidos, welcome my friends, we are so happy to see you once again."

"Hello Luis, good to see you, was there a problem at Plaza?"

"Nothing important, I was warned of a military exercise in that area so we changed to here to be safe. How is the plane?"

"Perfect, we had no problems."

"Very good, let's get the work finished then we will have time to talk."

At the same time that Slick was re-fueling the Navajo and Pete was supervising the bagging and weighing of the marijuana, Rosemary pulled on to Interstate #4 in Sam's big four door Mercedes, she planned a leisurely drive to Leesburg. She'd drive past the airport into town, have lunch, then return to begin her spying activities. Her heart was pounding just thinking about what she was about to do.

The Navajo was ready to go at 10:35, Luis invited Slick and Pete to relax for a few minutes under a tarp that his men had strung between the 2 trucks.

"My friends, have some cold water or coke, sit down for

five minutes, it is very hot. I have a letter from the lady for you Señor Slick."

"I have one for her too."

"I am happy with her work at the hotel, she takes her job very serious."

"Thank you for giving her the chance."

The three partners had decided earlier not to say anything about the problems that might be waiting back in Leesburg, if they were wrong, why give Luis any reason to worry.

"We hope to be making another flight in about a week, as always, we will call Carlos when we are ready."

"Have a good flight my friends, vaya con dios."

The Navajo began it's take-off roll at 10:55, twenty five minutes later at 11:20, it crossed over the shoreline out into the expanses of the Caribbean Sea. At the very same time, Rosemary drove past the Leesburg Airport and continued on in to town where she planned to have lunch.

"Well my man, in about nine hours the mystery will no longer be a mystery, we'll either be drinking a beer and laughing at ourselves or heading west."

"You think if things have gone to shit Rosemary will be able to figure it out?"

"She's pretty shrewd, didn't take her long to figure out what we're up to."

Three hours later the south shoreline of Haiti appeared on the horizon, the skies ahead were clear, the Navajo was performing beautifully. Pete was at the controls, Slick was looking at sectional charts that covered the states of Alabama, Mississippi and Louisiana.

"You getting ready to escape?"

"Just in case, looks like we could make it as far west as central Louisiana on one load of gas, there's a million airports to choose from."

Eleven hundred miles north, Rosemary was chatting with

Chuck, the manager of Leesburg's flight school, he had already shown her about how much money she could expect to spend while learning to fly. Now they were going to walk out and take a look at a Cessna 150, the plane the school used to train pilots.

As Chuck was demonstrating to Rosemary what various parts of the small Cessna did, a local police car slowly drove by.

"Hi-ya Sheriff!"

"Howdy, Chuck!"

"You catch those guys yet?"

"We'll get em tonight!"

The officer continued his slow patrol of the flight line, Rosemary couldn't believe what she'd just heard, she felt her face flush, her heart was pounding, she was having a little trouble breathing, Chuck didn't seem to notice.

Within a few seconds she had regained a semblance of composure.

"Who's he trying to catch?"

"They think there's a plane coming back here tonight carrying drugs, the sheriff's been watching it for a couple of weeks."

"Oh my, that's terrible, I hope he catches them."

Rosemary tried her best to act interested while Chuck showed her around the Cessna, she desperately wanted to get away from the airport so she could phone Sam. Chuck finally finished his spiel, Rosemary thanked him for his time and promised she'd be back within a week to sign up for flight training. They shook hands, Rosemary walked as casually as she could back to the Mercedes, her knees were trembling. Chuck watched her as she departed, he had totally misinterpreted her flustered condition, Chuck the cool pilot was sure that the sexy young lady had developed a crush on him, irresistible stud that he was.

"Sam, it's very important that you call me right back at this number."

Sam jotted down the number of the phone, he knew the area-code she was calling from. Ten minutes later he dialed the number from another pay phone at the corner Shell station.

"What's up?"

"Sam, thirty minutes ago I heard the local sheriff tell a guy

that they would catch the smugglers tonight when the plane came back."

"Son-of-a-bitch. Well, I guess that makes it pretty damn plain."

"What do you want me to do now?"

"Look, it's still early, get back over here and gimme that radio, I'll take it along as a back-up, then you go straight to ur house and stay there in case they have to leave a message."

"Okay, I'm on the way."

"Good work, we owe you big time."

"Oh Sam, I was so scared I almost peed my pants."

"You did good doll. Now, get ur ass outta there."

While Rosemary was racing towards Tampa in Sam's big Mercedes, Pete and Slick were enjoying the pristine view of the beautiful Bahaman Islands. Mother Nature was co-operating to the max, the weather was picture perfect, the sky was so clear that one could see at least a hundred miles in any direction.

At 5:25, Rosemary screeched to a stop in front of the nursery, she pulled the keys out of the ignition, grabbed the marine radio and ran to Sam's office.

"Mata-Hari, grab a chair and relax, I want to hear the whole story."

Rosemary went over the afternoon's events, she was hyperventilating before completing her recollection, Sam was howling with laughter.

"I told you that those fucking idiots couldn't keep a secret, even if Sheriff Bubba hadn't tipped you off, you'd have seen all kinds of action as it got closer to dark. How the hell they ever catch anybody is beyond me."

"You were right, I couldn't believe my ears."

"Okay kid, get home and take it easy, your day's work is done, you did a hell of a job, I'm damn proud of you."

While Rosemary was driving across Tampa to her house, the Navajo was flying along the east side of Andros Island, it would be dark in a little less than an hour. They'd make the low level dash across the coast of Florida in about an hour forty, then it was another hour fifteen up north to the drop zone. The weather continued to be perfect, the plane hadn't missed a beat.

Sam met Nevada and his new driver on the outskirts of the city, they drove off in the direction of the drop zone. At 6:45, Sam unlocked the padlock and swung the gate open, a few seconds later the two vehicles were hidden behind the trees. The lights were all set up before 7, now all they had to do was wait for the plane to give them a call.

As Sam was setting out the lights, Slick and Pete were descending down to the run in altitude of five hundred feet, the coast of Florida was dead ahead at seventy miles. There was enough moonlight to illuminate any ships that might lie ahead.

Twenty minutes later the Navajo zoomed across Highway 1, then Interstate 95, and out into the Okeechobee swamplands, about an hour to go.

"I'm gonna climb up to about five thousand and turn the lights on, you all set?"
"Ready as I'll ever be."

Sam checked his watch for the thousandth time, it was ten minutes until eight, he double checked to be sure that both of the hand held radios were turned on and on the right channel, they both were.

"Nevada, you want another beer?"
"Why not."

Sam pulled a pair of Buds out of his cooler, as he was about to hand one to Nevada, the radios crackled.

"Happy Hooker two---------------."

Sam switched one of the radios off, picked up the other one and listened.

"Happy Hooker two nine, radio check."
"I read you Hooker. I checked ur fishing hole today, you better find a new one."
"Roger, understand."
"Slick, you hear that?"
"Fucking A! You were right, that cop was watching us."

"I better get my ass in the back."
"Okay, lets drop this shit and get the hell out of here."

"Five minutes!"
"Almost ready!"

"Two minutes!"
"Door's coming open!"

"Get ready! Get ready! Ready! Ready! Ready! Go! Go! Go! Go! Go! Go! Go! Go! Stop! Stop!

Slick pulled up and started the 2nd pass, Pete had managed to throw out 6 bales, he got 8 on the 2nd pass, 8 on the 3rd and the remaining 7 on the 4th and last pass.

"Okay, we're empty, let's haul ass."
"Let's get the tank out while we're still close to the ground."
"Pass the tools."

Slick handed the bag of tools back to a gasping Pete. He disconnected the fuel line at the coupling and released the straps.

"I'm ready to toss it, how's it look down there?"
"About two minutes, it's dark as hell up ahead."

Pete leaned over Slick's shoulder so he could see out the windshield, *"I'm going to open the door, slide the tank out about a foot, then I'm going to jam myself between the side of the plane and the tank. When you slow her down and give me the word, I'll give it one big shove with my legs, that ought to do it."*

"Sounds good, I'll give you a ready, ready go."
"Looks okay now, not a sign of life down there."

Slick pulled the power back and lowered the flaps to half. Pete opened both halves of the cabin door, he then slid the tank into the middle of the floor and guided one end of the tank into the door opening. He then sat against the side of the plane, swung the tank until it was aiming directly out the opening. Finally, he cocked his legs behind the end of the tank, *"I'm ready!"*

Slick pulled the nose up about twenty degrees above the horizon, the airspeed bled off rapidly, *"Ready, Ready, Go!"*

Pete gave a mighty shove with all the strength he had remaining in his legs, the tank went out the door like a torpedo leaving it's tube, *"It's gone!"*

Slick lowered the nose to recover from the stall, picked up flying speed and headed north.

"I'm gonna throw the rest of this shit out too."

"Yeah, get rid of all that crap."

Pete closed the top half of the door, threw out the boards, bungees and straps, house cleaning done, he pulled the bottom half of the door closed. Slick added power and started climbing.

"Gainesville dead ahead about a hundred miles."

"I'm gonna lay down for a minute and catch my breath, my ass is draggin."

A little later when Pete took his seat, Slick explained his plan.

"I'm gonna approach Gainesville from the north so they'll think we're coming down from Atlanta."

"Sounds good, then what?"

"We'll gas up as fast as we can and head north west, I want to get the hell out of Florida before the cops in Leesburg figure it out."

At 9:50pm, Slick radioed Gainesville tower, he reported fifteen miles to the north and asked for landing instructions. The tower operator cleared them to enter the traffic pattern, there was no other traffic. The Navajo touched down at 10:10, the flight had lasted 11 hours and 12 minutes.

Slick shut the engines down next to the Shell sign, the smiling attendant was standing by.

"Howdy boys, you need some gas?"

"You bet, fill her up."

Pete helped the gas man take off the fuel caps, Slick borrowed a rag and checked the oil, neither engine had used half a quart. Pete paid for the gas, thanked the attendant and jumped back in the Navajo, Slick was already in his seat.

"You ready?"

"Let's do it."

The hot engines both barked and farted but started without too much coaxing, the Navajo was ready for take-off at 11:05, they

were 24 hours into the mission. The tower operator told them to report when clear of his zone and cleared them for take-off.

At 11:12, Slick reported 10 miles south, the tower operator
wished them goodnight and cleared them to switch radio frequencies. They were really 10 miles west, but the tower operator didn't
know that, Slick turned to a heading of north-west and continued
climbing, all they had to do now was find some nice quiet little airport way the hell away from Florida.

"Where we going?"

*"If we fly five hours, we'll be eight hundred miles away
from here, that would put us somewhere in Louisiana, we could
land at any uncontrolled airport, sleep in the plane until people
come to work, buy some gas and fly to West Texas or head a little
north and land in Colorado. By then we're gonna need some sleep,
we get a room, check in with Sam, get some shut eye, then find a
place to stash the plane."*

CHAPTER XVI

THE SOLUTION

Even though it was rapidly approaching midnight, the navigation problem couldn't have been easier. Interstate 75 passes just to the west of Gainesville, it heads north west until intercepting Interstate 10 which makes a bee line due west all the way to Los Angeles, California. Flying along at ten thousand feet in the middle of the night when the weather is clear, the busy highway below appeared as lighted lines going off into the distance. Slick simply aimed the nose of the Navajo in the general direction that the interstate highways pointed, nothing could have been more simple.

One hour after take-off, Tallahassee passed by to the south of the flight path, an hour fifteen after Tallahassee, Slick announced that they had crossed the border that divides Florida and Alabama, he might as well have been talking to himself, Pete was out like a light. Within forty five minutes, Slick began to see the lights of New Orleans, Pete was still asleep and not showing any signs of waking up.

Slick's urge to sleep was getting stronger by the minute, he was beginning to nod off several times each minute, flying along in an airplane while sleeping is not good for one's longevity if you happen to be the only pilot awake.

The sectional chart showed an uncontrolled airport on the outskirts of Lake Charles, a small city fifty or so miles west of New Orleans, there was also a VOR located right on the airport. Even if the airport lights weren't on and they couldn't be turned on by keying the mike, as bright as the moonlight was, Slick felt sure he'd be able to find the runway.

Over the city of Lake Charles, Slick made sure the radio was on the published frequency for airport advisory, he keyed the mike button 5 times and, POOF, like magic the parallel rows of runway lights came on. Flaps half, gear down, a wide base turn to final, full flaps and touchdown. A very tired pilot pulled off the runway, followed the taxi ramp until he saw where other planes were, pulled over and parked between 2 other aircraft.

The change from engines running to silence woke Pete, *"Where are we?"*

"Lake Charles, Louisiana."

"I gotta pee."

"Me too, follow me."

Slick opened the two halves of the cabin door and stepped down to the parking apron. Pete was right behind him, they walked to the edge of the cement and pissed in the dirt.

"Jesus, it's after four, how long have I been out?"

"Couple of hours. As soon as I zip up my fly, that's what I'm gonna be, out."

The sun peeking in the front of the Navajo woke the slumbering smugglers.

"Oh Jesus, nothing like an aluminum bed, my fucking back is broken."

"I could have slept on nails, man I was beat."

"You did good El Slicko, If I'd had to fly those last two hours we'd a never made it."

Slick opened several of the sectional charts and laid them side by side on the cabin floor. They drew an imaginary arc to the west within range of a full load of fuel, there were tons of options, any where from Wyoming to New Mexico. Their next stop would depend on whatever the weatherman had to say.

"Let's go see if there's anybody around."

The lineman sitting in the little office beside the fuel truck was surprised to see two men walk in from the runway side, *"Oh hi, where'd you guys come from?"*

"That airplane out there, we need gas and a phone to call flight service."

"Sure, no problem, use my phone, the number's on the wall."

While Slick called the flight service station to check on the weather to the west, Pete went out to help re-fuel the plane, what Slick found out made their direction of flight an easy choice to make.

"The weather's the shits to the north, flight service said the first storm of winter is kicking ass over and around the Rockies, no

problem to the south, we'll just keep chugging west along Interstate
Ten. There's plenty of un-controlled little airports west of San An-
tonio, we can grab another tank of gas and keep going.

And that's what they did, they headed west. Half way between San Antonio and El Paso, they landed at Ozona for fuel, five
hours later the Navajo was safely on the ground at Stellar Air Park
about 30 miles south of Phoenix. Somewhere between Ozona and
Phoenix the flyers had decided to continue west to the Los Angeles
area and park the Navajo where it had been before at El Monte. El
Monte was a quiet little place, they'd leave the plane there, contact
Sam and figure out what the next step was.

The flight from Stellar Air Park to El Monte would take almost exactly 2 hours, therefore the 2 sleuths wanted to take-off after 7pm, that way they'd land at El Monte after 9pm when the tower
shut down for the night. That would complete their flight from Florida to California without talking to a single sole on the radio. If by
chance the word had been put out to keep an eye out for such and
such a Piper Navajo, no use making it easy for them by telling tow-
ers all across the country who and where you were.

"You think those two babes are still hanging around that
bar in Manhattan Beach?"

"If not them, some just like em."

"I could use some coke and a little pussy, they had both"

"Pedro my boy, you flash that wad of hundreds and you're
in like Flyn."

Slick parked the Navajo in one of the many empty transient
slots, they tied her down, gave her a kiss on the cowling and a pat
on the nose and went looking for a taxi.

"That's one good fucking airplane, I'm gonna miss her."

"Damn amazing machine."

The taxi fare from El Monte to Manhattan Beach was $80
dollars, Slick stuck the key in the lock to his apartment at 10:45pm,
it had been a very long couple of days. All Slick wanted to do was
sleep, but there was still work to be done, calls had to be made, girlfriends and partners needed to know where they were and that they
and their assets were safe.

The first stop was the pay phone down by the bar where Pete's tag team was known to hang out.

"*Hi, it's me, how's things?*"

"*Oh, fine, very quite, you okay? I'm so glad you called, I was getting worried.*"

"*Everything's okay, we're back at my pad.*"

"*No kidding? You Know Who really wants to talk to you, he said no matter what time for me to find him.*"

"*I'm at the phone close to our bar, you still have the number?*"

"*Sure.*"

"*Go tell him, I'll be right by the door having a well deserved beer, I can hear the phone when it rings.*"

"*I'm on the way, should be about half an hour. If I can't find him, I'll call.*"

The phone rang at 11:40, Slick picked it up on the second ring.

"*Hello.*"

"*Slick, how's ur ass?*"

"*Great, how you doing, Sam?*"

"*Jesus, you guys made it all the way to California, you really hauled ass.*"

"*We figured the farther away the better.*"

"*Good thinking. Look, everything here is quite as hell. I think the local coppers at Leesburg were trying to make a big bust all by their lonesome. I don't think they got anybody else involved but we can't take any chances just because of what I think.*"

"*Yeah, I don't think either me or Pete would want to fly her south again, we'd always be looking over our shoulders.*"

"*Why don't you guys relax for a couple of days, Nevada's due back in a week with the loot, then we'll get together and split everything up and have a bunch of beers. Maybe you can find somebody who wants to buy the plane, how much you think we could get?*"

"*It's worth about a hundred and fifty, we could probably unload it real fast for a hundred to a hundred and ten. That's a steal.*"

"*I think we better get rid of it before somebody figures out that the owner doesn't exist, what you two think?*"

"*We agree.*"

"*Okay, see what you can do, ur girl wants to talk, she's got some more quarters, catch you later.*"

Slick could hear Sam tell Rosemary to come to the phone.

"*Slick?*"

"*Hi, doll.*"

"*When are you coming back, I can't wait to tell you what happened.*"

"*Couple of days.*"

"*Hurry, it's a wild story, ur not going to believe it.*"

After another beer, Slick went back to the apartment to get some sleep, Pete tried to score but struck out. The girl he'd been working on turned out to be a lesbian, he staggered back to the pad drunk, tired and horny.

In the morning Slick called several aircraft brokers who had ads in Trade-a-Plane, he called an outfit in Texas who claimed to buy and sell more Navajos than anyone else in the world, within a minute he was talking to the Navajo Man. The Man said that if Mister Allen's plane was as good as described, he'd write a check for a hundred and twenty five thousand on the spot, but first, the Navajo would have to be examined by a mechanic of his choosing. Such a mechanic worked at a Piper dealership at Van Nuys Airport. Slick, pretending to be Roger, Mister Allen's pilot, agreed to fly the plane to Van Nuys the next day, assuming that the Navajo Man could make the arrangements with the mechanic. He gave Slick the phone number to reach the mechanic and told him to call later in the afternoon for an appointment.

"*Pete! There's a Navajo broker in Dallas who says he'll give us a hundred and twenty five grand if the plane passes his mechanic's inspection. He'll probably try to jew us down to a hundred or so but fuck it, we got to move it before things unravel.*"

"*Fucking A, a quarter of a hundred is almost as much as a quarter of one twenty five, the difference is only six thousand and change.*"

"*Shit, I never thought about it, what the hell do we do with a hundred thousand dollar check payable to Carl Allen?*"

"Mister Carl Allen goes to the bank the check is written on, shows his I.D. and buys a hundred thousand dollars worth of American Express travelers checks."

"I didn't know Mister Allen had any I.D."

"He can get some pretty damn fast, that fucking Nevada has about five different passports, drivers licenses, library cards, everything, he can fix us up."

Slick called the mechanic in Van Nuys. Yes, he'd heard from the Navajo broker in Dallas, and yes, he'd be happy to take a look at their machine, his fee was $250 dollars, he'd need the log books and three hours to do the inspection. Slick told the mechanic he'd call back as soon as he got the log books sent down from Oregon.

Half an hour later, Rosemary had the log books in a box and was on the way to Tampa Airport to airfreight the package to Los Angeles.

The illegal fuel line had to be removed before flying the Navajo over to Van Nuys, it took them about 15 minutes to do the job, they were getting good at it.

"What about the seats?"

"If they buy the plane, Sam can box up the five at the nursery and ship em air freight, the ones in the van are history."

They picked up the log books at LAX, then drove across Los Angeles to El Monte, the mechanic was waiting for them at Van Nuys.

The Navajo mechanic was impressed with the mechanical condition of the plane.

"This plane is in damn good condition, I've always had good luck with that engine shop. I'll pass my blessing on in the morning, where's the seats?"

"In Oregon, if he buys it we'll make sure he gets the seats, there's only five."

"Don't worry, he'll make you an offer, this thing's like new."

Pete gave the mechanic his fee and they flew off. Slick was ready for a few drinks, he was starting to feel human again.

Slick got through to the Navajo broker at 11am, the used plane salesman went off on a long yarn about the substandard paint job, only 5 seats and a bunch of other shit designed to prepare a person for an offer of less than expected. After 5 minutes of whining, Slick was surprised that his offer was as high as it was, $112,500.00.

"I'll talk with the owner and call you back this afternoon,"
"Okay, now remember, that offer is COD here in Dallas."
"I'll tell the owner."

"Pete, the dirty bastard beat us down to a hundred and twelve point five, COD."
"COD what?"
"We get the check when we show up with the plane in Dallas."
"That's easy, let's go to Dallas."
"I'll go call Sam right now so he can get those seats and carpet shipped."

The wheels were rolling. Sam said he had a guy who would box the seats and get them to the airport. The seats would be shipped to Dallas-Ft. Worth, hold for Slick. Sam said he'd try to locate Nevada to get the ball rolling on the fake I.D.

Slick called the broker back and told him that Mister Allen had accepted the offer, weather permitting, the plane would be sitting on the ramp in front of his office at Dallas-Fort Worth Airport in 2 days.

The following morning the 2 ex-smugglers invested another $80 dollars in the taxi business, they were airborne at 9:30am. The route was an exact backtrack of the route of a few days earlier, refuel at Tucson and continue east. It was supper time before they landed at San Antonio for the night. Dallas was only a couple of hours farther to the east. The Navajo was behaving perfectly.

Pete and Slick found some of the bars where they'd drank and chased pussy when they were hot young Air Force jet jockeys. Everything was the same except the new jet jocks looked younger. The girls looked the same, young and eager to get their hooks into some fine young man, especially an officer and gentleman of the United States Air Force who had a much brighter future than the local cow-pokes and Mexican laborers.

Slick tried to dazzle a pretty Mexican girl with his Spanish speaking ability, sorry, she had a date later with the love of her life, a 22 year old 1st lieutenant from New Hampshire.

"His mom and dad are in for a hell of a surprise when he comes home with that hot little Mexican dish, I wonder how she'll fit in with the society ladies back home."

"She's probably the first piece of ass he ever had."

They laughed and reminisced about some of their recent adventures, it had been a wild couple of months, wild and profitable, they would each have about half a million after splitting up the money from the last load and from the sale of the Navajo.

The hotel van dropped them off at the airport at 7:30, they were in the air by 8:15 and on the ground at Dallas-Fort Worth by 11:30. Pete hired a van and driver, he took them to the Delta Air Cargo office where they picked up the 5 large boxes that had come pre-paid from Tampa. On the way back to the plane, they had the driver stop at a travel agency where they paid cash for one way tickets to Tampa, their flight departed at 4:30 that afternoon, there was a plane change in Atlanta, scheduled arrival time was 9:50pm.

The Navajo was soon fitted with it's carpet and 5 seats, Pete had the van drop him off at the terminal where he'd meet Slick later, they didn't want the Navajo broker meeting the person who would return to cash the check one day as Mr. Allen. Slick fired her up and taxied down the ramp to the broker's office, the 10 or so Navajos out in front were a dead give away that he had arrived.

Mister Navajo met Slick on the ramp, he was all smiles, he'd probably make a fast twenty to forty thousand dollar profit on this baby. Slick handed over the log books and the signed FAA Bill of Sale, Mister Navajo handed over his company check, the deal was done. No, he had no luggage. Yes, he'd appreciate a ride to the passenger terminal.

"Thanks for the lift, you'll have no trouble finding a buyer for that Navajo, she's a fine machine and I'm going to miss her."

"Thanks for bringing her down, hasta la vista."

"Hi, it's me."

"Hi, me, where you?"

"Can you pick us up tonight at ten?"

"Sure, oh goody."   .

"How's things?"

"I talked to your friend today, he says it's very quite."

"Good, see you tonight."

Rosemary was waiting with a big smile on her face, having no luggage to wait for, they walked straight out to her car.

"You want to hear this now or later?"

"Right now, I want to know what you had to do to get them to spill the beans."

Rosemary's story was all the better because she was so excited while telling it. The part where Chuck asked the sheriff if *"He'd caught em yet"* and the sheriff answering, *"Later tonight"*, and Rosemary's reaction of hyperventilating and almost passing out had them all in stitches.

"That's exactly how it happened?"

"Exactly."

"You see, Sam was right, those stupid fucking rednecks just had to brag about something in front of this hot looking broad so she'd know what studs they are."

"Oh fuck, that's funny. I can see the headlines, "COPS MISS BIG DRUG BUST BECAUSE OF MACHO PROBLEM."

"Where to?"

"The house."

"Oh Slick, can't we get some opium, you know what it does to me."

"Okay you horny bitch, swing by ur place, I'll dig it up."

"Oh, that's good."

"I haven't done anything yet."

"I mean it feels good when I smoke this stuff, and then when we make love it feels even better."

"I guess that's why all those Chinese Emperors always kept it around."

After a couple more hits, Rosemary led Slick off, she was at the point of not taking no for an answer, hell, so was Slick. Life is hard.

The three partners met for coffee at 10am, Sam was in the best of moods.

"You should have seen the look on Rosemary's face when she ran in the shop, she couldn't believe what had happened, I guess she damn near passed out when that dumb fucking pilot an cop started talking about smugglers, can you believe how stupid people are?"

"Your predicted it almost exactly to the letter."

"I guess I've had too many dealings with these fucking red-neck cops. God damn! They're dumb. Well shit, guess we're out of business."

"Yeah, I'm gonna make myself scarce for a while, think I'll meet my Colombian doll in Costa Rica, what about you, Pete?"

"I think we should cool it at least for the rest of this season, if we do it again we should plan on a big plane and one big score, it's too risky making this many runs."

The threesome discussed various possibilities. It was agreed that Slick would do some investigation into bigger old cargo planes, it would be ideal if they could make one run in a plane that had the range to take-off from someplace cool like Alabama or Mississippi, fly all the way to Colombia. Then, be able to take-off with 8 or 9 thousand pounds of pot from a runway as short as Plaza. They'd have to find a place where they could land with the load, it would be impossible to throw that much stuff out unless they could find a World War II bomber and drop the whole load at once.

Slick did some quick math, if they could bring in 10,000 pounds, they would gross $3,400,000 dollars. The pot would cost $600,000, another $200,000 for the plane and expenses would leave $2,600,000 to be split up 4 ways. Even if they just abandoned the plane, each share would be $650,000.

The second problem was based on bringing in a load of 6,000 pounds and expenses of $150,000, that would leave each of the 4 with about $400,000. Projects well worth looking in to.

"I got two hundred and twenty thousand in my car, they'll

have the rest ready in a couple more days. When we get the call, Pete, you fly up to get it, Nevada will take you to his man and fix you up with some Carl Allen I.D. so you can get that check cashed. You guys ready for a couple of beers?"

Slick did another math problem, there were lots of numbers that had to be balanced.

"Pete, how much you got left of that ten grand?"
"Six thousand four hundred, call it six."
"How bout you, Sam?"
"Nine, I spent about a thousand."
"I got a little over five."

The waitress replaced the coffee cups with bottles of beer.

```
$  6,000
$  9,000
$  5,000
$ 20,000
```

```
$  20,000   cash bag
+$220,000   first payment last load
=$240,000
 -$ 36,500  ½ the cost of last load of pot to Mouse
=$203,500 divided by 4 =  $50,875
```

That would leave: $112,500   check for the plane
                     +$188,000   final payment last load
                     =$300,500 divided by 4 = $75,125 share each

"Well shit, that ain't bad, we all did pretty good for a couple months work."

"You can say that again, when Pete called me I was down to my last dime, now I'm half a millionaire."

"Let's get that big plane, we'll make you a full fledged millionaire in one lousy day."

"Yeah, why not, the hardest part is having the right con-

nections down south, we got that, all we need now is a big mother fuckin plane and a place to land."

"Speaking of down south, did you guys call Luis?"

"Pete had a long conversation with Carlos when we were in California."

"Shit, we forgot about ur broad, what should we give her, she saved our ass."

The three going out of business executives agreed on $10,000 for Rosemary's spy job.

"Don't worry, she'll be happy as hell with that, she loves this shit."

"She's a good broad, I like her ass. Let's meet at the lake house tonight, we'll give the loot the light treatment, take out ten for Rosemary, split up the rest, then we'll burn some of those steaks and suck down some of that wine. Pete, you got any coke?"

"Plenty."

"Sounds like a party."

Slick went back to the lake house to take some steaks out of the freezer, Rosemary was out by the lake getting a little afternoon sun.

"Well my little spy, tonight you're going to be ten thousand dollars richer."

"You guys are too generous, it was only half a day's work."

"You earned every cent."

"This has been the wildest adventure of my life, I'm going to miss it but I need to get away from Florida, I have a lot of sad memories here. Nothing sad about the last few months hanging out with you and the gang, you know what I mean."

A flabbergast Slick asked, *"Where you gonna go?"*

"I'm going to take an art course at La Sorbonne in Paris, my classes start in January, you want to go with me?"

"I'll come for a visit, I'm not much into art."

"What are your plans?"

"We're gonna lay low for the rest of the year, then we'll see what happens."

"Be careful, you can't get away with it for ever."

"Sounds like you're saying goodbye."

"Not yet, I'm going to spend Christmas with my mom, then fly to Paris and look for a place to live. Thanks to you guys, I won't have to scrimp."

"Well shit, I'm going to miss you."

"I'm not dying, we'll still see each other."

"I've never been to Paris it could be fun. Look, I'm going to get the hell out of here in a couple of days, you wanna come out west with me for awhile, we could hit Vegas and put everything down, double or nothing."

"Sure, for two weeks, then I've got to get back here and make tons of arrangements."

Slick went inside and set up the ultraviolet light, he couldn't help but wonder what was going on inside Rosemary's head, did she know or suspect about the Colombian girl or was she just getting away from all the reminders of her dead husband.. He'd never ask and he doubted that she'd ever tell.

The men huddled in Slick's bedroom checking the new bills with the ultraviolet light while Rosemary and Sarah sat outside sipping wine and talking about France. After subtracting Rosemary's $10,000, each share was $48,375. When the money had been checked and divided, the three smugglers came outside to join the girls.

"Sam, did you know that Rosemary is going to art school at La Sorbonne?"

"Where's that?"

"Paris."

"You like them frogs?"

"Sam, that's the most famous art school in the entire world."

"Could-a fooled me."

"We have to get her a really chic outfit for Paris."

"That sounds like a job for you girls, but I'm gonna pay for it."

"Sam, you are too sweet."

Pete's travel agent friend called and invited him over to her house for drinks, the dinner party was down to 4.

"Guess that shows you a lot about his priorities, he could-a hung around here and bullshitted with his two best buddies, what happens, he dumps us for some skinny broad with little tits."

"He struck out big time in California, he worked on a chick about three drinks worth before she told him she was a dyke."

"The dirty slut."

"Oh Slick, how do you know she was a lesbian, maybe she just said that because she wasn't interested in him."

"She looked a little dykey to me."

"And what does a dyke look like, pray tell?"

"You know, like----."

"Like they want to lick ur pussy and cut off my dick."

"Thanks for the clarification, Sam. How is it that I always understand everything you say?"

"Cuz I talk English, not bullshit."

The next afternoon Rosemary modeled her new leather outfit complete with a little red beret, she was going to be the best dressed student at the Sorbonne, she looked hot.

"They'll want to use you as a model, you look like a million bucks."

"Thanks to you guys, you know how much she paid for this? More than six hundred dollars."

"You're worth every nickel."

Pete's girlfriend got him a ticket to Boston for the following day, Nevada needed him for at least 2 days to get the I.D. package fixed up. Slick and Rosemary were going to drive up to Atlanta with all his cash and the opium in the metal suitcase, then catch a nonstop flight to L.A., that much cash in a place that could conceivably be hot was making him a little nervous. They'd hang out at Manhattan Beach until notified that Pete had cashed the check from the Navajo broker and Sam had got the final payment for the last load of dope. They'd all meet somewhere for the final split, then it was going to be adios for awhile.

Three days later, Slick opened a savings account at the Bank of America branch in Redondo Beach. The bank had a special going on, if you kept your savings at a minimum of $5,000 dollars for the following year, you got a free medium size safety deposit box and the deal was good as long as you kept 5 grand in your account. An hour later he had opened another account at a Home Savings and Loan branch, they had also thrown in the safety deposit box since Mr. Adams had opened his account with such a tidy little sum. All of his cash was now safely tucked away either in the Cayman Islands or in new safety deposit boxes or savings accounts. All told, Slick had amassed just a little more than $450,000 dollars with another $75,000 due to come his way when the final payment for the last load and the check for the Navajo were divided up. Now, instead of worrying about having to sell his classic 1955 Thunderbird, Slick was thinking about buying himself an airplane, how things do change.

On their 4th day in California, Slick and Rosemary went on a spending spree, the plan was to unload all the counterfeit money in one day and be done with it. They drove south down Pacific Coast Highway to Beach Boulevard, then north until reaching an Orange County suburb called Westminster. Westminster had been taken over by Vietnamese refugees who'd fled their country just before it fell to the communists in 1975, the entire area was now known as Little Saigon.

Little Saigon had become a wide open, almost wild west town controlled by the Vietnamese crooks who'd been ripping off the US Taxpayers during the war in their homeland. When things went to shit they had used their money and clout to be on the 1st planes out, the money and gold they'd accumulated was so bulky that many of their countrymen had to be denied seats on the overloaded departing planes.

A wide open town run by the Vietnamese Mafia seemed a perfect place to pass a couple thousand dollars in excellent counterfeit notes. The 1st liquor store Slick walked in to was just what he was looking for.

The little Vietnamese lady minding the store spoke little or no English but she had no trouble handing him a $22 dollar bottle of Kahlua and making change for the fake hundred Slick handed her.

The next liquor store was even better, three giggling young

Vietnamese girls were behind the counter, they almost lost it when Slick tried to talk to them in their language, he was out the door in a matter of minutes with another bottle of liqueur and $80 dollars in change.

The scene repeated itself over and over. Only once did Slick use real money. A very wise looking and talking older Vietnamese woman who'd probably been a madame in a whore house in Vietnam, scared Slick into buying a pack of gum with some real coins before he scurried out of her establishment.

By 4 in the afternoon, he'd spent every last phony bill, the trunk of the T-Bird was full of a mixture of expensive liqueurs and wines. Of the $1,740 dollars in fake money he'd started with, Slick now had $1,025 in real money plus all the booze. Hopefully, the liquor stores would pay the protection racketeers off with the fake money, then the hoods would pass it on to their Don, the Don would have them whacked for trying to pull a fast one. There's so much crooked shit going on in Little Saigon that Slick felt sure the Vietnamese would blame each other for the sudden surge of counterfeit money. Some poor dumb shit gang leader would probably meet his end in a day or two over his and Rosemary's liquor rampage. Too bad, if they hadn't been such a bunch of crooks they wouldn't have let a bunch of commies run them out of their own country.

Later that night Slick hoisted a double Black Russian and proposed a toast, *"Rosemary my dear, lets drink to Nguyen Cao Ky, Madame Ky and the rest of the crooks who jumped ship when things got a little too hot for their chickenshit asses."*

"I don't know who you are talking about but I'll drink to them if we can smoke some you know what."

Slick broke out the opium. He and Rosemary spent the night enjoying the spoils of a good harvest.

CHAPTER XVII

THE HIGH ROLLERS

Ten days after the last flight, Pete called from Dallas, *"Slick, I got her cashed, Sam's gonna meet me in Vegas tomorrow, can you get over there?"*

"Fuck yeah, how'd it go?"

"A real hassle. Look, I've got reservations for all of us at Ceasar's Palace, I get there at four thirty, Sam and Sarah's plane lands at six, see you there."

"Shit hot, did Nevada come up with the rest of the money?"

"All of it."

"Dinner will be on me, I unloaded all the funny money."

"Sounds like a party."

"Okay buddy, see you tomorrow."

Slick was elated, he'd really been missing the excitement and the action of the past several months, not to mention Sam and Pete.

"Rosemary, pack ur bags, we're going to Vegas."

The next afternoon Slick and Rosemary cruised along the strip, Sammy Davis Junior was at the Sahara, Buddy Hackett was at the Tropicana and Elvis was at Ceasar's Palace, Vegas was in full swing.

"Oh god, Elvis Presley. You think we could get in to see him?"

"In this town, a hundred dollar bill can get you almost anything, I'll try to set it up for tomorrow, tonight we have business to take care of, then we're going to a party."

Their room was fantastic, the four poster canopy bed was fit for a king, you could almost swim in the bathtub, there was even a phone in the bathroom. They decided to try out the monstrous tub before the others arrived and things got busy, ten minutes later nothing could be seen but bubbles with two heads sticking out the top. Slick found the switch and turned on the jets, now the bathtub was a Jacuzzi, bubbles were all over the place. The streaming jets had an arousing effect on Rosemary, her hands had an arousing effect on Slick, the next thing he knew, she was having her way with him.

"Jesus, that feels good."

"Be quiet."

The combination of hot water and strenuous lovemaking had a predictable effect, Pete's call caught the horny duo sound asleep.

"Slick, wake up, I'm here and I want someone to drink with, what the hell you doing sleeping in the middle of the day anyway?"

"This crazy woman thinks I'm eighteen years old. How you doin, Pedro?"

"Only thing I'm lacking is a broad."

"A problem with a simple solution in Las Vegas."

"Meet me downstairs at the main bar."

"Gimmee fifteen minutes."

Pete was all smiles, the two semi retired smugglers greeted each other like the friends they were.

"Good to see you man, I've been bored shitless, I miss the action."

"Me too, pruning the roses doesn't hack it. How's ur girl?"

"Couple more days and she's my ex girl."

"She's really going to France?"

"Sure as hell. It's okay with me, now I don't have to bullshit her about going south."

"You think she knows?"

"These fucking broads can smell strange pussy from a hundred miles. You said they hassled you in Dallas."

Pete went into a long description of all the crap he had to go through to finally get the check cashed, the bank ended up calling the Navajo broker to make sure he had issued a check to a Carl Allen. The bank wanted to know why Mr. Allen didn't just deposit the check in his account like 99 percent of other people did. Pete's answer was that he was going on a long holiday and he wanted to convert the check to American Express Travelers Checks.

"I finally acted like I was getting pissed off and asked the

guy what business was it of his what I did with my own money, quit annoying me and get me my checks so I could catch my plane or take me to his boss, what the hell was this anyway, Russia."

"What he say?"

"He whined about some irregular banking practices, then he took me to one of the tellers and told her to take care of me. Then the fucking broad wanted to know why I wasn't signing all the fucking checks and was I aware that if someone stole them unsigned the bank was not responsible. I said I knew the rule, thank you and goodbye. Anyway, I ended up with a hundred and ten thousand in five hundred dollar traveler's checks and two thousand five hundred in cash. When I walked out of the bank they were all looking at me like I was some kind of nut."

"Well at least you got it done. You think I should bother to go up to Oregon and close the post office box?"

"Fuck it, when Mister Allen doesn't pay his rent, they'll cancel it."

"Yeah, ur right, How's Sam?"

"Shit, he's doin fine, you know that fuckin nursery's gonna show a profit this year."

"No shit? I thought it was just a front."

"That's how it started, now he's selling flowers like mad, Sam's the local expert on all kinds of tropical plants, all the little old ladies love him."

"He's a real charmer, if they only knew."

Pete ordered 2 bottles of Budweiser, Slick filled him in on what he'd learned about big cargo planes and where you buy one.

"I spent a couple afternoons hangin around Burbank Airport, there's a bunch of old pieces of shit layin around over there. Any of them could be bought and fixed up for the right amount of money, but the guys I talked to said the DEA is starting to ask a lot of questions when people who don't have anything to do with cargo airlines start paying cash for planes that seem to have only one use."

"That makes sense."

"Why don't we buy a plane in South America, have Luis get us a place to park it, make sure the thing is in good mechanical shape and make a one way trip to Florida, unload the bastard and

haul ass. That way we don't have to worry about the fucking Feds, narcs, cops, DEA and everybody else trying to mess with us. In Colombia the army brass and all the cops are on the payroll, shit, they'll probably help us load the dope on the plane, what-da-ya think?"

"You know how to fly those things?"

"Not yet, but I can sure as hell learn, I'd hang around down south with my girl, fly the plane until I got the hang of it, make the arrangements with Luis, call you, you come down for a holiday load up and we're off. Ten hours later we land on some deserted airport, unload, hide the shit, give the boys up north a thousand pounds at a time or whatever they can handle and it's all over within a couple of weeks."

"Sounds good, Sam's gonna love the idea, that's the main thing he's been worried about, the narcs snooping around some big old plane."

"You think ur buddy the Mouse would front it?"

"Why don't we front it, that little prick's in pretty hot water with the law, we ought to stay away from his ass, let's see what Sam thinks. How much we talkin about?"

Slick borrowed a ballpoint from the bartender.

"If we brought in ten thousand pounds, we'd have to have six hundred thousand for the pot and whatever the plane cost, let's say a hundred grand. We'd gross three million four hundred thousand minus seven hundred thousand leaves two million seven hundred thousand divided by three equals nine hundred grand each, Jesus Christ, that's a bundle."

"You mean if we had a plane big enough to carry twenty thousand pounds we'd each end up, with two million?"

"Fuckin A, why not, if we got busted we'd be in just as deep a shit for ten thousand pounds as for twenty thousand."

"Two million in one day, wouldn't that be sweet."

"Yeah, but don't forget, twenty thousand pounds would mean over a million in advance for the dope, I'm not sure I'd be willing to put up four hundred grand, that's damn near all I got."

Sam and Sarah checked in a little after 7, half an hour later the men met to talk business, Sarah and Rosemary went window shopping at the chic shops that are part of the Ceasar's complex. Sam thought the idea of launching from Colombia on a one way mission was outstanding, of course that would require at least one of them spending a lot of time in Colombia which was no problem as long as Slick was still gaga over his Colombian doll. They all agreed that the biggest problem would be in finding the right place to land. They needed a place far enough away from town where a big plane could land without attracting any attention. The airport would have to be deserted at night so that a big plane could unload a big load into a big truck and then the big truck could drive away unnoticed and disappear to it's hiding place. The setup would require a lot of homework but the payoff would make it all worth while.

"We got nine or ten months to get it all set up, there must be at least a hundred airports we could check out."

"Who says it has to be a airport, couldn't we use a field or a deserted stretch of road, how bout one of those abandoned housing developments that went bust in the last couple of years, shit, there all over the place."

"Shit Pete, that's a hell of an idea, nobody's looking for airplanes to drop out of the sky and land on some rural road in the middle of the night."

"Anyway, we got plenty of time to figure it out, let's split this loot up and go have a couple of martinis and a big juicy steak. I got a hundred eighty from Nevada, that plus the first payment of two hundred twenty equals four hundred thousand, that about right?"

"That's right on, we took off with a thousand one hundred and seventy five pounds of dope, that comes out right at four hundred thou."

"Okay, Slick, figure it out."

Slick, the team accountant jotted some numbers on a piece of hotel stationery:

$180,000 last payment
$112,500 Navajo
$292,500 divided by 4 = $73,125

"*Each of us get's seventy three thousand plus a little change, then I got to give you both a little back, I got rid of all that counterfeit.*"

"*Give em seventy three, dinner's on you tonight, Slick.*"

"*Sounds like a deal.*"

Pete counted out a hundred and forty six, shinny new $500 dollar traveler's checks, "*Like the bitch at the bank told me, until you sign each of these, anybody can cash them.*"

"*They're going right in my safety deposit box except for five or six that I'm going to invest later tonight, did I ever tell you about my system on the roulette table?*"

"*I can't fuckin wait.*"

"*Let's go find the broads, I'm starving.*"

Slick took them to an off the beaten track steakhouse that had been recommended by the girl who signed him up for a safety deposit box, she had been right, the food was outstanding.

After dinner, Sam wanted to have a drink in each of the 7 original big name hotels along the strip, they started at the Sahara on the south end and started working their way north. By the time they hit the Flamingo, nobody was feeling any pain, Slick had tried his system at each club, so far he'd lost almost a thousand of his hard earned dollars.

Pete had strayed to the cocktail lounge where he'd spotted several available looking girls, Slick and Sam went straight to the roulette table.

"*Slick, you gotta explain this system to me, I don't have a fuckin clue what ur trying to do.*"

"*It's simple, I pick six numbers that come next to each other on the wheel, they form sort of a little pie section. Sometimes if you're lucky, the ball will land in that little pie several times in a row, as you've seen tonight, so far I haven't hit a single number so it ain't foolproof.*"

"*Maybe you've got the wrong pie.*"

"*I'm gonna try the same six numbers, I'm due to hit.*"

They approached a table that had no players, Slick asked for a hundred dollars in one dollar chips, Sam did the same. Slick put two chips on the 7, 11, 20, 26, 30, and 32, Sam put two of his chips on top of each of Slicks.

The croupier spun the wheel and flicked the ball in the opposite direction, *"No more bets."*

Round and round went the little ball. *"Seventeen."*

The croupier scooped all the bets.

"You see that, seventeen is right next to our pie, that ball moves over one number and we're winners."

Slick repeated his bet, Sam followed suit, the croupier flicked the ball, *"No more bets."*

"Thirty two."

"Hot damn!"

"First fuckin number tonight, about time."

The croupier gathered up all the losing bets, he then paid Slick and Sam 35 to 1, so they each got 70 chips back.

"Place your bets."

They both repeated their bet except they doubled the bet on 32.

"Sometimes these numbers repeat."

"I'm just followin your lead."

"No more bets."

Sam's eyes were glued to the little ball as it went round and round, it finally slowed down, jumped out of one number and finally stopped on the 11.

"Son-of-a-bitch, that fuckin ball jumped out of thirty two."

"We still got a winner."

"Oh yeah, so we do, I'm startin to like this game."

Pete strolled in with a sexy looking doll on his arm, *"This is Virginia, she says she's lucky."*

"From the looks of those tits, I'd say ur the lucky one, those things real?"

"Of course."

"Place your bets."

They all scattered their bets on the sacred numbers, when Pete's date leaned over to place her bets, everybody including the croupier got an eye full, this chick knew how to advertise.

"No more bets."

Round and round went the little ball.

"Double zero."

"Where'd that fuckin number come from?"

The croupier scooped up all the chips.

"Place your bets. You gentlemen want some drinks?"

"Hell yes, this is hard work."

"Comeon pie, do ur stuff."

The little ball went round and round, drinks flowed, the pie started doing it's magic, Pete's date started squealing and showing more flesh, Sam and Slick doubled, then quadrupled their bets, Sarah and Rosemary stood back and watched.

"No more bets."

"Seven! Fucking seven!! Pay us baby!!"

The croupier pushed huge stacks of chips across the table to Slick and Sam, he pushed a much smaller stack over to Pete's hooker, Sam flicked a twenty five dollar chip back to the croupier as a tip, *"Thanks buddy, that was a good spin."*

"Thank you sir."

"Count em up, we gotta hit the road."

The croupier stacked all the different colored chips in equal piles, the hooker had $310 dollars and she hadn't even fucked anybody yet, Sam and Slick each had over $2,000 in winnings and it had all happened in about ten minutes.

"Jesus, Slick, this is too fuckin easy, couple more hours and we'd own this joint."

"Yeah, Sam, they build all these fancy hotels because everybody always wins."

They marched triumphantly to the cashier's cage to cash in the winning chips then went out front to catch a cab to their next destination, the Sands.

"How'd you do last night?"

"Pretty good I guess, looks like a pretty big pile of chips and money over there."

"You and Sam really had a crowd downstairs at the dice table."

"That fuckin Sam loves craps, he was hot there for awhile, how long did he hold the dice?"

"I don't know, fifteen minutes, the whole table was going nuts, that one guy in the cowboy hat had stacks of black chips, he must have won twenty thousand."

"How about Pete's hooker?"

"She was dropping green chips in her purse as fast as she could."

"What a great town, you got any aspirin?"

"You better get up, we're supposed to meet them for breakfast at eleven, Sam and Sarah are leaving at two."

Slick counted his loot, he had chips from 5 different clubs totaling a thousand three hundred, he had two thousand six hundred and change plus three of the six travelers checks he'd started with.

"Wow! After dinner and everything else, I'm two thousand four hundred ahead, that ain't bad."

"Now, maybe you can get tickets for Elvis tonight?"

"Guaranteed."

There were a lot of goodbyes to be said, Sam and Sarah kissed Rosemary, Slick kissed Sarah and embraced his friend, Sam. Pete told Sam he'd be back in a couple of days, Pete's hooker almost broke into tears, she truly liked these people who treated her just like one of the gang instead of like an alien.

As Sam and Sarah's taxi departed, Virginia remarked, *"They seem so nice, especially Sam, he's a special man."*

"That he is, that he is."

Pete broke up the wake, *"Bloody Mary's are on me, Slick, try to get four Elvis tickets, Me an Virginia would like to join you."*

After a nap, Slick went down to the casino. Over by the Black Jack tables, he asked one of the dealers who he should talk to in order to get tickets for a show that was sold out, the dealer pointed out a cool looking guy standing between the crap tables.

"Tony's the floor boss, he can fix you up."

Slick walked up and introduced himself to Tony and told him the situation, Tony listened, asked Slick to wait a few minutes and walked away. Ten minutes later he returned, *"It's taken care of, you go to the head of the line tonight, ask for John, tell him ur Slick, he knows ur coming, he'll have your tickets, it's all set."*

Slick started to pull some money out of his pocket, *"No, no, you just take care of John, I'm glad to help."*

"Thanks Tony, I can't thank you enough."

"Hey, it's what I do. See you after the show."

Elvis was fat but it didn't matter, the women went wild, the red faced tub of lard could still do a number on the girls.

"How in the world did you get these seats?"

"After the show you have to go back stage and fuck him, that's how."

"Oh Slick, you are the greatest, I've been dreaming of having sex with him since I was a teenager."

Elvis closed the show with his rendition of *My Way*, Rosemary was in ecstasy, Slick thought the burned out crooner was going to pop a blood vessel. As The King wrapped up, Rosemary had almost reached orgasm, Slick had tuned the noise out and had drifted a couple thousand miles south.

"Wasn't he terrific!"

"Yes my dear."

"I'm so horny, you don't mind if I fantasize a little next time we make love?"

"Whatever turns ur crank."

Slick met Pete in the morning for a bloody Mary, they had a few things to discuss. They decided to tell Rosemary nothing about future plans, as far as she was concerned, they were retired, any talk of future missions she may have over heard could be brushed off as pure fantasizing. They would stay in touch by phone, Slick needed to know how things were in Florida. The Mouse's legal problems were a real worry, if the little turd went down, Pete was sure he'd sing like a bird to keep his ass out of jail, he was making sure all his assets were well protected just in case. Pete would do what he could to find out to what extent the cops in Leesburg were pursuing the case of the plane that never returned, they had the van, it was registered to Carl Allen at a P.O. Box in Tampa. Four other vehicles had been also, they had all been sold off in the days since the last mission.

"You mean my Mercedes is gone?"

"Yeah, long gone, that dirty old Mister Allen sold it along with Sam's big four door, my green one and the four by four. They're all paid for and signed over, history."

"*How'd he do it so fast?*"

"*Sam knows a guy who moves a lot of cars, the guy don't ask no questions. Trust me, if the cops from Leesburg follow the paper trail back to him, he'll say he never met Mister Allen, he only met someone who was acting as his agent, paid for the cars and sold them to his buyers, end of story.*"

"*Anything else they could trace back to any of us?*"

"*There's only one fly left in the ointment, that fucking little worm, Mouse, he knows way too much about me and Sam. You're laughing, all he knows about you is that you're a pilot and me and Sam call you Slick.*"

"*You think he's going down?*"

"*Sam thinks he's fucked, he's running out of money, his partner has rolled over, the Feds are putting big time pressure on him to cop a deal, Sam thinks they will make him an offer he can't refuse, they may already have.*"

"*And Sam thinks he'll go for it?*"

"*When they say to him, twenty years maximum security with a bunch of horny, muscle bound cons who are always looking for a tight new asshole or five years probation, what do you think?*"

"*Yeah, ur right, he ain't no Sam.*"

"*Sam thinks he might not rat on us because we're still providing him with money and we will continue to do so, at least he thinks we will. I mean, there's no reason for him to blow the whistle on us, he's got plenty of guys he can fuck who the Feds already know about, why bring us in.*"

"*I hope ur right, keep ur eyes and ears wide open.*"

"*Anyway, we'll be laying low for the next couple of months, everything should be clear as a bell before we make another move.*"

"*Doesn't the little prick know what would happen to him if he fucked Sam?*"

"*He knows, one of his Cuban buddies got a little out of line a couple years ago, Sam really fucked him up, you saw how Sam looked at him, he knows.*"

"*I'm surprised he's still alive.*"

"*We needed his money.*"

"*We don't need it any more.*"

"That's a point, I wonder if the little prick has figured that out yet?"

Pete motioned for the waitress to bring another round, "What about my Virginia?"

"Great girl, I like her, no bullshit there."

"I like hookers, you always know exactly where you stand."

"Shit, they're all hookers, they're all sellin that pussy, some take money, some take houses, they all take something."

"Ain't that the fuckin truth."

"Look, Pete, why not hang around here another night, I'm pretty sure I can get tickets to the Sammy Davis Junior Show. This fuckin Vegas beats the shit out of that dog shit bar in Manhattan beach, besides that, I'm gonna miss ur ass."

"Why not, I've had enough of that travel agent bitch watching herself fuck in the mirror, let's go out and kick some ass tonight."

It was Slick's job to take care of the tickets, a short conversation with his new pal Tony solved that problem. The fucking pit bosses in Vegas seemed to have one hell of a "cosa nostra", there didn't seem to be anything they couldn't get done. Pete was in charge of arranging dinner, Tony directed him in the direction of one of his fellow pit bosses who was into "haute cuisine" within minutes, everything was arranged. It was going to be a very special evening.

Rosemary slept in, Slick drove Pete out to the airport, Virginia had left a little earlier, she and Pete had promised to stay in touch, they'd really hit it off.

"Well old buddy, take care of urself, remember you gotta constantly check ur six or somebody will sneak up behind you."

"We'll be okay, tell Magda I'll be down for a visit, maybe sooner than you think."

"Why not, they can't haul you off if ur not around."

"Relax, Slick, we're gonna be okay, not to worry."

The two friends shook hands, Pete turned and walked into the terminal, Slick drove off wondering what travails awaited his friends."

"You want to stay another night or go back to the beach and smoke opium?"

"We better get back, my flight to Tampa is day after tomorrow, I have to pack and I want at least one more session with my favorite man and my favorite drug."

"Your wish is my command."

During her last two days in California, Rosemary and Slick smoked a little of the forbidden flower, ate a lot of rich foods and spent as many hours in the sack as their bodies would allow. Rosemary vowed that should the law ever approach her concerning the activities of her one time boyfriend and his pals from Tampa, she'd swear that the only thing they ever talked about was sex. Slick promised that he was one hundred percent retired from the smuggling game, he'd had all the excitement he needed to last two lifetimes. Now he was going to disappear for awhile in some far away country where nobody knew who he was and no-one knew how he could be reached by phone.

Slick walked Rosemary to the departure lounge, they had enough time for a good-bye drink before the final boarding call.

"You have fun, art school in Paris sounds like every girl's dream."

"Luckily I married right and had a crook for a boyfriend, most girls can't afford it."

"You earned every bit of it, ur a hell of a girl."

"You be careful Slick Adams, you don't think for a moment that I believe that drivel about you being retired do you?"

"You don't?"

"Not for a second, you still have that look in your eyes."

CHAPTER XVIII

THE AFTERMATH

Slick had a little business to take care of before getting out of town. He made a deal with the apartment manager to split the difference with the 4 months he was still ahead in the rent. It took another day to settle up with the phone, electric, gas and water companies. He put $25,000 in travelers checks in his pocket, parked the T-Bird in his brother's garage, got a ride to Los Angeles International, purchased the ticket he'd reserved earlier, called Pete and told him where he'd be the next day, then boarded a plane bound for San Jose, Costa Rica.

At the same time as Slick's jet was departing Los Angeles, Rosemary was driving north from Tampa towards her mother's house near Atlanta. She'd been a busy girl, there are a lot of little details that one has to take care of before leaving home for a long period of time. She'd even asked one of her dead husband's partners in the law firm to do a little snooping around down town to see if there was any scuttlebutt going around about a couple of people she vaguely knew through an old friend of hers. She had told the partner that she was a little worried about some of the company her friend was keeping, he had promised to keep his ears open, she was to call him before leaving for Europe to see if he'd heard anything.

While Rosemary drove north, Sam chatted with the Mouse in his latest hotel room, he'd been changing hotels rather frequently of late. Mister Mouse was very depressed, things hadn't been going his way in what seemed to him a long time.

"Ramon, I'm just about the only friend you got left, I'm gonna have another two hundred grand for you in a week or so, we're still working, you still get a quarter of whatever we earn, don't fuck it up."

"Sam, these bastards are really leaning on me."

"Ramon, ur gonna need money, who else you gonna get it from?"

"They know who you are, Sam, they want to know where you fit in." Ramon was almost pleading.

Sam got right into Ramon's face, *"I don't fit in! They don't know nuthin unless someone tells em. If someone tells em I'm gonna know it's you and that ain't gonna be good."* The words had come out as guttural sounds emitted from an angry animal.

Sam continued the lecture, when he was done, Mouse was one hundred percent convinced that Sam was the only chance he had to survive. Sam would protect him even if he went down, he would have him killed badly if he caved in. It was simple, the choice was clear, all he could ever tell the feds about Sam was that he was an old friend who owned a nursery. Poor Ramon, he was in one hell of a dilemma.

Sam drove home feeling a lot better, he was sure that Ramon the Mouse had got the picture, he'd lied about having another two hundred grand in a couple of weeks, he had it right now but he needed Ramon to think there was still money on the way. Sam would meet with Pete in the morning so he could bring him up to date.

As Sam pulled into his garage, Slick's plane was landing in San Jose, he cleared customs and grabbed a cab, destination downtown, *"Hotel El Presidente, por favor."*

It was as if he had never left. The manager at the El Presidente greeted him by name, then showed him up to his old room on the second floor. After a quick shower, Slick walked across the street to Lucky's Piano Blanco, the luscious Roxanna rushed over to greet him with a soft kiss on the lips. *"You come back."*

"I missed you."

"Oh, Señor EsSlick, you are the bad one. Where is the sexy girl?"

"No more."

"You tell the truth?"

The flirtation went on, Slick couldn't believe the change that had come over Roxanna, the last time he'd seen her she'd acted very coy, now she was coming on to him. Maybe she needed money, who knows, nobody could ever outguess these women.

Pete met Sam at the nursery the next morning, they went for a walk out back to be sure their conversation was private.

"I had a little heart to heart with the Mouse last night, I'm pretty sure I convinced him never to get you and me messed up with

his other problems. He thinks we're still working so he'll have money coming in. The dumb little bastard has blown everything but a hundred and fifty in the Caymans, how much did he have down there?"

"Shit, I don't know, me and Slick put over half a million in his account when we went down there in October, since then we transferred about two hundred grand to Luis, I don't have a clue how much was there before."

"Whatever was there is almost all gone, jesus, what a lame brain, we gotta keep him thinkin that we're still workin so he thinks he'll still be getting a quarter of whatever we earn."

"So you didn't tell him we sold the plane?"

"Oh fuck no, I didn't give his last two payoffs either, I want to be deep in debt to him so he covers our asses."

"Good plan."

"You heard from Slick?"

"He's back in Costa Rica."

"He really likes that Latin pussy."

"You saw those pictures."

"Rosemary's gone, she came by to say goodbye to Sarah, France is a good place for her, she knows too much."

"I'll call Slick later and bring him up to speed."

Sam and Pete talked a little more about Ramon, Pete was having a hard time being convinced that the Mouse wouldn't rat on his partners to get a softer deal with the Feds.

"I told Slick I thought when he had the choice between five years probation and a bunch of cons butt fucking him, he'd go for the probation in half a second."

"I promised him that if our names came out, what would happen to him would make a little butt fucking the least of his problems."

"He take you serious?"

"I was very serious."

"I bet the little prick about shit his pants."

"He got the picture."

While Pete and Sam were discussing Ramon's fate, Slick was having breakfast in bed with Roxanna, he was feeling pretty cocky about having stolen her away from her other admirers, she was feeling a hundred dollars richer.

"I like you Señor Eslicko, you are a good lover and a nice man."

"I like you too Roxanna, you are a great lover and a very nice lady."

"You like me as good as Eva?"

"Yes, I'm with you aren't I."

"Why do men like her, she is skinny and has leetle tits."

Slick's truthful answer would have been, *"great pussy and fantastic blowjob,"* but of course he fibbed and said something innocuous then changed the subject.

"What time do you have to go to work today?"

"Two, but my seester, Olga, can take my place if I am busy."

"Is she as sexy as you?"

"You will like her."

The phone rang, Slick picked up the receiver, he was informed by the hotel operator that he had a call from The United States.

"Slick, that you?"

"How's it going, Pete?"

"I just wanted to tell you what's going on, I gotta make it fast, I only got ten dollars in quarters."

Pete relayed the story of the meeting between Sam and Ramon, they both got a good laugh at Ramon's expense.

"You think he'll keep his mouth shut?"

"According to Sam he will, I guess Sam put the fear of god in him."

"I hope so, I'd hate to see you two get fucked around because one of his other deals goes sour."

"How long you gonna hang out there?"

"A week or so, maybe forever, you ought to see what's lying next to me."

"You fucking dog."

They set a time for Pete's next call, should anything important come up before then, he'd call and leave a message at the desk.

"Ur ex old lady left town."

"Excellent, see ya later old buddy, watch ur ass."

"Don't worry about me, I'm headin up north a couple hundred miles to look at airports."

"Good idea, talk to you later."

Slick hung up and went back to his breakfast, he was relieved to know that at least for the time being, things were cool in Tampa. His eyes then drifted across to Roxanna who was sitting there munching on a mango seed stark ass naked, suddenly all thoughts of his buddies and their problems vanished as though they had never existed.

Three days later, Slick was back with Eva, Roxanna was a little too much of a premadonna, beautiful and sexy but a pain in the ass. Good old Eva, she didn't let anything get under her skin, so what if Slick had shacked up with that big tited bitch for a couple of days. Now she had him back and nothing in the entire world made her happier than walking out the front door of the El Presidente hand in hand with El Señor Slick knowing that Roxanna was glaring at her from Lucky's across the street. The pecking order of different species is a thing to behold.

Slick had talked to Carlos in Colombia, they were ready for him any time, just call one day in advance and everything would be arranged. Carlos passed along greetings from Luis as well as from what he described as a very excited Magda.

Pete called at the appointed time, he had lots of interesting little tidbits to pass along. Ramon had met with his gang of high paid lawyers, they had demanded a ton of money to continue defending him, Ramon had said he'd be back the next day with the money, no one had seen him since. Sam figured he'd hired a plane to fly him to the Bahamas, from there he could go anywhere in the Caribbean, Central America or South America. As long as his money lasted he was free as a bird.

"What do you guys think?"

"Sam knows he had at least one account in some bank in Nassau a couple of years ago, maybe he had a stash hidden away in case of a rainy day. There ain't no doubt that he's had millions in his hands in the last ten years, maybe the little prick was smarter than I thought."

"*Sounds like it's a win situation for you, he doesn't dare come back now.*"

"*That's right, Sam is clicking his heels together, there ain't no deals gonna be offered him now, they catch him, he's gonna be locked up without bail, there's so many people pissed off at him now, he'd probably die of a heart attack before somebody got to him with a shank.*"

"*Maybe I'll run into him in Colombia.*"

"*Shit, you never know, he knows a lot of people down there. When you goin?*"

"*Day after tomorrow, I'll be staying at the same hotel, you got the number?*"

"*Sure, wait a minute, I got more.*"

"*Shoot.*"

"*Rosemary called me at the nursery, I laughed my ass off.*"

"*What was so funny?*"

"*The way she talked, like some secret agent from a spy movie, "You know who this is?" I said, yes, she told me to go to the payphone at the Seven Eleven and wait for her call. She was really excited, one of the lawyers from her old man's firm had been talking to one of his buddy lawyers who worked in the DA's office in Orlando about some dope peddler they were building up a case against. The guy had got caught red handed with more than a hundred pounds of pot somewhere north of Orlando.*"

"*So far I don't get it.*"

"*Just listen. The guy they caught was from Tampa. They'd just found a van they're sure was part of a smuggling ring near the airport at Leesburg, the van is registered to some non-existent guy from Tampa, they put two and two together. It all adds up, they think they've caught part of the Leesburg gang, ain't that the funniest thing you ever heard?*"

"*The dumb fuck must wonder what the hell they're talking about, he's probably just a small potatoes salesman.*"

"*They got him with a hundred lousy pounds and now they're makin him into Al Capone. He'll probably be charged with every dope deal they haven't figured out around there for the last ten years.*"

"*Shit, that's great, why would they go looking for us when the case is already solved. What I can't figure out is why was this lawyer telling her about some pot smuggler."*

"That was my exact question, she'd asked this lawyer who she said was her old man's best friend to keep his ears open because she had a girlfriend who's boyfriend was dealing with drugs and she wanted to warn her if the guy was hot."

"I'm glad to know what she found out, but I wish she'd keep her nose out of it."

"She left a couple of days ago, she's probably drinking wine on the Left Bank listening to some faggot frog bullshit about how France won the war single handed."

"She's gone. Good. I don't want her stirring up any shit."

"I'm gone too, call you in a week."

Slick lay back on his bed to digest what he'd heard. He decided not to be pissed off at Rosemary, she was just trying to help out, what the fuck, he'd never met any of those lawyers, they probably didn't know he or his partners existed.

As far as Ramon the Mouse making a run for it, Slick could only wonder one thing. Why had he waited so long? If he'd taken off a few months earlier he'd be a hell of a lot wealthier, stupid fuck probably believed the slimebag lawyers could get him off.

I wonder what he did with Tina, damn, she was a hot looking little slut. Shit, you don't suppose he took her along? Nah---he needs to be inconspicuous and that she ain't.

Slick kissed Eva adios and headed for Colombia, no news from Pete in the last two days was good news, nothing to report meant nothing bad had happened, maybe they were indeed home free.

Carlos was there to greet his friend from up north, as always, he had things fixed so Slick slid right through customs and immigration.

"Señor Slick, bienvenidios, Come, follow me, someone is waiting to see you. Later tonight we will all meet for some drinks and seafood, Luis is happy you are here."

"Good to see you, Carlos, how's everything?"

"Fine, everything is fine, Sam and Pedro, they are well?"

"They're doing great, everybody is safe and sound."

Magda rushed into Slick's arms, damn, she was beautiful, damn, she felt good.

Later they met, Luis was in a happy mood, he'd loaded 2 tons of pot on a DC-3 earlier in the day. The evening was strictly for fun, having made a quarter of a million US that day, Luis was in the zone, he toasted Slick and his lady and everybody else he could think of. The men would meet in the morning to discuss future plans, this night was for drinking and eating and enjoying, they did just that.

The following morning, Slick gave Luis and Carlos a detailed briefing on what had happened in Florida and a brief sketch on ideas and plans for the future. Luis laughed as Slick finished, apparently this wasn't an original idea. Renaldo the pilot, knew some people who specialized in aircraft for precisely this kind of mission. Once they had the plane, they would finalize the plan, there were many details but nothing that couldn't be done, there was plenty of time, the next season was far away.

Slick and his lady left on a tour, neither he nor she had ever been to any country in South America except Colombia, that was about to change. Their first stop was Maracaibo, Venezuela. Carlos had recommended a hotel that was famous for it's Flamingo dancers, the place wasn't fancy, but late at night things really got wild. Slick was in heaven, he liked joints like this, he liked towns like this and he thought he'd never get enough of the woman he was with.

Four days later they flew back across Colombia to Panama City, the capital of Panama. The plan was to take a look at the Panama Canal, then catch a flight south to Peru or Chile. Panama City was one of few major airports in the region where you could catch flights to most of the major cities in South America.

Slick also noticed that at every airport they landed, there were tons of old piston engine passenger and cargo planes coming and going, these planes were still being used in great numbers by the local airlines. As the United States modernized it's airline fleets with jets, thousands of piston engined aircraft became available,

Central and South America bought them up at fire sale prices. Finding the right plane somewhere in the southern hemisphere didn't look like it was going to be that big of a problem.

As they walked away from the Avianca Boeing-707 that had delivered them, a huge old four engined DC-6 powered up for take-off, the engines sounded beautiful. Slick stopped to watch the take-off roll. It was way too long for what he had in mind, but, jesus, what a load that baby would carry, how did 4 million for one day's work sound?

After half a day watching ships pass through the locks at the east end of the Panama Canal, Slick left Magda in their room and went back to the airport to see what he could learn. After wandering around for awhile, he ran into a half Panamanian, half Swede named Patricio Jansen who was the general manager of one of the local cargo airlines. Patricio was an absolute gold mine of information, what he didn't know about cargo planes, you didn't need to know. Patricio described the range and load carrying capabilities of half a dozen different types of cargo planes he had flown during his long flying career, two sounded as though they'd fill the bill, The Convair 440 and the Douglas DC-4. The Convair was the smaller of the two, it had two big 2000 horse power engines. The main drawback of the Convair was it's range. To fly from Colombia to northern Florida an extra 600 or 700 gallons of fuel would have to be carried in the cabin. After stripping everything unessential from the plane, they might be able to take-off with a payload of 10,000 pounds of dope.

The DC-4 was fitted with four, 1450 horsepower engines, it would carry a 20,000 pound payload 2,000 miles without batting an eye, it's only drawbacks were the size of the aircraft and the length of the runway required to get airborne with a heavy load.

Patricio's company operated 3 DC-4s, one of them was in the hangar being refitted with a new engine, Slick followed Patricio out back to take a look.

Considering it was a 4 engine aircraft capable of transoceanic flights, the DC-4 wasn't as big as Slick thought it would be. It wasn't small but it wasn't anything near the size of the huge DC-6 that he'd watched take-off the day before.

If Patricio was curious as to why Slick needed a large cargo plane, he didn't ask, what he did ask is, how could he help Slick buy the right aircraft for whatever job he had in mind. He assured Slick that he was well connected with most of the cargo operators in Central and South America and he would be very interested in helping Slick and his people find their plane. Slick liked Patricio, he promised that when and if it got down to the nitty gritty, he would be in contact. *"I am aware of the problems that a gringo can encounter while trying to do business south of the border, we will definitely need help when the time is right, I will call or visit you when our plans are more solid."*

They shook hands and parted company, Slick hadn't been bullshitting, he had every intention of staying in touch, when they made their move, they'd need help and Patricio was obviously a man who knew his way around airplanes and the Spanish speaking bureaucracy. After all, all he'd ever done was mess around with planes and permits and all the other bullshit that goes along with flying.

When Slick got back to the hotel, he had an inspiration,. He called Patricio at the cargo company, *"Patricio, do you think it would be possible for me to fly along on a cargo run one of these days, I'd like to get a little feel for the capabilities of the DC-4."*

"Sure, why not, you can spend a day with me, it's hot and noisy but you will enjoy flying a real airplane."

"Great, I'll call you when we get back from our trip, should be about a month, thanks for everything."

"Okay my friend, see you then."

Shee-it, what could be easier, hang around with Patricio, slip him a few bucks, learn how to fly a DC-4, have him make the arrangements to buy one, buy one. Who would suspect a thing, just another cargo company buying another plane, all of the sudden it disappears over the horizon never to be seen again, and it's a 2 million dollar payday, sweet jesus, this was going to be fun.

"Come my dear, I met a man who told me where to get the best lobster in Panama, I had a great day today, let's celebrate."

Magda figured the Panama Canal must have been a lot more exciting to Slick than it was to her, but she didn't care, every day she spent with her man was a celebration. How was it possible to live in hotels and eat every meal in restaurants and buy so many expensive things? He seemed to spend more money each day than she earned in several months. These men who flew the marijuana planes were not only brave, they must earn huge sums of money, more than she could calculate, much more than she had ever seen, she must be dreaming.

"*I'm ready.*"

"*My, my, don't you look gorgeous. I think you are getting more beautiful every day.*"

"*It's because you buy me such nice clothes.*"

"*Sweetheart, you'd look great in a flower sack.*"

How was it possible that this man who lived like a king, who could have anything and anyone he wanted acted like all he wanted was her, was treating her like his queen, this definitely must be a dream. Fantasy or not, she would do everything she could to make the dream last as long as possible.

While Magda was wondering how she managed to fit in this dream-like life style, Slick was feeling pretty lucky himself. Lucky that he had this dream girl who was not only beautiful and physically perfect, she was passionate beyond belief plus being the nicest girl he'd ever known. Yeah, he was a pretty damn lucky guy.

Peru was interesting, the Inca treasures that the Spaniards hadn't stolen were fascinating, but, damn, Peru was poor. For every person living like a human, there were thousands living in utter squalor.

Chile was a total surprise, the people were smart, well educated, proud and handsome. Almost everything worked, the food was great and the place buzzed with night life.

Maybe the best kept secret in South America was Paraguay. Rumor had it that thousands of Germans had fled there after WWII, the people sure looked as though they had a lot of Aryan blood mixed in with whatever other types of blood they'd started with. What ever the mix was, the final product was outstanding, Slick couldn't help but stare at some of the beauties who adorned the streets, maybe old Hitler was right, there is a little magic in that nazi blood.

Rio de Janiero, the capital of Brazil sucked, the main industry there was simple, try to rip off tourists, you couldn't even trust the hotel safety deposit boxes. They soon tired of the hordes of beggars and thieves and departed, it was time to rough it. Slick had met a fellow American in Chile who had raved about a little village on the west coast of Ecuador where he'd spent several months fishing and just relaxing. Getting there was not all that easy. First, they flew from Rio north to Caracas, Venezuela, then west to Bogata, Colombia, spent 2 days in Magda's capital city, then caught a flight to Quito, Ecuador. From Quito they traveled west by bus to the coastal town of Esmeraldes.

Esmeraldes was like stepping back into previous generations. The people there lived by the barter system, the fishermen traded some of their catch for corn, cooking oil and whatever else they needed to live, the farmers did the same with portions of their crops, the system worked well, it had been working for hundreds of years.

One entrepreneur in Esmeraldes had taken a great risk by investing everything he had in the construction of a tiny sports fishing resort complete with rooms, restaurant, boats and guides. His gamble was beginning to pay off, his only means of advertising was word of mouth and the word was getting out, there are lots of fighting fish to be caught off the coast of Esmeraldes.

Slick dazzled the owner of the resort with his Spanish speaking ability, Magda had been a good teacher, he was now quite fluent. The price tag was so small that Slick was caught off guard, they could stay at this cute little resort right on the water for an entire week for less than one night at the rip off hotel in Rio. Of course, the price quoted was only for the room, food, drinks and fishing trips were all extra, still, this place was a bargain.

That night at the bar, Slick made arrangements with Juan, the resort owner, to charter a boat for the next morning, it was time to have some real fun. Juan asked what kind of fish the Señor and his Señora wanted to catch so he could have the right baits ready, Juan would be the guide for this special guest.

By 11 the next morning, they had caught 3 big Wahoo, 2 Mahi Mahi and several other reef fish. Juan suggested they head a little farther off shore where he could see sea birds circling, maybe they could catch a yellow fin tuna.

They found the birds, Juan picked the bait and within ten minutes they'd hooked something big, the reel was screaming, whatever it was was taking out line at a tremendous rate. Juan was yelling, Magda was shrieking, the reel was smoking, Slick was holding on for dear life, finally, the fish stopped it's run, good thing, there wasn't a hell of a lot of line left on the reel.

Twenty minutes later, Slick had recovered about half the line, sweat was pouring off his body, Magda continuously doused him with cool sea water, Juan continued to shout encouragement, this fish wasn't going to give up without a fight. Every time Slick thought he had the battle won, the fish would take off on another hi-speed dash, taking out the line that Slick had worked so hard to recover. Finally, the fish ran out of steam, Slick was making steady progress, good thing, he was losing steam himself. Magda was peering over the side looking for the first signs of the fish as it came up from the depths, Slick knew she saw something when she screamed, *"Dios mio, es muy grande, es enorme."* Juan moved to her side with his gaff, he was constantly warning Slick not to pull too hard, *"Tranquilo Señor, tranquilo, poco mas, poco mas, tranquilo, tranquilo."*

Finally, the fish came to the surface, Slick could see the bright yellow fins and the shinny green head of a very large yellow fin tuna, slowly he pulled the fish closer to Juan and his gaff.

Swoosh, Juan sank the gaff deep in the head of the tuna, the battle was over, now all they had to do was somehow get this monster over the side of the boat. Juan's first move was to run a piece of rope through the gills of the huge tuna, that way, if they dropped it, they wouldn't lose it.

Magda pulled on the gaff, Slick and Juan reached over the side and grabbed hold of the fish, with adrenaline working to the maximum and several big grunts, they were somehow able to get the magnificent fish over the side. Fish and all, they fell exhausted to the bottom of the boat, the fish twitched a few times and died, the three excited fishermen tried to catch their breaths. Magda embraced Slick, sweat, fish blood and all, she was so proud of her man, she gave him a kiss one might expect for protecting his woman's honor in a duel to the death.

When Magda and Slick finally untangled, it was Juan's turn, he grabbed Slick, embraced him, pounded him on the back then embraced him again, apparently catching a big fish is a pretty big deal here in the town of Esmeraldes.

There was still work to be done. Slick helped Juan drag the fish to the shady side of the boat, they then covered it with several burlap sacks, Juan then poured several buckets of sea water over the burlap. He then got the boat going in the direction of the resort, Slick steered so Juan could keep dumping water on the prize fish. Magda broke out two cold cans of beer for the men and a juice for herself, Slick proposed a toast to the best Captain in Ecuador, Juan toasted the fish, then to be polite he toasted the beautiful Señora, they were all smiles.

As they approached the resort, Juan began shouting for his employees, as soon as the boat was tied up, an army of people jumped in to help get the fish out. The army carried the fish up the rickety dock where they hung the fish by it's tail next to a sign with the Resort's name on it. Juan sent one of his men off to find a camera, he then asked Slick and Magda to pose with him beside the fish, he needed proof that this monster was more than something in the imagination of another bragging fisherman. The camera arrived, fifteen or twenty pictures were taken, Juan was so proud he was about to burst. Finally, the army carried the fish to a waiting antique pick-up truck, they all vanished down a dusty road.

After a much deserved nap, Slick and Magda went to the bar for cocktail hour, Juan was there in all his glory. Slick discovered what all the excitement had been about, this tuna was the biggest fish that had ever been caught by any sportsman in the short history of sports fishing in the town of Esmeraldes. It had weighed in at 102 kilos or 225 pounds, as of this moment, Juan was the champion guide in town, and in a small place like this, that was a big deal. The roll of film had been put on a bus bound for Quito, it would be developed and back in 4 or 5 days. Juan would select the best pictures to be blown up, soon, everyone in Ecuador would know of his resort, he would soon be very busy thanks to Señor Slick and the beautiful Señora, drinks were on the house.

It was a great party, everyone in town came by to meet the conquering heroes. Slick sent one of Juan's employees out to buy a case of rum, two cases of coke and several blocks of ice. Platters of fresh fish were served, the Yellow Fin Tuna was good, the Wahoo was great, the Mahi Mahi was out of this world. Wow, this day to day struggle to survive here in the third world is really tough.

The struggle continued, Juan traded some of the Yellow Fin Tuna for a dozen spiny lobster, his chef barbecued the tails, they were served with lime juice and melted butter. Slick thought his taste buds might explode in ecstasy.

The photographs came back, there was one great shot of Magda, the fish and Slick. Slick loved the picture, Magda had blood on her clothes, arms and cleavage, which there was plenty of. She looked radiant, nothing was blocking any portion of the fish and the sun was at just the right angle. Slick made a deal with Juan. In exchange for that great negative, Slick would take several of the photos that Juan liked and get them blown up in Quito, then send them back by bus when they were ready. Juan liked the deal, they sealed it with a double rum and coke.

Slick took another look at his picture and shook his head in amazement, damn few women in the world could turn a photograph of two sweaty people covered with blood and a dead fish into a sexy work of art, Magda had done just that. She was one hell of a woman. He wondered how many other girls he'd known would have been embracing and giving him a juicy kiss on the bottom of a dirty old boat in a puddle of blood just to celebrate catching a smelly fish, damn few. Damn few.

A week later in Quito, Slick took Juan's chosen negatives to a photo studio and ordered some blow-ups, he found a travel agent near-by who confirmed seats two days later back to Panama City. His next task was to place a call to Pete, they hadn't talked in almost 3 weeks. He left a message for Pete to be at the usual place at 5pm.

At exactly 5, he placed the call to the payphone that they called the usual place, Pete picked up the receiver on the first ring, *"Señor Slicko. I presume."*

"Señor Pedro, how goes it?"

"Oh wonderful, we're selling flowers like mad, one more

fucking daisy or tulip and I may lose my mind."

"I'll be in Panama in two days, I made friends with a guy there who's gonna take me flying with him in a DC-4, I think it's our next plane."

"How much can it carry?"

"More than twenty thousand pounds, in a couple of days I'll know how much runway and everything else we need to know, it's got four motors but it's not that big."

"They got any for sale down there?"

"They're all over the place, cheap too."

"I've found some very interesting places you and I need to look at when you get back, there is a totally deserted housing project that never got any farther than streets and driveways, the streets are straight and a mile long, there isn't anybody within ten miles."

"I like it."

"I spent a couple of days in Jacksonville, about forty miles outside of town there's a public airport that has one roving security guard at night, he drives around the airport about every two hours, then he leaves. I've been out there talking with him twice, he could be had for peanuts."

"Does anybody ever land there at night?"

"Yeah, lots, it's a lot like Leesburg, there's cars and vans parked all over the place."

"We'll take a look, I'll be back in a couple weeks. Everything else okay?"

"Quite as a mouse, we haven't heard a word about Mister Mouse, no pun intended."

"No shit, the little fucker just hauled ass, I'm proud of him."

"So is Sam, he's happy as hell."

"You still seeing the travel agent?"

"Nah, I got sick of her. I'm back to Sam's next door neighbor's wife, she's a better fuck anyway. You'll never guess who picked me up the other night."

"I give."

"Lola."

"No shit, how's she doin?"

"She's the same, lookin for another sugar daddy, man, she's got a nice ass."

"I told you."

They bullshitted a little longer, Slick promised to call from Panama after he'd flown the DC-4.

"How's Magda?"

"One hundred percent perfect, she's a keeper."

"Okay buddy, take it easy."

Slick went up to the room where Magda was waiting, she was sitting in front of the window combing her hair. She was wearing a violet silk nightgown that Slick had bought for her in Chile, a ray of sun light was shining on her and she looked like an angel. *"Mi amor, I missed you, can I have you for awhile?"*

"What part of me do you want?"

"I want all of you, every part, I love you."

THE EPILOGUE

Sam: Last anybody heard, he still had the nursery and it was still going great guns. Nobody ever heard of Sam getting in any trouble with the law, nothing serious anyway.

At last report Sam and Sarah were together and seemed as happy as ever. Those who know say he still pays cash for everything, he and Sarah take lots of trips, he certainly doesn't seem to be hurting for money.

What Sam has been doing since that frantic season with Slick and Pete is anybody's guess, if he stayed in the import business, he isn't talking, whatever, he's still a scary loyal guy who you'd want on your side when the shit hits the fan.

Ramon the Mouse: If Ramon ever came back to the US, he did it under a completely new identity, as of last report he hasn't been seen or heard from by any of the old gang. Slick has his own suspicions, but suspicions don't mean jack shit.

Pete: Pete got overpowered by cocaine for a rather long time and kind of lost it. He pissed off tons of money on dope and broads. He got hooked up with a bunch of dope peddlers who thought they were big shots only because they were stoned on their own product ninety percent of the time.

Pete's job was sort of a high class delivery boy with the new mob, he'd drop off dope to people who sold it in ever smaller quantities and more important, he picked up money owed his outfit. On one such trip, Pete and his boss had been on the road for quite some time and were about ready to return to Florida to pick up more stuff and hide the money they'd collected. What happened next is almost unbelievable.

Pete and the boss (Who must have been stoned on his ass or the dumbest mother fucker who ever lived) were staying at a cheap motel in the area where they were distributing their product. The boss developed quite a thirst, but being stoned on coke, he didn't want to drive to the liquor store and risk being busted for driving under the influence. (Good law abiding citizen that he was) So, the genius called a taxi and asked the driver to run off and bring him back a case of Dom Perignon Champagne. The old man who owned the cheap hotel became suspicious when he saw a thousand dollar case of booze being delivered to a twenty dollar a night room. He called his son, the local sheriff, to discuss this unusual turn of events, the son said he'd be over in a few minutes for a visit and to investigate.

Snorting cocaine gives people a strong thirst that can only be quenched by large quantities of cold sweet liquid, champagne doesn't hack it. Pete had snorted about ten lines and he was dying for some Pepsi, there wasn't any in the room, so he left to walk down to the corner store for another bottle.

While Pete was away from the room, the son of the motel owner arrived, he was off duty so he was dressed in civilian clothes and driving his own car. His dad told him which room had had the case of champagne delivered, the son walked along in front of the motel until he was at the window of the room where Pete's boss was. God knows why, but the curtain was open enough that someone interested could peek in, the sheriff was interested, he peeked in. Inside he saw a big man lying asleep on one of the two beds, between the beds there was a table with a glass top. On the table there was a big pile of white powder, the sheriff may have been a bit of a hick but he instantly suspected what the pile of powder was. He ran back to his dad's office to call for back-up.

As Pete walked back towards the motel with the bottle of Pepsi, two sheriff's cars passed him at high speed, neither had their sirens on. To his amazement, they pulled into the parking lot of the motel and stopped in front of his room, Pete crossed to the other side of the street and stood behind a tree to see what was going to happen. The two uniformed sheriffs were joined by another man and the manager of the motel, the old guy produced the master key, the other guy in street clothes stuck the key in the lock, they all disappeared inside Pete's room with guns drawn.

Due to all the cocaine he'd snorted, Pete's brain was fuzzy, but fuzzy or not, he realized there was nothing he could do to help his boss, he was fucked. The best thing Pete could do was to get his ass as far away as he could before somebody connected him with what was going on at the motel. He nonchalantly strolled back down the street in the direction he'd come from. He checked his pocket to see how much money he had, only then did he realize how badly he had screwed up. His wallet was in the room right beside that big pile of cocaine, in his wallet was his driver's license along with everything else you carry in a wallet.

The boss was really fucked, the three sheriffs found an unbelievable cache of treasure. The pile of white powder was indeed cocaine, more than half a pound. Pete had been cutting the cocaine with whatever druggies use to cut cocaine before selling it, that's why it was in one big pile for the world to see if they happened to peek in through the window. Under the beds the cops found even more treasure. In two canvas bags, there was almost seventy pounds of marijuana, under the other bed there was a large suitcase, besides some clothes, the suitcase contained over three hundred thousand dollars in cash, the sheriffs couldn't believe their eyes, they had hit pay dirt.

Pete walked to the convenience store where he'd bought the Pepsi, from there he called one of the local boys who the day before he'd delivered dope to, within minutes, the drug connection was on the way to rescue Pete.

Thus began two years of life on the lam for our fallen hero, fortunately, he had access to some of the money in the cache or things would have been really tough.

Pete found out later that the boss man had been so loaded on a mixture of champagne and cocaine that he didn't even remember getting arrested. Of course he was guilty, he was sentenced to a very long time in some hot shitty prison. In order to get out before he was old and gray, he made some deals with the law, many of his former associates were arrested on various charges. They never caught Pete, he moved away from everybody who knew him until the heat was off. Years later when he finally came back to Florida, nobody seemed to care about some old has been petty ass drug dealer. The cops always figured that Pete had been a very small link in the chain, no big shot would have been dumb enough to leave his wallet lying around, would he? The law never connected Pete with that other gang of flyers who had been active years earlier around Leesburg.

Rosemary: Rosemary spent two years at La Sorbonne, she studied all forms of art, she discovered that her forte was photography. In the years that followed she sold a lot of photographs to different magazines, her husband had left her quite a pile of money, allowing her to travel the world in search of the perfect picture. As far as anybody knows, she's still out there somewhere looking for her prize winning shot.

Slick: Slick and Magda stayed together for almost two years. He met someone in Panama who was connected well enough at the US Embassy to get her a tourist visa, after that they spent some time traveling around the land of milk and honey. Slick knew the end of their love affair was near when she started pestering him to have some babies, she went back to Colombia to visit her mother and to find the father of her future children.

Slick didn't like what was happening to his friend, Pete. The effect of too much cocaine is so obvious to outsiders, it's strange that those who use it never seem to see what's happening. Regardless, Slick departed and didn't leave any phone numbers.

A couple of years later, Slick took the balls of money to his bank, he told the bank manager that he'd found the damaged money under a house that he was renovating, a month later the bank credited his account with $14,300 dollars.

Over the years, Slick and Sam stayed in touch, usually just a call once or twice each year. During one such call, Sam invited Slick to meet him in Florida, he had something important to talk about. When Slick arrived, he was surprised that Sam handed him more than $75,000 dollars in cash, it was his 1/3rd share of the money Mouse had never been paid. Sam said he'd given Pete his share some months earlier, they both lamented what had become of their old friend and partner.

Exactly what Slick's been up to since the days of The Leesburg Gang is hard to say and he ain't talking. Slick spends a lot of time traveling around the world, he's always got plenty of cash and he's always with some delicious looking woman. Maybe he made some good investments with his share of the earnings, maybe he made some more flights, nobody knows except him and like I said, he ain't talking.

There are some interesting little footnotes: Sometime in the late seventies, there was a very interesting article in all the newspapers that subscribe to the Associated Press. It seems as though a DC-4 cargo plane had been found parked at Fernandina Beach Airport some 40 miles outside Jacksonville, Florida. The airport manager had wondered about the plane but he hadn't said anything to anyone for three or four days. When the police finally came to take a look, they discovered that the plane was unlocked. Inside, they found marijuana residue. It was estimated that a plane that size could have carried as much as 25,000 pounds of marijuana non-stop from South America to Northern Florida. The FAA said the DC-4 had been registered to a company in Panama. When the company in Panama was questioned, they had documents to prove that the aircraft had been sold to a company in Colombia, further investigation could find no trace of the Colombian company.

Another footnote: Three stories from Florida newspapers, all concerning cargo planes that landed somewhere in Florida, in each case, the planes had obviously carried loads of marijuana. These three stories are all dated before 1980.

Plane # 1, A Super DC-3 landed on the ranch belonging to the governor of Florida, the plane was unloaded and abandoned, it's cargo was estimated at 6,000 pounds.

Plane # 2. A Convair 440 was found abandoned a little to the west of Cape Kennedy on a road in a housing project that had never gotten any farther than roads and driveways. In the airplane was evidence of marijuana. There were also two extra fuel tanks that would have given the C-440 enough range to fly non-stop from South America. Experts estimated that the Convair could have carried as much as 12,000 pounds of marijuana.

Plane # 3. A DC-4 was found abandoned on a deserted stretch of highway north of Lake Okeechobee. In the DC-4 there was marijuana residue. Around the plane, there was evidence of at least 2 different trucks that had undoubtedly been used to haul the illegal cargo away. The DC-4 could have carried more than 25,000 pounds of illegal drugs non-stop from South America to where it was found.

After 1980, the idea of flying in a load of dope, unloading and abandoning the plane, really caught on. There are literally hundreds of accounts in Florida newspapers, some landed at airports, some in fields, some on roads some in the Everglade Swamps, damn few were discovered before the cargo was long gone.

The ingenuity of the boys who brought in the crop could fill volumes. I know one very well to do ex smuggler who refused to trust anyone else with any knowledge that could get his ass put away, his solution was simple, he was a one man gang. Jay bought a Cessna 206. He put enough extra fuel in it to be able to fly from southern Florida to Colombia, his route was simple, direct. Jay flew directly across Cuba straight south to Colombia. In Colombia, he loaded five hundred pounds of marijuana in his single engine Cessna, toped off the gas tanks and headed for home. When he landed in Florida right at the public airport, nobody thought twice about a single engine plane doing anything as crazy as flying all the way across the Caribbean Sea. Later, Jay unloaded the pot into his van and drove home. At his leisure, he filled little plastic bags with one ounce of marijuana, then he became a small time dope peddler for which the penalty is a slap on the fanny. By selling the marijuana an ounce at a time, Jay was getting more than a thousand five hundred dollars a pound for his cargo, gross for the flight, $750,000 dollars. Jay made 3 flights, then he retired with over a million dollars in his safety deposit box, he never got caught, he was never suspected of anything worse than being a bit of a nerd.

You notice I said "The Boys Who <u>Brought</u> In The Crop" because when the laws were changed giving long mandatory jail sentences to marijuana smugglers early in the 80's, most of the amateurs got out of the game, all the smart ones anyway. Since then, marijuana has been mostly in the hands of organized crime, it's no longer an adventure, it's now a deadly business where you get your balls cut off and your wife and kids get killed if something goes wrong.

So, what happened here with Slick and Pete and Sam and Mister Mouse is pretty much a thing of the past. It was a hell of an exciting time, tons of money was made by some of those who had the guts to give it a try and were successful. Some others who had the guts fucked up and died in fiery crashes of overloaded planes or just disappeared and were never heard from again.

> Finally, the answer to the sixty four thousand dollar question, *"No mom, no matter what you might think, Slick Adams ain't me."*

ISBN 141201065-9

Edwards Brothers Malloy
Thorofare, NJ USA
August 4, 2016